UNIVERSE OF TWO

UNIVERSE OF TWO

A Novel

Stephen P. Kiernan

WILLIAM MORROW
An Imprint of HarperCollins*Publishers*

This book is a work of fiction. References to real people, events, establishments, organizations, or locales are intended only to provide a sense of authenticity, and are used fictitiously. All other characters, and all incidents and dialogue, are drawn from the author's imagination and are not to be construed as real.

FIRST EDITION

Library of Congress Cataloging-in-Publication Data has been applied for.

Library of Archives Canada Cataloguing in Publication information is available upon request.

ISBN 978-0-06-287844-1
ISBN 978-1-4434-5737-8 (Canada)

20 21 22 23 24 LSC 10 9 8 7 6 5 4 3 2 1

To the Hibakusha, and to the veterans of Los Alamos as well

UNIVERSE OF TWO

But come now, tell me
about your wanderings: describe the places,
the people, and the cities you have seen.
Which ones were wild and cruel, unwelcoming,
and which were kind to visitors, respecting
the gods? And please explain why you were crying,
sobbing your heart out when you heard him sing
what happened to the Greeks at Troy. The gods
devised and measured out this devastation,
to make a song for those in times to come.

—*The Odyssey* (trans. Emily Wilson)

1 .

I MET CHARLIE FISH in Chicago in the fall of 1943. First I dismissed him, then I liked him, then I ruined him, then I saved him. In return he taught me what love was, lust, too, and above all what it is like to have a powerful conscience.

On first impression, Charlie was weak-chinned. To my girl-friends I might have called him a milquetoast, soft as an old banana. Which only goes to show how smart a nineteen-year-old girl is about anything. Now I know better. It turns out the greatest kinds of strength are hidden, and move slowly, and cannot be stopped by anything until they have changed the world.

Which he did twice.

I am not exaggerating, I was there on both occasions. One time I helped him, and the other time I hurt him. I hadn't intended any harm, but there's no denying that I used my influence to make him do terrible things. Irreversible things. He forgave me, that was in his nature, but I haven't forgiven myself—even now, all these many years later. Some deeds are like tattoos, and the ink of regret is permanent.

How did it start? As innocently as the chiming of a bell when a shop door opens.

I was in the back office when I heard it ring, letting me know a customer had come in. At that moment I was frustrated, opening a shipment of sheet music for the high school chorus Christmas show. It was goose bumps chilly in the store, because we rarely had cus-tomers till afternoon and my mother wanted to scrimp on heat. But it wasn't the cold that bothered me. It was the company that we used for sheet music supply. Their prices were the best, and their delivery the quickest. For some reason, though, they triple-sealed their packages, using that thick brown packing tape with the bad glue smell, so that it was all but impossible to get them open. Like breaking into Fort Knox, just to get the four-part harmony pages for "Jingle Bells." Mr. Kulak, the high school principal and choir director, would be in to pick up the sheet music during his short lunch break. It was eleven thirty and I was nowhere near getting that package open.

"Anyone here?" the customer called.

"Be right out," I hollered, which my mother would have said was not satisfactory customer service, but then again, she was never the one who had to deal with that tape.

It was amazing that life during the war continued with that much normality. To me, Chicago seemed starstruck. Movie matinees every Saturday after we closed early, they swept me away. The follies coming through town. Boys home on leave who would squire me around, their best pal toting a friend of mine too. We'd go to a show with them in uniform and us in patched-up nylons, feeling grown up. In spite of whatever hijinks they might have been dreaming of, all those boys really hoped for was a decent good-night kiss. Which I gave, easy as a penny. What did it cost us, anyhow, to allow them that? With what they were going to be facing? Some of my friends wouldn't smooch a soldier on the first date, in case he got the wrong idea, or they got a reputation for being fast. But I would have kissed a hundred boys in uniform, just to give them something about home to dream on while they went and did the world's worst job.

Still, there were plenty of days that the world felt upside down. So many boys were gone in the service. My brother, Frank, the born natural at fixing cars? He'd enlisted at nineteen. Now he was stationed in England, working in a motor pool. Who knew when we'd see him again?

Far worse, we all knew families who had received the horrible telegram. Some mothers would never be the same, like Mrs. Winchester, the best soprano in our church's choir until her Michael came home in a coffin and she didn't sing anymore. Some fathers became bitter and silent, like Mr. Winchester, who perched on his front stoop and glared at people like he was daring them to start something.

Sorrow was in the air. Sometimes it seemed like half the people in that city were walking around with broken hearts of one kind or another.

So maybe a package I couldn't unwrap was a small complaint, maybe I was self-absorbed and unaware. But what did I know? My life was so small then. I had no idea.

I'd tried peeling that tape off with my hands, only tore off an inch or so, and it made my fingers hurt. I found the big scissors, but they barely managed to snip off the extra strip on one corner. Still, I was determined.

"Anyone here?" the customer called.

"Be right ooouut," I sang back, not much concealing my annoyance. Then the big scissors slipped, and though I pulled back quickly, the point of one arm jabbed me in the forefinger.

"Damn," I grunted, though louder than I should have.

"Is everything all right?" the customer asked. "Is there some kind of trouble?"

"No trouble," I sang out, before jamming my finger in my mouth, sucking the metallic taste of blood. "Be right there, I completely promise."

Cursing in front of a customer? My mother would have wrung my neck. But she was off at her Monday war wives' luncheon, not due back till one. I straightened my skirt and stopped before the little mirror to make sure I was presentable. A lock of my hair had come out from its comb, dangling in front of my face. I was in the middle of arranging it back into place when I heard the chord.

In the olden days, they used to have trumpets come out and play a fanfare before the king spoke, to shut everyone up I suppose. And plenty of paintings of angels have cherubs making music in the background whenever something big is happening.

This chord? It was a hallelujah. A call from the heavens. Or at least from a guy who knew what an organ could do. Because I scurried out of the office and there he sat at the Hammond spinet model, our entry-level instrument. He didn't choose the church model, with its classy cabinet and thirty-two-note bass pedals, and Dubie's Music did not carry the concert model because it was too glamorous and expensive to sell in Hyde Park.

What I saw? A fellow, skinny as a bread stick, wearing oversized pants and perched on the spinet's throne with his eyes closed. He had his left hand on the low manual, right hand on the high manual, left foot on the bass note, right foot on the volume pedal, announcing for all the world every bit of the meaning and grandeur of a G-major chord, fully voiced, with all the trumpet stops open.

I know which key it was because I have perfect pitch. It's not a talent, I was born that way. Maybe this is an advantage when sizing a customer up by what chord he plays first, but I promise, it is an affliction at the Christmas show when they sing "may your days be merry . . . and *bright*," and on that high note all the sopranos go flat.

"Well, well," the skinny guy said, opening his eyes as he switched off the organ. He turned to me with a grin like a ten-year-old who'd just unwrapped his Christmas present. "Not bad."

"Sorry I made you wait—"

But he was already off the bench and holding his hands toward the organ. "Would you play for me, miss? Please?"

I hung back by the door. Most customers would have said miss, or please, but not both. Also guys didn't usually buy organs. They mostly brought a gal, let her choose, then dickered over the price. "Sounds like you can play it just fine yourself, mister."

"Not a lick," he said. "Only G major." He gestured again, like an usher showing me to my seat. "Please?"

"Sure," I cooed, sashaying across the sales floor. "This is the Hammond spinet, built right here in Chicago. Two manuals of forty-four keys, plus a full octave of bass pedals, the largest-selling organ in the world."

He made a face. "Why would anyone want to be the largest-selling anything?"

"Honestly?"

"Wouldn't you rather be the best-sounding instead?"

I sized him up. A little nervous, he had black marks on his fingertips, like he held a pencil all day. Not an indicator of musical passion, I'd say. Back then, I was constantly assessing people, measuring them. The fact that I always found myself superior had not yet dawned on me. "The sales *are* a sign of sound quality, sir. Of the public's appreciation."

"I see. But if you would please play—"

"Of course." I slipped out of my shoes, so as not to scuff the bass pedals. "There are percussion and vibrato controls, plus drawbars for each manual, so you can customize your tone."

"Thank you, but I only want to hear it."

"Coming right up." He was an odd one, all right, but sales were slow and I wasn't going anywhere. I switched the instrument on again—which meant I had to stall while it warmed up. That little delay is one of the pleasures of the organ, how it reminds you that it is a machine, air filling the bellows, organizing itself for you. "Hammond uses ninety-one tone wheels, sir, machined to a mere one-thousandth of an inch. The transformers are sealed in wax, so the organ stays in tune regardless of changes in humidity."

He nodded, too polite to expressly tell me to shut up, but if you're paying attention, customers give plenty of signals when they want less talk, more music.

By then the spinet model was ready anyhow. I adjusted this and that drawbar, eased back the volume pedal, and sat up straight—posture always the last thing to check before playing—then trotted into my usual demonstration repertoire: "Isn't This a Lovely Day," "Monkey on a String," "Cheek to Cheek." He stood close by, watching my fingers move, maybe my feet on the pedals, nodding a little with the beat.

"No no," he said after I stopped. "I mean, very nice. But do you have something slower, please? Maybe more sonorous?"

Sonorous. I didn't know what the word meant, but I was certainly not going to say so. Maybe I had a sale on the hook, and here it was only Monday.

Business wasn't great, to be honest. As a hobby, my father belonged to the Chicago Amateur Radio Operators Club. Most guys were interested in broadcasting, or finding other radio buffs hundreds of miles away, but Daddy's pleasure came from repairing the club members' radios—tinkering and soldering in our basement. The armed forces decided that his skills could be put to better use. He'd left early that year to serve in a communications center near San Diego.

So, with my mother at the helm of the cash register, I went to work at my father's store in Hyde Park: Dubie's Music, selling accordions, pianos, and organs for the few buyers who remained in that corner of sweet home Chicago.

Of course that put all my hopes on hold. I'd been accepted to the Oberlin Conservatory of Music in Ohio, a premiere organ school with two dozen instruments to learn on. Which was thin ice all around: My family had no money for college, if anyone had gone it would have been my brother as a future breadwinner, and deep down I doubted I was good enough to play at that level. I might dream about a scholarship, or a loan of some kind, but only after the war was over. Meanwhile, any skinny guy who played a decent G chord was definitely worth my time.

"Happy to," I said. "Sonorous it is." I pulled out some sheet music, flipped through, and saw *Chopin's Nocturne no. 2*. Now that's a sentimental old sop, I know, and I'm no great fan of the key of E-flat major. But the composition has lots of room, air all through the melody, then busy little bursts before everything spreads out again. I started at a nice, brisk pace.

"See how responsive the spinet model is, sir?" I kept playing while I talked. "All the sustain you want for long notes, all the precision for the trills."

Then we were both quiet. It had been a while since I'd played that piece, so I was busy reading the pages. It actually was a pretty enough composition after all. I struck the last notes, a pair of E-flats three octaves apart, and sat back with a sigh.

Skinny guy didn't say a word. He just pulled out a handkerchief, reaching past me a little too close for a stranger, until I realized he was wiping a bit of blood off the keys, from my finger that had been poked by the scissors. He stepped back, folding the handkerchief into a neat square before tucking it away in his pocket without a word.

I closed the sheet music. "How's that for sonorous? Are you falling in love?" That was as flirty as I knew how to be.

"It's all right," he announced. "I was curious about what a non-cathedral organ would sound like. What you have here is a well-made calliope."

"A calliope? Does this place look like a circus?"

"In Atlantic City, for example," skinny guy continued, "there is an organ with seven manuals, one thousand two hundred and thirty-five stops, and thirty-three thousand, one hundred and twelve pipes. It took eight years to build, ending in 1932." He looked smug as a dog with a fresh bone.

"I bet it sounds horrible, something that giant and noisy. I bet it's deafening."

"It is a bit muddy," he admitted, "or so I've been told."

"Oh, so you've never heard it for yourself. What makes you so all-fired opinionated about organs, anyhow?"

"Until recently I was a chorister at Christ Church Cathedral in Cambridge, Massachusetts. Which has a lovely, two-manual pipe organ."

Well, *la-di-da*, I thought, easing down from the bench, sliding my shoes back on. "For a nonpiped instrument, mister, this one here is a beauty. Perfect for churches, concert halls, recording studios, and the finest homes. There's nothing better for sale anywhere."

"Oh, I didn't come in to buy anything." He smiled. "I wanted to listen."

I put my hands on my hips. "Well, then you're wasting my time."

His face made a surprised expression, eyes wide and the eyebrows way up. "I suppose I am," he said. "I'm sorry. How might I make it up to you?"

That was how he wound up in the back room with me. He took the scissors from the unopened box and put them aside gently, as if they were a sleeping cat. We made conversation. Turning eighteen in three months, he was sure to be drafted.

"You aren't going to enlist?" I asked him. Lots of fellas made a big boast about doing such a thing. That was my kind of guy.

"Look at me," he said, holding his bony arms wide. "Not exactly a born warrior. The only way I'd survive beyond an hour is if I stood sideways, and made too thin a target for a rifleman to hit."

But, he said, he was a bit of a math whiz. His uncle, a professor at the university, had brought him into a team of young guys doing calculations for the government.

"They try to make it sound manly, saying it's classified and so on," skinny guy continued, all the while using his fingernails to pick one corner of the thick brown tape upward. "But really it's plain mathematics all day."

I'd been no slouch at math myself, in high school, which I had only graduated from that June, and probably would have won the math award if I hadn't been a girl. But it was not like today, with calculators and computers and so on. We had slide rules, and long-form division. Not to mention that any student skilled at math, boy or girl, gets the award now. Well, some of the time.

"Not too boring," he continued. "And miles better than getting killed. Or worse, having to kill someone else."

Which gave me something new to think on. I'd worried plenty about Frank and the other neighborhood boys getting killed. But before then, I hadn't spent ten seconds considering what it would be like for them to kill someone.

"How old are you?" he asked, direct as you please with such a personal question.

I never gave anyone that information in those days, yet I answered this boy right out: "Nineteen."

"Oh," he said, registering that I was older.

"Since last month. What's all this math for, anyhow?" I'd taken a seat on the desk, legs crossed ladylike and acting casual, like guys came to help in the back room every day, yawn. My mother would have had kittens, right there on the office floor.

"No one knows," he said, making tiny progress in getting a little flap of tape loose. He pinched it between his thumb and forefinger. "It must be important, though, because the assignments come from way up in the military."

I straightened my sweater. I'd heard plenty such talk before. "You don't say."

Meanwhile he tightened his grip and pulled straight up. All three layers of tape came away in one fat strip, making a ripping sound as the box popped open.

"There you go," he said, the coil of tape dangling from his hand like a just-killed snake. He turned to drop it in the wastebasket, then held that skinny but surprisingly strong hand out to me. "Charlie Fish."

"Brenda Dubie," I said, shaking hands. "Pleased to meet you."

"Nice to meet you, too, Brenda."

But neither of us let go, for a second there, neither one. Talk about a chord playing.

The little bell on our front door jingled again. I whirled to see Mr. Kulak striding into the store, taking off his hat. I rushed forward to meet him, not doing anything wrong, but feeling anyhow like I'd just been caught red-handed.

2 .

THE BOYS OF THE Metallurgic Lab at the University of Chicago worked at gray metal desks, with wooden chairs on wheels that creaked at the least movement; drawers that resisted, complained, and sometimes refused to open; flimsy in- and out-boxes on the desks' front corners; and bare bulbs overhead. In winter, the room smelled of dry heat, iron from the rusty radiators. In summer, the scent was boys' sweat.

All the desks were arrayed in a circle—so that no mathematician was ranked above another, and each received equal amounts of daylight from the wall that was all windows. The older workers did a geometric calculation, however, determined that desks to the south received 11 percent more light, and claimed those places for themselves. But some younger boys found the southern advantage to be seasonal, true only in summer, and they took proud possession of the northern desks. The debate over whose calculations were correct resurfaced whenever the workload was light, complete with competing formulas chalked across the big front blackboard.

There were two exceptions to the circle: one desk space open for the unit's manager to enter and exit the circle, and a desk by itself near the door, which Cohen occupied. A recent Columbia graduate, he was disliked by everyone.

Charlie toiled in a middling desk, not caring to join either side in the location dispute, preferring to wrangle his assignments into order with what seemed, compared with his peers, to be of limited brilliance but limitless patience. He would work and work a problem, without complaint, however long it took to find a solution.

"That is why, you tiresome boy," Cohen said on his way past, dropping a new assignment sheet atop Charlie's overflowing in-basket, "you get to do arcs. And they want this one pronto."

Arcs, meaning curves: how an object moves through space, where on a sphere to place electrical connections, what navigation path will help a vessel avoid a problem at sea. The other boys worked on concrete tasks: how much weight a ship could carry on deck before becoming top-heavy (which they guessed had to do with tank transport), what temperature a metal would reach during bursts of intense pressure (which everyone assumed meant the barrels of gunships), plus the raw number-crunching of supplying fuel, bullets, uniforms, tires, bandages, meals, coffins.

The primary difference in his work, Charlie gradually realized, was *pi*. No one else was reckoning with the irrational number. Because every arc problem involved *pi*, he could never arrive at a precise answer. It would always be approximate.

Charlie scanned Cohen's latest assignment sheet. This time the object weighed 10,000 pounds, was released 11,000 feet in the air at a speed of 357 miles per hour. What would its arc be, how long would it fall, and how far away would it land?

Charlie took a pencil and began to draw on the assignment sheet. He liked to start every problem with a picture, to visualize what he needed to know. But halfway through the sketch, his hand went still. His mind had wandered to the young woman he'd met on Monday, Brenda, and the pleasantest thirty minutes in Chicago since August, when he'd arrived from Boston. Granted, she was a regular weathervane of moodiness. But she played the organ like an angel. And when he tore off that packing tape, her face had brightened like the sun coming out. Monday was his only day with a longer lunch break, though, which made getting back to that organ store feel further away than next spring.

Humming to himself, he drew the problem again: altitude of release, dotted line of the downward arc. To represent the target, he used a swastika.

"Does anyone think it is possible for Cohen to be a more inefficient jerk?"

Charlie knew who'd said it without raising his head. Richard Mather, Andover grad, snatched from Yale for a place on this team, winter home in Manhattan and summer place on Long Island, an unapologetic snob and an expert at baiting all of them into debates. On his desk Mather kept a framed photo of his sister, a smiling, tomboyish blonde holding a tennis racquet, which he would wave periodically before the noses of the other mathematicians. "Look all you like, suckers, because you will never get close."

"Shut up, Mather." That was Santangelo, a kid from Milwaukee whose hair was all tight coils. As a result Cohen called him Steel Wool, purely for the pleasure of annoying him. Santangelo was a mad-dash genius at arithmetic. If you walked up to him out of the blue and said, "Three hundred and fifty-seven times six hundred and twenty-four," Santangelo would shrug and answer, "Two hundred and twenty-two thousand, seven hundred and sixty-eight." "Divided by sixteen?" He'd blink twice and say, "Thirteen thousand, nine hundred and twenty-three." Then he'd bend back over the lab notebook he was filling with calculations as fast as he could scribble them.

Now Mather had his hands on his hips. "Because you know I'm right, Santangelo?"

"Because you are such an itch."

Mather swaggered away from his desk. Charlie knew: argument was this guy's favorite way of procrastinating. "Let's review the facts."

A groan went up from the room.

"First, look at how he delivers new assignments, fifteen minutes after the workday starts. Every one of us has already begun something, has prioritized our tasks—"

"Which in your case includes lots of talking."

"Second, Steel Wool, consider how he distributes our chores willy-nilly, this desk to that, when half a minute spent organizing his sheets beforehand would enable him to deliver them in one pass through all the desks, saving time and reducing distraction."

"Mather, will you please shut up?" Charlie rarely contributed to the parleys, but he was sick of trying to solve arcs while a brighter kid gabbed the morning away.

"Ah, Fish takes the bait." Mather sidled around the circle of boys. "You answer me, then. What do you think of our wonderful boss?"

Charlie put his pencil down. He hated Cohen. The guy had two ways of speaking: commands and criticism. Incapable of telling a story or carrying on a conversation, either he was telling you what to do, or he was belittling what you had done.

"Suddenly he's shy," Mather crowed. "Isn't that cute?" He snatched Charlie's pencil away, holding it like a microphone. "No comment on the scandal, Mayor Fish?"

"All right," Charlie said. "He's annoying. And bossy."

"There." Mather flourished the pencil overhead like a conductor's baton at the end of a symphony. "The definitive response."

"Also smarter than you," Charlie added, and the room erupted in jeers.

"Well said, Fish," Santangelo cried, as Mather dropped the pencil and played at hangdog while shuffling back to his desk.

The hall door swung open and Cohen returned, Professor John Simmons following two steps behind. All the math boys stood.

"At ease, fellas," Simmons chortled. "As you were."

John Simmons was the least pretentious man in the building. He greeted people in the hallway, did not close his office door even for secure calls, and took the time to learn the boys' names. But no mistake, he was also second in command, head of the physics department in Denver, acolyte of the Nobel Prize–winning genius Arthur Compton. He also happened to be Charlie's uncle, which was how the boy ended up on the math team. His mother had asked her brother to keep a fragile fellow out of battle.

Simmons walked through the room shaking hands, introducing himself to the new arrivals, then taking his place in the circle's one-desk gap. He told the boys to be seated.

"Fellas, I don't mind you clowning around in here a little bit," Simmons said, with a half-suppressed grin. "But there is a war on, you know. There are rooms exactly like this—in Munich, Berlin, perhaps Tokyo—where bright young boys like you are working day and night on calculations to help them hurt us. And hurt our country."

With the group properly sobered, he began slowly pacing. "I'm here this morning to tell you that our project has been given additional status and urgency. Last night I was informed that all of you are now ineligible for the draft."

A restrained cheer went through the room.

"Not so fast." Simmons stopped in place. "You now answer to the United States military. Starting in January your paychecks will come from Uncle Sam. I imagine at some point someone in a uniform will come in here and give each of you a rank. You will receive orders, and you will obey them."

Giving that idea time to sink in, he recommenced pacing. "Our project's security level has been heightened, too, from classified to top secret. From here on, it will be a court-martial offense if you tell anyone what you are doing here—not your buddies, not your girlfriend, not your family. Who your boss is, what you do all day, how many pencils you go through, every single thing here is now confidential military business. Loose lips on your part will be treated by my superiors as an error on my part, which would make me . . ." He paused to glare at them. "Unpleasant. Any questions?"

There were none. For once even Mather had nothing to say.

"Our work will intensify. Your tasks may seem odd, but I assure you, they are essential to the war effort. You'll learn more about that soon. When you do, you may wish for the days when you were in the dark."

Simmons stood to his full height. "Get to work, boys. And remember: there are other rooms, exactly like this."

The professor strode off—with one curt nod and one word, "Charlie," his only recognition of his nephew.

Cohen came to the front. "Everything on your plate, clear it by Friday."

The math team groaned.

"Quit whining, babies. Every job in your box must be done, documented, and on my desk before you leave for the weekend. Monday morning is a whole new ball game." He strutted out the door, his walk a stiff imitation of Simmons's.

Charlie frowned at the problem on his desk. *Pi*, that numerical elbow, made everything difficult. He took up his pencil, saw that Mather had broken the point, and found a fresh one. He was stalling, though, because he could not answer a basic question: What crazy giant gun would it take to shoot a bullet that weighed ten thousand pounds?

3

CHARLIE FISH CAME TO the store every Monday. We'd chat, we'd flirt, one time we split a sandwich—egg salad he'd brought from a deli. He told me about growing up in Boston: singing with various choirs, being the youngest in his college class, how his mother loved to stroll on Saturday mornings beside the Charles River, the crew boats darting up the river like giant water bugs. Eventually I put him to work in the back room and he made no complaints. Soon, though, he'd ask me to play. And why not? In another month he'd be a draftee. What harm could there be in giving him something to hum when he was far away? Often he sang along, a fine tenor, steadier than I'd expected.

One way I've been lucky: I never had to live without music. My mother started piano lessons when my outstretched fingers only spanned three keys. Those years I was hoping to attend the conservatory helped me develop a discipline. Even now, though my hands are wrinkled and weak, I manage to touch the ivories for a few minutes every day.

Sometimes afterward I linger on the bench, and imagine all those soldiers far from home, with bad food and foreign landscapes, their clothes stained with the scent of fear. I bet they whistled and hummed and sang to themselves all the time. Something calm when you're afraid. Something busy when you're bored. Something sad when you're missing home or your girl.

Performing for Charlie, those afternoons in 1943, felt like living in a snow globe. The world's brutality made our haven of innocence all the sweeter.

While I could have impressed him with classical pieces, at work I preferred playing trendy stuff: "Oh What a Beautiful Morning," "Paper Doll," "That Old Black Magic." My favorite that fall was "Oklahoma" because the Hammond could make the wind come sweeping down the plain on one set of keys, while on the other set the last syllable *aaahh* of Oklaho*ma* was still in the air. These days I can still play those tunes from memory, but I don't do it often. They sound insubstantial as cotton candy.

Charlie liked sadder songs. Whenever I asked him what next, he'd suggest "As Times Goes By," or "You'll Never Know," or a classical piece like "Moonlight Sonata." While I played, he would stand close beside me, maybe humming the melody, always watching closely. Funny thing, though. These days I play the ones he liked all the time, and they don't sound fluffy. They still touch the heart.

"Why do you like those blue tunes, anyhow?" I teased him one Monday.

"Maybe it's what playing them does to the organist."

"Go on." I waved him off. "What's the real reason?"

"How the organ sounds," he said. "How notes continue, and how they fade."

"Whatever do you mean?"

"It's physics—what the wind does to make a note. That's no accident." He smiled. "Science makes the air sound beautiful."

I thought maybe Charlie was showing off. But there I was, playing for him as fancy as you please. That morning I'd styled my hair to look nice in back too. Which he would see while I was on the bench. Maybe we were playing the same game.

I remember one spring when I was still in my sixties, I saw a movie about the courtship rituals of birds. The grebes did a kind of ballet, it was that elegant, with one bird mirroring the long-necked moves of the other, until they both went running away across the surface of the water. The birds of paradise swept their wings out, puffed their chests, and danced around on tree branches. And the whooping cranes? They leaped and spread their wings and went crazy wild for each other. Oh, that movie made me ache to be young again. It also reminded me that my courtship with Charlie was pain-fully reserved. More than a month after that first handshake, we had not touched again.

The other thing I noticed was that each Monday Charlie showed up a little later. It made me nervous, for one simple reason. My mother.

The war wives' group had the use of the function room only till one o'clock, when the Hyde Park Chamber of Commerce board met. Then it was a two-block walk back to the store. You could set your watch by when my mother would come striding in—1:05 and never a second later, taking charge and wanting a full update on every littlest thing that happened in the sixty-five minutes she'd been gone.

Each week Charlie arrived later past noon. I began to feel squeezed, and would have to hurry him out the door. He was always nice as peaches, and let me shoo him off without a complaint. He'd stand on the sidewalk and gawk through the big window, wave or do jazz hands, something to make me smile before shuffling back to his math office—wherever it was. If I asked what street, he'd go cute and change the subject.

One week he didn't arrive till almost quarter to one. I was triple disappointed. First, there'd be no time for helping with chores. Sec-ond, I'd only have time to play about two songs, and I'd spent the week learning five that together sent a little flirty message. Third, we'd barely have any time to visit before I'd have to send him along.

But Charlie seemed in the opposite mood. He was gabby and casual, humming to himself while he wandered around the store. The clock above the register read twelve minutes till one. He opened the covers of several pianos, playing that old standby G-major chord in various octaves. When he lifted the hood of the Chickering baby grand, trilling tunelessly up and down the black keys, I couldn't take another second.

"Did you come to buy a piano today?" I said. "Or to kill time?"

Charlie stopped fiddling and smiled at me. "You look especially good today, Brenda. That knot there, up so high, I have never seen that before."

"It's called a chignon." I slid onto the bench. "It took me three tries."

"Well, it was worth it."

"Thanks," I said offhandedly, but was secretly pleased down to my toes. That chignon had cost me an hour, and Charlie's compliment repaid every second. I switched on the spinet model, playing test chords so I could start the new tunes as soon as it warmed up.

"Please don't hurry," Charlie said. "We've barely had a chance to talk."

"Oh, I just have the music all through my veins this afternoon," I insisted, pulling out sheets for the songs I'd practiced.

"Did you do up your nails too?" He pointed, and I stared at my fingers like they belonged to someone else. "What's the occasion?"

"Just a Monday." I shrugged. "Plain old Monday."

I noticed the clock by the register read eight to one, and immediately started in on "Moonlight Becomes You," which I figured he would love because it is full of diminished chords that sound sad but also like they're leaning toward something. I had barely finished the intro when Charlie came over and switched off the organ.

"Hey," I said, sharper than I'd intended. "What's gotten into you, anyhow?"

"That's the question I have for you, Brenda. Do you only want an audience? Do you not want to talk to me anymore?"

"Oh, Charlie, it's the flat opposite of that," I confessed. "I'm always glad when you're here. I wait all week for the next Monday to come along."

Just like that, I started spilling the whole pot of beans. While half of my brain was bossing me to shut my yap, the other half was telling and declaring, as if this boy were headed off to the front the next morning. How smart he was, how nice and polite. I was giving away my entire reserve. "Also I have to get back to work by one, and on the days when you get here later than usual—"

At that I glanced out the big front window, and the jig was up. Here was my mother, low-heeled shoes and gigantic brown purse, coming up the sidewalk like a plow truck clearing snow. The clock read four minutes to one. Lunch had ended early.

Charlie didn't seem to mind that I had trailed off in midsentence. He followed my eyes and retreated from the organ, clasping his hands behind his back.

"—though you would hardly think a bowl of pudding would cause such a fuss," my mother complained, unpinning her hat as she barreled through the door. She had a habit of starting conversations right in the middle, whether you were there for the beginning or not, and would bristle like a porcupine if you asked what she was talking about. I learned it was best just to play along.

"Did someone spill?" I prompted.

She was tucking her huge purse behind the register. "What? Of course no one spilled. But Elise insisted on having seconds, which is its own house on fire, with all the weight she's carrying these days, hips like a whale—although come to think of it, whales don't actually have hips, do they?—and meanwhile Nancy Burgoyne had not had firsts, and merely said no thank you to be polite."

Only then did Charlie come into her sight, over by the baby grand. "Brenda," she purred, not taking her eyes off him. "Why didn't you tell me we have a customer?"

"You hadn't taken half a breath so that I could."

"That's all right," she said. "I forgive you."

It has long been my belief that after a child is of a certain age, the parents' primary role is to cause embarrassment. To prove that point, my mother clapped her hands together and, with an expression as authentic as a bouquet of plastic flowers, minced over to Charlie. He wore a grin the size of the front grille on an Oldsmobile.

"How do you do, Mrs. Dubie?" He held out that strong hand. "I'm Charlie Fish."

"Pleasure to meet you, Charlie," my mother chirped, shaking hands while eyeing him all over. "Are you in the market for a piano today?"

"Nooo, ma'am," he said, wagging his head like some old Lincoln Park bluesman testifying a song. "I'm here because Mr. Dubie is out of town, as I understand it, or I would be speaking with him myself."

"I see," she said. "This is a business matter of some kind, then?"

"Nooo, ma'am," he repeated. "I am here in Chicago, far from my home back east, for an assignment with the war effort. I haven't been able to make many friends due to my responsibilities. But I have been lucky enough to make the acquaintance of your charming daughter, Brenda."

They both turned and looked at me. I felt like a goldfish in a round bowl, exposed to any and all.

Charlie pressed on. "I've come today to ask, though I have no family nearby who can vouch for me as a decent young man, if I might take Brenda out to a show on one of my evenings off from the war effort. Would that be acceptable to you?"

All at once I was peeved. How about asking *me*? First things first, mister.

"Charlie, you seem like a good, polite boy," my mother announced. "And I'm of a mind that manners still matter a great deal in this madhouse world."

Charlie nodded. "Maybe more than ever."

She sighed. "I suppose it would be all right, if you weren't out too late."

"Nooo, ma'am," he declared for a third time. "Not a chance of that. My work starts very early in the morning."

"Do you drive, Charlie?"

He shook his head. "It would be strictly walking or cabs for us."

"Good. I've always maintained that driving was a job for husbands. You people are too young."

"Yes, ma'am," Charlie said.

"Very good," she said, preening like a mother hen. "I approve."

"Thank you, ma'am. If you'll excuse me, I need to get back to work now." He strode by me, a skip in his step, pausing to tip his hat. "See you soon, Brenda."

"Yes, soon." And he was gone.

"What a nice young man," my mother said. Which was a wonder, since she had never acknowledged any boy I'd dated before enough to have any opinion of him at all.

"He won't buy an organ," I said, "but he has many good qualities."

She stood beside me, looking out at the street where Charlie had paused to wave before hurrying off. She hooked her arm in my elbow. "Oh, he'll buy an organ, all right."

4.

THAT AFTERNOON IN THE math room, Mather did not come back after lunch. Charlie returned from the organ store to see Mather's chair empty, the normally tidy desk a messy splay of papers. Mather's photo of his sister was gone too.

Santangelo stood by the front windows, dancing a little jig. "Gentlemen, a great pimple in the world has now been popped."

Laughter rang through the room.

"Back to work, you lazy dogs," Cohen snapped, hurrying in from the hall. "You especially, Steel Wool." Setting a cardboard box on the desk, he swept Mather's papers in unceremoniously.

Charlie bent to his calculations. Because he'd spent the better part of the morning imagining where he might take Brenda on their date, he'd made little progress on his assignment. The real question was which Brenda he would be taking out: the cagey girl who masked her insecurity with sass, or the sweetheart whose face went soft when she switched on the organ. One of these Brendas was entertaining, but the other was lovely.

Meanwhile Santangelo could only watch Mather's things disappear into Cohen's box for so long before sauntering over to Charlie. "Quite the going-away party."

"He got promoted," Cohen snapped, grabbing all of Mather's pencils in his fist, and tossing them into the box. "If you must know. Reassigned to New Mexico."

"What could there possibly be in New Mexico?" Santangelo asked.

"Sand, I think," Charlie ventured. "Mountains?"

Cohen was opening drawers one by one, dumping the contents into his box, but he paused to sneer. "Every time I think you boys could not be any more stupid—"

Santangelo wagged a finger at him. "Stupid is not the same thing as being deliberately kept uninformed."

"New Mexico . . ." Cohen began, but he checked himself. "You don't need to worry about New Mexico." He addressed the whole room. "Probably none of you do. Let's accept that it's important military strategy. If it works." He slammed the last drawer. "Mather jumped past all of us to get there, leap-frogged our whole business. Even me."

"Is that why you're peeved?" Charlie asked. "Because he was promoted instead of you?"

Cohen tipped Mather's in-box tray into the cardboard box, papers tumbling. "Where do I start with you idiots?"

"I have an idea," Santangelo said. "When we ask you a question, why don't you actually answer it?"

"Because I can't." He bustled out of the circle of desks toward the door. "I'm not allowed, and you're too stupid to figure it out for yourselves."

"Mather was right," Santangelo said. "You're a power-hungry jackass."

It hit him like an arrow between the shoulder blades. Cohen dropped the box on the floor, pencils flying up, and Charlie considered that several boys in that room could probably describe in great detail the effect that happens when a falling object lands, and the force causes pieces to rise in the opposite direction.

Cohen turned slowly, like a gunfighter. For the first time, they realized that he was physically fit, lean and muscled.

"Steel Wool, I would really enjoy teaching you a lesson based on four years of boxing at Columbia," Cohen growled. "But it wouldn't be worth the inquisition I'd face afterward. You're too numbskulled to learn anyway."

"Maybe we wouldn't call you names," Santangelo said, "if you showed us some respect."

"I would if you deserved it. You could know everything you want, if you used your thick heads." Cohen scanned the room. "Fish. What are you calculating right now?"

"The arc of an object launched at three hundred and fifty-seven miles per hour."

"Right. And is there anything that actually goes that speed?"

One of the far-desk boys raised his hand. "The Flying Fortress?"

"Bingo. The B-29. What you're calculating, you dunce, is aerial trajectories."

"Fine," Charlie said. "But why are we fiddling with all of these different drop altitudes? It's not like we're going to fly over Tokyo at eleven thousand feet, and expect to be welcomed with roses."

Cohen stood still, waiting, watching them sort it out.

"It can't be a bomb," Santangelo offered. "It must be some other kind of weapon, like a tank, and they want to drop it from lower so it doesn't smash on landing."

"Eleven thousand feet wouldn't change anything," Charlie said. "A tank only needs fifteen hundred feet to reach terminal velocity."

"Point proven." Cohen bent and picked up the box. "Stupid as a box of bricks."

"We're asking reasonable questions," Santangelo insisted.

"Not for me to answer." He swaggered to the doorway. "But I will tell you this."

They waited, and Cohen took his time.

"First, the name calling ends now, right now, or I will put you in the hospital, inquisition be damned. Second, if you all don't finish those trajectories today, I won't be the one who drops you out of a bomber."

Cohen slammed the door behind him. The boys were quiet. Charlie ambled back to his desk. "Maybe . . . ," he said eventually. "Maybe they'd do the run at night, so it would be safer to fly at eleven thousand."

"Could it be like our version of a kamikaze?" asked the boy at the back. "Would we stoop that low?"

"This is war," Santangelo answered. "There's no such thing as low."

5.

HE WAS LATE, WHICH in my book was not the way to impress a girl. It was Saturday night, I'd given him my home address, and we were going to grab a bite before seeing a picture. I was ready on time, maybe a bit early to be honest, but the kitchen clock cuckooed six times and there was no knock at the door. I flipped through a magazine, went to the john to check my teeth in the mirror, fortified my lipstick. I perched on the piano bench facing out, my leg jiggling.

"Brenda," my mother said, smoking a cigarette at the dinner table. "For the love of Pete, will you relax?"

Easy for her to say, sitting pretty as if we were playing hearts and she'd just won the jack of diamonds. Yet I knew she was right. I wanted the interest of boys, it was important to my self-image, so I kept my makeup fresh and my dating calendar full. Jerks were rare, and despite the war—maybe even to spite it—life was a lark. There was plenty of time before I'd need to get serious. Till then any fella would do, so long as he behaved himself and was nice to my girlfriends.

But Charlie Fish? Deny it all I might, that boy gave me ants in my blood. Today I like to think I knew already that he was something special, but that would be rewriting history. I didn't yet see the strength that was deep inside, waiting for its time. I also didn't see the strength he would call forth in me, and how it would make my innocent years seem trivial as jigsaw puzzles.

At six thirty I went into the kitchen. Bad idea, because I couldn't resist the bowl of pistachios my mother left on the table. I started cracking them open, popping one after another in my mouth without thinking. By the time Charlie arrived, I'd gobbled half the bowl, leaving me salt-mouthed and with a lump in my belly.

"Sorry I'm late," I heard him tell my mother in the front room, while I poured a glass of water from the pitcher in the fridge. "With the snow dumping down like that, there were no cabs."

I peered from the kitchen. My mother was crushing out her cigarette. "You walked from Ellis Avenue?"

"And Fifty-Ninth, yes, ma'am. They're housing us in the university's empty dorms."

She rose from the table. "Well, let's get you dried off."

Just like that, my mother had found out where he lived, information I hadn't been able to pry loose in ten Mondays of conversation. She raised her eyebrows at me as she bustled by.

"What?" I said to her. "What?"

"Hi, Brenda," Charlie said. "Sorry I'm late. And soggy."

His hair was soaked, the shoulders of his coat drooping. Appealing as a wet cat. "I didn't know it was snowing," I said, looking away so as not to embarrass him further.

My mother scurried back with two towels. "Charlie, how about we don't let you catch a chill and ruin your evening?" She handed him one towel and used the other to rough up his hair.

"Thanks so much, Mrs. Dubie." His voice was muffled by the towel.

"You can leave that coat here to dry while you're out," she continued. "I'll lend you one of Frank's."

"Frank?"

My mother froze. "You don't know about Frank?"

Charlie ducked out from under the towel. "Should I?"

"Of course you know about Frank," I sang out, while my mother gave me a look made of daggers. "My brother in the service. Who is overseas now."

"Of course," Charlie said. He turned to my mother. "Of course." He smiled, and it was so quick I wondered if he had winked at me. "Brenda has always called him Francis."

My mother's expression softened. "She has?"

"Out of respect, I guess," Charlie said.

That was the first time I suspected he and I might make good coconspirators.

"Well," my mother conceded, "I suppose that is more respectful." Then she reverted to her busy self. "His coat won't fit, but it'll do till you get Brenda home—at a reasonable hour, by the way."

"Which reminds me." Charlie gave me a wink. "We ought to skedaddle if we don't want to miss the newsreels."

"You should." My mother dug in the hall closet for Frank's winter coat.

There's no nice way to say it. Charlie looked ridiculous. The coat's shoulders were so broad, its sleeves did not begin till almost his elbows. Which meant he had to roll them up, never a good look with the lining showing. Also it smelled a bit of mothballs. We had a quiet walk to the diner, snow falling in tiny flakes. My fingers were cold because I hadn't been able to find my gloves from last winter. I stuffed my hands in my pockets, fingers curled over thumbs. In memory, I see us from a distance, strolling a snowy sidewalk without speaking, friendly as the one and ten bowling pins. At the diner, we slid into opposite sides of a booth and the awkward silence stretched longer.

Finally Charlie cleared his throat. "Would you like to tell me about Frank?"

I fidgeted with the pepper shaker. "My older brother. He enlisted two years ago."

"You have a brother." He folded his hands like a judge. "Funny how that never came up."

"You haven't exactly volunteered an encyclopedia about your family either."

Charlie made that surprised face of his. Maybe he wasn't used to a girl giving him backtalk. "I told you I'm from Boston. I have a younger brother and two sisters I'd gladly tell you about later. What's Frank doing?"

"Running a motor pool in England. He could get bombed, but he's not in battle."

"I never realized before how many people in a war are not actually fighting."

"But he's still far from home, and my father is gone too. That's what makes my mother such a wreck."

"Your mother is a wreck? She seems fine to me."

"Well, what would you know?"

Charlie looked surprised again. "That's true. I barely know her."

Why was I peevish? I don't know. Maybe I thought it was like being coy. The chemistry I had with Charlie felt like the first time every winter that I went skating on Lake Michigan. The ice could be a foot thick, trucks out by the fishing shacks, my girlfriends already charging ahead. But for me those initial steps out onto the ice still felt dangerous. I might fall through. I might pass over the one weak spot in the entire frozen bay, and drown before anyone noticed. So, every year, I was peevish with my friends that first day, tentative. Then I was over it, skating as confidently as they did till March came and the thaws put our skates away till next year.

Maybe I felt with Charlie, for the first time, that something was at risk with a guy. Maybe, too, the other boys had made me the littlest bit spoiled.

The diner did not help. The menus had coffee spill marks on them. The food did not come for ages. I was still stuffed with pistachios. I was not trying to be a prima donna when I asked for more water, but the waitress never brought it. Charlie asked nicely twice, but still no water. I could have demanded it for myself, I suppose, but nobody wanted to be that kind of girl in 1943.

Charlie apologized, he paid, and afterward he put back on the coat that made him look eleven years old. The walk to the theater was only three blocks, but in fresh snow it was a trudge. He sang a bit of some Italian song that sounded like a march. Which was funny, though I didn't laugh. My hands were freezing, and somehow I blamed Charlie. No good-night kiss for this fella.

Then the theater saved the night. There was no line at the ticket counter, no one waiting for popcorn, and when we ambled into the half-lit rows of seats, we saw that we were alone. It must have been the snow. There was no one else in the whole place.

"I hope you don't mind that I arranged a private viewing," Charlie said with a big smile, his arms wide like a showman.

"So expensive," I marveled. "You shouldn't have."

And we were friends again. For the newsreel, we sat right in the middle. It opened with the usual marching-band music, and the image of an eagle in an attack pose. The horns sounded flat, F notes bending sourly down toward E, but I blamed that on the projector. The news began with a launching of two new navy ships, which were gigantic. One of them, the announcer said, was the most heavily armed cruiser ever. Next we saw Red Cross volunteers packing boxes of food, medicine, and cigarettes for Allied prisoners of war. Gary Cooper, last year's winner, awarded the 1943 Academy Award for best actor to Jimmy Cagney for his role in *Yankee Doodle Dandy*.

"I loved that picture," Charlie whispered to me.

"Me too," I whispered back. Then, I don't know where the impulse came from, but I jumped up, running to the far right-hand side of the room and the back row. After a bewildered second, Charlie saw the game in it and trotted after me.

The movie was about a military ship that might be haunted, because the captain kept doing odd things. The first officer was supposed to be heroic, because he was handsome, but he kept striking poses in profile that made him look like a mannequin. At one point Charlie stood in the aisle and imitated one of the poses, his chest puffed out and chin pointed up, and when I laughed—as loud as I pleased—he ran across the center seats and sat on the far-left side, down front. Oh, I came skipping after him.

If that picture was actually suspenseful, we were having too much fun to notice. We sat in probably ten places, each time making more of a racket, each location tumbling into each other a bit more as we sat. As fun a date as I can remember.

At last the credits rolled, the end, and it was perfect, perfect. We sat in our front-row seats, not going anywhere.

"That is the best movie I have ever seen," Charlie said.

"That is the best movie I have ever *not* seen," I replied.

We stayed till the lights came up, and then a minute more. "Let's wait till the crowd thins out," he said. I was so pleased I could have pinched him.

Now, all these years later, I wish I could recall the name of that movie. I would gladly watch it, from the recliner in my little assisted-living apartment. Would it all come back to me? There is the moment I ran to the back. Here is when Charlie posed in the aisle. This is when our hands touched on the armrest between our seats. Could the silly scenes and weak dialogue replay that night? Or better, bring Charlie's presence back to me? I would watch every movie made in 1943, no matter how boring, to have my hand accidentally brush against his for half a second one more time.

At last we idled up the aisle and he helped me on with my coat. As Charlie put on Frank's, I realized he didn't like it either. He was being a good sport. Outside, the snow had stopped, a plow truck came through tossing the mess to the curb.

I took his arm. "Sorry I was a pill at dinner."

"They should have brought you more water," he said. "I will never go back there."

"Oh, had you been to that diner before?"

"No." He laughed. "But I'm still not going back."

We stopped for coffee, and made small talk, mostly about movies we liked. He checked his watch and suggested we mosey if we wanted to avoid the wrath of mother. Outside, the trees were draped with white. A man stood singing on a street corner, he wore a long tweed coat and Charlie dropped a coin in his hat.

We had crossed the street when the man began his next song.

Oh Danny boy, the pipes the pipes are calling
From glen to glen, and down the mountainside.

It was a sentimental old tune but he had a good steady tenor, and the lilt of an Irish brogue. "That man has excellent pitch," I said.

"Fine vibrato too," Charlie replied.

Which caused me to pause in my walking and listen.

But come ye back when summer's in the meadow,
Or when the valley's hushed and white with snow.
Tis I'll be here in sunshine or in shadow,
Oh Danny boy, oh Danny boy I love you so.

I thought of my father, stationed in Southern California, his letters giving no hint of when he might come home. And my mother, no wonder she was bossy, without his ever-patient ear for her concerns. And Frank, not in the line of fire but not safe from bombs either, and far from Chicago. Sure, I wished I'd gone off to Oberlin to study the organ. But all these people were suffering in some way, and I was a silly, selfish girl. All I wanted was for us to be together, busy and arguing and talking about everything easily and casually like we did before the war.

All that time the man was singing, his breath rising like each note was a cloud, while Charlie had moved his arm up to around my shoulders.

You'll come and find the place where I am lying,
And kneel and say an "Ave" there for me.

However blue I might sometimes be, I still had boys and movies and home, girlfriends to gossip with. How much greater Daddy's and Frank's loneliness must be. It broke my heart a little, and on that snowy sidewalk I started to cry.

That's when Charlie opened that stupid giant coat like the flaps were wings, and pulled me inside to his chest. I burrowed right against him. The sadness I'd been feeling for months, but telling myself over and over that I didn't feel, all came pouring out of me, and I became a weepy, runny-nosed, sobbing mess.

Charlie put his skinny arms around me and held me close. "It's okay," he said, which was silly because he didn't know what I was crying about. But my head fit right exactly in under his chin, while he wrapped all that extra coat around me, and kept saying it anyhow. "It's okay, Brenda. It's all going to be okay."

6

LATE IN THE DAY, Santangelo shuffled through the gap in the desks with a manila folder under one arm. Charlie was not so much solving a trajectory problem as wrestling with it, his body curled around the papers, which made their own arc across his desk.

"Charlie," Santangelo whispered. "Take a look."

"An interruption," Charlie sighed, sitting straight. "Short but sweet, I hope."

After glancing over his shoulder—two newer boys labored with a Marchant calculator, a cumbersome but useful device—Santangelo opened the folder to reveal a map. Unfolding it end over end, he spread the sheet atop Charlie's work.

"I have to finish this pile today," Charlie protested, tapping his pencil on the gray metal in-box.

"Half a minute." Santangelo pointed to the top of the map: New Mexico.

Charlie sighed. "Are you chasing Mather, so he can annoy us one last time?"

"That's the whole thing." Santangelo was still whispering. "I've gone over this map twenty times. I can't figure out where they sent him."

"What are you talking about?"

"There's one university physics program, in Albuquerque, but it's all astronomy. A guy on my high school's national science fair team, two years ahead of me? He's in the graduate program there. I phoned him, and they have no math boys there. Not one."

"So?"

"So look at this map. There's Holloman Air Force Base. Opened last year."

"In the middle of nowhere."

"Yup. No town nearby, nothing on the map but blank space. I doubt there's electricity out there, much less physics labs."

Charlie raised one corner of the map, eyeing his unfinished work beneath. "What's your point, Santangelo?"

"Don't be thick. Something enormously secret is going on down there. It all lines up, see? Mather—smartest guy here, I hate to admit it—gets promoted to a place that is practically invisible, on the same day we become top secret, on the same day we become military guys. We are in the war now."

"We have always been in the war."

"No, I mean *in* it." Santangelo checked on the far-desk boys again, then leaned closer. "This New Mexico deal is so big it's entirely secret. Either they told Mather, or he figured it out like Cohen was trying to help us do—"

"Cohen wouldn't help a cat out of a tree if its fur was on fire."

"Except for all those hints he gave. If we shared the problems we're solving, we'd be able to piece this together."

Charlie tilted his chair back. "Uncle John said we'd learn what's up soon enough."

"Yes, and wish we hadn't. But Mather knows now."

"No offense, Steel Wool. But I really need to get today's arcs sorted out."

"Fine." He snatched up the map, trying to fold it brusquely but finding the creases uncooperative. "Somewhere in the middle of all that nowhere, our boy Mather is living the high life, thanks to our drudgery right here."

"What makes you think it's the high life? Two days ago, you were saying it was some place horrible."

Santangelo paused in his folding. "Didn't you see how furious Cohen was not to be picked? He knows what's out there, he wants a piece of it. Frankly, Fish, so do I."

"You are letting your imagination run way ahead of you. Blank space on a map, if it means anything, certainly does not signal a luxury resort."

"After this December Chicago weather, I would be happy with a dose of sun and the rest would be gravy." The map accordioned into itself at last, closing neatly. "I'll tell you what else." He poked Charlie's papers with one finger. "The answer to every arc question is the same. Sooner or later, everything falls down." He tucked the map back into his folder. "Then it goes boom."

"I'm not interrupting anything here, am I?"

Both boys whirled to see Professor Simmons in the doorway, a smile on his face.

"No, sir," Charlie said. "Only a bit of collaborating."

"Glad to hear it." He hooked a thumb at the air over his shoulder. "Say, Charlie, when you're all done collaborating, would you stop by my office?"

Charlie gave Santangelo a look of fire. "Be right there, sir."

Simmons swept away down the hall.

"Collaborating?" Santangelo snickered, but Charlie ignored him. He had evening plans with Brenda, and work had made him late way too many times. He would rather arrive in her good graces, and not have to spend the evening apologizing. But any chat with the boss was bound to eat time. As Cohen had trained him, he turned the pages on his desk facedown, then hurried after his uncle.

The metallurgy program was spread all over the university. The math building was not fancy: drab walls, bulletin boards with little on them but thumbtacks—evidence of announcements for students before the war all but emptied the campus. Charlie hustled down the hall, humming to keep his courage up. All the classrooms he passed were dark. In fact, the only light came from the department chair's office at the end of the hall.

There was no secretary at that hour, so Charlie knocked on the outer door.

"Come," Professor Simmons said. He waved a hand in welcome.

"Hi, Uncle John," Charlie said. "Sir."

"Hello, son." The professor gestured to a chair and Charlie sat. "Let's get right to brass tacks, shall we?"

"Yes, sir." He thought the office smelled of bay rum cologne.

Simmons lifted a sheaf of papers, a thick folder of problems worked and solved. "Your work here has been careful and accurate, Charlie, with very few errors."

"Thank you, sir. I—"

"But slow. It's too . . . you're too slow."

"That's my strength though, Uncle John. No matter how hard a problem is, I keep at it, keep plugging away."

"But our work is urgent. And when I see you lollygagging, chatting away—"

"He came over to my desk uninvited, sir—"

"Please." The professor held up a hand for silence. "I want to keep you here, Charlie. You're a good boy, and I don't see you as much of a fighting man . . ."

"Probably not, sir."

"I promised my baby sister I would look out for you. But your work? It has to get speedier, or you'll have to go."

Charlie nodded, his mouth gone dry. He'd turned eighteen six weeks ago. Army or navy, he could guess what a future outside of the math team would be. The war took what it needed, and didn't care what opinions an eighteen-year-old boy had on the topic.

"May I ask one question, sir?"

Simmons folded his hands on the desk. "Of course."

"Well, pardon me if it sounds impudent, but everyone else is dealing with rational numbers. I have all these complicated fractions of curves."

"Yes. I've been quietly making sure you get the work that matters."

"But arcs, Uncle John? They're impossible. What makes them so all-fired important?"

At this the professor smiled. "Charlie, Charlie."

"Like I said, no disrespect meant."

"You need a bit of history." Simmons stood, and went to the blackboard. "Trajectories have been a concern of war makers since . . . well, since the Middle Ages." He drew a primitive catapult, with a dotted line that ran from its bucket, over a wall, to the ground on the other side. "If you have to dig up your ammunition, heave it onto a cart, haul it to the battlefield, and only after all that work can you fire it at your enemy—knowing that if you miss, he'll fling it right back at you—well, pretty soon you realize that trajectory is one of the most important concepts in warfare."

He ambled back to his seat. "Now imagine that the rock you are planning to throw costs millions of dollars. And to catapult it, you must risk the lives of thousands of men. You'd want to make sure that rock hits exactly where it is supposed to, destroying exactly what it is intended to destroy. Otherwise you've squandered all that money and wasted all those men."

Simmons lowered his hands and sat forward. "You follow me, Charlie? You'd want to make goddamn steel-trap iron-clad sure."

Charlie nodded. "I follow you, sir."

"Like it or not, son, modern warfare has become a race. Hitler has his panzers and rockets, the Japs have their fleet and their fighter planes. Right now we are in a mad dash to catch up. I landed you this assignment as a favor to your mother. But to put it plainly, you are doing a mediocre job. It will not do, you hear me, Charlie? In a race to victory, mediocre will not do."

Charlie stood. "Loud and clear, Uncle John. I hear you loud and clear."

The professor also rose from his chair, the smile back on his face. "See? I knew this talk would be good for us both, Charlie."

"Thank you, sir."

"Of course." He held out his hand.

Charlie shook it, and left the office at a run.

7

HE HAD NEVER TASTED eggnog before. When my mother poured Charlie that nice big glass of it, and clinked her glass against his, cheers, and he took the big, gulping, enthusiastic swallow you'd expect of a polite boy, thank goodness she didn't see the expression on his face three seconds later. While she turned to check the oven, he looked like a gargoyle who'd just drunk gasoline.

"Wow," he managed to say, shuddering, "that is really something."

I caught his eye, and handed him my glass of water. Charlie nodded gratefully, filled his mouth and swished it around.

By then my mother had straightened. "Give that casserole five more minutes, and then we'll eat," she said, taking a decent gulp herself.

The three of us stood in that tiny kitchen, smiling for three different reasons. Who would have predicted that my mother would have a helpful role in our romance by giving Charlie and me secrets to share together? In retrospect, perhaps she could have. Maybe we were amateurs, and she knew exactly what she was doing.

"Come on," she called, charging into the living room. "Let's watch the snow."

My mother had turned off the table lamps but left the front steps' light on. Great fat flakes fell past as I stood at her elbow watching. A gust of wind made them all change direction at once, like a school of tropical fish.

"Sure is pretty," Charlie said, joining us. His glass was nearly empty, and I imagined he'd made a stop at the sink along the way.

"Do you get much snow where you come from?" my mother asked.

"We do," he said. "I'd say Boston gets buried twice a winter."

"Sing something," I blurted. "Some Christmas song."

Charlie made his surprised expression. "Really?"

"Great idea," my mother cheered, dropping into a chair. She raised her glass to him. "Knock yourself out, kiddo."

Charlie gave us both a look, then leaned to the piano and played an E. I already knew—from his humming beside me while I played the organ, from snippets of songs here and there—that he could sing on pitch. Plus he'd told me stories from his years in the choir. Still, maybe my favorite thing he had done up to that moment was playing that note, so he would be on key for us. And then he began.

O little town of Bethlehem, how still we see thee lie
Above thy deep and dreamless sleep the silent stars go by.
Yet in thy dark streets shineth the everlasting light.
The hopes and fears of all the years are met in thee tonight.

We clapped, he blushed, it was adorable as kittens.

"Let's open gifts," my mother cried out. Sometimes she could be worse than a kid.

"Honestly, Mother. It's not Christmas yet."

"Charlie has work tomorrow." She made a face. "Just one won't spoil anything."'

There was no point in arguing. My mother was flexible as a brick. We'd skipped a tree that year, to save money, and the old fireplace hadn't been safe to burn things in for years, so our presents lay in their wrapping on the hearth. Meager, to tell the truth, what with the holiday packages for Frank and Daddy mailed weeks ago.

"Charlie first," my mother insisted, lighting a cigarette. "Pick that big box."

Now when it comes to unwrapping, I am a shredder. So is my mother. We believe in getting to the goods as quick as we can. Not Charlie. He found the taped places, and slid a finger under them to open the paper without tearing. By the time he was done we could have used the wrapping paper all over again. I wanted to give him a shake.

"This is a really large gift," he marveled, weighing the box.

"For the love of Pete, kiddo. Open it." My mother gulped her eggnog.

It was an overcoat, black as coal with a velvet collar. "My goodness," Charlie said. He put it on, discovering that it was double-breasted, smoothing the front down with his hand. "I feel like Humphrey Bogart."

"Well, well." My mother half-hid a smirk behind her eggnog glass. "Brenda, doesn't he look smashing?"

I felt a little clench in my heart. I was not in love with Charlie Fish. I liked him well enough, and he was sweet as cinnamon candy. But he was so skinny, almost frail. I had higher hopes. Still, I hated when he had to cancel a date because of duty, and I liked our little confidences. Any Monday he didn't visit the shop, I'd spend the whole afternoon at the spinet model, trying to lift my mood with show tunes. Now my mother's urging was not helping to clarify matters.

"He does," I said at last, because it was true. "Smashing."

He went to the hall mirror and examined himself. "Well, hardly. But now I'll be warm." He turned to us, beaming. "It's wonderful. Thank you."

"Brenda next," my mother bossed, ever the dictator. "Open your gift from Charlie."

The woman knew what she was doing. He handed me a small box, long and narrow. Wrapped in graph paper. Can you imagine anything less romantic? Light green, covered with square grids. Granted, Charlie had drawn a little spruce tree on it, a few holly leaves, and in the corner what I guessed was either the sun or a star, sending rays in all directions. At least there was a personal touch.

Today I wish like anything that I had saved that paper. I wish I had those little drawings, sketched with a red pencil, probably made in stolen time at his math office. I would frame them in silver, hang it on my apartment wall, and call it "Before." That is, before everything happened with us, and to us. Before I learned to cherish his kindness. Instead I tore it all away, ripped open the box, and then had to catch my breath. Gloves—beautiful calfskin gloves the color of butterscotch.

"What is it? What did he give you?"

"One second please, Mother."

I touched the one on top, soft as spring leaves. I slid one finger inside, and felt some kind of fur.

"They're lined," Charlie pointed out, "so they'll be warm as well as fashionable."

"How did you know?" I asked him.

"The night at the movie. Your fingers were white the whole time."

"Charlie, they're beautiful." I slid on the gloves, then stood and gave him a quick hug. He was still wearing the handsome overcoat. "Thank you."

"Sure." He ducked his head a little. "Any time."

I glanced at my mother then, expecting her to want to open her first gift, but she was taking a drag on her cigarette. She let out a huge blue plume, then tapped her lips with one fingertip, over and over.

All through dinner I was chatty. Charlie had given my mother matching ashtrays, three of them, monkeys who see and hear and speak no evil. She held them up and cackled, then gave him a poke in the arm.

"You are an all right guy, Charlie Fish. You are all right."

Which was better than I could have hoped for. The food was good enough, the lights stayed low, the snow turned to rain, but we didn't care. Sometimes Charlie would say something that sounded like math, about how air moves in waves through organ pipes for example, and I would think: this is not the guy for me. Other times I would glance up from my plate and he would be looking at me, straight on and not hiding it one bit, and what girl doesn't like to be admired a little?

During dinner my mother was prickly as a cactus with me, as usual, but to Charlie she was ripe peaches and sweet ice cream. When the meal was done, and he'd brought the last plates into the kitchen, she told us to vamoose while she cleaned up.

"I need to get back to the dorm anyway," he said. "Lights out is at eleven, and I have early duty tomorrow."

My mother, wearing yellow rubber washing gloves whose fingers were almost worn through, threw an arm around his neck. "Merry Christmas, Charlie Fish."

"Thanks for a great dinner. And for the Humphrey Bogart coat."

"It's nothing, kiddo," she said in a Bogart voice. "Brenda, walk him to the door so he doesn't get lost along the way." She made a sweeping motion with her rubbery fingers, then cranked the hot water on and began washing dishes.

Of course it was awkward at the door. How could it not be? Maybe some kids are sophisticated about such things by that age, but not us. As Charlie pulled on his coat, snug as he did the double-breasted buttons, I slipped my new gloves on again.

"That was a really nice evening, Brenda," Charlie said. "You saved my life with the eggnog—"

I silenced him with one gloved finger on his lips. Charlie started to make his surprised face again, startled wide open, until I stood on my toes and put my lips where that finger had been.

You never know about some people. You think you do, you have an expectation, and then they turn out to be something else entirely. I would never, for example, have imagined that Charlie Fish would be a good kisser.

I could not have been more wrong. Charlie pulled me to him, suddenly very much strong and in command, and kissed me for all he was worth. I found myself grabbing the hair on the back of his head—where did an idea like that come from?—while he swept me closer and our bodies pressed together their whole length.

There is no shame—I say this now as a frail old lady who has not been smooched in a long, long time—no shame in enjoying a kiss at nineteen. Or any other age. Sooner or later the kisses will stop, this is a certain thing, one day there will be a last kiss, and I would venture to say that for every single human being, it will come too soon.

Today I would gladly exchange every remaining hour of my life to have one minute more with Charlie Fish, just one, and to spend it kissing. Like days, the kisses of a life are numbered. Perhaps that makes each one all the more precious. And none so special as the first.

Then he released me. It took us a few seconds to untangle. "Merry Christmas, Brenda." Eyes bright, he swept open the door, damp and cold poured in, and out went Charlie Fish into the slushy December night. I could hear him singing the "Hallelujah Chorus" as he skittered away up the street.

I stood there a full minute, stunned by the strength of desire I felt for this unimpressive fellow—a sensation I had never known a glimmer of with the boys I'd smooched after a night of dancing or a show—bringing the gloved fingertips to my mouth, touching my lips, fully perplexed and utterly changed.

"Brenda?" my mother called from the kitchen. "I'm running out of rack space. Would you please get in here and dry?"

8 .

SANTANGELO WAS A TERRIER with a rag in his mouth. He would not let it go.

Every noon, he'd invite a different guy to join him for lunch. Half a sandwich along, he'd start asking about that boy's math, what was he working on lately, a regular interrogation that continued either until the guy became suspicious, or Cohen rang the one o'clock back-to-work bell.

"Damn that bell," Santangelo said, falling into line. "I feel like a pet."

But one afternoon he sidled up to Charlie's desk in better humor. "I'm putting it together," he confided. "Everyone has a separate part, but they all interlock. It's a jigsaw puzzle."

Charlie made less conversation than anyone else in those days, as he strove to accelerate his output. Outside it might snow all day, and he would only know when he left the building at night. If the hour was reasonable, he went to Brenda's, but many nights it was too late. Dorm proctors locked the doors at eleven, and he had missed lights-out only once—going back to the math rooms to spend a miserable night on the floor. Once had been enough.

"A puzzle?" Charlie continued with his work. "Figure anything out so far?"

"Well." Santangelo sat on the adjacent desk—which, after its prior occupant shipped off to the army, had remained unoccupied. "There is a major installation somewhere in New Mexico. I've seen the numbers. They're using tons of construction materials, plus heavy equipment like bulldozers and bucket loaders. There is at least one mine."

"A mine? What in the world for?" As he spoke Charlie drew an *x* on his page, to represent an impact spot one thousand feet off the ground. That was his latest assignment, and he could not imagine anything more useless. Calculate the falling time, aiming, and variables for an object released at thirty-five thousand feet, but stopping a thousand feet off the ground. Why not start at thirty-four and end on the earth, like all bombs do? Raising his eyes, he realized Steel Wool was waiting for an answer. "Maybe all that equipment is so they can put in a swimming pool for Mather."

"I admit it sounds flaky." Santangelo bent closer. "But I know one thing."

"How's it going, girls?" Cohen snapped from the doorway. "Fish, you guppy. Always glad to see you have time to chat."

"He came over to my desk."

"He came over to my desk," Cohen mimicked in a falsetto, before ducking back down the hallway.

"Most annoying human on earth," Charlie grumbled.

"What does he care anyway?" Santangelo asked. "It's not like your uncle is going to heave you."

"That is exactly what he means. I am sitting in the bucket of a catapult. Snip the rope and wheeee." He made a curve with his hand, as though it were sailing off somewhere.

"Not a chance." Santangelo stood. "I haven't figured out yet why arcs matter so much, but you're the only guy working on them. If they heave you, no more arc math."

"Please." Charlie pointed at his full in-box. "I really have to finish today's pile."

"Well, excuse me," he said, hands in the air as if Charlie held a gun. "I forgot. Director's nephew, no time to talk." Santangelo turned away, feigning hurt. But he brightened at a new boy's desk.

"Hi there. What are you working on today?"

Charlie bent over his arc problem. He'd already calculated the falling time from thirty-five thousand feet to one thousand: forty-three seconds. But the object couldn't be a bomb, or his task would have ended with an impact on the ground.

Meanwhile two more assignments sat in his in-box, and it was already a quarter till four. If he skipped dinner again, he might get to see Brenda for an hour—assuming he could solve the problem on his desk at all. Charlie drew an arc from the top corner of a sheet of paper to an inch above the bottom. Everything else was a mystery.

By the time he finished for the day, he was alone. Cohen had popped his head in at seven to announce that he was heading home, and told Charlie to put finished papers in Simmons's in-box. Now Charlie gathered his things, pulling on his new coat before switching off the lights. Again the hall was dark except for the office at the far end. Charlie assumed it was the custodial staff, until he heard a cough from within.

"Uncle John?"

"Charlie? Is that you?"

"Yes, sir."

The boy stood in the outer room beside the secretary's desk, wondering whether or not he should leave his work there and hurry along.

"Come on in," the professor said. "You may as well."

"Sorry to disturb you," Charlie said, inching into the office.

"No, it's good timing. Are those today's calculations?"

"Yes, sir." Charlie held them forward. "All three trajectories."

Simmons took them, opening the folder and flipping through the pages. "Any idea what you are working on, Charlie?"

"None at all, sir."

He waved the papers that concerned the object stopping its fall at one thousand feet. "None at all? Such discretion becomes you."

"Oh." Charlie realized he was being credited with understanding something, when he actually had no idea. "Thank you, sir."

"What strikes you as meaningful, in this calculation?"

Charlie felt a small rise of panic. Glancing around, he noticed the rough drawing of a catapult still on the blackboard. "I suppose the question is how to stop the rock from hitting the ground, so it will cause even more damage."

"Exactly." Simmons clapped his hands together. "You understand completely."

Charlie shuffled his feet. "Sir, I don't mean to—"

"It's all right." The professor held his hands up as if in protest. "I've been saying it all along. No matter how much work you give them, bright boys' minds will not sit still all day."

Charlie had no idea what his uncle meant. "I suppose not, sir."

"You suppose not." Simmons returned to his desk, gathering a sheaf of papers. "Well, let's get down to business." He tossed down a folder an inch thick. "Charlie, here are the results from your first six weeks here. See for yourself how many substantive errors you made in that time."

He read the upside-down cover and saw three red checks. "Wow. Sorry, Uncle John. I had no idea you all were keeping track of that sort of thing."

"Who do you think we work for here? We keep track of everything."

Charlie shifted his weight from foot to foot. Warm with his coat unbuttoned, he realized he had not been invited to sit this time. "Yes, sir," he said.

"Here is your second six weeks." The professor tossed another folder on the desk. It was thinner, but with only one check on top. "More accurate, but less work completed. That period ended in December, about the time we had our last chat."

"Yes, sir."

"And here—" He took the papers Charlie had just brought, added them to a third folder, and dropped it on top of the other two. "Well, you can see for yourself."

It was thicker than the other two combined. But the cover had so many red checks, Charlie had to lean closer to count. "Nine?"

"That's right, Charlie. Nine substantive errors. Each one of which, if we didn't catch it, would cost equipment, or money, or lives." He flattened his palm on the stack of folders and sighed. "You did what I asked you to do, you sped up. But your accuracy went all to hell. And that's assuming today's pieces are correct."

Charlie stood straight. He found himself looking out the window: an early February night in Chicago, cold rain angling across the glass. He realized he did not know what day it was. He had not seen Brenda in weeks. The window also contained the reflection of his uncle's back, which was ramrod upright.

"I'm not good enough," Charlie said.

"'Good' is the wrong word," Simmons said. "You are a good person, a good citizen, and you have an excellent work ethic. But when it comes to arcs, Charlie Fish can be accurate, or he can be fast. But not both." He let that sink in. "Bear in mind, I am not showing you any other fellows' folders, and none of them looks perfect either. Because you have worked on trajectories, however, you are not someone I can simply let go."

"I'm sorry, Uncle John. I don't follow you."

"You know things about our special catapult. I can't send you off to the army now, or turn you loose on the streets of Chicago when there are spies everywhere. Some Kraut might capture you, and learn what we're doing here."

"I can keep a secret—"

"Don't be naive, Charlie. These people will cut off your fingers one at a time until you spill. They will drug you and ruin your mind, purely for sport. There is no shame in saying that you could not withstand their torments. No one could."

"I suppose so, sir."

"The question is what to do with you now." He stood and went to the window, surveying the street below. Half a minute passed. "How are you liking Chicago, son?"

"I like it well enough, Uncle John."

"I love it here. This city is full of vitality and muscle, without all the pretentiousness and self-importance you find on the East and West coasts. I prefer Chicago to pretty much everywhere else." A bit of moisture had fogged the lower part of the window, and Simmons rubbed it clear with his thumb. "My superiors want to move me, this whole kit and caboodle, to a more secure location."

"New Mexico?"

"What?" Simmons whirled to face him, then checked himself. That easy smile came back to his face. "Charlie Fish. In a world where everyone is bragging about themselves all day long, you are much smarter than you let on."

"I don't know about that, sir."

"Don't be humble with me. I've got your number. But here's the wrinkle." Wiping his wet finger on his pants, the professor returned to his desk. He stacked the three collections of Charlie's calculations together. "I can't have folders with more red on them than all the Valentines you and I will get next week. It stands out. And trust me, Charlie, certain kinds of standing out are not good."

"I'm willing to do my part and then some, Uncle John."

"Of course you are," he said. "But you've become the one thing that neither I nor this country has time for right now." He held his hand out.

Charlie, realizing he was being dismissed, shook that hand. "What is that, sir?"

"A problem."

9.

THE BEING-LATE PART I grew accustomed to, though not without a struggle. Ever since boys first started paying attention to me, in tenth grade when I developed, I always had punctuality rules. Ten minutes late on the first date and there would never be a second one. Fifteen minutes on a subsequent date and he'd better have an explanation that defied gravity. Plus an apology that included candy, flowers, or both. Twenty minutes late and his mother better have died.

Partly it was a matter of supply and demand. There were many fewer guys during the war, while I still did my socializing with the same five gals, and my best friend Greta leading the charge. You would think that made the boys choosers and the girls beggars, but the way I figured, scarcity meant a girl had to value herself more highly, so boys would respect her.

Partly, too, it came from my mother. My father was the bread-winner and provider, but that didn't mean she lacked for power. Dinner was at seven, for example. Sharp. If he was down in the basement fiddling with radios, and didn't hear when she called from the top of the stairs at five minutes till, too bad. We'd sit and eat anyhow, in a terrible silence that Frank and I would lie low under, like cows waiting out a thunderstorm under a tree—feeling bad for Daddy and what was waiting for him once he realized the time. We'd hear his tread on the stairs, see his sheepish face peek around the corner, and my mother would greet him with a visage of ice.

Oh, the pleas for mercy we'd hear that night. Frank and I would wolf down our food and rush our dishes into the kitchen, while

Daddy tried to regain Mother's good graces. All she would do was point at her ear so he knew where to aim his apology. Say what you will about the severity of basic training, that woman would have made an excellent drill instructor.

The thing about my punctuality rules with the boys is that they worked. Holding myself high made them line right up. But the first time Charlie Fish was tardy, it was that night of the snowstorm, and he'd been drenched. With my mother drying him off, there'd been no chance for me to set the ground rules. The next time, he was even later.

"Oooh," I fumed, pacing as the minutes passed. "If he stands me up, I will fry that boy."

"It's wartime," my mother replied, not bothering to look up from the crossword puzzle she was doing in pen. "Boys are not in charge of their schedules anymore. Why don't you practice your scales?"

I sat at the piano sure enough, but all het up. After a clumsy start, I began running through the majors and minors in every key. It did help to pass the time, and my mood softened as I worked up and down the notes, but I resented her anyhow for being right.

When Charlie finally arrived, it was a solid hour past our arranged time. "I had a last-minute meeting," he explained, nose running and breathless. "It couldn't wait."

To his credit, he'd brought flowers, no easy thing in wintry Chicago. I put them in a vase, then went ahead and had dinner with him anyhow. I might be self-important, but I wasn't the kind of girl to stay home and pout. Charlie found a Polish place with steamed-up windows and amazing sausages. Pretty soon he had me laughing about what the clues would be in my mother's ideal crossword puzzle. Seven-letter word for proper gentleman? *Yesmaam.* Twelve letter word for heaven? *Cleankitchen.* I forgot all about that hour of fretting.

Date by date, I grew accustomed to his tardiness. Always ready on time, just in case, I adjusted my rules to accommodate his unpredictable schedule. I'd sit with my mother while she puffed away on one cigarette after another, triple the amount she'd smoked before

Daddy left, reading a gossip magazine or helping her with the occasional crossword clue. If Charlie was late, I'd let him buss me on the cheek and out we'd go without a fuss. Somehow he wore me down.

But Valentine's Day is different. Particularly in your nineteenth year, when events having to do with romance begin to matter in new ways. By then I'd stopped dating other boys, unless it was in a big group for the movies or some such. No one was getting smooches from me either. That had stopped on Christmas Eve, thank you very much. I hadn't exactly announced these things, because I didn't want Charlie making assumptions. But we were close enough in our conversations that by February he must have known. Granted, I pecked that sailor from Indiana home on an eight-day leave, the one who was such a dazzling dance partner. But when our lips touched, I thought of Charlie. Like a beach ball with the nozzle left open, all the fun went out of it.

Whether I admitted it or not, out loud or in my secret heart, Charlie had become my fella. The skinny math kid. It didn't feel like I was settling, though, for all my airs. More like choosing something out of the ordinary. My girlfriends might not have understood, except Greta, who wanted us all to have serious fellas. Frank would have squinted one eye at me and said, "Really?" My mother revealed as much of her opinions as a sphinx. Not one word for or against. That was as out of character as if she'd come down to breakfast one morning having grown wings.

I hardly noticed. I was busy getting excited about Valentine's. The Monday before, Charlie had stopped in at the store like he used to before his work got so busy. He brought a deli sandwich for me, roast beef on rye with tomatoes and Thousand Island dressing. Nothing for himself, though, he couldn't stay. While I ate, he explained that his assignment was changing again, he was sorry not to have been around more, and he wanted to make it up to me. So: Six o'clock sharp on Valentine's Day. We'd go out for a fancy dinner. We'd hold hands the whole time.

"I promise," he said, and to the young girl I once was, those two words were more delicious than any sandwich ever. I answered that

I would dress to the nines for him. And secretly told myself that I would kiss him every chance I got.

Charlie rushed in at almost seven thirty. He had no flowers, because the store closed before he could get there. He wore his usual work clothes, drab as a sidewalk, because he didn't want to run back to the dorms to change and then arrive even later. He claimed he'd bought some chocolate for me, but that was in the dorms too.

Charlie looked pale, like a person kept too long inside. There was perspiration on his brow, though it was mid-February. He wrung his hands and apologized and asked if we could sort it all out on the way to the restaurant before we lost our reservation.

I took a page from my mother. I mean, I was wearing my best blue dress, which I had altered for the occasion. Also I was good enough to get into a conservatory. Also he had promised. So I held myself tall and aloof, and tapped one finger against my ear.

But that backfired, because he leaned close and said, "Brenda I am as sorry as I could be," and he was still breathing hard from running, which I felt in my ear like an electric charge, down my neck about to my toes. I shivered from it.

If my mother saw, she hid it well. Her nose was buried in a new book, about a boy in Boston who was an apprentice at Paul Revere's silversmith shop. All she did was lower the book and say, "Charlie, how nice to see you. I hope you and Brenda have a fine evening." Then back up with the book, a ribbon of cigarette smoke rising from behind it.

I put on my coat and the gloves Charlie had given me, haughty as a duchess, and waited by the front door so he could open it for me.

"Oh, right," Charlie said, doing just that, but the moment of hesitation would cost him, oh yes. That, as I breezed past him, was my decided plan.

I gave him the same treatment on the walk to the restaurant. Sure enough, they'd seated someone at our table. Seeing my annoyance, and Charlie's desperation, the maître d' had mercy and squeezed us into another spot. But the space was too small, and back by the kitchen doors—which swung every fifteen seconds the whole meal as waiters rushed in and out. Plus the place smelled like pea soup.

"How was your day, Brenda?"

"Don't even start," I snapped. Which was foolish, because it left so little room for peacemaking conversation. My Valentine's Day was ruined, but not beyond repair.

I wanted oysters, but they'd run out. I ordered soup.

"That's all you want?" Charlie said. "Soup?"

"Minestrone is very good for you," I answered, smug as a bishop. Which killed another sally at conversation. I was making everything worse.

In a way, that exchange revealed our relationship in miniature: Charlie's good intentions and my overinflated sense of myself. It would harm that night, and it would taint our future. Eventually, when I learned how far he surpassed me in the things that really matter, only then would I become the person I ought to have been from the start. I don't want only to live that night over again, I want to change the whole beginning. I should have been humble, I should have been kind. Instead I sat with arms crossed and a pout on my face. Some jack-o'-lanterns are more becoming.

Charlie tried again. "Brenda, I know I messed up, because of my work duties—"

"You made me a promise, Charlie Fish." I was forgiving as a steel beam.

"—but you look terrific tonight," he persisted. "That dress flatters your figure beautifully."

"I know," I said. "I myself sewed the waist in."

Oh, if I could reach back through time, I would give that girl such a shake. There was a war on, and this sweet boy was part of it whether he wanted to be or not. Yet all she could think about was herself, and how he had inconvenienced her. She will have only one first Valentine's Day with Charlie Fish. Wouldn't she want to make it unforgettably sweet?

Instead I made a big show of unfolding my napkin, and raising it high, almost above my head, before dropping it in my lap. I don't know what that was supposed to signify, but something about deep annoyance, I suppose.

Charlie looked exhausted and dewy-eyed. He kept trying like a champion anyhow, offering me a bite of his steak (I refused), asking for a taste of my soup (I declined). He talked about the movies coming out that weekend, and which ones we might enjoy.

"Oh, I don't know," I said, shaking too much salt into the soup. "Maybe."

The meal was eternal. At some point my knight accepted defeat, hurrying through his food, saying thank you but no, we did not want to hear about the special Valentine's Day dessert, paying the check as quickly as he could. We trudged home in silence, the wind bitter at our backs. He didn't do his usual humming, though often as not that would result in both of us singing as we skipped down the sidewalks. Maybe he didn't want to risk it, and have that nice habit ruined by my temper. When we reached the front steps, Charlie said he was sorry but he couldn't come in. He had early duty again, and it was a long walk back to the dorms.

"Well." I held out my gloved hand, determined that this was the last I would see of that tedious Charlie Fish. Really, what had I been thinking to have spent so much time with him? "This will go down in history as my worst Valentine's Day ever."

Charlie took my hand, but he did not shake it. He held it between both of his. "Mine too," he said. "I wish I could have made it all better."

His face looked so crestfallen, I couldn't help myself. I leaned in, lips to his sweet lips, two seconds and no more. I told myself to consider it a kiss good-bye. Then I ran up the steps, leaving Charlie Fish out there in the cold.

THE MOMENT HE AND Santangelo returned from lunch, Charlie knew something was different. When he'd left there were papers on his desk, facedown as usual, and now they were gone. Charlie's gait slowed. His can of pencils was empty. The in-box too.

Charlie slumped down into his seat. "Damn."

"What is it?" Santangelo asked, peering over. "Oh."

"Yup."

"Rough business, Fish."

Charlie opened one drawer, confirmed that it was empty, and did not bother with the others. Santangelo saw, and backed away to his desk.

"Yes, better get busy," Charlie said. "No point in both of us joining the army."

"Fish." Cohen stood in the doorway with a cardboard box that Charlie suspected held the former contents of his desk. "You're wanted. Double-time."

Santangelo bent over his papers, but he whispered as Charlie hurried past, "Good luck."

Professor Simmons's secretary was typing with a pencil between her teeth when Cohen led Charlie in. She pointed at a chair. Before Charlie could sit, Cohen placed the box there, then gave him a pat on the back.

"You weren't all bad," he allowed. "Compared with some others. See you after the war."

Charlie swallowed hard, too nervous to reply. Cohen vanished down the hall and the secretary returned to her typing. Over the thwack of the keys he could hear his uncle in the inner office, talking. First the disaster with Brenda, and now this. And what about the problem he'd nearly solved before lunch? Who would do it now?

Simmons put the phone down, and instantly his secretary called out, "He's here."

"Good, good."

Charlie had taken only one step forward when his uncle charged out of the office, trademark smile on his face. "There's my fine young fellow." He slowed by the secretary's desk. "Get me Enrico on the phone. I'll be back in five."

The woman turned to a Rolodex, took the pencil from her mouth, and used the eraser to flip through the cards.

"Come along, Charlie. No time to waste."

Charlie gestured toward the cardboard box. "Should I bring—"

"You won't be needing that." He strode off, Charlie scrambling in his wake.

The math team occupied the top floor of a three-story building. Now he followed the professor down four flights, to the basement. He did not need anyone to explain what this meant in the department's hierarchy.

The glass door of one room let out a strange bluish glow, and Simmons knocked before entering. Charlie followed close behind, but not before noticing a hand-painted sign on the door: *Beasley's Dungeon*. A man at a workbench was bent over something, a kind of strange pen in his hand. The room smelled of heat and old shoes.

"I have a new one for you, Beasley," Simmons said in his most affable voice.

Goggles on his face, Beasley did not look up. "Shall I shoot myself now, and save us all the headache?"

"Grouchy," Simmons stage-whispered, "but an excellent teacher."

"I am not a teacher," Beasley said, concentrating on his work. "I am an expert. There's a difference."

They waited until Beasley sat back. As methodically as a machine, he wiped the strange pen on a sponge that hissed from the contact, placed the pen on a stand, and covered it with a welding mask. Spinning on the stool to face them, Beasley removed his goggles and donned thick black glasses. He resembled an annoyed bird, narrow and beakish, with the glasses perched low on his nose, as if they were about to fall off. "What failure have you brought me this time?"

"This is Fish," Simmons said, "the smart fellow from upstairs I told you about."

"Has he soldered before?"

"Total novice. I mentioned that earlier."

Beasley grimaced. "I was hoping you'd been joking."

Simmons laughed. "Always the dreamer." He checked his watch. "I have a call."

"You do know I am being asked to produce more down here, not less, right?"

Charlie was astonished at Beasley's blatant disrespect for the department chair, but he marveled more that his uncle allowed it. In fact his trademark smile was undiminished. Maybe it was about more than warmth, maybe there was resolve too.

"I'm counting on you to teach him so he increases production from this lab."

Beasley pursed his lips. "I am not a teacher." He pouted on his stool, then touched his glasses upward, though they continued to hang every bit as precariously on the end of his nose. Charlie thought they were somewhere between aristocratic and comical. "Look, I'll give him the basics, all right? Safety rules, some circuits. But you can't expect me to do my job if I'm spending half my time babysitting."

"I don't need a babysitter," Charlie spoke up at last.

"It talks?" Beasley snorted. "You are so uninformed, swaddling infant, you don't even know what you need."

"Try, Charlie." Simmons gave his elbow a friendly squeeze. "Try not to punch him in the jaw."

And he hurried off to take his call.

As the door closed, Beasley stood—though to Charlie it seemed more as if the man were unfolding himself, long limbs straightening until he stood six and a half feet tall. His wrists were long and knuckles large, and he had a giant Adam's apple. Charlie thought of a bird with an extended bill, perhaps a crane of some kind. More than anything, though, he felt an impulse to reach forward, to push those glasses up the bird's beak before they fell off.

"Wait," Beasley said, switching off the light that Simmons had left on. He crooked a finger in Charlie's direction. "Follow." He moved with a strange, large-jointed walk, and Charlie thought: not crane, stork.

"This is your station." He pointed at a desk that was cluttered with wires and electronic components. "Notice that it is at the opposite extreme of the room from mine. Notice that you work with your back to me. This is deliberate, to minimize chatter and interruptions."

Charlie picked up one of the components, a strip of stiff wire with a yellow lump of ceramic material in the middle. "What will I be doing here?"

"You're unacquainted with this project? What kind of imbecile are you?"

"You know, I am about at the end of taking insults from you. A guy two minutes into a new assignment can reasonably expect—"

"Oh no, you're not." Beasley wagged a finger. "Your days of being insulted by me are only beginning. You are more likely to fail here than anywhere else in this building."

"You don't know that. You don't know one thing about me."

"Oh?" Beasley snatched the component from Charlie and pointed its wire at him. "Charles Fish. Brought straight from Harvard, where you were majoring in math and on track to graduate at eighteen—a fact you keep so quiet, not even your dorm buddies know. You also sang in the university choir, which makes you as pathetic a creature as I can imagine."

"How in the world did you—"

"Finally, you are the nephew of John Simmons, metallurgy boss, and owner of the phoniest smile this side of Lake Michigan." He tossed the yellow component back on the desk. "Right so far?"

"You have one hell of a nerve."

"Fish, your uncle's influence ends at that doorway. In a dungeon, the guard serves the prisoner's sentence right along with him. In a dungeon, the guard is king. And I am not here to win a war, I'm here to avoid having to kill anyone."

"Really?" Charlie stepped back. "On that, actually, we agree."

"I'll throw the confetti later. Tell me, how do you know when water is very cold? Quick, now."

"Well, it's ice, I suppose."

"You suppose? Pathetic."

Charlie crossed his arms. "What's pathetic about that?"

"How can you tell when water is very hot?"

"It boils."

"Progress," Beasley said. "But I won't get my hopes up. Now." He lifted off a rack one of those strange pens. "How do you know when metal is cold or hot? Does it freeze or boil? How can you tell?"

Charlie puzzled that over for a second. "I don't know."

"HOT," Beasley yelled, pressing the pen's tip against Charlie's arm.

"Yow," Charlie jumped back, rubbing where he'd been touched.

Beasley shook his head slowly, a picture of disappointment. "It wasn't hot."

Charlie reddened with anger. "No."

"But you couldn't tell by sight. There is no way, looking at a piece of metal, to know if it is hot or cold or"—he thumbed the metal pen's tip—"Room temperature." He put the device back in its stand. "These soldering irons can reach seven hundred and fifteen degrees. If you ever touch something in my work area, I figure the third-degree burn you'll get will serve as education and reprimand all at once. But if I come over to your station for any reason—to borrow a tool or check your work or blow my nose—and you have left a hot iron uncovered, I will find the first possible opportunity to stick it in your eye. Got me?"

"You were telling the truth," Charlie marveled. "You really aren't a teacher."

"Lesson one is ended." He pointed at a stool. "Sit."

"Would it be entirely too much to ask for a bit of context?" Charlie hooked his foot on the stool and rolled it closer. "What is this department, and what are we doing?"

Beasley crossed his arms. "I'm permitted to tell you that we receive electronic designs from somewhere outside this building, and my job is to build them. Every part is top secret, every assembly is urgent. That's what I'm doing. What *you* are doing, other than slowing my work? I have no idea. But I will placate my director, and with luck the war will end before either of us murders the other."

Charlie sat on the stool with a sigh. "Are you always this disagreeable?"

"Are you kidding?" Beasley sniffed. "Today I'm in a *good* mood."

Later the stork announced that he was going to lunch, and that "Harvard boy" should organize his station. Alone, the first thing Charlie did was switch the overhead lights back on. He returned to his desk, scooping up a handful of the components. They were all pieces of colored ceramic, roughly the size of a dime, with stiff wires sticking out of both ends. He found goggles, a welding mask.

Was this odd laboratory how he would manage to stay in Chicago? Was this a means to seeing Brenda again? The room was dusty and smelled of burned metal. Charlie went to the lavatory and returned with towels to wash and dry the desk. They came away gray. As an afterthought he wiped the stool, too, and the towels turned black. But he hummed as he cleaned, his mood improving.

Beasley reappeared gnawing on a piece of jerky, and gulping from a bottle of pop. He chewed with his mouth open, forcing Charlie to turn his head. There were packages of jerky in Beasley's shirt pocket, which he dumped out on his desk. Then, his face in a sour expression, he went to the doorway and switched off the overhead lights. Beasley returned, chewing audibly.

"Lesson two, Harvard," he said, finishing the soda along the way, tossing the bottle in his metal waste bin, which clanged nearly as loudly as a church bell. "I am not teaching, I am demonstrating." He sat at Charlie's station, belched, and leaned over the desk. "Observe."

For about one minute, he showed Charlie how to operate the soldering iron, how to set the temperature, and how to keep the tip clean. "I do this for you once, Harvard. After that, you're on your own."

Beasley uncoiled gray wire from a spool. When he touched it to the soldering iron, the soft outer layer vanished in a whiff of buttery smoke. The remaining core melted into a little volcano-shaped droplet. He made point after point, his hands deft and precise.

"It's called tinning. You tin a component into place. You snip off the surplus wire. You tin another component. Done."

Beasley rummaged in a bin, found a flat metal plate with rows of small holes, and set it in front of Charlie. "Tin all of these points. Don't bother me till you're finished."

At that, Beasley made his storky way back to his desk. Charlie was glad to be left to himself. It seemed easy, and he started right in.

The outer layer would not melt. The core would not stick. The gun tip clogged with metal. Charlie sat back, breathing deeply to control his frustration, then tried again. Hours passed. The sponge dried out. The lighting was terrible.

"Pop quiz," Beasley announced down his nose, holding out a hand as he stood beside Charlie's station.

Charlie passed along the soldered plate. "I haven't got the knack yet."

Beasley touched his glasses, though they remained precisely as low on his nose. "Well, well."

"Am I doing okay?"

He handed back the plate. "You are the worst at soldering I have ever seen. No one else in my experience comes close."

"With a little practice, I—"

"With a lifetime of practice, you might advance all the way to mediocrity." He peered at the control panel of Charlie's iron. "No wonder. Your temp was set at two-ninety. That's too cold to make anything but a mess."

Beasley wrote something on a piece of paper, placing it facedown on a filing cabinet beside Charlie's desk. "Shut down, Harvard. Go home. Come again tomorrow to fail another day."

"I'll keep practicing, if you don't mind. At the higher temperature."

Beasley ambled to his desk and snapped off the light. "You are permitted in here only when I am present, and I am leaving."

"I'm a slow and steady kind of worker. How can I improve if I can't practice?"

Beasley opened the dungeon door, sweeping his arm to indicate that Charlie should precede him. "My sincere advice to you is to go home, and stand awhile in front of your bathroom mirror."

"My mirror?" Charlie shut off his own desk lamp, making his way to the door. "What would that accomplish?"

"You can contemplate what you will look like with an army helmet on."

The next day Charlie turned his instrument hotter, and the wire melted, the iron made the wet sponge hiss. The basics were exactly as Beasley had demonstrated.

But he still didn't make neat volcanos. Instead the wire clumped up on his iron. He wiped and wiped the tip on his sponge, but the clumping continued. Also the smoke had drifted away when Beasley demonstrated, but with Charlie it rose right up his nose—sweet-scented, but piercingly hot. He managed to solder a total of two points successfully before lunch.

Occasionally he spied on the stork. The man was a master, that was clear: cleaning and tinning and moving pieces with dexterity, never lifting his head except to stir one gloved finger through a bin of components, searching. When he finished a plate, he would clear his throat, gnaw off a fresh plug of jerky, and start the next.

Charlie could not imagine how many hours it had taken to

develop that level of skill. A thousand, probably. Here he was, ten hours in, nine hundred and ninety to go.

"Buckle down," he told himself. This was only the first full day. Soldering might be his only way of staying in Chicago.

In fact, the afternoon went better. A hotter iron did make the wire behave. One component seemed to melt into place properly, and when he snipped away the extra wire, he noticed that Beasley went still for a second at the sound. Still it took hours, and all of his focus. He was concentrating so hard, his nose inches from the hot iron, the tap of a finger on his shoulder startled him.

"What?" Charlie jerked upright.

The finger belonged to Beasley, who extended his hand. "Show."

Charlie's lower spine hurt from staying bent over for so long. He glanced at the clock, it was five already. The afternoon had flown. "It's pretty rough."

"Show."

After covering the hot iron, Charlie handed over his plate. Beasley peered here and there, nodding. "Simmons neglected to tell me that you were mentally retarded."

"You should watch your mouth."

"Should I?" He flipped over the paper he'd left on the filing cabinet the day before and read aloud: "nine rows, eighteen contacts each." Beasley dropped the paper in Charlie's lap. "That was what you needed to do to get a C on this examination. One hundred and sixty-two contact points. Instead I count, let me see . . . if I allow this half-done area, it's forty-one. You failed by one hundred and twenty-one."

"Soldering is harder than I thought."

"Fish, you dolt. *Life* is harder than you think. Show me your technique."

Charlie picked up the hot iron, and began pressing the wire to it.

"Stop," Beasley said. "Stop before I throttle you."

"What?" Charlie asked. "What am I doing wrong?"

"Never touch the iron directly to the wire. I told you that. All it will do is clump."

"You most certainly did not tell me—"

"I am now repeating myself, which I detest."

Charlie rolled his stool backward, calming himself. When Simmons told him to resist the temptation to punch Beasley, he'd thought the man was joking. Not anymore.

"Pay attention this time." Beasley demonstrated, placing the iron against a point on the square. "You heat the component, not the wire. The wire melts into place."

Charlie was too angry to reply. The man's instruction had deliberately omitted a basic step.

"I'm taking a meal break," Beasley said. "Though your stupidity makes me sick."

He had reached the door before Charlie managed to reply. "Why are you so deliberately annoying?"

The stork paused in the doorway, turning slowly, perhaps so that his glasses would not fall off. "Because I am not theoretical, Harvard. I am real."

"What are you talking about?"

"I am a licensed electrical engineer." Beasley waved an arm at the room. "Everyone else here is theoretical. Math theory, physics theory, chemistry theory, and nothing gets done. You theoreticians scamper around this place like ants. And about as usefully."

Charlie shook his head. "Do you always exaggerate like this?"

"Exaggerate?" He strode back, hackles raised, and waved Charlie's unfinished plate in his face. "You are working on electronics that our military men will depend on with total faith. Do it right and Americans live, do it wrong and they die. So far, Harvard, you have done every single thing wrong." He tossed the plate on the desk, components scattering. "And you think I exaggerate. Grow a conscience, will you?"

Beasley was gone before Charlie could answer—not that he had any comeback ready. Even with a less abrasive instructor, he was out of his depth and he knew it. A person could not learn soldering in a day and a half, not well enough for soldiers to bet their lives on. He rose from the stool, poked his head out the door to make sure the hallway was deserted, then climbed the stairs two at a time.

The secretary was gone and he knocked on the professor's outer door. Instead of waiting to hear any welcoming words, though, he barged in. "Uncle John."

"Charlie." Simmons sat at his desk, looking up from his papers. "I guess I should have expected to see you."

"I don't mean to seem ungrateful."

"But you wonder what you are doing in the dungeon."

"With the most difficult human being I have ever encountered."

The professor nodded, waiting.

"Doing a task I am wholly unqualified for," Charlie continued. "With a teacher who despises me for no reason I have given him. And soldiers' lives are at stake. And any burn I get is my fault."

Simmons maintained a serious expression. "All done?"

"I don't even know what this soldering is for."

"That didn't seem to bother you when the work was arcs."

"True." Charlie felt caught. "That's true."

"Son, you are going to encounter all sorts of people in life. You have to decide which ones you allow to determine your fate, and which ones are bumps in the road."

"Beasley feels bigger than a molehill."

Simmons rose and went to the window. He lifted one leg to put his shoe on the sill, and leaned an elbow on his thigh. Charlie thought of a football coach, giving a halftime pep talk.

"There is always more to know," Simmons said. "There is always a backstory that makes simple things look complicated."

"Beasley, for example?"

"His mother's family name is Kozera. They are Poles. One night last spring, Nazis killed the entire family. Aunts, uncles, grandparents, cousins, all of them. So here is this young man, an outstanding engineering student in Rensselaer, who has spent every summer of his life with his family in Warsaw. And they're all gone. What does he do next? Pick up a gun? Enlist? No, he volunteers to use what he has, skills which prove to be quite valuable. Personality issues aside, he creates a highly productive electronics laboratory, which is helpful to national defense in a way neither he nor I is permitted to tell you. Some people consider Beasley a war hero."

Charlie ran his hand over the back of a chair. "I am supposed to respect him, then? Or have sympathy for him?"

"Maybe not. Maybe no one is allowed to treat people the way he does, no matter what they have lost or what they accomplish." Simmons returned to his seat. "But you have a choice to make, about how large his influence will be on your life."

"He seems determined to have me fail."

"Well, like it or not, this is your shot, son. Most boys don't get as much as one, which you had already in the math crew. The dungeon is opportunity number two. There won't be a third, not because I can't keep a promise to my baby sister, but because at that point we're out of options."

"What if I can't learn soldering well enough though? What if I'm terrible at it?"

Simmons sighed. "Plenty of young men make better soldiers than you might expect. And many soldiers get through a war and come out the other side just fine."

"What should I do?"

"You'll need to write your own story, Charlie. I can't devote any more time to you, there's too much work. Sometime down the road, I imagine you sending me a note, maybe three words long. *Get me out*—and I'll have it done by supper time. Or, if you treat Beasley as a way of strengthening your determination, knowing that bigger challenges lie ahead, you might send three different words. *Ready for inspection*—something like that. If the work's good enough, I'll make sure you advance quickly."

As he listened, Charlie dug a fingernail into the wood of the chair back. "There is no way around this guy, is there, Uncle John?"

"Make the most of this opportunity, overcome it, and you will earn yourself a ringside seat at history. It would be a hell of a shame for you to miss it."

"The history of this war, you mean?"

"Charlie." Simmons let his shoulders drop. "I can't tell anymore whether you're being sincere, or discreet about something you've already figured out."

"I am genuinely in the dark here." Charlie advanced till his thighs touched the desk. "As your nephew, I'm asking. What do you mean? The history of what?"

The professor looked down. He seemed to discover the piles of work on his desk. He placed both palms on the stacked papers, then raised his head, looking his nephew in the eye. "I mean of all time, Charlie. I mean the history of the human race."

11.

MY MOTHER WAS WAITING up when I came home on Valentine's Day. Or, to be more accurate, when I let myself in she was plopped down in one of the living room's overstuffed chairs, smoking a cigarette. There was only the one lamp on, over the piano, so the room was dim. She seemed surprised to see me.

"Dinner's over already?"

"It is." I hung my coat in the hall closet.

"Did you have a nice time?"

"So-so." I headed past her for the kitchen where I switched on the lights.

"The food was less than excellent?"

I peered into the icebox. "The company was less than excellent."

I heard her exhale, then. It was not just the smoking, there was attitude in it. One quirk about Frank and Daddy being gone, with all of their male noise and activity, was how sensitive my mother and I became to each other's expressions. That exhale had the weight of what a year before might have required a long parental lecture.

I came to the kitchen door. "What?"

"What happened?"

"Mother. I am allowed to not like a boy, if I want."

"Of course you are."

"A girl deserves to feel special, sometimes." I felt myself almost about to cry, just saying it. "She deserves more than hours of waiting, sloppy clothes, no flowers, a bad table, boring conversation. She deserves more than an apology."

My mother took a long drag on that cigarette. The end of it glowed.

"Go ahead," I told her. "I'm sure I'll hear it eventually anyhow."

"Brenda." She put her cigarette in the ashtray. It was the speak-no-evil monkey, one of the Christmas gifts from Charlie. "Sit down here half a minute, sweetheart."

Sweetheart? I was in no mood for sugar talk. I was still angry, and frustrated, and wanting to shout at someone. But she patted the arm of the other overstuffed chair, and what else could I do? "This is not a great time for a lecture, Mother."

"Good thing I don't have a lecture to give you."

So I came and perched on the edge of the chair, and waited. My mother stared off out the window, not in any hurry.

"I miss your father," she said at last. Right out loud, plain as a piece of toast. "The longer he is gone, the more I feel like I have not been a very good wife."

"What? What are you talking about?"

"Calm down, Brenda." She picked up her cigarette for a long drag, holding it before the exhale. "We can have this conversation without getting hysterical."

"All right," I said, sliding back into the arms of the chair. "I'm listening."

"My girl." She turned to me and smiled. "When I married your father, I wasn't two years older than you are now."

"I have no intention of marrying anytime soon."

"Neither did I. But it turned out marriage had intentions about me. So I went fast, married fast, babies one and two. Why wait, right?"

I didn't know what to say. We'd never had a conversation like this.

"The problem is," she continued, "when it comes to your father, I have always had an inflated sense of myself. I had more education, came from a better-off family. He was this good guy, this very nice guy, who sold organs and tinkered with radios. I'd studied biology, played tennis, was nearly as good in math as you are."

"You played tennis?"

"So I made the rules," she said. "From big things like how you and Frank would be raised, to little things like what time we ate dinner. Your father's the breadwinner, but I've always been in charge."

"And look how well it's worked out for us all."

"Not all." She set her cigarette back in the ashtray, smoke rising. "Not everyone."

I waited for her to elaborate, but she had nothing more to say. "I'm not going to marry Charlie Fish," I said.

That seemed to rouse her. "Now that your father is gone, I have a different appreciation for his effect on my life. Now I know how kind he is, and how much I depend on that kindness, every day."

"You can tell him when he's back."

"That's exactly what I was thinking about when you came home. I don't know how, yet, but things will be different around here when the war is over. I'm going to try being less of a dictator. There will be a lot more appreciating instead."

There was a string of fabric loose on the chair arm, and I worried it free with my fingernails. "I never really thought about how you and Daddy got along. It was just the way things were, like the air in the house."

My mother nodded. "To you, he's your old papa. But to me, he's still my valentine. I'd give anything to be able to talk to him tonight. To sit with him while you're on a date. To have him reading in that chair, and reach over to give my hand a squeeze."

"I'm sorry." I said it in a small voice.

"If Charlie's not the guy for you, I won't meddle. Or," she smiled for one quick glint, "I'll try not to. But I want you to think about what this war is going to do to the guys you'll meet two and three years from now."

"They'll be so happy to be home. When this war ends, it is going to be a huge party everywhere."

"I hope so," she said, studying her smoky exhalation. "But there will also be lots of damaged goods. Guys who got hurt, or saw terrible things, or did terrible things because they had to. Who knows what kind of husbands they will be? You're a sweet girl, Brenda, with a young heart. They will have the hearts of old men."

She paused, smoking awhile, leisurely as a stroll on the beach. The kitchen clock cuckooed ten times. I thought: at least this disappointing day is almost over.

"I worry about Frank this way, too, but that's another conversation. All I'm saying is that Charlie is likely to come out of this war in okay shape, not all messed up inside."

I worked that fabric string into a little ball. "Because he's not in combat?"

"Because he's a decent human being. And more substantial than you give him credit for. You say you don't like this boy, but you might consider yourself lucky to have found him. The problem is that you, my girl, are more than a little bit spoiled."

"Mother." I made a face. "I am hardly—"

"You are, and you know it. Mostly I don't mind, because it means that you treat yourself as a valuable person. Which you are. You'll like who you like, regardless of what your old mother says. My only advice is, don't be too quick about what you throw away."

"What is that supposed to mean?" I was still peeved about the spoiled comment.

"It means, my sweet baby girl, just what I said. It's good to be proud, but don't let pride make you a fool."

"I'm not overly proud, and I am definitely not a fool."

My mother gave me a long, calm look. It was all I could do not to squirm.

"Let me say it this way, then." She took a last pull on her cigarette. "Don't do what I did, and consider yourself so superior, you miss twenty years of times you could have been kind. It's the worst kind of regret. Brenda honey, don't be me."

Then, with one last dragon breath toward the ceiling, she ground the butt out in the ashtray like she was putting it to death.

There wasn't another word between us on the topic that night, nor the next few days. The whole discussion was moot anyhow, because February melted into March, that month inched like a snail toward springtime, and Charlie Fish was scarce as new nylons. The more I mulled over our last date, the more I knew I had behaved like the perfect anti-valentine. No wonder weeks went by and he never turned up.

April arrived with letters from Daddy and Frank, both of whom wrote that they were well and safe. They used the same words, well and safe, which reassured my mother but made me suspicious. The crocuses did their brief purple display, daffodils rose and passed, the trees began to bud. But Charlie remained a no-show.

Well, fine. I worked twice as hard, sold more organs than in the Christmas rush, and started group piano lessons for beginners. In any quiet moment, I switched on the spinet model and learned the latest show tunes—not the classical material I'd need for the conservatory after the war, and never anything sonorous. Toe-tappers only.

It didn't work. The guy had a kind of glue to him. Memories had stuck in my brain. Many mornings I'd wake up, and lie in bed remembering how he opened doors for me, let me go first, stood when I returned from the ladies' room. I was not smart enough to feel regret about Charlie, not yet. Just longing.

A cute guy came in accordion shopping. When I put the straps over my arms, he smiled like a toothpaste billboard. "That instrument's looks just improved by a country mile," he said.

Normally a flirt that bold would steel my determination to land a sale, at full price. I gave him about half my usual demonstration, happy as a clown, then had to put the thing down. "Sorry, mister," I said, "it feels a little heavy today."

My girlfriends asked me on double dates, but my heart wasn't in it. Somehow quiet Charlie had spoiled me for the guys who were rowdy and loud. Polite Charlie stood in the way of the quick dancers and quicker kissers. One fella, out on the sidewalk after a night a gang of us went bowling, gave me an overfriendly squeeze good night, and his hand strayed oh-so-accidentally to the side of my boob. Oh, I gave that corporal a good smack in the chest, calling him fresh and not caring who heard, but he just laughed and winked at his pals. I walked myself home that night, thank you very much.

After that I stayed in for three Saturday nights in a row. I felt about forty years old.

My mother watched all of this with her usual eagle eye, but keeping any opinions to herself. Thinking back, I can only admire her restraint. I'm sure she knew exactly what I ought to do, but stayed mum so I could sort it out for myself. Instead I clung to my superiority, showing the world a girl unconcerned with any such silliness as a boy, bored by the melodrama of it all—while inside a little hopeful part of me began to wither.

The shop door's bell rang, I hurried out of the office, and it was never Charlie. Just a customer, curious about Hammonds.

"Good afternoon," I'd say, coming forward, poised as a beauty contestant, but aching inside. "How can I help you today?"

THE PARTICULAR MISERY KNOWN as Beasley appeared to be inexhaustible. No matter what Charlie did, his lab boss found an opportunity for scorn. Gradually, though, this strategy won the tall man what he wanted: Charlie's silence.

Through February and into March, all Charlie did was tin points on a steel plate. When he showed Beasley his progress, the stork's response was to scrape the work away.

"Try again tomorrow," he'd say.

"What was wrong with that one?"

"Shoddy technique, Harvard." He'd toss the blank plate back to Charlie. "One bump and your device would need repair. Soldiers' equipment gets bumped every thirty seconds all day long."

So Charlie would try again, slow and steady. If he began humming to himself, Beasley would yelp like he'd received an electric shock. Any time he made progress, the stork insisted otherwise. As the weeks passed, though, an unexpected thing occurred. Charlie began to find pleasure in the work. There was a satisfaction to it, like mowing a lawn with particular care. Eventually he completed an entire plate in one morning. With a solemn air, he brought the work over to Beasley's station.

"Why are you bothering me?"

"Look." Charlie held the plate out.

Beasley gave it two seconds of scrutiny before tossing it aside. "Fast work is not automatically good work. Dozens of those points would not conduct if you tried them."

Charlie deflated. How could the stork have known such a thing?

That afternoon he observed from his station as Beasley finished an assembly. His last step was to take a square red device with two wires, and touch one to each end of his project. A white light came on, and the needle on the front indicator jumped to the right. The next time Charlie finished a plate, he waited till Beasley left the room, then used the red device to test his work. The light stayed off, the needle remained to the left. Point by point he tested, finding eight where the soldering was sloppy enough to prevent electricity from flowing.

"Eight," he muttered, shaking his head.

"Might as well be eighty," Beasley remarked, returning to the room. "If one contact is bad, the whole plate won't conduct." He stork-stepped over to Charlie's desk. "Imagine a battlefield littered with dead soldiers, all because of you."

He held out his hand, and Charlie gave him the red device without a word. A few days later Charlie mastered a plate, and Beasley tested the device spot by spot. The needle jumped every time. "Congratulations," he said. "Nine weeks, and you are now a rank beginner."

Charlie bit back a mouthful of acidic replies.

"Now." Beasley sketched on a sheet of paper. "Build this."

Charlie took the design to his station, turning the page this way and that.

One sheet of paper, but it took him six days. Along the way, he learned a trick: if he wanted to join two wires together, he could heat them first, and the soldering material would sponge them into one, like a tomato-sauce stain spreads on a white shirt.

"Congratulations, Harvard," Beasley deadpanned, after Charlie demonstrated the technique with pride. "You discovered wicking."

Wicking. He wondered what other methods Beasley was withholding. Meanwhile the stork assigned harder designs, which required measuring the wire precisely for each step in the circuit, then adding it without breaking connections Charlie had already tinned. One design was so tight, he had to start over forty-five times.

"Does it have to be so tight?" he asked across the lab.

"Electrons move at one speed," Beasley snapped. "Build the components half as far apart, you've made your device twice as fast. Don't whine about the laws of nature."

Charlie turned back to his desk, and began attempt number forty-six.

The following week he finished his most complex design yet. It appeared tight and precise. But when he borrowed the red testing device while Beasley was out buying jerky, the plate would not conduct. He checked each point and they all worked fine. But the full plate was as dead as a gravestone. When Beasley returned, Charlie had no choice but to bring the plate over.

"It won't work. I can't figure out why."

"Simple." Beasley gnawed off a piece of jerky. "I gave you faulty gear."

"Why in the world would you do that?"

Instead of answering, he snapped his fingers. "Fetch."

"Fetch what?"

"The last three plates you made. Exam time."

"Are complete sentences really too much to ask?"

"Fetch."

Muttering, Charlie brought two other circuits from his station. Beasley took them, touching his glasses upward though they hung as low as ever, then frowned at the plates.

"Terrible," he said at the first one. "Terrible," he pronounced the second. "And this one . . ." He held the plate close enough to smell it. "Garbage."

He tossed all three in the trash bin with a clang. "I gave you failed components because you were ruining too many good ones, and we don't have enough to spare."

"And you couldn't be bothered to tell me, while I tried over and over to make them conduct?"

Beasley shrugged, turning to switch on his iron. "You never asked."

Charlie stood there, wringing his hands into fists, feeling the explosion build in his chest. Beasley must remain a bump, must remain a bump. He stomped back to his desk, grabbing a piece of paper. On it he wrote, "Get me out."

Was that it? Was he finished? Good-bye, Chicago? Good-bye, Brenda? Charlie turned the paper over like it was top secret math. "I'm taking the rest of the day off," he growled, switching off his equipment.

"It's only eleven thirty."

"I need to bring some people some sandwiches."

"Why don't you quit altogether?" Beasley asked. "That's what failures do."

"Because it would give you pleasure," Charlie seethed, jamming his arms into his coat. "Because it would make you right."

He charged out, slamming the door so hard it wobbled back open again.

1 3 .

THE LONG STALEMATE BROKE on a glorious morning in May, and I cannot take any credit. Just before noon, who should show up at Dubie's Music, decently dressed and carrying a bag of sandwiches from the neighborhood deli?

"Is this okay?" Charlie poked his head in the door. "Is now a convenient time?"

"Mother?" I called, without taking my eyes off him. "Did you set this up?"

"What's that, Brenda?" she said, emerging from the office with her arms full of files. Immediately she broke into a smile. "Why, Charlie, how nice to see you again."

She was innocent, I had to admit it. No actress in all of Hollywood could fake guilelessness as well as she wore it right then.

"I brought us all sandwiches." Charlie raised the bag. "I hope you don't mind."

"Mind?" my mother fawned. "Charlie, you are always so thoughtful."

"What about your ladies' group?" I asked.

"I can miss one Monday, for Pete's sake," she said. "Hold on a minute."

She went back to the office and we were alone. Frozen with uncertainty, I didn't say a word. He hummed to himself, key of F. I examined my fingernails. Had he always been that skinny?

"I can leave, if you'd rather," he said.

"Don't be dumb," I said. "You brought a sandwich. You might as well eat it here."

He stepped closer, holding something out. "I also brought this. Sorry it's late."

A chocolate bar, big as a license plate, with a special Valentine's Day wrapper. I imagined it was the one he'd left at his dorm those months before. I took it, but lacked the self-possession to so much as say thank you. In fact, there were two oratories I could have delivered—one a snippy rehash of slights past and time passed without him showing up, the other a repertoire of tender conversations I'd had with him in my head. That was the one I wanted to say, but lacked the courage to say. So I made not a peep.

"Heeeeere we go," my mother sang, shuffling her feet in tiny steps as she carried in a folding card table, opened it in the middle of the piano area, and pulled two benches up. "Fine dining at Dubie's Music."

Of course she hogged one side completely, so I had no choice but to sit beside Charlie. He was careful as a surgeon, holding strict posture so as not to touch me inadvertently. "How's business?" he asked.

"Slow," I said.

"That's not quite accurate, dear," my mother corrected. She leaned toward Charlie. "Brenda had a sale every day last week."

"You don't say," Charlie marveled.

He reached for a napkin, and that was when I saw his hands. All over, I could see little brown sores. "Holy cow," I blurted, not thinking. "What happened to you?"

"I'm sorry," Charlie tucked his hands under the table. "Just minor burns."

"Let me see," my mother demanded, snapping her fingers. "Come on."

Charlie raised his hands for her to inspect. She turned them over, slid his sleeves up to show his wrists, pursing her lips in disapproval. "How in the world did you do this?"

"They have me doing different work over at the university now."

"No more math?" I asked.

He shook his head. "Soldering. I'm not very good at it, but I'm trying."

His smile was so modest it galled me. Your hands are covered with scars, I wanted to shout, and grab them and lotion them smooth. What monsters did this to you? But all I did was hold my sandwich, showing as much compassion as a tree limb.

"What do they need soldering for?" my mother asked, letting his hands go.

"I'm not allowed to say."

"Then it must be important."

Charlie shrugged.

"My father does soldering," I volunteered, surprising myself. "He has a whole setup in the basement."

"Is that right?" Charlie asked. "Does he ever get burns?"

"Not that I recall," my mother said. "All I really know is that Frank Senior has spent many happy hours down there."

Then she turned and gave me the high beams, so I would understand exactly what she was doing next. Interpreting silence for approval, she took a deep breath and sallied forth. "You know, Charlie, if you ever thought a little extra practice would help . . ."

"That's exactly the problem," he said. "I'm only allowed to solder when my supervisor is there. If I could work another few hours, I think I'd improve much faster."

"Well then, it's settled," my mother said.

"Excuse me?" Charlie replied, focusing. "Did I miss something?"

"You come for dinner this week, and we'll eat early so you can get down to that workshop and sharpen your skills. You'll be an ace in no time."

Charlie made his surprised expression, the wide-eyed one that always softened my heart. He put his sandwich down, and stared off into the middle distance. He was humble, that Charlie Fish, but he had dignity too. "That is generous of you, Mrs. Dubie. But I would not want to intrude on your household if I was not entirely welcome."

"So it's really up to Brenda," she said, all brass and tacks. With that she took a big bite of her sandwich, and both of them became quite busy not looking at me.

One time as a kid at the community swimming pool, there was a dare among us girls to see who would go all the way down and touch the drain. It was not that hard, if you started with a good big breath. But what I remembered afterward was the pressure of it, the squeeze that water exerted on my lungs—or maybe the pressure was outward, the air inside me wanting to come out. In that moment at the folding table, I had the same feeling: there was a pressure on me, and something inside was trying to escape.

"It's my mother's house," I said. "Anyone she invites is welcome by me too."

Charlie turned and faced me, and I suspected he wanted more. He deserved more too. I just didn't know how to give it yet.

"Then it's settled," my mother announced despite her mouth being full, but not without fixing me with a glare like her eyes were flamethrowers. If Charlie noticed, he was too polite to let it show. "You come Thursday, I'll roast us all a chicken. And after lunch I'll see if I can find some ointment for those burns."

The bell hanging on the front door tinkled just then, a rube-looking fellow in a too-small hat wandered in. He peered around as if he did not know where he was. I knew how he felt.

Casual as you please, I picked up my sandwich. "Mother," I said, "would you mind taking this one please?"

14.

ARRIVING AT WORK THE next day, Charlie spied Santangelo near the entryway. He jogged over, calling out, "Hey, Steel Wool."

"Charlie, hey." Santangelo swung the door wide. "How's life in the basement?"

Charlie fell into step beside him. "I never thought I would be nostalgic for arcs. What are you third-floor guys up to these days?"

"Oh, there's no one up there anymore."

"They canned all of you? Who's doing the nation's math?"

"Nobody got canned. We're all reassigned. What about you?"

"Soldering." He stopped, lowering his head. "What for, I have no idea—and I'm not very good at it." With effort, he raised his face again. "Where'd they reassign you?"

"The Manhattan Engineering District. With the group working beneath Stagg Field."

"The football stadium?"

"Sports are on hiatus for the duration." Santangelo leaned closer. "You have no idea, Fish. We lined a squash court with graphite, and inside it they are breaking the laws of nature."

"Are they?" Charlie snickered. "And what's your job?"

He laughed. "I man the crank."

Charlie laughed, too, though not knowing why. Perhaps Santangelo's excitement was contagious. "What's the crank do?"

"Raises and lowers the control rod, the one that makes the reaction go critical."

"I have no idea what you're talking about."

"It's downright comical." Steel Wool raised his arms, conjuring an imaginary squash court. "Bigwigs stand up in the balcony, you know? They wave like emperors, I loosen the rope, the rod drops, and the Geiger counters go insane. Chain reaction, bingo. Then they lift a finger, I tighten the rope. The rod rises and the reaction stops." He glanced up and down the empty hallway. "It's incredible. They actually control the pile."

"What's a pile?"

A sudden look of panic crossed Santangelo's face. "I shouldn't be talking to you, Charlie. I thought you knew more."

"What are they controlling, Steel Wool?"

"Can't say," he answered, moving away down the corridor. "God. Forget all that crap, okay? It's nothing. Just . . . just fancy math."

"What is it, though?"

"Forget it, all right? Forget I said anything." And he bolted up the stairs.

Charlie stood alone, listening as Santangelo's shoes ran flight after flight. What was he supposed to forget? What did any of this talk mean? At last he turned, making his way down to the dungeon. It smelled of stale air.

As Charlie hung up his coat, Beasley went to his station and switched on the iron. "Next lesson: how to sweat." He tapped the desk with a forefinger. "Pay attention."

Before Charlie had settled in, Beasley arranged two plates. In one smooth motion, he melted soldering material into the gap between the plates. The hot metal seeped into the seam, cooling like a metallic glue.

"Conductive, solid, waterproof." Beasley stood. "Try sweating your failures together first, so you don't ruin something of value." He ambled away. "Not that anything you make possesses any value."

Charlie spent the day sweating. There were gaps, spills, mistakes that did ruin components. By day's end, though, he had run one bond successfully for the length of two plates. It was the fastest he had learned any new technique. He brought the completed assembly across the lab for inspection. "How's this?"

Beasley barely gave Charlie's work more than one eye, before tossing it aside.

"What?" Charlie asked. "How is it?"

"Sloppy, incomplete, and ugly." Beasley continued soldering. "I am going to talk to Simmons about you tomorrow. As far as I am concerned, you are officially CTD."

"CTD? What's that stand for?"

He pointed his index finger at the floor and made a swirling motion. "Circling the drain."

1 5 .

HE ATE NEARLY THE whole chicken. I'd been too little to remember when Frank went through his growth spurt. But I could not recall ever seeing a human being tuck into a meal like Charlie did that night. My mother gave all three of us decent portions: chicken, rice in gravy, warmed carrots. Charlie was finished before I'd taken three bites.

He put his fork down, then noticed how much was left on our plates. "That is mortifying," he said. "I'm sorry, today I had to skip lunch—"

"Are you kidding?" My mother laughed. "Nobody around here ever says anything nice about my cooking. You just paid me the perfect compliment."

It wasn't true. Roast chicken was her signature dish, with salt and onions and pale crescent moons of celery, winning cheers from our family every time. But I was smart enough not to contradict her.

"Here," she said, taking his plate. "Let's load you up right this time."

She shuffled off to the kitchen, Charlie calling after her, "I haven't had home-cooked food in a solid year."

My mother returned with a plate piled high. "I can't imagine the cafeteria meals. The taste. The dirt." She feigned a melodramatic voice. "You got here just in the nick of time."

We all chuckled. I couldn't remember the last time my mother said something that made someone laugh. Charlie's second helping went down slower, but she persuaded him to have thirds. After dinner, she made sweeping motions with her hands.

"Shoo," she said. "I'll take care of the dishes. Brenda, please show this starving wolf to the basement. And, Charlie, make yourself at home down there."

"I really appreciate dinner, ma'am, and the chance to practice some more."

"Don't you go all ma'aming on me," my mother said. "Just get busy."

I swung the narrow door open, switched on the light, and started down—calling back to him, "Watch your step."

In fact, the stairs were crooked as a cowboy's teeth, but they'd always been that way, I'd just never paid attention to it before. I felt a flinch of embarrassment, until I heard Charlie exclaim from above me.

"Look at this place. It's immaculate." He'd spied the worktable.

"Daddy likes things tidy."

He stood beside the plank bench that served as a seat. The table-top was clear and clean. Soldering tools hung on a particle board against white-painted outlines, so anyone could see where each one belonged. Spools of wire dangled in easy reach.

"It's as organized as an operating room," Charlie said. "Where does he keep his components?"

Not knowing what a component was, I shrugged. "Maybe in there?"

Charlie saw where I was pointing, to the chest of narrow metal drawers. He slid the top one open, revealing those odd little electronic things, in racks that arranged them by size. "Your father is a genius."

I didn't know what to say. I certainly had never thought of him that way.

"I'm realizing that I work in a garbage heap," he continued. "We waste hours, digging through bins to find components." He turned to me with his eyes bright. "It makes sense here. The organization of it all makes sense."

"I'm glad," I said.

Then there was a pause, a strange, awkward moment, which I felt down to my toes, but Charlie did not catch. I went to the place

I always sat, three steps from the bottom, while Daddy worked. I'd been sitting on that step since I was a little girl, while he told me stories about men whose radios he was repairing, or the HAM operator who had connected with someone in Norway. I would watch, no idea what he was doing with those wires and tools, thinking it was silly how he poked his tongue out when he was concentrating. I was just his daughter, keeping him company. We were soldering ourselves together. The world went away, and we became a universe of two.

Charlie slid onto the bench—good posture, like I'd learned on the organ—and began plucking things from the drawers. "This is great," he whispered.

A stranger thought occurred to me: One day, I might have a daughter, too, who might sit and watch her father from the stairs, learning about patience and craft, enjoying their quiet bond. And then the most peculiar notion of all, that the person she'd be keeping company might be this boy, right here.

Charlie switched on a soldering iron. "Your father is teaching me without even being here. That's how smart his organizing is."

"He has his ways," I croaked. But Charlie was so enthralled, he did not notice that I'd choked up. "Be right back."

"Sure, okay," he said, turning a dial, and I trotted back up those crooked steps.

My mother was drying the dishes. "Everything swell down there?"

I just gave her a hug.

She laughed and made a face. "What's that all about?"

I couldn't say. I scurried up to my room, and closed the door. I sat on the bed for a while, looking out the window at nothing. San Diego, England—the people I loved were far away. I knew, too, that if they made it home, *when* they made it home, life would not go back to the way it had been. I'd finished school, Frank would be a veteran and all grown up. My father would want to spend every possible minute with the wife he'd missed for so long. I couldn't imagine him wasting evenings alone in the basement.

No, the days of sitting on the third-from-bottom step were over. Life is always rushing away from us, I know that now, but that night it was a new idea. I wrapped the bedspread around myself, my grandmother's old quilt, reds and blues in a flying geese pattern she'd sewn while pregnant with my mother. And I had myself a good pout.

"Brenda?" my mother hollered from downstairs. "You need anything?"

"I'm fine," I yelled back. "Be right down." But for a long time, I didn't go anywhere.

Gradually I recovered, hurried past her reading in the overstuffed chair, and headed straight to the basement. Halfway down the stairs, I realized I'd brought along my quilt. Meanwhile Charlie had finished something, I could see a little teepee of metal plates shielding the soldering iron, but he was not at the table.

"Charlie?" I called out. "You still here?"

"What the heck are these for?" He poked his head out from the unlit storage area, back behind the furnace. He was holding an organ pipe nearly his own height. "Is your dad building a cathedral down here?"

I pointed at the soldering table. "What about your practicing?"

"I needed a break or I would have burst into flames." He approached with the pipe. "But honestly. You don't sell cathedral organs."

"There are only a few pipe repairmen in Chicago," I explained, "and they're all expensive. My father does the small jobs. He figures churches will refer customers to him down the road."

"This wouldn't be too hard to fix though." Charlie held the pipe horizontally. "The seam has split, that's all."

"Any fix is hard when your repairman is in San Diego till who knows when."

"Don't the churches complain?" He ran his sleeve down the pipe and it came away gray with dust. "This must have been down here for years."

"I guess the war is teaching patience to all kinds of people," I said. "Even me."

It slipped out, but Charlie didn't let me get away with it. "What are you impatient for, Brenda?"

"Oh, I don't know. Knowing more, I guess. Understanding more." I shrugged. "Maybe being grown up."

"I think the war is making that happen pretty fast anyway," he said. "Being eighteen today is completely different from being eighteen five years ago."

Neither of us had more to say about that. "Get back to work, you," I said finally. "Enough chat. You've got to earn that chicken supper, or else next time instead of the bird, my mother will skin *you*."

"Yes, my joyous work. Because I didn't do it enough already today."

I was glad to change the subject. "What's the trouble?"

Leaning the organ pipe against the wall, Charlie shuffled back to the soldering table. "I'm trying to build a very tight assembly, but I can't find a tape measure." He scooped up a bunch of short pieces of wire in various colors, all with gray blunt tips. "I'm estimating, but the lengths aren't right."

I leaned over the thing he was making, and each connection was a separate piece of wire, like he was using cut-up cannelloni. "Why are you doing it this way?"

"This is how I was taught. What do you mean?"

"Don't get touchy," I said. "It's just not how my father does it."

"Oh really." Charlie crossed his arms. "You're going to teach me now?"

"Jerk." I crossed mine too. "If you don't want to know—"

"No, please." He tossed the wire scraps back on the table. "Enlighten me."

I rolled my eyes. "Charlie, even I can tell that measuring piece by piece takes forever. Look."

I picked up one of the spools, and stood over the work he'd abandoned. "Clip one end to the starting place, and bend the wire"—I unwound the spool over each of the components, like it was yarn, making one continuous line—"Till you reach the end. My father doesn't measure anything. He touches the iron where the wire has to connect." I reached the last component and pressed the wire onto it. "Done."

Of all the times I'd seen Charlie's shocked expression, that one won the contest. His eyes followed my wire its whole length, while his jaw hung slack.

"Careful there," I teased, "or some bird will build a nest in your molars."

He closed his mouth, but leaned over the table like he was reading scripture. "Do you know how ingenious that is?"

"Hardly," I laughed. "It's just what my father does for his radio friends."

"Believe me." He started to pull the bench over, but stopped himself. "Thank you, Brenda. You have no idea."

And he kissed me. It wasn't slow and smoldering, like our lovey smooches from before. But it wasn't all brotherly quick-on-the-cheek either. Somewhere in the middle.

I'm not sure he gave as much thought before kissing me as I gave it after. I still think about that kiss now, all these decades later. How authentic it was. How sincere. Often I wish my young self had seen this unguardedness as a strength, rather than a weakness. But wartime culture does not prize vulnerability. I had a lot to learn.

He plopped himself down and started a new board. Using Daddy's technique, and humming some sweet melody, he finished in about ten minutes. "What do you know."

"Are you going to get sore if I tell you another thing of Daddy's?"

"Sore? Hardly."

I leaned past him to switch on the light that hung over the table. It reminded me of the day we met, when he had reached to clean up the spots of blood. Then I climbed the stairs and turned off the overhead.

"Daddy says a light behind you casts a shadow on your work. That's why organs have lamps right over the sheet music. If the church is dark, you can still see the notes."

"Boy." He smiled, his face open as a dictionary. "There are going to be some changes at work tomorrow."

Well. I could have eaten half a pie. Charlie Fish might be a whiz, but I was helping him. Maybe my sense of superiority wasn't entirely imagined. Maybe I was good for more than selling organs and accordions.

He set up another design. Again, ten minutes. I think he was humming Peter's theme from "Peter and the Wolf." *Bah-bum barump-bump-bum.* After that he tried harder ones, tighter ones. Along with the melody, he bounced a little on the bench. I wrapped myself in my grandmother's quilt and watched, third step from the bottom.

When the kitchen clock made its cuckoo call, it broke my reverie and I stood. "Time for Brenda to get to bed."

Charlie did not lift his head from the worktable. "Is that ten o'clock already?"

"Try eleven."

He jumped up. "It's already eleven?"

"Ten was an hour ago. Twelve is an hour from now. It's amazing how it works that way."

"You don't understand." Charlie switched off the iron, tossing the little pieces back into their drawers. "They lock the dorms at eleven. I'm going to be late."

"I'd say you already are."

He stopped, deflating, shoulders dropping. "I guess I am."

"Go ahead and keep working, Charlie. I'll leave my quilt. You can sleep on the couch."

"Is that okay? Will your mother mind?"

I folded the quilt, putting it down to one side. Then I came down the steps, leaned over, and gave him a proper kiss—no hurry, no pretending it wasn't happening. When I pulled away, his eyes were scanning my face, like he was searching for something.

"G'nite, Charlie," I said.

He was still sitting there, taking it all in, as I made my way back upstairs.

I woke before my alarm. With a boy sleeping in the house? Who was not a member of my family? Of course I did. Putting on my robe, I tiptoed downstairs. There was no one on the couch. The basement door creaked, and I'd only descended halfway when I saw him.

Charlie was sound asleep at the workbench. Near his hands lay things he had soldered, wires and pieces and who knows what. But also, leaning against the shelves, on the floor, all around him, there were organ pipes. Some were knee high, others taller than me, surrounding Charlie as if he were part of an organ himself. And wrapped around his shoulders? My grandmother's red and blue quilt.

Charlie Fish might be sheepish, not strong enough for a world at war. But he was a decent guy, and I felt something inside me melt a little. Then a hand stroked my lower back, and it was my mother with a finger to her lips. She motioned me back upstairs.

"Why don't you get started on your day, and I'll bring him some coffee?"

I wanted to be the one bringing coffee, but accepted that my mother had it right. In the kitchen she gave me a hug like I'd given her the night before. What in the world? I went upstairs and turned on the shower, and while I waited for the water to get hot I thought about Charlie, and how he had brought some kindness to our house.

By the time I came back downstairs, one red swipe of lipstick for courage, he was seated at the table chowing through a mountain of bacon and eggs, plus gulps of coffee whenever business got slow.

"Good morning," he sang out, bright as a cheerleader. His hair was cowlicked in back, like a nine-year-old. But Charlie gave me such a long, direct gaze, I had to turn away. The quilt was heaped on my chair; I folded it on the way to the stairs. It smelled differently, not like the basement. I held it to my face, then realized what the scent was.

I returned, pouring myself some coffee as I sat, and hoping he hadn't been watching. "You fixed the organ pipes, didn't you?"

"They were all seam problems." He drew a line in the air with his knife. "I used the sweating technique and they sealed right up. Easy."

The thought occurred to me: My father would gobble this guy up. Someone who liked soldering, and could fix organs? I could imagine him winking. "Baby girl, where'd you find this one?"

"Easy or hard, it was helpful of you," my mother said. "That church will be so pleased." She started to open the morning paper, but as I sat down she paused. "You know what, Charlie?"

"What's that?" he said between forkfuls.

"It was nice to have a little noise in the house last night." My mother glanced at me then, oh it was quick, but as complete an assessment as if she had measured my pulse, temperature, and blood pressure. "I've missed you hanging around the store too," she continued. "I hope now that you can come by more often."

"Well, I hope so too," he said, blushing ever so slightly. He brought the coffee cup up to his lips, then put it back down without taking any. All my life since, I've remembered that moment, when he put the coffee cup back down. Because you never quite notice as it's happening when a door in your life is opening, but sometimes, later you can look back and think: *then.*

"Provided . . ." Charlie cleared his throat. "Provided all parties feel that I am welcome."

I lowered my head, despite all my swagger unable to say a word. I mean, his scent was on my childhood quilt.

Before that day, what I'd wanted was for boys to pursue me, to pay for dinner, to confer a status on me. The bigger a deal they were, the bigger a deal I was. But this time, with this guy? What I wanted was him. His calm, his intelligence, his humility.

I sat like a lump, turning all of this over in my mind. My mother waited another few seconds before opening the paper, raising it in front of her face. "Charlie, I think I can safely say that is how all parties feel."

It was my turn to blush.

CHARLIE AMBLED INTO BEASLEY'S Dungeon at twenty to ten, as relaxed as a gambler holding aces. Beasley finished some flourish on a piece he was making, before speaking at the bin of components he was poking through.

"Must be nice, being a man of leisure during wartime. Wander into work any hour you like."

After hanging up his coat, Charlie crossed to his desk at the same easy pace. A stack of wiring designs sat in the middle, all other materials shoved aside. He gave the top one a slow study, switching on the soldering iron as he read. Then he went to two other desks, carrying their lamps over to his station.

Beasley had been watching the whole time. "What, Harvard needs special light?"

"Light from behind casts shadows. I want to see my work more clearly."

Beasley sniffed. "You'll see all those mistakes so much better now."

Charlie took fifteen minutes to organize his station, arranging components by color, and then by size. It was a pleasant chore. Imagining Brenda now at work in the store, remembering how soft she looked while sitting on the basement stairs, he had to restrain himself from whistling. And when she came down with her hair wet from the shower that morning, she had lost all severity. Innocent. Lovely.

It was time to use what he had learned. Pulling out a bare plate, he secured the soldering wire to the first component, then used Brenda's technique, bending the wire to the next one, and the next, to the end.

By then the iron was at full heat. He brought it down gently, here and here and here, whiffs of smoke rising as he tinned each spot.

He stood abruptly, letting the stool roll back into an empty desk with a bang.

"How about a little quiet around here?" Beasley snapped.

"How about a challenge?" Charlie said, bringing over the finished plate.

"Fish, you are challenged by tying your shoes."

Charlie set the plate by the stork's elbow. "Done."

"What, you quit already?"

"Done, I said."

Beasley straightened, touching his glasses with the usual undiscernible effect. He gave Charlie's work a hasty scan, then did a double take. "This isn't how you do it."

"It can be."

"Nothing's measured. It's loose and loopy. It'll never work."

"Why don't we test it?"

"Not worth the bother. This looks like a child did it."

Charlie reached for the red testing device. "Let's see if it conducts."

"Back off." Beasley swatted Charlie's hand aside. "Why do you insist on being humiliated?"

"Maybe you've given me a taste for it."

Beasley held up the red testing device's two wires. "When this fails, I am going directly to Simmons to get you transferred."

Charlie leaned back against an empty desk. "Test it."

Beasley touched one wire to the start of the design, and lowered the other to the finish. The white light came on, the indicator needle jumped to the right.

Charlie clapped his hands once. "There. Now what are you going to tell Simmons?"

"Nothing." Beasley put the red device away. "The man is an idiot. I mean, he's a genius, he's helping to transform physics. But you can be a genius and still be an idiot."

"Why won't you tell him what I've done?"

"Because I am a genius who is not an idiot. And you." He scowled. "You are an idiot who is not a genius. If I contribute to your advancement, I will endanger all the people who don't know how genuinely incompetent you are."

Charlie took his plate back. "You don't want him to know what I can do."

"Such a dreamer." Beasley picked up his soldering iron again. "Your work is so sloppy, if I showed it to Simmons he would punish me. Instead, when the history of this war is written, I and the dungeon will have an illustrious place in the record. But you?"

He cleaned his iron on the sponge, once again making that hiss. "You will be too mediocre to mention. As you were in math, if I heard right. Why, even your girlfriend—"

"How do you know I have a girlfriend?"

"It's my business to know your business. That's how a genius avoids surprises."

Charlie glanced through the window of the hallway door, and chuckled. "Well, I don't know how to break it to you. But here comes a surprise."

Beasley spun on his stool as Simmons strode into the lab. "Good morning, gentlemen." He smiled as always, effervescent. "Everyone having a good day?"

"Sure." Beasley made a show of returning to his work. "War is nothing but fun."

"If you say so." He waved a slip of paper. "Charlie, I was pleased to see your note."

"Yes, sir." He stepped forward, the plate still in hand. "I wanted you to see this."

"An assembly? So?"

"I built it in fifteen minutes."

"Fifteen?" Simmons studied along the length of the wire. "Smooth work." He turned to Beasley. "It conducts?"

"It does," Charlie declared. "Wonderfully."

Beasley shrugged. "It worked one time. But it's casual technique. Unreliable."

"Maybe." Simmons looked from one man to the other, then placed a sheet of paper on a desk. He scribbled on the page before handing it to Charlie. "Make this."

"Sure." He ambled to his station, strumming through the organized drawers to gather components. Simmons stood by, while Beasley sat at his desk, hands hanging.

Charlie went to work, humming Beethoven's sixth symphony.

Beasley snorted. "If you please, Harvard."

"Won't be much longer," Charlie said. Finishing the assembly in ten minutes, he checked it against the original drawing before handing it over.

Simmons took the plate to the red tester, and it conducted. "You knew he could do this," he said to Beasley, "and you didn't tell me?"

"Fish has been pathetic till now. He only started decent work this morning."

Simmons rubbed his jaw, as if calculating something. "Charlie, come with me."

He started for the door, while Charlie grabbed his coat. Then he remembered something, doubling back to switch off his iron and cover it with a welding mask. "Wouldn't want anyone to hurt himself."

"Harvard," Beasley called out.

He turned at the door. "Yes?"

Beasley was standing now, his soldering iron put aside. "I never liked you. Not for one second."

"Yeah?" Charlie said. "Well, your zipper's down."

Instantly Beasley bent to see, waist and neck jerking forward to check his crotch. Of course it was not down at all. But the abrupt motion made his glasses fall off the tip of his nose. He caught them in both cupped hands.

For Charlie, there was an unmistakable thrill of triumph. It lasted, however, only as long as Beasley kept his head down. Because when the stork lifted his face, Charlie discovered what those glasses had hidden: small eyes, a pinched face, the most frightened person he had ever seen.

Simmons was already a full flight ahead on the stairs, and Charlie hustled to catch up. By the time he reached the office, the secretary waving him in, the professor was already seated at his desk. He waved the finished assembly in the air. "Son, if I had not seen you make it that fast with my own eyes—"

"He's on the line now," the secretary called.

Simmons pounced on the phone and spoke without a greeting. "We're ready."

He listened, his trademark smile returning. "Of course I'm sure. It's seamless, stable, and quick to make."

Despite the smile, though, Charlie saw something in his uncle's demeanor, the seriousness of it, that made him realize this conversation barely involved him. It was about something else, and he was a small part.

Simmons paused again, nodding, grinning wider than ever. "In fact, we have exactly the right guy for the job. Dutiful, humble, obedient. You could start detonator production immediately."

Suddenly Charlie was seized by a sense of dread. Where did detonator production take place? Had he succeeded his way out of Beasley's clutches, without thinking far enough ahead? Now that Brenda was allowing him to see her real feelings, the last thing on earth he wanted was a promotion to somewhere else.

Simmons set the soldered plate on his desk. "I could get him to you in a week."

Charlie began to sweat inside his shirt. What had he done?

Simmons hung up without a good-bye. He grinned up at Charlie. "I knew I was taking a risk with you, but here's a tangible result. You followed orders and you delivered."

Charlie swallowed hard. "Yes, sir."

Simmons sat back in his chair, hands clasped behind his head. "Congratulations, Charlie Fish, and pack your bags. You are on your way to New Mexico."

17.

THEY TOOK HIM FROM me.

Just when I was beginning to understand what the presence of Charlie Fish could do to my life, they removed him from it. With a whopping three days to pack and make arrangements. He was sweet enough to spend several hours each morning visiting with me at the store, but whenever I played for him I could see he was distracted by all the chores he had to complete. As soon as I finished, he'd hurry off to tend to some detail or other. They did not allow him time to visit his family, instead promising an extended leave at Christmas. Which I doubted he would actually receive. They did not give him a mailing address either. Charlie said he'd be told when he arrived. It only increased my vulnerability that I had to wait to get a letter from him before we could be in contact.

"Brenda?" my mother called up the stairs. "Hurry up. He'll be here any minute."

I stood from the bed and crossed into my parents' bedroom, at the front of the house, to examine myself in the full-length mirror. I wore a favorite dress, navy blue with white piping, trim but not too fancy, and a baby blue hat pinned snug into my hair. An overcoat would hide my dress from Charlie, but I would know about it, and perhaps he might sense the care I had taken for him.

Downstairs my mother was busy digging in the fridge and packing the picnic basket, quick as if she had four hands.

"You're sending Charlie off with the family basket?"

My mother did not so much as glance at me. "And what of it?"

"Didn't Daddy give you that for an anniversary present? Won't he be upset when it's gone?"

She stopped stock-still in the middle of the kitchen. "You worry about all the wrong things. Here—" She handed me two glass jars. "Fill these with water, would you?"

"It's a fair question."

"Brenda, please. It's not like we're picnicking every Sunday these days. Charlie can return the basket once the war is over."

"And if it lasts another five years—"

"Then a picnic basket is the last thing we'll be fretting about." She snapped her fingers twice. From the sink I saw her pour an entire percolator of coffee into a canteen tin, which she capped tightly and tucked into a corner of the basket. After filling the first water jar, I packed it too. The basket was stuffed, and I found myself counting.

"Eleven sandwiches? Mother, it's not like he's crossing the Sahara Desert."

She spoke while lighting a cigarette. "Little girl, you have no idea what's ahead of him. Besides, with no family to see him off, an extra sandwich or two does no harm."

"Or ten." I snorted. "Maybe you want to be the one he's courting."

She gave me a look then, a slow burn. "I don't know where to begin to answer a wisecrack like that." She exhaled smoke and left the room.

I was tucking the second filled jar away when the knock came at the front door.

"I'll be right back down," my mother said, hurrying up the stairs.

"You couldn't answer the door first?" I hollered after her.

There was no reply, and I realized what she was up to. My mother wanted me to greet Charlie. Today I'd like to give her a dozen roses for trying to teach a self-absorbed girl. But right then I was only annoyed, and the second knock didn't help.

"Come the heck in," I yelled, trotting over to swing the door wide.

"Hi, Brenda," he said, making a little bow. "Hey, nice hat."

"Why thank you, Charlie." I patted it as though to check if the pins had come loose, wondered where I had learned such an old lady gesture, stepped backward out of his way, and almost tripped on the rug. I caught myself though, and just as quickly suppressed any sign of embarrassment. "Come on in. My mother is just finishing making you a feed wagon."

Charlie wore his Christmas overcoat with a loose suit under it. He dragged two duffel bags in behind him. It struck me as a little pathetic, that everything he owned could fit in two dull green canvas bags. The war diminished everyone.

"A feed wagon?" He removed his hat. "What's that?"

"Nothing," my mother said, skipping down the stairs. "Brenda said officially nothing. Nice to see you, Charlie."

"Thanks, Mrs. Dubie. Super dress, too, Brenda."

"It's an old one actually," I demurred.

My mother put her hand on my arm. "Thank you, Charlie, I'm glad you like it." Then that hand gave me a nudge.

I sighed, rolling my eyes. "Thank you, Charlie—"

"And you're glad I like it?" He grinned and gave me the quickest little wink.

What a perfect way to appease my mother without taking her side against me. "Something like that, yes."

There was a honking from the street, and we peered out as one. "Already?" My mother checked her watch. "I called for a cab at eleven."

"I wouldn't mind being early," Charlie said. "So I can buy a snack at the station."

I laughed. "My mother thought of that. Though you may need a wheelbarrow."

"Go," she said to him. "And, Brenda, you fetch the basket."

In the kitchen, an idea occurred to me. I could write Charlie a note, some simple thing for him to find late in his trip, when he'd eaten down into the stack of sandwiches. I grabbed paper and sat at the table, but my brain went blank. What could I say that wasn't too corny, didn't give my dignity away, stoked his desire, preserved my virtue, and brought him safely home?

Maybe if I'd thought of it sooner, if I'd had an hour to make up something perfect, I might have done something that bold. Today I wish I had confessed everything, made promises for the whole future, because I was heartsore and he wasn't even gone yet. But I knew myself too little to be so frank, to have such nerve. Instead I tapped the pencil eraser against my teeth, hoping for inspiration, until my mother barged into the room.

"Sitting here? The taxi's waiting and you're actually sitting here?"

"Sorry." I stood, grabbing the basket, and left that paper on the table. I can still picture it today. *Charlie,* my imagination wishes it could write, and fold, and tuck deep inside, *I will miss you so.* Instead, for all time, that sheet is blank.

We had a nice little chaos, the three of us, loading everything into the taxi. It was a gray March day, a slow melt under way. My mother gave directions so the cab took us the long route, along Lake Shore Drive. But the lake's ice was softening, the water a gunmetal gray. The snowbanks were crusty, too, with black gravel from winter traffic.

"Mother," I said, "it's not exactly gorgeous this time of year."

She narrowed her eyes at me. "Who knows when Charlie will next see a decent body of water?"

He stared out the window. "I have no idea."

After that we rode in silence. Charlie managed a bit of song, humming so quietly at first I thought it was coming from outside the car. I could have said something, to warm him in the time ahead. But my mother's presence stifled me, I was self-conscious. As the road curved and traffic swept past, I sat in the middle and felt like a human knot.

"...though I suppose dampness makes it feel colder," my mother said out of the blue, in one of those conversations that started in her mind long before she gave it voice.

"It does," Charlie agreed, affable as ever. I was going to miss that boy.

"Turn here," she instructed the cabbie. We'd reached the river, a white plate of ice with a melted blue-green sluice down its middle, and swung left onto Wacker Drive, toward the Randolph Street Bridge. The only longer route we could have taken was if we went home and started over again. Still, we arrived at Union Station too soon. I'd been there once before, when an older cousin married a well-to-do lawyer from Oak Park. They held the reception in one of the side halls. I'd been ten, a flower girl in a pink dress, giddy with the glamour of it all.

This time it was a Friday, and the station was strictly business: men in suits and fedoras who carried briefcases, women in low square heels that made a hammering sound on the pavement, soldiers swaggering here and there. Everyone knew what they were doing and where they were going. Meanwhile, Charlie strained to hoist his duffels out of the trunk, a strap going over each shoulder, and by the way he leaned I could tell one bag was much heavier than the other.

"Do you want to shift some things around?" I asked him.

"I'll fix it on the train," he said. "Guess I don't have much experience at packing."

His eyes roved over my face, like he was seeing me for the first time, and only had a second to take in my features. I felt Charlie's attention keenly, like a too-bright light, and I had to turn away. My mother was checking the picnic basket, asking if he had his ticket yet. He patted his jacket pocket, and we set off for the Great Hall.

They say the cathedrals of Europe were built with high ceilings in order to draw the faithful's eyes toward God. I'm not sure how Chicago's Union Station was intended to inspire people, but I sure felt the majesty of it. All the bustle, the soldiers striding by in uniformed groups, men lounging by the walls in a cloud of cigarette smoke, the shouts of porters and baggage men—all of these nonetheless dwarfed below the great, vaulted skylight, which I knew from an eighth-grade project was 115 feet over our heads. Sun streamed in the high windows at the far end, casting beams down on the wooden benches. Dirt and shoe scuffs on the white marble floor seemed mean and meager compared to the expanse of commerce and bustle. I felt a swell of affection for Chicago, my hometown and the only place I knew, and wished that Frank and my father were there.

Beneath one of the arches, Charlie had stopped to read the track assignments. My mother stood between us for a moment, but seemed to realize it and stepped away.

"Excuse me, but I need to visit the ladies'," she said. "Charlie, I hope this is a great experience, and you help our country find victory and peace, all right?"

"Yes, ma'am." He held out his hand for her to shake. "Thank you for all of the—"

"There you go, ma'aming me again." She pulled him close for a quick hug. "Take care of yourself, kiddo."

Then she was hooking the handles of the picnic basket over my arm, and leaning to speak in my ear. "I'll be back in a bit. But Brenda? Don't be afraid to feel things."

"What is that supposed to mean?" I asked, jerking away.

She had already started off. "I'll meet you after, right here."

Amid the noise and chaos, we were alone. My stomach fluttered like I was about to cross a rush-hour highway. But I straightened my spine, boldness coming from somewhere inside me, and took a lapel of his coat in each hand. "Charlie" was all I could say.

"Brenda," he said, looking down at me. He cleared his throat as if about to give a speech. "You are the best thing that happened to me in this whole city."

"Well, I would hope so," I snapped, my usual bluster. But he tilted his head to one side, and I knew to give him a break. "Sorry, go ahead."

"I'm not glad to be leaving. It might be exciting, maybe even important. But I will be thinking of you the whole time." He looked directly into my eyes, though it caused him to blink again and again. "When this war is over, I would like your permission to come back here, and investigate how it feels for us to see each other again."

"Investigate? Did you say investigate?"

He bobbed from side to side. "Go easy on me, Brenda. I'm new to fancy talk."

"Then speak to me in your regular talk."

"All right." Charlie tilted his head back, eyes on the skylight. "Listen to this room for a second. Just listen to it."

I closed my eyes. At first it was all sensations, my hands on his lapels, the nearness of his body.

But then I calmed. There was a rushing sound of people and echoes. I heard the conversation of women passing by. The thrum of train engines like a bass note. Two men laughed over by the shoe shine stand. Someone yelled. A child's shoes slapped the marble, chasing a cooing pigeon. I opened my eyes and Charlie was smiling at me.

"It's beautiful," I murmured. "Who knew?"

"Now imagine how fantastic an organ would sound in here. A huge, powerful one, hundreds of years old, like in some vast European cathedral." He began to hum, some old hymn, low in my ear so no one else would hear, just for me.

"Charlie." I pushed and pulled on his lapels. "Who knows how long this war will last, and how it might change us? If you want to investigate, that would be okay with me."

"Really okay?"

"Very okay." I nodded. "Investigate away."

We stood for a minute then. I was trying to memorize him, getting the last possible bit, like how you finish the water in your glass before you rise from the table. One more sip. A guy rushing past tapped Charlie on the shoulder.

"Sorry, boss, but do you know what time it is?"

"Can't you see what you're interrupting?" I snapped.

Charlie checked his watch. "Five of noon."

"Thanks, boss."

The man hurried off, and Charlie sighed. "My train leaves in twelve minutes."

I felt pressure in my throat, like I might choke. "I guess you'd better go."

He leaned forward and kissed me, slow and gentle, and I found myself grabbing the back of his head again, pulling him closer. In memory, I see us cinematically, as if from a camera on a high balcony:

a skinny guy in a black overcoat bending to kiss a girl wearing a light blue hat—it probably happens there all the time, several times a day, but these two are so painfully young—while the world swirls around them on its sprint to a future no one can foresee, and yet somehow they make a kind of mooring, a fixed place around which, for that one moment, everything turns.

Then we parted. Charlie looped the duffel straps over his shoulders, I handed him the picnic basket, he waddled off into the crowd. The basket brought his load closer to being in balance, but he continued to lean to one side as he made his wobbly way.

I stood perfectly still, as though I were made of glass, until he was out of sight. Charlie was gone. Gone. The Great Hall's wash of sound continued as though nothing had happened. If that room had an organ, I would have played something wounded and mighty. I glanced around and there she was, ten yards away, watching me like a guard.

"Mother," I said. She rushed forward, all of a parent's care written on her face. But some deep well of venom surged inside me, and I snarled, "Eleven sandwiches? *Eleven?*"

She stopped abruptly, as if I had slapped her. In the same instant her expression changed from affection to something else, not anger, but almost bewilderment. She shook her head. "Who in the world ever taught you to be so cruel?"

I stammered, unable to muster a reply, while she turned on her heel and charged off to the taxi stand.

"We will never see that picnic basket again," I called after her. "And you know it."

She did not break stride, barging between two soldiers and disappearing in the crowd. I stood half a minute fuming, people passing intently on my left and right. Then there was nothing for me to do but follow her home.

18.

AT LONG LAST THE engine eased, the train snaked through several slow turns, and they chugged into Lamy, New Mexico. Charlie checked his watch: thirty-three hours since they had rattled out of Union Station.

His skin had a sheen. His legs felt full of blood. His mouth tasted as sour as old milk.

The train shuddered to a halt and a conductor bustled through the car, opening a door at the front. Charlie dragged his bags out to the station platform, setting them in the shade with the picnic basket on top. Only one passenger boarded the train, a white-haired man with a worn carpetbag. The whistle sounded twice, long and loud, which struck Charlie as extravagant for such a minor stop. The locomotive revved, bellowing smoke, and away the small train rolled: up the line, around a bend, continuing west.

Charlie's ears needed time to adjust to the quiet. He felt greasy, and numb with fatigue. A burro brayed. Two pigeons cooed and strutted past, reminding him of the doves in Union Station. The air smelled of dry earth.

In that moment, he began the practice of writing Brenda a letter in his head, a habit that would soon become second nature. Eventually it would seem as if events had not occurred until he had told her.

A hacking cough sounded as loud as if it were directed in his ear. He turned to see that his sleepy traveling companion had also descended at that stop. The boy had boarded at Charlie's last layover, and as other passengers reached their stops, for the last five hours he and Charlie had been the only riders. Now he stood beside two suitcases, absently digging in his pockets. Little though Charlie's experience was with such things, he thought this was the look of someone with a magnificent hangover.

Charlie knew a ride to Santa Fe was supposed to be waiting for him when he arrived. But there was no car, and he did not know if his train had been early or late. Assuming his bags were safe, he wandered off.

The views were not the green trees of New England. In all directions the land was barren, bland, and brown. A dog awakened in the middle of the road, lifting its head to sniff in Charlie's direction, then lying back down without having bothered itself to bark. But there, on a rise above the town, stood a stone church, dignified and graceful.

He strode off to it, as though that had been his destination all this time. So many hours spent sitting had dulled his muscles, Charlie thought, feeling his heart pound and his breath grow short as he climbed the hill.

The church's front doors were open, and from the wood's weathered look he suspected that they had not been closed in years. He tiptoed in, though why he needed to be quiet he could not say. The pews were gone, save one against a wall. The window openings were empty, too, colored glass glinting here and there on the floor. A scent of rodents soured the air. There was no organ.

To test the acoustics, Charlie sang a few lines of the "Ode to Joy."

Freude, schooner goetterfunkin
Tochter aus Elysium
Wir betreten feuertrunken
Himmlische dein heiligtum
Deine zauber binden wieder
Was der mode schwert geteilt . . .

His voice trailed off, knowing its roughness would have made Charlie's college choir director growl in dismay. He dropped onto the pew, knuckling both eyes until he saw stars. Someone outside started honking a horn, blast after blast.

"So annoying." Charlie rose to see what the matter was, feeling light-headed from the motion, arriving at the doorway.

"Come on," a man in military green yelled from below. Standing beside a battered school bus painted the same green, he waved an arm. "Get a move on, bub."

Charlie remembered what his uncle had said: He would be treated like royalty. He would work with the smartest people in the world. His labors might one day be considered heroic.

"Not quite," he told the empty church. "Not yet, anyway."

And he shuffled his tired bones down through the dirt.

The man who had waved him down turned out to be holding a rifle. Charlie went to fetch his bags. "Sorry to hold you up."

The guard shouldered his weapon. "Not a place to wander off, sir."

"Sorry," Charlie said.

"Nice picnic basket, though."

Charlie noticed the soldier was smiling. "I have sandwiches left. You hungry?"

"Hell yes. Sir."

Charlie handed one over and stepped onto the bus. The dark-skinned driver greeted him in Spanish. Charlie nodded hello, noticing that the hungover man sat hangdog a few seats back.

"Any chance you have another one in there? To save a starving pilgrim?"

Charlie opened the basket. "Help yourself. That last jar has coffee in it too."

"Angel of mercy." The man grabbed two sandwiches, unwrapping one and taking almost half in a single bite. "Ham." He spoke with his mouth full. "A benediction. I owe you my life."

Charlie took note of the other passengers—from the empty town they seemed to have materialized out of thin air, all of them Hispanic—as he hoisted the duffels overhead and sat behind the hungover man.

"I guess we're still some distance from our destination," Charlie said to him.

"Nineteen miles to Santa Fe, then a company car forty miles up to The Hill."

"Company car?"

He finished chewing before answering. "You'll see. Probably an old truck."

"You've been here before?" Charlie asked.

"New as fresh paint. But the professor who hired me told me what to expect."

"Where are you headed?"

"Same place as you." The man turned the sandwich and bit the other side. He was making shapes. "Project Y."

"I'm sorry. What's Project Y?"

The man recoiled, then calmed. "A joke. Never mind." He turned forward. "Thanks for the eats."

Suddenly an idea occurred to Charlie. What if Brenda had left him a note in that basket? Any kind of good wishes would be wonderful. He opened the top wide, pushing away the last sandwiches, the jars of water. There didn't seem to be anything.

But he wasn't satisfied. He stared out the window. If the situation were reversed, he would certainly have left a note for her. He tore into the basket again, shoving things aside, digging everywhere, but there was nothing.

He slumped back in his seat. Of course. Brenda was not the hidden-note type. Damn desire, though, he thought. He had been fine all this long way, and now his imagination had made him miserable.

With a grinding of gears, the bus lurched forward. The driver slowed at a crossroads and the bus shook, a screech of metal on metal from the front.

"Have mercy," the hungover man said, pressing his eyes closed.

A mile farther, the bus needed to turn onto a paved road, and it brought another shudder and screech. Charlie checked, and the other passengers dozed or conversed in quiet Spanish. The vehicle was clearly unsafe. Why were they not worried?

"We're going to die on this bus," the hungover man said before dozing off.

The ride to Santa Fe took an hour, Charlie trying to sleep, too, but he'd napped enough on the train. The bus rattled along. He hummed to himself, bits of a French song he'd learned in college, but it felt as false as whistling past a graveyard. Gradually they began to pass houses with small corrals in back, then clusters of homes, and eventually they entered the city. They passed adobe houses, shops, street markets, until the driver brought them to a final squealing stop.

"*Bueno*," he said, clapping his hands as if in self-praise. "*Bueno*."

"Here we go," the soldier announced. "East Palace Avenue, number 109. Everybody off."

The hungover man grabbed his suitcases and stumbled out of the bus. Charlie, his bags overhead, decided to let the other passengers off first. As they streamed past, he could not help noticing their dress: wide-brimmed hats, brightly colored cover-ups like blankets with an opening for their heads. Through the window he saw them line up outside the stores, where they sat against the wall and settled in to wait.

"You always a lollygagger?" the soldier asked.

"Not usually," Charlie closed his picnic basket. "It's a long ride from Chicago."

"That'd take the wind out of anyone's sails." Hoisting Charlie's duffels onto his shoulder, the soldier trundled down the bus steps. "Welcome to Santa Fe."

A wooden canopy shaded the sidewalk, like something out of an old western movie. The gate of 109 East Palace hung wide, opening into a courtyard. The soldier set the duffels inside the gate. Charlie balanced the basket on top and sidled into the office.

"The top item is your pass for The Hill," a woman was telling the hungover man, who slumped in a wooden chair. Striking, with bright red lipstick, she handed him a folder. "Don't lose track of it."

The room was sparsely furnished: filing cabinets, metal desks like he'd had in Chicago, a little corner fireplace in which quiet coals glowed. A boy occupied a chair to one side, his legs tucked up like some sort of elf. The walls were bare but for a calendar that, on closer inspection, was from 1941.

"I imagine you are unaccustomed to military ways," the woman continued. "Few civilians are. But I promise, carrying your pass at all times will be as useful as wearing shoes."

As she spoke, she handed the hungover man's travel papers to the boy. He crumpled each page into a ball and dropped it onto the pile forming between his feet.

"Normally we have food for new arrivals," the woman said. "Not today though. But most people prefer to have an empty stomach the first time they make the drive."

"One question," the hungover man said. "What is my mailing address?"

"The mail. How could I have forgotten? Everything is censored, incoming and outbound. Don't seal your envelopes, please."

"I'll have no privacy?"

"No location information, no names of coworkers, no stories about what you're working on." She smiled. "We're all encouraged to stick to our knitting."

"If those topics are forbidden, what does that leave for a fellow to say?"

"I'd suggest focusing on the weather. It's quite sunny here, as you'll see."

"The weather." He rubbed his face. "I'd been hoping to share more than that."

"I sympathize." She touched her lipstick with the tip of a pinkie. "We are all learning to adjust our expectations. There are women on The Hill who do not know what their husbands do all day. That is the reality, and I live by it too." She smiled again. "Your address is Box 1663, Santa Fe, New Mexico."

"Sixteen sixty-three." The man stood, tucking his folder under an arm as he moved away. "Thank you, I think."

The woman nodded to the boy, who immediately tossed his pile of crumpled papers into the fireplace, where they smoked and then flared. Charlie watched the papers burn, until he noticed she had extended her hand toward him. He shook it briskly. "I'm Charlie Fish. How do you do?"

The woman gave a quick laugh. "Pleased to meet you, Charlie. I'm Dorothy McCay, and I was actually reaching for your papers."

"Oh. They're in my bag." He pointed over his shoulder. "Be right back."

"No hurry. I'm not going anywhere."

But he did hurry. Charlie was nineteen, farther from home than he had ever been before. He suspected he was in way over his head. Even the hungover man had a self-possession Charlie envied. Digging out the documents, he resolved to do his best at every moment.

Dorothy opened his papers to scan the top. "I hope you enjoyed the trip from Chicago." She flipped through the documents so quickly he could not imagine she was actually reading them, handing each page to the boy as she'd finished it, then rose and went to a filing cabinet. By the time she returned with Charlie's folder, the boy had crumpled most of the travel papers.

"The top item is your pass for The Hill." He peered in to see a cardboard rectangle the size of a driver's license. Dorothy continued: "I think you heard my lecture on keeping it with you. Your housing assignment is in a barracks, for which I apologize."

"Why would you say that?"

She smiled. "Construction on The Hill has not kept up with the flood of new babies, much less the growth in staff. Your assignment is in TA-6, Detonation. Your packet has a map so you can find it." She handed him the folder. "Any questions?"

Charlie thought the hungover man had asked a useful one. "My mailing address?"

"Box 1663, Santa Fe."

"That's the same number you gave the other fellow."

"And everyone else on The Hill too." She nodded. "We all live there now."

He wanted to probe further, but the boy tossed Charlie's crumpled papers into the little fireplace. It was like erasing his past, consuming it in a tidy fire.

Outside, the hungover man occupied the only bench, head in his hands. As Charlie sidled over and sat, the man straightened. "So, I overheard that you're Charlie Fish. I'm Giles Crosby, straight out of Princeton's Applied Mathematics."

Charlie's eyes went wide. "As in Einstein?"

"I've seen him twice in the hallway. Therefore I take full credit for his success." He made a small bow. "Feel free to send flowers and money."

"Terrible thing, really, not to be thanked publicly, after all the man owes you."

Giles smirked. "I'm glad you appreciate how I've suffered."

"It's the same for me." Charlie was smiling now. "At the University of Chicago—"

"Bastards, all of them." Giles gritted his teeth. "That place is notorious for not recognizing how twenty-year-olds are revolutionizing the world."

Charlie mock-sighed. "We are woefully underappreciated."

They sat companionably for half a minute before Giles spoke again. "I've actually heard you fellows in metallurgy have been going great guns."

"Just nosing forward an inch a day."

"The first controlled chain reaction in history? That's not nosing, friend. That's elephant-trunking." Giles scratched himself under one arm. "You managed not to blow yourselves up too. Bully for that." He heaved the sigh of a general learning he had lost a platoon in battle. "Now we've reached the big time, and I feel miserable."

Charlie opened his folder, then closed it without looking inside. "It's not my business, but maybe if you cut down on the drink . . ."

Giles bristled. "Is that what it looks like?"

"Near as I can tell."

"We're at seven thousand feet, chum. Altitude hits me like a hatchet between the eyes." He chopped a hand toward his forehead. "You don't have a headache at all?"

"Come to think of it, I felt one back in Lamy. I blamed it on travel."

Giles dug in his pocket. "It'll worsen. Project Y is three hundred feet higher."

"Project Y again."

"Now you know what it means. And yes," he sighed. "You're right about my condition. I had a six-hour layover in Denver, and arithmetic took over."

"Arithmetic?"

"Giles plus layover equals hangover. For which your ham sandwich proved medicinal. Here." He opened his palm to reveal a small white pill. "Feel better."

"No thanks," Charlie said, recoiling. "What is it, anyway?"

"Suit yourself." Giles tossed it in his mouth, swallowing without water. "Aspirin."

The bus from The Hill arrived late. But it was in better condition than the one from Lamy, with firm seats and brakes that did not scream. The driver paid attention.

He needed to. After twenty miles of flat pavement, they turned uphill onto a dirt road that surpassed anything Charlie had imagined. Potholes and bumps. Gut-wrenching washboard, when the entire bus and everything in it jarred from side to side.

Once they crossed a bridge with a small sign—Rio Grande—the climb began. They navigated perilous switchbacks, sharp corners with a cliff on one side, no guardrails, and the bus swaying to the edge time after time.

"I spoke too soon," Giles whispered from across the aisle. "This is when we die."

Charlie swallowed dry-mouthed, while another stretch of washboard rattled his innards, and the next swerve attempted to pitch them off the cliff.

"How about that view, people?" the driver yelled over his shoulder. "Right?"

Charlie glanced out at the landscape below, the multicolored cliffs and jutting mesas, but a rut jerked the bus sideways. Wedging his feet to brace himself, he realized: there is nothing beautiful about being terrified.

"Alchemy," Giles said, leaning across the aisle. "Know what I mean?"

"Pardon me?" Charlie was not inclined to conversation.

"The Egyptians pursued it first, then the Chinese. In the twelfth century it became a Western obsession too."

"Sorry, I'm half asleep. What are you talking about?"

"Alchemy, Charlie. The theory that with the right method and ingredients, a base metal like mercury could be turned into a pure one, like silver. People believed it would provide a pathway to immortality. The ultimate challenge was changing lead into gold, because it does not tarnish or decay. Gold stays perfect forever."

"The place we're going is trying to make gold?"

"A military version of it, yes. You'll see soon enough." Giles slid closer in his seat. "It is not possible to turn lead into gold. But it may be possible to split uranium into barium or radium."

"And what's the value of that?"

Giles cupped his hands and made them into a ball. Then, as he spread his hands apart with fingers wide, he whispered, "Pooooosshh."

The bus lurched and they both grabbed their armrests.

"Alchemy," Charlie muttered. "Whatever in the world."

Two hours later, dusk settled on the land, the cliff casting long shadows into the canyons. The ground grew level, and the driver downshifted.

"East entry, people. Present your pass, and I'll be waiting by the gate."

Charlie followed a queue to the guardhouse. More like a shed, he mused, with a sign on the front: Los Alamos Project, Main Gate. They were surrounded by high barbed wire, with bright lights shining all around. The air smelled sweet and clear. By contrast, the guards wore helmets and uniforms, and carried rifles.

This time Charlie did remember to bring his papers, and he

found the cardboard pass. He worked a kink out of his neck. The journey was nearly finished. Giles fell in behind him, digging in his pockets again. Then he started patting them, one by one.

"Hello," Charlie said, handing his pass to the guard. The man scowled like a bulldog. He studied Charlie's face, then examined the pass with the same flat expression. He handed it back and waved him on, no words said.

Charlie had returned to the bus before he realized that Giles was no longer behind him. He turned.

"The damnedest thing," Giles was telling the bulldog guard. "I had it with me when I got on the bus."

"It's true," Charlie said, ambling back. "I was with him when he got it, back at the East Palace Street office."

Two guards appeared and stood in front of him.

"Move on," Bulldog said.

"I can vouch for him though," Charlie persisted.

"Don't worry yourself about me—" Giles began.

But the guard poked his chest with a finger. "You keep quiet. And you," he snarled at Charlie. "This would be a good time to mind your own business."

Giles waved Charlie on. "We'll get it straightened out."

"All right," he said. "If you're sure." He returned to the bus, watching the guards pat Giles down. As the last passenger to reboard, Charlie happened to glance to his right, where the guard was opening the gate. All at once the weight of the situation fell on him: in a few seconds he would venture into a place he knew nothing about, to work for people he had never met, and he was not allowed to tell anyone about it.

"Rough trip?" the bus driver asked.

"A bit," Charlie allowed.

"You'll settle in quick. My advice is to stick to your knitting."

Charlie started up the bus steps. "That's the second time I've heard that."

The driver closed the door. "Won't be the last either."

Charlie took a seat, the guard waved them on, and he rolled into Project Y.

19.

MY MOTHER PUT A plate of meat loaf before me, then sat at the table across from me. "He's probably getting there about now."

I was no fan of meat loaf. In fact I considered it the most boring meal on earth. Which she knew perfectly well. But I was still all diplomacy. I felt her anger at me still simmering, and I had no intention of bringing it to another boil.

"How awful," I said, "to be traveling all this time."

Since Charlie Fish kissed me in the Great Hall of Union Station, I'd had two workdays, five meals, and a good night's sleep. He had probably needed every one of those eleven sandwiches. I was not about to bring that up again either. I ate the meat loaf like a good, dutiful daughter, and it was not an act.

Apparently, meanwhile, all the organ buyers of Chicago were on Charlie's train too. The first day, after the taxi brought us from Union Station, we did not have a single customer. I practiced for hours, and was interrupted by the little bell jingling not once.

The next day we had foot traffic, folks test-driving a Hammond, and one fellow who played an accordion at absolute top volume, before banging it down on a piano bench and saying it was too loud.

The rest of the week? Tire kickers, a man who was visibly drunk, a woman asking directions to the library. One dad brought in his ten-year-old princess, who was too shy to sit on the spinet model's bench, yet he scowled the entire time I demonstrated. Finally I cajoled her into playing a Tinkertoy tune, which I praised triple what it deserved. When she slid off the bench, he took her hand and they left without a word.

It didn't matter that I learned the latest show tunes. That I tightened my introductory patter down to three sentences. That I became an expert on lipstick application, a doyenne of the sales floor dress, an ambassador of welcome to every person who opened the door of Dubie's Music and made the little bell ring. No one was buying. Or haggling. Or putting down one thin dime of a deposit.

And from Charlie? Silence. All of my sales energy had to be faked, to hide how blue I was. I'd wake up thinking about him, how he made me laugh and opened the door and always insisted I go first when we'd spoken at the same time. I dwelled on memories of him asking for a slow song and watching with soft eyes while I played. On and on like that, until it was an effort to get myself out of bed.

I came down for breakfast, not speaking till I had a piping hot cup of coffee. My mother was reading the morning paper, but I could tell she had one eye on me.

"What?" I said.

"Nothing." And she buried her nose back in the paper. "Not a thing."

I counted on work to revive me. Retail can be fun if the customers pour in and the register runs and the goods move along. When a whole city loses interest in your store? When hours go by without a walk-in? And you're only there out of duty to your family, when you'd rather be at a conservatory improving on the organ? There's a reason retail halfway rhymes with jail.

Was it the war? How could it be? We were finally winning in the South Pacific, capturing the Marshall Islands, for example. Hitler was on his heels too. I knew that because one night my mother interrupted her before-dinner cigarette and forced me to read the evening news: the British air force had bombed Berlin.

I put the paper down. "Why do you think business is so slow?"

She laughed in surprise, a billow of smoke snorting out. "That is not what I expected you to say. Germany matters, you know."

"Of course it does. But honestly, why do you think?"

She considered. "Maybe people are too tired to make music. Or too sad."

"But they need it more than ever. Yesterday in the grocery I heard two different people whistling 'As Time Goes By.'"

"Whistling isn't putting money down on an instrument you have to learn to play, especially one that's not easy. Organs might be too hard for now."

It was my turn to ponder. "Maybe we should start carrying harmonicas."

She picked the newspaper back up. "That, my girl, is a smarter suggestion than you realize."

But we didn't. Instead the days stretched long, spring dragged its heels, and customers were as rare as lottery winners. One afternoon I did the closing, while my mother bought groceries and went home early. Which meant that she saw the mail first. When I came home, in the middle of the kitchen table there sat a letter, addressed to me and postmarked Santa Fe. Still sealed, too, though I could imagine my mother's temptation.

I snatched the envelope and bolted upstairs, practically tearing it open on the way. In my room I closed the door and sat on the bed.

"Dear Brenda, How are you?"

I have always hated letters with questions in them, even if they are asked purely for manners' sake. Don't people realize there is no way to answer? I scanned down Charlie's scrawl, looking for where the meat of it began.

"I live in a . . ." and after that it was blacked out.

"I've made a new friend, a chemist named . . ." and the same censoring.

"Our work is like alchemy. Each day we . . ." and blacked out again.

The back side was worse. By the time I finished page two, and reached Charlie's sign-off—"Take care, and please say hello to your mom"—all I knew was that he was working hard, the food was decent, and the weather was great. The weather.

I trudged down the stairs like I'd experienced some kind of defeat.

"How's Charlie?" my mother asked, standing at the sink with her back turned, as if that would prevent me from knowing how crazy curious she was.

"He says hi," I answered, and like a perfectly cruel daughter, I said no more.

Dear Charlie: I'm fine, but don't bother asking in the future, okay? Because I could have yellow fever and pneumonia put together, and get over them both before your next letter reached me. Also what do all the blacked-out parts mean? Are you giving away military secrets as a hobby?

All these years later, I sit in a rocking chair on the terrace of my assisted-living facility, and debate which is a greater wonder: That I thought this opening was somehow funny? That in my mind it conveyed to Charlie how desperately I wanted to know everything about his life in Santa Fe? That I thought the tone contained enough familiarity for him to sense my deep affection? Or that he saved it, actually kept it in his papers like something important—though reading it later caused me pangs, to see how prickly I could be, while he was alone and so far away?

What he was actually doing, I still had no idea, and that ate at me. Why the secrecy? How could a math and soldering guy possibly be involved in something that required such high security? I could not begin to imagine.

I sealed my reply in the morning, news about the slow sales and the loud accordion guy, trying to make him sound comical. It may have come out mean. I left it in anyhow.

When I asked my mother for a stamp, she gave me five. "It's good of you to write back so promptly."

"What are the extras for?"

"You have lots more free time than Charlie. You don't have to take turns. You might want to write him again before you receive his next letter to you."

"Oh, I might?" I scoffed. "We'll see."

"No harm in a suggestion," she said. "Proud girl."

I flounced out to the mailbox, dropped the envelope in, and headed to work. It was a sunny spring day, birds and flowers and a dog that writhed on its back in the grass of a little park. For some reason, that dog about floored me. By the time I reached the store, it had sunk in: this was going to be my life for the foreseeable future. Not movies, but mail. Not soft kisses, but licking envelopes.

As I unlocked the front door, I felt the blues come over me like never before. Charlie was gone. Till who knows when. And I, who still had home and family and friends, had mailed him a letter full of trite and bratty things. I would have to send a better one right away. As soon as I got home that evening.

I wandered around the store, switching on the church model, which had seen so little use there was dust on the console. As it warmed up I wiped the organ with a chamois cloth, so lightly the keys did not play. My mother declared that random notes were the opposite of professionalism: never touch a key until you mean to. But as I settled onto the bench, my elbow hit a B-flat—a quick bleat, and I swear it pulled at me.

I opened a few stops, wanting a reed sound, and played that B-flat again, this time on purpose. Why did the note seem so different? So poignant? I had played B-flats in pieces since I was four years old, no weightier than any other note. One of my standard audition pieces was in the key of B-flat. Yet this time it meant something more.

My left hand played an octave lower, another B-flat, and then ar-peggiated the major chord: B-flat, D, F. It sounded plaintive. Sincere. Without any plan, my left hand moved on to spell out a G-minor: B-flat, D, G. The chords had two of their three notes in common, the difference between them was small. But I went back and forth—

slowly, in a solemn procession—B-flat to G-minor, and it was like the organ knew how I felt.

I was the kind of musician who did not compose, who disliked improvisation. The risk of hitting a wrong note was too great. But those two chords expressed my emotions better than words. While my left hand alternated between them, my right hand played, five times, a slow, quarter-note D, followed by rest.

Simple, obvious, but it worked. The music said what I wanted to say. B-flat, G-minor, and the high, ringing D that linked them. It was like a march. I was the drummer boy and the fife player, both, and the wounded soldier limping home too—all made possible by the unique power of the organ. With strings, there's a moment when the bow reaches its end and has to change direction. With horns and woodwinds, sooner or later the player has to breathe. But an organ note can simply continue, tirelessly, while two chords pass feelings back and forth: yearning, longing; affection, sorrow.

When my mother came bustling in, I switched the organ off. She paused at the door, aware that she had interrupted something. Then she continued into the office, where she did paperwork for the rest of the morning. And the chords continued playing in my heart.

The afternoon was quiet as the week before, spring advancing, but this year without graduation-present customers and wedding-gift parents. My first anniversary at Dubie's Music approached, and a job I'd been loving had turned to mud.

Where was Charlie? What was he doing? Why had I sent such a trivial reply?

On the way home, I saw a couple kissing against a building. Some kids chased each other around a tree. A pigeon trotted along with its head bobbing, staying in my path without flying away for a full block. But nothing could make the sun come out.

At home I went straight to my room, fishing out the stationery that I saved for thank-you notes and special occasions. I parked myself at the little desk and began.

Dear Charlie,

Please forgive my last letter. It was terrible and petty. This is all new to me. As it is to you, too, of course. So I will make dumb mistakes until I learn better.

Since you left Chicago, the music is gone. No one pops into the store. There's no you to learn new pieces for. Spring is happening all around me but I do not feel it. In your letter you used the word "alchemy" and I do not know what it means. This is a secret I have kept from you: Sometimes you use words I don't understand. I do not want to pretend anymore.

I sat back, astonished. Every sentence contained a confession. Reading this note after the last one, and thinking I had gone stark crazy. I slid the paper into a drawer, and went downstairs.

My mother was in the kitchen. Feeling like I'd be terrible company, I went to the living room—where the piano sat with the cover open like an invitation. I slid onto the bench, fiddled with classical pieces, started a ragtime tune that made me feel like an imposter, and finally gave in to what I wanted to play.

Two chords from my left hand, while that mournful D wafted high above. Back and forth, that one note as my mooring, I let myself drift.

Maybe I had never really felt anything before. I didn't remember being upset when Frank and my father went away, though I sure missed them now. Charlie seemed to have opened a door in my heart, and behind it was a room full of melancholy.

I cannot say how long I sat there, repeating myself on those keys. As evening came on, the room grew dark and eventually the reverie broke. When I stopped playing, the immediate sensation was not of relief or catharsis, but embarrassment: my mother had been in the next room that whole time, listening to me carry on with my two chords.

I marched into the kitchen, ready to say I don't know what. She was sitting at the table, the newspaper crumpled in her lap, tears streaming down her face.

It stopped me like a crossing guard with his hand up. "Are you all right?"

She shook her head. "No. I'm not all right, and neither are you."

"What do you mean?"

She wiped her face roughly on her sleeve. "Little girl, we need to change some things around here. Both of us. We can't keep on like this."

20.

EVERY DAY BEGAN WITH Midnight kneading Charlie's stomach. Other fellows in the barracks fed her scraps, or poured her basins of milk. A few found catnip somehow, and left a little pile for her to squirm against. But each night, she chose Charlie's bed.

Midnight's rounds were famous all over The Hill. No fence could contain her, nor guard control her. She spent daytimes wandering around the technical area, immune to speeding trucks, and passed her nighttimes prowling—which worried the boys more, because the canyons were yowling with coyotes. Every ten days or so she limped in with a wound in her side or scratches on her face, the cause unknown.

Once the barracks fell quiet, and light spilled in the windows from a bare bulb outside the entry, Midnight would make her way inside. After visiting several bunks in the long room she would reach Charlie's, two-thirds of the way down on the left, onto which she would jump soundlessly, tongue-wash her paws of the day's dust, snuggle herself against the small of his back or the bend of his knees, and become tiny in sleep until the sky pinked and the first risers stirred. Then she would stretch fore and aft, yawning wide with her small teeth showing.

Next she would climb on top of Charlie, and with alternating paws she would knead his stomach, knead and knead, as he woke and stretched and stroked her ears until the ebony animal narrowed her green eyes and purred. Why she chose Charlie, no one knew but many envied.

That morning he scratched under her chin. "Detonation day, kitty. Maybe today I'll have my first one." The cat responded by leaning into his fingers.

Giles passed on his way to the latrine, pausing to release a magnificent fart. "Blasphemy," he said.

"You are a pig." Charlie put a pillow over his face.

"In honor of detonation day," Giles said, bowing. "And may I observe that this cat is training you nicely for your girlfriend. What a touch you'll have when the war is over."

Charlie blushed. Giles knew how often he was lovesick about Brenda. But he'd never yet put a finger on her, and the very idea of it made him squirm.

Then again, to Charlie any sentence that contained the phrase "when the war is over" was entirely fantasy. The war would never be over. Not with Hitler beating back the Russians and firing rockets at Britain. Not with Japan apparently willing to spill the blood of every citizen capable of carrying a rifle, rather than accept defeat. The newspapers had made much of the Battle of Eniwetok, for example: Of the three thousand five hundred Japanese soldiers defending that little island, all but one hundred had died. And those survivors were considered a national disgrace.

The Hill was supposed to solve these problems, though after six months Charlie still did not understand how. Giles promised to explain, but free time was rare, and usually devoted either to festivities at Fuller Lodge, or bonfires behind the barracks where the boys gulped beer and rum like Prohibition was returning in the morning. Charlie's days brimmed with work, too, and tasks of crushing complexity. Who had room for the big picture?

"Compartmentalization," Giles called it, a word he labored to pronounce that night by the bonfire. Rum made him more thoughtful, but less articulate. "Know what I mean?"

"I don't," Charlie said, himself half a dozen drinks behind.

Giles speared a stick into the coals, spiraling sparks skyward. "A man cannot be a security risk if he knows only his job, and remains ignorant of the larger enterprise."

"But that's the opposite of how science works," Charlie said. "Advances happen when people collaborate, and challenge one another's ideas."

"Spoken like the fanatical communist you obviously are." Giles laughed. "My advice—"

"Stick to my knitting, yes." Charlie worked an invisible set of needles in the air. "I'm finishing a scarf right now."

"Fish, my fine friend." Giles drew the stick from the fire, blowing on its glowing tip. "You may be an innocent, but you are still capable of learning."

Now Charlie watched him waddle in his boxers down the center of the barracks to the latrine. Sitting up, he deposited Midnight at the foot of the bunk. "Good kitty." From his locker, he dug out soap, razor, and toothbrush—then checked in the mirror and put the razor back. As he shuffled away, the cat nestled into his pillow.

The barracks were made to hold sixty boys in two long rows, with room between bunks for a locker and chair. Instead the administration had shoehorned ninety boys inside. There was no privacy, no air circulation—yet some at Los Alamos maintained that these fellows were lucky. Others had to raise families in cardboard houses with unsafe furnaces. Or they lived in trailers with walls as thin as a tin can: ovens in summer, iceboxes in winter.

Everyone on The Hill, within days of arriving, knew the story: A remote plateau that four years earlier had housed no more than a boys' school was now home to six thousand people. There were daily power outages and frequent water shortages. Yet new workers, many green with nausea from the trip, stepped off the bus from Santa Fe every day. Some of the more senior scientists had taken to sleeping beneath their desks.

Charlie might have tried that himself had he been assigned a regular place of work. But his tasks alternated between lab and field. Today was a field day, detonation day, which he tried not to think about too much. Either he would have his first turn, or he would not. Meanwhile his next rotation for a shower was not until Sunday, which meant that tonight he would sleep on sheets gritty with sand.

"Maybe that's the definition of being in a war," he said to Giles the last time he'd gone to bed unwashed. "You're away from your people, and you wake up dirty."

Giles shook his head. "There is only one definition of being in a war. Someone is trying to kill you."

Charlie reached the line for the sinks, counting heads to realize that his turn would put him at the one on the far wall. Thanks to a plumbing error, that sink had no cold water—both spigots ran scalding hot. Fine for shaving, misery for brushing teeth.

Later, back at his bunk, Midnight having embarked on her rounds, Charlie made the bed before jogging to the mess hall. The food was bland but plentiful, and he ate a heaping plate of scrambled eggs. He also poured himself some milk, but after one sip he pushed the glass away.

"I was surprised you tried it," the boy across from him said.

"Ever an optimist, I guess."

"I don't know how they do it." The boy grimaced. "The milk has been sour every damn day since I got here. Do you think they do it on purpose?"

Charlie tucked in to his meal. Around him the room crackled with energy, boys late for duty or returning from working all night. The room was loud, his chair bumped by workers hurrying past. Finally Charlie took his coffee outside to drink in the shade.

Project Y had become a hive of activity. Trucks roared past, jeeps ferried officers between duties, boys poured in and out of the fenced tech area. A pickup idled through, its bed crowded with dark-skinned women in colorful garb. Locals all, the cleaning staff.

Some midteen boys ran past pell-mell, and Charlie knew they were headed to the equipment dump, where faulty gear and old machines went to die. Those kids had wreaked havoc a few weeks back, when they found an old searchlight in the heap. Being the children of scientists, they repaired it with found parts, taught themselves Morse code, and one night had themselves a fine time flashing obscene messages into the sky—until a transport plane misread the signal and nearly crashed into the canyon.

Chastised and punished, the boys also became famous on The Hill. Mischief was to be expected. The school was disorganized, its teachers mostly spouses of lab workers. Enrollment might grow by ten in a single day, and teenaged boys were not likely to sit attentively in class when perfectly good junk piles beckoned. As they dashed past, Charlie had half a mind to join them.

His daydream was interrupted by a battered old power wagon rattling up, its horn honking needlessly. A bald young man leered out the window. "All ashore them's going ashore."

Charlie squinted at him. "Monroe, I'm not sure that's what you actually mean."

Monroe, a troublemaker's glint in his eyes, gave an infectious laugh. "It means I have commandeered this here truck, we're running late as molasses in January, and today is detonation day."

"One minute." Charlie grabbed the tailgate, swinging up into the truck's back. A dozen other boys made room, while two lay across a bed frame. "What's that for?"

One fellow shrugged. "Brunder lost a bet."

Charlie did not know who Brunder was, or what wager would cost a man his bunk. But as Monroe hit the gas and the truck careened away, Charlie grabbed the nearest bedpost and held tight.

The road climbed to Fuller Lodge and Bathtub Row—where Oppenheimer and the other brass lived—and skirted the busy tech area. They paused at a security fence, every boy raising his pass for the guards to check, the soldiers as humorless as tombstones. Monroe opened it up again, spinning gravel.

In minutes they reached Tech Area 6, a rutted dirt road that forced Monroe to slow. Nonetheless, on reaching the staging area, he slammed on the brakes. All four wheels locked, and the truck skidded sideways to a halt.

The site boss, a swarthy giant with hands as wide as canoe paddles, observed without comment. He'd arrived three weeks before, never told anyone his name, and somehow that made him terrifyingly intimidating. Charlie and the others hopped right down, while Monroe and another fellow wrestled with the bed frame and mattress.

"Planning on a nap today, Monroe?" the site boss said.

"No, sir. I was thinking this'd make a fine test object, to measure detonation yield."

The site boss scowled. "Doesn't look like a meaningful control object to me."

"Maybe not, sir," Monroe answered, undaunted. "But it could be, if you think of it as Hitler's bed." He wore a jack-o'-lantern's grin. "Or Himmler's. Or Rommel's. Let's see how high we can launch one of them bastards."

"Tell you what," the site boss said. "You fellas hustle all day, and we'll bring that mess up to the concrete bowl. Deal?"

To Charlie, the little cheer that went up reminded him of high school, boys riling themselves up before a game. Detonations at the concrete bowl required remote operation, and there was only one person who could build reliable triggers.

After only a few months, Charlie was well known for his wiring work. He was the one the site boss ordered to the tech buildings by Ashley Pond. "Solder me a relay," he'd growl. "One that sends two signals at once."

Charlie would do the math, design the assembly, and sit at a soldering table till the work was done—his workmanlike patience in full force—at ten, at midnight, at dawn. He'd deliver the device to the site boss, who invariably already had one from army supply, and who would hold the two pieces side by side in his huge hands.

"Decent job, Fish," he'd say. "The army's unit is sweated, though, so it's waterproof. Maybe we'll try yours next time."

Another time he said, "Theirs is twice the weight of yours. I bet it's sturdier." He turned and dropped both assemblies on a flat rock. The army one held up. Charlie's burst into pieces.

The site boss's instruction was more humbling than Beasley's. Nothing personal, just factual assessment. That's what made today potentially special: the site boss had not pulled Charlie aside to reveal flaws in his gear. "Okay," he said, striding away downhill. "Let's go. Solid science, no injuries."

Charlie followed, the batteries heavy, but he didn't mind. His arms had grown stronger. Also he enjoyed the weather, a cooler day, high clouds. The trees shading them, he'd learned, were ponderosa pine: tall, reddish, littering the ground with needles.

"Site number one," the site boss said, pulling out a stopwatch. "Let's see how long it takes you fellows to set a charge and establish a safety zone. Go."

The boys jumped into action, Charlie affixed wires to one of his batteries, and detonation day was under way.

The boys scurried to and fro like bees whose queen was gunpowder. Before each blast, the site boss sounded an air horn, and the crew scampered off behind the trees. After the lunch truck made its delivery, Monroe was first to grab his shovel and head back to the work site. Charlie tagged along.

"Thing I don't get, Fish?" Monroe had a sway-hipped walk, like a horse on a steep downhill. "Why we're inventing something so crazy complicated, when we already know about the Halifax."

"The what?"

"You oughta get out more." Monroe picked a stem of switchgrass and nibbled on it. "Only the biggest explosion in history."

Charlie leaned against a tree, the bark warm through his shirt. "I'm listening."

"Nineteen-seventeen, all right? Halifax is a harbor, way up in Canada someplace, and here you've got two ships. One's a damn fool, driving too fast, wrong side of the highway. Other one's snailing along, careful as a truck delivering eggs, on account of it's carrying half a million pounds of TNT. They collide, ka-boom. But big. Killed two thousand, injured nine thousand. Blast so huge, it emptied the harbor of its water."

"Incredible."

"Damn straight," Monroe laughed. "Fish flopping round and old sunk boats and who knows what. Though of course that means a tidal wave soon after, when the water comes rushing back. Anyhow, the explosion blew down every house and outhouse for three-quarters of a mile. Windows broke for ten miles around, and one sixty-one miles away." He took the grass stem from his mouth, pointing it at Charlie. "Now I know what you're thinking . . ."

"You do?"

"Sure. That last window must have been mighty weak to give out from an explosion sixty-one miles away."

Charlie chuckled. "Now that you mention it."

"Must have been cracked already, is what I figure. Elsewise some kid put a baseball through it and blamed it on the blast." Monroe inspected the tip of the stem. "Thing I want to know, though?"

"What's that?"

"Why we need to build a big Gadget here, us folks slaving away, when all we oughta do is christen a new ship the *Halifax II*, fill its hold with hell yes, and sail it where we want to do our business. Am I right?"

"Well," Charlie grinned. "One problem might be Germany. They'd torpedo anything that entered their waters."

Monroe glared at him. "Well damn, Fish." He threw the grass stem away. "Why you gotta be a spoilsport?"

"It might work on Japanese ports," Charlie offered, but Monroe had already stomped away.

"Let's go, fellas," he yelled up the hill. "Back to it. We got us a bed to blow up."

The afternoon moved briskly. At day's end no one was injured, though Monroe had forgotten his hat and managed to get a sunburn on his dome.

When the tests were complete, the technicians collected their gear and gathered around the site boss on the hill, where he stood watching with crossed arms. Monroe came last, almost shy, dragging his feet till he reached the outside of the group. "Hey, Mister Charlie, what time you got over there?"

"Let me see." Charlie made a show of lifting his sleeve to check his watch.

"All right," the site boss growled. "We all know it's quarter till five. If you boys run the equipment back to the trucks, you can blow up the damn bed."

The crew let out a huzzah, and suddenly the long day's fatigue vanished. They hurried back for the rest of the gear.

Charlie delayed, sidling over to the site boss. "Sir, I was wondering—"

"What is it, Fish?"

Charlie patted his rucksack's side pocket. "Maybe we could try one of mine?"

He sighed. "Put me in, Coach. Something like that?"

"For fun," Charlie said. "For the whole crew."

The site boss opened and closed his giant hands. "You seem like a nice kid, Fish. Probably all your life, you've been a guy who did a good job, who stood out. But I don't think you understand the situation here on The Hill. I don't think you realize what standing out can lead to."

Charlie felt he was in another of those moments when he had no idea what someone was talking about, and the best approach was to say nothing. He watched as the boys hauled equipment up the incline to the road.

"All right," the site boss sighed. "Give us a three-way charge."

"Yes, sir," Charlie said, lifting his batteries again. "Thanks so much."

"But if it leads to other things, remember. You asked for it."

Charlie was already running to the trucks. The crew piled in back for the half mile to the concrete bowl. Charlie rode in Monroe's passenger seat, urging him to drive slowly for once so he could choose the right device.

"Relax," Monroe said. "Worst that can happen is we all get killed."

Rounding the bend above the bowl, they saw deer in the clearing. Monroe sighted down one finger. "If I had my twenty-two right now, damn but we'd have a fine dinner."

The bowl was a circle two hundred feet around, made of concrete a foot thick. It was concave to help in recovering exploded materials.

Safety dictated that observers stand well back, making remote switches the only way to detonate.

By the time they parked, the does were long gone. The crew's enthusiasm remained high as they unloaded matériel, arranged explosives in three piles, helped Charlie set his wires. The site boss stood on a rise above the bowl.

Monroe picked two fellows to help him carry down the bed, placing the mattress precisely. The metal frame spanned only inches above the explosives. He savored the moment with a grin. "Now, Brunder," he said. "Don't you wish you'd got with that gal like you bet me, instead of it coming to this?"

As Charlie unspooled wires, walking backward, Monroe brought a handful of sticks to the crown of the ridge. The site boss watched him stab the sticks into the ground, adjusting their height with a tape measure.

"What are you up to now?"

"Angles, sir." Monroe pushed the last stick a fraction of an inch deeper. "I can sight down these sticks, and see which matches the peak of the bed's flight. A little geometry and we'll know right off how many feet high it went."

The site boss tried to suppress a smirk. "You're measuring the yield."

"Exactly, sir." He adjusted a stick. "See, and all them other fellas said you was a stiff know-nothing, but I always disagreed with them."

Now the site boss smiled openly. "No matter how often they insisted."

Also grinning, Monroe shook his head. "All day long, it seems sometimes."

"Okay," Charlie said, arriving on the ridge. "Almost there." He attached wires to the battery's positive and negative bolts, then to a switch he'd pulled from the rucksack.

The site boss's smile faded. "How much powder did you boys set there?"

"Whatever all we had left, sir." Monroe shrugged. "I don't rightly know that anyone weighed it."

"Well, damn," he said. Then he cupped his hands around his mouth. "You boys take better cover. Move it back." He waved the crew farther into the trees.

Charlie checked the last connection. "Ready, sir."

The site boss pursed his lips. "We ought to be back by now. It's Saturday night."

"All due respect, sir," Monroe said. "But we done a good week's work. It'd make our whole weekend to blow a little harmless steam off here."

"It won't be harmless if someone gets hurt."

"Sir?" Charlie squatted beside the switch. "I am ready to make a detonation with my trigger, my very first."

"Oh hell," he conceded. "Probably be a dud anyway." Raising the air horn up with a straight arm, the site boss gave a long blast. Charlie unlocked the switch, then paused.

Monroe dropped to his belly, behind the row of sticks. "Nighty-night, Adolf."

At that, Charlie drove the switch closed with his full weight.

The explosion shot dirt and debris in all directions, a blast of gravel and dust. It roared, too, louder than the air horn and with greater percussion, its echo returning from the cliffs behind them.

But the true surprise was the bed: It soared higher than anyone had expected, end over end with a balletic poise, mattress stuffing flung every which way like a pillow burst in barracks horseplay. The frame pieces landed on the concrete bowl with a clang that made the boys' ears ring.

Charlie stood over his device. In the excitement he had bent the firing arm. But it had worked. He couldn't wait to tell Brenda. Smoke lingered at eye level, acrid and gray.

The boys were laughing, applauding. Someone lifted the bed frame, its slats curled like a handlebar mustache, and threw it in the air. It landed with another clang.

Only then did Charlie notice the truck inching down the rough trail behind them. It was not a battered rig like their crew used. It was new, rust-free, and a yellow light on the roof circled as if it were some kind of police car.

The effect was immediately sobering. The crew tightened into a cluster on the bowl, except for the three men still on the ridge.

Monroe rubbed his chin. "We're gonna catch it now."

"Don't you do any talking," the site boss said. "Not one word."

The truck swayed as it crossed the open scrub, not hurrying, its pace conveying a regal kind of power, as if to say of course the subjects will wait, while that yellow roof light turned steadily like a slow alarm. When the vehicle reached the ridge, the driver halted, and they could hear the hand brake drawing tight.

The passenger door opened and a man in black shoes emerged. Slender, his hair brushed hard back from his face, he had a forward lean, as if he were in the middle of an argument. He wore a gray suit, and stepped with care to keep his shoes clean.

The site boss squared his shoulders. "Good afternoon."

"Hello," the new arrival said, though to Charlie it sounded like hail-lo, with a click in the middle. The diversity of nations represented on The Hill—Germany, Denmark, Norway—had turned everyone into an expert in accents. This man, Charlie would have bet a Russian, rubbed his hands together, then clasped them tight. "I am Bronsky."

"Good to meet you, sir," the site boss said. "How can I help you today?"

"You are authorize? For this just now detonation?"

"Not exactly, sir. We'd finished our assignments for the day—"

"Your boys will cleans up mess."

"Of course, sir."

"You betcha, right quick we will," Monroe interjected, which brought a silencing scowl from the site boss.

"I observe this detonation has three-part device. How you did trigger it?"

He pointed to Charlie. "Our team has a specialist."

Bronsky turned. "May I please see?"

Charlie handed him the assembly. As the man examined his work, tilting it this way and that, he could not keep his tongue. "I got too excited, sir, and damaged the firing arm. But it's only my first one."

Bronsky raised his eyes to examine Charlie too. "What your name is?"

"Listen," the site boss said. "We're sorry, sir. This was only a prank after a long week. I apologize if we wasted any munitions."

"Please to answer," the man insisted. "What your name is?"

Charlie swallowed. "Fish, sir, Charles Fish."

"Fishk. Well done." He cleared his throat. "Rest of crew will please to police site."

With the device still in his hand, he minced back through the dirt and climbed into the truck. After the driver turned around, they swayed up to the trail with the yellow roof light still slowly spinning. No one spoke till the truck was out of sight.

"Who was that?" Charlie asked.

"Igor Bronsky," the site boss replied. "My director's boss's boss. And exactly what I was warning you about."

"You warned me?" Charlie said. "When?"

"Ninety-four," Monroe interrupted, bumbling up the ridge. His sunburned head radiant, he waved the longest of his measuring sticks like a miniature flag. "Can you believe it?" he cackled.

Arms high, Monroe faced down the hill and shouted to the crew. "We done blasted Hitler ninety-four feet in the air."

Dear Brenda,

I had the most amazing day. Your Charlie may be in trouble, but it might turn out to be a good kind of trouble.

He wiped a bit of dirt off the page, frustrated because he had already scrubbed his hands. A shower would really do the job, but that was still a full day away. Charlie took in his surroundings: the barracks a whirlwind of activity, boys washing themselves, or folding laundry, or mock-sparring. Saturday night and the pressure of the week was about to release.

For him that meant square dancing at Fuller Lodge: a string band, a caller, older folks ready to teach the steps to beginners like Charlie. He liked how wholesome it felt.

Some tech workers were already outside, meanwhile, deep into their beers. Others sat on the floor, a bunk between them, playing two-bit poker and passing around a bottle. One checked his hair in a locker mirror, while another splashed on cologne, so everyone knew they had dates.

> All week we work for as long as there is daylight, with only Sundays off, so nights like this have extra meaning. I suppose it might be like the prom, back in high school. I went stag and it was not much fun. But I bet a pretty girl like you had guys begging for a dance. I bet you wore a smashing dress, too, your hair done up with that French braid I can't forget.
>
> If you had been my prom date, I would have danced every song with you. But all I would have been thinking about all night was kissing you. That, and maybe—

The lights went out. A groan came from up and down the barracks so immediately, it seemed rehearsed. Power failures were a fact of life on The Hill, the slender wires installed for a boys' school no match for the demands of thousands of people and dozens of labs. But blackouts always seemed to come at the least convenient times. The barracks master lit a lantern by the door, its dim light casting long shadows. Charlie brought his face close to the page. He could barely make out his handwriting, and he hadn't gotten to the detonation yet. Much less how he missed her.

"Enough, Charlie." Giles strolled over with a beer. "Finish your love letter tomorrow."

"I wanted to tell her about today while it was fresh in my mind."

"You can't mail it till Monday anyway." Giles took a long drink. "Have a beer on your way to the dance. The guys want to celebrate your first detonation."

"Honest?"

"Well." Taking a swig, he ambled away. "I do, anyway."

On The Hill a beer cost pennies, and no matter what other shortages occurred, the supply remained plentiful. As Charlie approached
the bonfire, Giles handed him a cup of beer and made space for him
in the circle. Most of the fellows were concentrating on a drinking
game, drumming on their laps and taking turns making fast hand
signals. An error meant someone had to chug.

"You're not playing?" Charlie asked Giles.

"Monochopsis," Giles said. "Know what I mean?"

Charlie sipped his beer. "No idea at all."

"The persistent feeling of being out of place."

"Oh, I know that well. The only time I don't feel it is in choir
practice."

"You sing?" Monroe staggered up. "Warble us a lick."

"Not right now."

"Come on, choirboy." He swigged from a whiskey bottle. "Do it
before I up and fall over." He held the bottle forward. "I'll give you
some courage."

"Thanks anyway." Charlie bowed back a few steps. "I'm off to
the dance now."

"Monroe, the thing I want to know," Giles said, grabbing the
bottle for himself, "is why a couple of drinks turns your vocabulary
into a cornpone cartoon."

"Kentucky luck." Monroe smiled. "Booze brings up my blood,
is all."

Giles nudged Charlie. "Be good." And he tilted the bottle into
his mouth.

"Always," Charlie said, backing away from the bonfire. He
waited till he was fully in the dark before pouring out the rest of his
beer.

The walk to Fuller Lodge was pleasant with the power out. The
residential side of The Hill lay under a canopy of stars so plentiful,

compared to anywhere else he had lived, it could have been a different sky.

He marveled that some people were expert in the heavens, knew the stars' names and brightness and locations. Maybe he would try astronomy, once the war was over.

That again. Once that unimaginable time should come. Meanwhile he lived on a parapet of science as isolated as any feudal castle, the surrounding canyons more deep and protective than any moat.

Humming to himself, Charlie thought about the fellows back by the fire. They were all young, the average age on The Hill being twenty-seven. Even Oppenheimer, boss of the entire Project Y enterprise, was only thirty-nine. In part, that was why square dances suited Charlie so well: all kinds of young people, everyone far from home.

Also he enjoyed the freedom from worries about romantic entanglements. In a square dance you did not have one partner so much as four, moving through the steps as the caller named them: simple ones like the "Allemande Left" and "Promenade," which were like taking a playful walk; complicated steps like "Weave the Ring" and "Box the Gnat," where Charlie had to pay attention to left foot, right foot, left hand, right hand, and the sixteen ways he could confuse them; and moves that defied description but gave him keen pleasure, like "Ocean Wave" or the classic "Do-Si-Do."

He'd arrived not knowing one dance step, clinging to the walls like a moth for months, until an older woman spotted him.

"I've got a girl at home," Charlie protested.

"I'm twice your age," the woman laughed, pulling on his arm. "Besides, square dancing isn't about sweet talk, it's about losing the overwork blues."

He acquiesced, made a fool of himself with a thousand missteps—which girl was his cross and which one was his corner?—and laughed more that night than he had in the last five months combined. At evening's end the woman patted Charlie on the shoulder. "You come back here next week, all right, young man?"

He hadn't missed a Saturday since, except for those times the site boss gave him an assignment on Saturday to build something by Monday.

The gaiety at Fuller Lodge was so deliberate, so determined, the music did not even stop when the band took a break. The minute they put down their instruments, Willy Meehan—by day an Electronics Division leader—would break out his accordion, an instrument so large people called it his Stomach Steinway, to keep the party bouncing. No time for rest, just boisterous fun till the clock struck midnight.

At that, the room emptied in minutes. People might linger on the terrace, and sometimes romances occurred on the grassy knoll at the foot of Bathtub Row. But quiet came fast, the dance floor swept and everything made ready for religious services in the same room eight hours later. Charlie had joined the choir, prompted less by faith than by the desire to sing, though it meant an early morning after a late night. He would squeeze his whole week's joy into one twelve-hour burst.

Now he was passing the family apartment buildings, so hastily built they would have been called tenements back home, though they housed some of the world's preeminent scientific minds. Out of the dark came women's voices, a peal of laughter.

The power came back on. By then Charlie was facing the tech area, where men working late meant the lights were on in nearly all the windows. From Fuller Lodge, brightness spilled onto the outside patio, and music poured out to echo across the campus. Charlie felt like a swimmer, approaching a cruise ship at anchor.

The caller had a microphone, Charlie could hear him telling people to hustle and rustle, new squares were forming. He quickened his pace.

Fuller Lodge had been the main building of a boys' school. They'd left behind horse trails, a basketball hoop, and a main lodge made of logs—with antlered deer heads over the doorways and local Indians' rugs tacked to the wall. Here and there, long strings of crimson chilis hung to dry. There were large fireplaces at each end of the main room, with a piano pushed against the wall to make room for more dancers.

There were far more men on The Hill than women, no surprise given the disciplines that Project Y required. But there were
WACS, female technicians and administrators, wives whose husbands didn't dance, plus a few women scientists with reputations
equal to many of the men. After all, Marie Curie had won two Nobel Prizes for discovering radioactivity and more. Still, the lopsided
population meant that women had no rest on dance nights. It was
likewise considered polite for boys not to monopolize partners.

When breaks came, Charlie liked to wander out on the stone terrace. The tech area's lights reflected off Ashley Pond, reminding him
of Chicago skyscrapers shining on Lake Michigan. What was Brenda
doing? A time zone ahead, she was probably asleep.

"May I please to say hello?"

It sounded like hail-lo, and Charlie turned to see the slender man
with the brushed-back hair. Charlie couldn't help checking, and yes,
his shoes were still immaculate. "Mister Bronsky."

He made the slightest bow. "Mister Fishk."

Charlie waited, but the man said nothing more, and he felt he had
to fill the silence. "Are you enjoying the square dancing tonight, sir?"

"I do not dancing."

"I didn't use to, myself. I've learned how, since I arrived here."

"I come from Russia, where it is not time for dancing."

Charlie hardly knew how to respond. "Yes, sir."

Bronsky stared into the distance. "That assembly you use today. At concrete bowl. How you do arrange three detonations to
be simultaneous?"

"I make the connecting wires all the same length. One may have
an extra loop, but that's a small inefficiency for having all three go
off at the same time."

The Russian man nodded. "Make electrons travel same distance.
Simple."

"There would be more integrity if I created a timing device,"
Charlie replied.

Bronsky bent and wiped the toe of a shoe with his thumb. "You
can build device with more than three triggers?"

"Theoretically, I could make an infinite number."

Bronsky frowned. "I am not discussing of theoretical."

Charlie turned from the pond. The man wore an expression of deprivation, as if he were hungry. But there was plenty of food on The Hill. He wanted something else. Charlie felt like he was back at Harvard, taking an important oral exam.

"I don't know. I don't know how far soldering wire can carry a clean signal."

"Is easily determined. Trial and error."

"Yes, sir, but it would be hard to know what caused the error. Resistance in the material limits its capacity. Also, if you had too many triggers, the device could become unwieldy. For example, if the contacts need to be closer together than the width of the wire, making the device physically impossible to build."

Bronsky waited while Charlie continued to think the problem through.

"There's a reliability risk too. If you have one firing control for, let's say ten or twelve circuits, what if one thing failed? It would affect ten other things. I'd probably want redundancy, too, especially in a combat situation." He chuckled at the complexity of it all. "Can we go back to theoretical ideas instead?"

Bronsky waited, making sure Charlie had nothing more to add, before he spoke. "Perhaps, Fishk, please you are build for me device that triggers six, and we see what flaws we find."

Six. He'd never done more than three. It would take days of work—designing, soldering, trouble-shooting—and only if he quit the field team. "I could do that, sir."

"Good." Bronsky cleared his throat, began moving away in his cautious, mincing fashion, then paused at the edge of the light. "Perhaps please, by Friday, you are build for me ten of them."

Charlie threw his head back laughing. "Ten? Do you know how much time that would . . ."

His voice trailed off. The man had already vanished in the dark.

IT HAD TO BE submarines. I'd considered everything else Charlie could possibly be working on. For a while I speculated that it had something to do with the big new bombers. My girlfriend Greta said they flew so high, no Japanese defense plane or antiaircraft fire could reach them, so they bombed at will. Powerful. I liked imagining Charlie contributing to that strength.

At the movies I saw a newsreel about bomber factories in Wichita, Kansas, and Renton, Washington. Not New Mexico. Next letter, I asked point blank: "What are you doing down there?"

Charlie's reply dodged it with a joke. "We build the front end of horses. The other half comes from Washington, D.C."

Which made that letter like many in those days—you did not know how to read it. Was Charlie mocking my curiosity? Or was he forbidden to tell me, and trying to make light of it? A girl had no way of knowing.

I missed Charlie, his kindness, his attentiveness, his patience. But I hated the tedious communication, not knowing when I'd see him again. Life reduced to longing, requiring my mother and me to cope and worry. Families around us experienced such severe losses, sons injured or killed, we could not utter one word of complaint.

One morning she left the newspaper on the kitchen table while I sipped coffee, and I was bored, and scanned the headlines: The US Navy had torpedoed the *Lima Maru* of Japan. Two thousand seven hundred and sixty-five men had died.

That was the population of my whole high school, times four. I pictured our gym, packed for a basketball game, and tried to conceive of four times that many people. I knew those sailors did not all die at once, too, the instant the torpedo hit. No, they were in the middle of the ocean, and their ship sank and pulled them right down with it. They fought for air, they knew what was happening, they drowned.

It was gruesome, and fascinating. The maps and numbers of the war stopped being abstract. I could conceive of four gymnasiums of people. Destruction had come within the grasp of my imagination.

The very next morning, I read that the US Navy had torpedoed the *Petrella*. Two thousand six hundred and seventy men drowned. I began following the news, especially submarines: stealth, a water missile streaking across open sea, the surprise explosion, the devastating result. I could picture it all. I craved news of the next success.

Three weeks later, down went the *Sakito Maru*, taking 2,495 men to the bottom. My school times four, again and again.

Charlie had to be part of it. Of course, New Mexico was an odd place to develop ocean weapons. But to me, that made the idea all the more canny. Something in Charlie's math was useful to underwater warfare. Essential, perhaps.

In April the *Yoshida Maru #1* took a torpedo and sank with 2,649 souls. The next day I received a letter from Charlie.

> I hope spring has arrived in Chicago. It has been warm here already for weeks. They say the snow was insufficient this winter, and we may have water shortages. I would be okay with that if I could stomach the milk. Meanwhile, my work has intensified, and I don't get outside as often as I used to. But the square dances continue and they improve my mood. If only I could have one dance with you . . .

As usual, there were many blacked-out parts. I read the remaining words as if they were code, as if Charlie was communicating a special message only I would understand. Did dances mean successful sub attacks? Was not getting outside his way of describing the span of days without a sinking? What was the significance of bad milk?

A girl could drive herself crazy. But my mother had already decided we would not be going loco. If she said there would be changes, it had the weight of law. So: Dubie's Music was now open half days. We were not, she insisted, going to sit around all day despairing. Anyone who wants an organ badly enough will come in the afternoon.

We still had precious few customers, but somehow it did not feel as offensive, or as personal, if I only had to occupy myself for four hours at a time. When customers did arrive, I was in better humor.

One result of the reduced hours was that my organ playing, which had settled into a steady plateau when I was applying to conservatories, broke free. I would never play in the league of the instrument's giants, whose performances in the 1920s had drawn thousands. But I had definitely surpassed the amateur level. If the war ever ended, if I ever found a way to pay for Oberlin, if my acceptance there was still valid, I no longer worried that I would be out of my league.

One afternoon my mother came out of the back office as I practiced. "Brenda," she said, a mess of papers against her chest, "I bet there aren't three churches in Chicago with someone of your skills. You keep right on working."

She returned to the office, while I sat speechless. Not only had my mother spontaneously praised me, she also gave voice to my secret opinion of myself. The unusual thing is, it wasn't bragging. An organist's skill can be measured as easily as the time a runner needs to run a mile. Repertoire tells all. And the piece that had my attention the most? Bach's Toccata and Fugue in D Minor.

"Toccata" means touch, and that particular work required a great variety of touches: the trumpeting opening notes like a call to attention, flights of spriteliness, deep Germanic bombast. There were vast washes of chords, too, with Bach's brilliant arpeggios going nonstop in the high notes. Not to mention a finger-bender of a fugue in the middle, the melody like a bird flitting this way and that, then repeated in the other hand, then in harmony, then sideways.

Oh, and the call and response passage, that was like a soloist with his choir. Bach used the full instrument, every inch of its span. Technically the Bach toccata was not an especially difficult piece, but for me the fugue part was impossible. I needed a proper teacher but also relished my solo attempts.

My mother spent her free mornings at an armory, the Eighth Regiment's brick castle up by Thirty-Fifth Street. She refused to say what she was doing. Of course I nagged her to tell me. One night at dinner she'd had enough. "Suppose some Nazi guy grabs you and drags you into an alley."

"I'd kick him in the shins," I snapped back.

"Not if he had a gun you wouldn't. And he puts the pistol barrel to your throat and says, 'Tell me what your mother is doing at the armory.'"

"I would say I have no idea. She won't tell me."

She crossed her arms in victory. "And that is how it must stay."

The other change we made, at her insistence, was nightlife. Mine. She stayed home like always, her companions a book and a pack of cigarettes. I could gauge how good a novel was by her ashtray. The fewer the butts, the more the story had captured her attention. But she urged me to go out, to rekindle my friendships.

I told her I was fine, but actually I was scared. Would fun create a distance between me and Charlie? What would I do about the interests of boys—which were natural, but might come as a test I did not want to take?

Greta solved the problem. She'd been in my class: big-boned but gorgeous, with bright green eyes. Greta had curly hair so black, in certain lights it looked blue. With a roaring contagious laugh, that girl was fun as a carnival. She called one Wednesday and invited me to *Casablanca*.

"Seen it, thanks," I said. "Twice."

"Me too," she laughed. "Five times. But I'm ready to make it six."

"Who all is going?"

"You and me, like old times."

I glanced across the kitchen, where cigarette smoke rose from behind the evening paper. I did love that movie, how it was both funny and serious.

"Sure," I said. "You bet."

By the time Greta arrived, she'd found the four other girls from our regular gang, and we marched off to the theater together, a warm spring night with my pals. But I also noticed, when my mother answered the door, the presence of the other girls did not surprise her. "Hello, ladies," she'd said, like she'd been expecting them.

Well, and so what? Maybe she asked my friends to get me out of the house. We loved the movie, hollering the best lines, Greta squeezing my arm when Rick tells Ilsa, "We'll always have Paris."

No one shushed us. Everyone in the theater had seen it before. When Rick said the last line, it seemed like the entire place shouted along: "Louie, I think this is the beginning of a beautiful friendship."

So it began. Out most nights: movies, bowling, long walks by the lake. I shouldn't have worried. I missed Charlie no less. And I had something to put in my letters. In June the Allies invaded Normandy, newspapers filled with heroism and sacrifice. I did not sense that the beginning of the end might have arrived. Later that month, an American ship sank the *Toyama Maru*, and 5,400 Japanese died. Almost as many men as we'd lost in all of D-Day, gone from a single torpedo.

The next day we sank the *Nippon Maru*, taking 3,019 lives. I felt a dark thrill of connection to Charlie, and the incredibly complicated math it probably took to track down an enemy ship, and aim a torpedo to rush through the water true as an arrow, not diverted by waves or currents or a ship's evasive movements.

Today, it galls me that I remember precisely the number of lives lost in each sinking. I memorized them. I had no sense of thousands of actual Japanese boys drowning, their families' hopes and hearts going to the bottom of the ocean with them.

Yes, I know that Japan started the war, in the attack on Pearl Harbor. I know that sinking their navy was essential. But today, at my age, it does not diminish my patriotism to say that I grieve for the cost of the conflict on all sides. There is glory in victory, but it can be solemn, too, aware that all sides experienced the pain.

In retrospect, I wish Charlie *had* been working on submarines. A torpedo is a simple object, really, a kind of bullet. The truth was far more complicated, and therefore the effects of my ignorance would prove to be far more harmful.

Then the phone would ring, Greta would laugh uproariously, and off I'd go into an adventure. I had simplified the war so that I could withstand it.

Eventually—it was bound to happen—Greta suggested a dance. At Douglas Park, which I knew from high school was named after the guy Abraham Lincoln defeated in the debates, who went on to be a United States senator anyhow. I recoiled from the idea though. Dances meant dancing. With dancers. Why take the risk?

But I loved that park. There was a lagoon in the middle where my father taught Frank how to fish. I have a picture on my dresser my mother took that day: Frank, with the proudest ten-year-old expression on his face, holding up his first catch: an ugly catfish as long as my arm. I'm at a point in life where I do not care much about material objects, but that image is one I cherish.

Maybe I was justifying. I could have gone to that park anytime. And the girls were perfectly capable of dancing without me. But they pleaded. One whose mom ran a salon offered to do my hair for free. Then Greta asked me to be her backup, in case a certain Brian she was supposed to meet at the dance didn't show up for some reason. Which provided the excuse I needed to say yes.

I didn't go overboard. Didn't wear my best dress. Didn't accept the offer for my hair. The one special thing was that I wore the necklace my father gave me for my sweet sixteen, a string of tiny pinkish pearls.

"Don't you look nice," my mother said, peering up from her latest novel. "I don't think I've ever seen you go to a dance looking more like your actual self."

I put my hands on my hips. "Is that a compliment or a criticism?"

"I guess that depends on what you think about your actual appearance. Personally, I prefer authentic to false."

"I'm still not sure what you mean."

She let the book fall into her lap. "I already said you look nice. Just because you're back-dooring Charlie, you don't have to fight with me. It's your life, Brenda."

"I am not back-dooring anyone." I almost shouted it.

"Then we agree." She lifted the book again, giving it her full attention and then some. "Have fun, home by twelve."

I left the house seething. What was back-dooring, anyhow? My first stop was Greta's house. We were going to meet the other girls and then share a cab. The second we were outside, I asked her what it meant.

"I'm not sure," she said. She wore a yellow dress that showed off her bosomy figure. "I think it means cheating on somebody. Where'd you hear it?"

"Some book my mom is reading." I checked to make sure the clasp of my pearls was secure. "Do you think going to this dance means I'm back-dooring Charlie?"

Greta chuckled, throaty and free, enough to lift anyone's spirits. "Didn't he tell you that he's dancing every weekend? Does that mean he is back-dooring you?"

"Of course not. I totally trust him. In fact, his telling me is part of why I do."

"Then you only need to worry if you do something that you can't tell him."

"Greta." I gave her a quick hug. "You're the best best friend."

The band was fantastic. Usually in those days, half the musicians in a group were gone in the service, and you could tell. But this sextet was first rate, with an enormously fat clarinet player in front who could really swing.

His intonation was impeccable, never sharp or flat unless he bent a note on purpose. Every song the band would set things up, playing chords and a beat like making a stage for him to stand on. His cheeks would bulge and he'd lean back, and then out would blast a rush of notes, high and stylish and full of energy, like a fast-talking guy trying to whirl a girl into romance.

He seemed to know every song, too, because someone would call out a tune, and half a minute later the clarinetist would be playing it, and playing *with* it, eyes so wide in delight you could see the whites, while the rest of the band struggled to catch up.

I hadn't been there five minutes when a man—twenty-seven, I'd say, way out of my range—appeared and asked me to dance.

"Happy to," I said, and out we went. He was good, too, knew how to lead so a girl could trust him. Plus his hands never wandered one inch. After three tunes I thanked him and took a step away. He made a little bow, then tottered off to find another lass.

Which was perfect. Fun and no harm done. This must be how Charlie did the square dances: light as a feather, keeping his distance. A boy my age came along, red-haired and smiling too much for my tastes, and asked if I wanted to cut a rug.

"Thanks," I said. "I'm taking a break."

I saw him on the floor one song later. So no guilt. The clasp of my pearls kept sneaking around to the front, but I slipped it back and went on enjoying that knockout clarinet player.

Greta's Brian showed up after all, and they danced to every song. They shook and spun on the fast tunes, snuggled close on the slow ones, and later in the night they had a long smooch on the floor for all of us to see. Everyone clapped for the band when the song ended— except me. I was clapping for my friend.

The band leader announced that people should pair up, last dance. I sidled over toward the punch bowl. Scanning the room I saw Greta, not with Brian but holding the arm of some other guy—I spotted how whoa Nellie handsome he was, despite an arm in a sling—and they were arguing about something. I hurried over.

"What's the matter?" I said. Any guy who fooled with my friend was in for it.

"Here." He waved a hand at me. "Let's ask Brenda herself."

"Fine." Greta released his arm. "Go ahead."

The band started up, a sweet slow song. Couples were nuzzling around us. I wanted to get this guy out of Greta's hair—how did he know my name, anyhow?—so she could snuggle with her boy.

"What is it?" I shouted to be heard over the music.

Handsome shouted back. "I told her you were the prettiest girl at this dance, and I want to meet you, and dance with you, and marry you."

"What?" I said.

"I told him he was crazy," Greta yelled, "and you already have a fella."

"Greta honey?" Brian had reappeared on the dance floor. "Shall we?"

"You're nuts," I told handsome. "Leave my girlfriend alone and you get one dance."

"Brenda—"

"Go, Greta. I'll be fine."

By degrees she turned away, until Brian drew her close and they started to sway. When I raised my right arm as if to waltz, handsome took it and led me to the edge of the dance floor. It was less crowded, not as loud. Then he lifted my arm again and took my hand, resting the sling of his right arm on my hip, and we did a little side to side. I intended to say not one word. I hoped it would be a short song.

He studied his shoes a minute, not much of a dancer. For all his zeal, we were barely moving. When he raised his face again, the downpour began.

"My name is Chris Beatty, I was between you and Frank in school but, Brenda, I always thought you were beautiful and spirited and interesting, and I'm an airman now, a pilot assigned overseas, can't say where, but we were shot down and I dinged my arm, four surgeries, they sent me home to heal up so they can get me back to the war . . ."

He paused to breathe before charging ahead.

". . . and I've not been up to much but annoying my ma and tormenting my little sis who is in tenth grade, until tonight when some buddies dragged me here—"

He glanced past me, over my shoulder as if to spot his pals and prove that he was telling the truth, but then he continued like he was running downhill and his legs got going too fast. What girl wouldn't be flattered? It was adorable.

". . . I saw you across the room early on, and, Brenda, I've spent the whole night going back and forth do you talk to a girl when you're shipping back really soon, do you bother her, but then I remembered the one thing I have learned from this war so far—I mean besides how to fly and navigate and all—one thing that matters, because I learned it the hard way . . ."

At that his voice tightened the slightest bit, not in some masculine fakery, but as though he was about to cry. I felt it, too, in my throat, without knowing what he was going to say. He leaned forward, his body expressing some kind of amazing urgency.

". . . which is that everyone dies, everybody, I've seen buddies do it right before my eyes and the only question is when, what day is your number up, and did you make good use of the time you had . . ."

Then he reached forward before I could think, and hooked one finger in my strand of little-girl pearls. He leaned me ever so slightly toward him, as if to convince me, as if to make me believe.

". . . but if I let you walk away it might be the last time I see you, ever, so I started across the floor and then your friend stepped in before I could ask you to dance, or talk to me, or ask you please God to marry me, Brenda. Please. Please."

He wound himself down, he gulped and caught his breath. He released my pearls. A pilot. Who had been shot down. Who knew what he wanted. Who was, now that he stood before me, quite frankly, gorgeous.

"Don't be ridiculous," I replied. But I rose up on tiptoe to whisper close into the whirl of his ear, "Dance with me now, and we'll see about the rest."

CHARLIE SAT IN THE back of the pickup as it swayed over open terrain, trying not to vomit. Most crewmen perched on the gunwales, like dogs with their heads out the window. A bold few dangled their legs off the tailgate. But Charlie carried another new assembly, so he sat in the truck's well to protect it, his belly feeling every pitch and yaw.

Meanwhile the summer sun roasted him, the dust dried his lips, and he felt similarly sunburned by the remove he sensed from the crew. No longer did he work with them all day amid the ponderosa. They saw Charlie only when he had something to test.

At last the truck eased to a halt. The driver set the brake, tilting his cowboy hat forward. When it came to napping, Charlie thought, the man was a professional.

Bronsky climbed out on the passenger side, and with his strange fastidious steps to protect his shoes, he minced down to the bowl while unfolding a blueprint. Charlie stood and took deep breaths.

The site boss sniffed in his direction. "Fish."

"How are you today, sir?"

Instead of answering, he turned at the sound of his director's boss's boss calling for a measuring tape. One by one, Bronsky checked the measurements of the munitions circling the bowl—ten piles of TNT, every nest of yellow crystals equidistant from the center and from one another. Crewmen helped as the director called for adjustments of an inch or two in each mound of explosives, while the rest stood well back. To Charlie, they appeared as interested as if they were watching a chef prepare a meal that someone else was going to eat.

He climbed off the truck, cradling the assembly, and shuffled down the slope. The only crewman looking his way was Monroe, who he'd seen as recently as breakfast, his usual garrulous self, but who now greeted Charlie with a discreet nod.

"Fishk," Bronsky called, eyes on the blueprint. "Do your businesses."

"Hi, fellas," Charlie said, ambling out into the bowl. No one replied. He placed the assembly on the ground.

The work absorbed him: unwinding the wires to a safe distance, attaching the detonator. Absently, he began to hum. "Camptown Ladies," doo-dah, doo-dah. When everything was connected, Charlie waved to the site boss, who as usual sounded his air horn. Rather than telling the boys to move away, as before, now the blast signaled that they might return within visual range, to watch the fireworks.

Bronsky hovered as Charlie connected the assembly to a car battery. "Ready, sir."

"All clears," the Russian unit director cried out—the one of his many speech habits that the boys chose to mock behind his back, announcing "all clears" when they finished a meal, chugged a beer, flushed a toilet: "all clears."

A whole lexicon of ridicule was developing on The Hill. Los Alamos was nicknamed Lost Almost. A girl with shapely hips was known as a Project Y. Every time the water ran out or the power failed, the boys would cry "Shangri-La." The strangeness of their situation seemed to increase daily. Those who obtained driver's licenses saw not their name beside the photo, but a number, and their address was "United States Army."

"God forbid a policeman ever pulls me over," Giles said. "He'll think this is a play license."

There was no police force on The Hill, however, only MPs with open contempt for civilians, their tempers as sullen as hungry teenagers. There was no telephone for personal use either. For radio, there was a station that broadcast on The Hill only. Men world-famous in their scientific fields strode about in dungarees and shirtsleeves, often unshaved, unless a photographer appeared for some reason. The gents would resurface in suits, their faces sleek and fingernails clean. There was one teahouse halfway down the hill, and one restaurant, but it was above the rank and finances of barracks boys. They made do with the rare weekend trip to Santa Fe, riding there and back in drab green Army buses, their wallets full on the way down but empty on the way back, with little to show for the trip but a hangover and the occasional tattoo.

When a fellow staggered back into the barracks, the boys would greet him: "Did you meet any local girls?" Nearly always, he would grin in defeat. "All clears."

Now Bronsky unceremoniously unlocked the assembly, confirmed that the bowl area was empty, then jammed the circuit closed. The explosions were tidy, tests of control rather than yield, but nonetheless an entertaining sight. The boys who'd snuck their heads out from behind trees and rocks enjoyed eight bursts of light bringing eight bangs of noise, rushes of dust and smoke from the perimeter of the bowl, debris tossed in eight directions.

The crewmen cheered, Monroe yelled, "Hell yeah," but Charlie hung his head. Two piles had not gone off. A gray cloud rose, leaving a chalky taste to the air.

Bronsky marched down the hill to loom over one of the duds, eyeing it from every angle, then swept with his hand as if to dismiss the entire situation. Charlie stumbled down the slope, stopping at the concrete's edge.

"Next time Fishk, you leave assembly in truck until all else is connected. Yes?"

Charlie scanned the bowl: eight scars on the concrete, two mysteries. "Yes, sir."

"Disconnect these two," Bronsky said, pointing, though Charlie had already squatted by one of them, removing the feckless wires. "And please to throw in trash."

Only one thing could repair Charlie's spirits after a debacle like that, and when he returned to the barracks after dinner, that exact thing was waiting on his bed.

Dear Charlie,

I took your advice, or followed your example anyhow, and at the urging of my girlfriends, last Saturday I went to a dance.

Feeling a flash of insecurity, he glanced up to see that the barracks were nearly empty. A few boys napping at the far end. The gap in days between Brenda's last letter and this one was the longest since they had parted in the Great Hall of Union Station. Each day now, Charlie saw how much destruction could take place in a fraction of a second. With the expanse of time since their last kiss, any imaginable thing could happen. He swallowed hard before bending back to the page.

You would have loved it. There was a clarinet player with perfect embouchure, brilliant tone, and a clever idea every three seconds. Also his repertoire was limitless. People could call out any old tune, and half a minute later he'd be playing it. He kept us dancing till midnight. I only went out on the floor for a few numbers, but they were good fun, and I thought of you and all your square dancing.

The best gossip of the night is that Greta may have landed herself a fella, though I haven't had a chance to squeeze all the juicy details out of her. I saw them smooching during a slow song, so I hope he doesn't have to go off in the service anytime soon.

On she prattled, news and chatter, and it did Charlie's heart good. More than anything the letter said, its mere existence was a balm. She was thinking of him. She took the time to write.

"Before you, Charlie Fish," Giles said, sauntering down the barracks aisle, "no one had ever detonated six devices on one assembly. Eight is a fine achievement."

"Tell that to the man who wanted ten." Charlie lowered the letter. "But wait. You guys in Electronics heard already?"

"My friend, the minute you succeed, we will have to build feeder wiring for long-distance initiation. Your progress is our workload."

"No one tells me anything."

"I told you: compartmentalization. But I have worse news."

"And so far today you've been nothing but rainbows and unicorns."

Giles laughed. "That's funny, Charlie. You just made an actual joke."

"It was an accident. What's the worse news?"

"My division is developing electronics equipment for twenty-four detonators."

Charlie drew back like a trout doubting a lure. "But they want the firing to be simultaneous. How can you do that with two dozen terminals?"

"It's madness. My only question is whether they want you to be juggling knives or fire sticks while you perform this feat of magic."

Charlie grimaced. "Machetes, I believe."

"That's why God gave you ten toes. Any mishaps, you'll still have some spares."

"Seriously, though." Charlie put the letter aside. "If the goal is twenty-four, why would Bronsky have me work on ten?"

Giles sat on the bed beside Charlie. "I am untrained in Russian inscrutability. Maybe if he said twenty-four at the outset, you'd have replied that it is impossible."

"Well, it is. A basic short circuit would involve testing six hundred connections. Or is it six hundred squared?"

"All clears." Giles nodded at the letter. "Rainbows from your girl?"

Charlie smiled. "And unicorns."

"Have you informed the young lady yet of your plan to make a hundred babies with her, or die trying?"

"Get out of here."

"The things you utter in your sleep, Fish. The whole barracks knows." Giles shook his head. "Poor girl has no idea."

"Quit it," Charlie said, grinning and flushed.

The barracks' back door slammed, two boys entering with a rage of setting sun behind them. The forward one had a familiar stagger.

"Monroe, you infamous chemist and drunkard," Giles hailed him. "What mischief are you committing this fine evening?"

Monroe navigated to the nearest bunk, holding it for balance. "Celebration."

"You seem further gone than usual," Charlie said. "Are you all right?"

"Great, Mister Charlie. Better than eight out of ten."

"Ouch," Giles laughed.

"I've done something, though. Take a gander." Monroe lifted his shirt, and sticks of red dynamite were inked in a stack on his ribs, with orange sparks coming off its lit blue fuse. The whole area was ringed by angry skin. "Done it today in Santa Fe."

"What in the world?" Charlie asked.

"Of course." Giles threw up his hands. "A tattoo."

"Souvenir of our mission here." Monroe fingertipped the red area. "Tender as a new lamb though."

"Monroe," Charlie was incredulous. "You do know that we're working with TNT here, right? And not dynamite?"

Giles burst out laughing.

Monroe shrugged. "No one seeing this'll know the difference."

"It's scarification, regardless," said the person who'd entered behind Monroe, stepping into the light. "Ugly and permanent. Hello, Fish."

Charlie found that he had stood. "Richard Mather."

The mathematician from Chicago made a small bow. "I'm surprised to see you here. I didn't think your uncle had that much clout."

"I did it on my own," Charlie replied. "Or halfway, anyway."

"Please," Mather scoffed. "You aren't nearly intelligent enough."

"None of us must be very smart," Giles observed, "to be living in this bedlam."

Mather checked his fingernails. "At the moment I prefer it to both Belgium and Bataan."

"No argument there," Giles answered. "But, Monroe? Lots of argument with you. What have you done?"

"Become irresistible," he preened. "Handsome as a banty rooster now. Tell them ladies to line right up."

"You've defaced yourself. It's graffiti on your body."

"Easy does it," Charlie said. "Too late to lecture him now."

But Giles shook his head. "As if this life did not already give a person enough things to regret."

"Jealousy talking," Monroe slurred. "Some people can't handle a man so pretty."

"Exactly," Mather said. He leaned against a locker, sliding his hands into his pockets. "I'm breathless with envy."

Charlie remembered his constant interruptions in Chicago, the picture of his pretty sister who he swore none of them would ever touch. Were they supposed to be friends now, on this island of science? "Which division are you in?"

"Theoretical. Under Bethe."

"That's the genius crew," Giles observed.

Mather blinked blandly at him. "If the shoe fits . . ."

Giles snickered. "Humble too."

"Fellas." Monroe shook himself as if he had just awakened. "I'm dancing on over to Fuller Lodge for a bit. Aim to make a god-awful fool of myself, do things I'll regret for weeks, and I'd be right honored to have your company."

"Not me," Charlie said, waving the letter. "I have reading to do. Then I need to march myself over to the tech area, and figure out what went wrong today."

"That's you all over, Fish," Mather said. "Not that bright, but as persistent as a salmon headed upstream."

Giles's eyes went back and forth between the two, waiting for Charlie's riposte. When nothing emerged, he patted his friend on the back. "Don't underestimate our Charlie. This guy has already rewritten the world's rules for detonator switching."

Mather bent at the waist, looking downward, before rising with a smirk. "Just checking to see if I'd wet myself with excitement."

Giles bristled. "Well, aren't you a perfect pain in the—"

"Don't mind Mather," Charlie interrupted. "Unfortunately, he is every bit as smart as he considers himself to be."

"Also?" Monroe held one hand high. "He knows where to get whiskey. Them sick of rum can respect such a man."

Mather stood straight again. "You've all bored me. Good-bye."

He swept away down the barracks aisle, his manner entirely regal, Monroe wobbling along behind, his boozy scent following like a tail. Giles watched them, shaking his head, then turned to Charlie. "Sonder," he said, "you know what I mean?"

"Rarely do I know what you mean."

"Sonder is the realization that every other person has a life as vivid and complex as your own."

"So saith the walking dictionary."

"Shower night for me, so I'll leave you to your epistle," Giles said. "Are you planning to attend tomorrow's lecture?"

"I'll be choiring at the church service, if that's what you mean."

"No, the physicist Robert Sebring is speaking in the afternoon. Allegedly, he's going to explain what's actually happening here, and what we might accomplish."

"The end of compartmentalization?"

"Possibly. But my hope is for liberosis. Know what I mean?"

Charlie shook his head. "Not a bit."

"The desire to care less about things. It might do us all some good."

"Where do you find these ten-cent words?"

"Lying on the ground, Charlie, waiting for someone to scoop them up." He headed down the row of bunks. "Have a good night."

"I hope when you wash all the dirt off, there's still a person left inside."

Giles snapped his fingers. "Damn close to making your second joke of the day."

"I apologize."

Charlie shoved his pillow against the bed frame, settling against it, when who should jump onto his lap but Midnight. She squeezed her ebony body along his leg and began to purr. He rubbed under her chin before lifting the letter again.

> Dear Charlie, I took your advice, or followed your example anyhow, and at the urging of my girlfriends, last Saturday I went to a dance.

The guard returned Charlie's pass, waving him through the fence. Party music from Fuller Lodge echoed at his back. He climbed the creaking stairs and was chagrined to see a light on down the hall in his workroom. The bigger surprise was finding Bronsky there, perched on a high stool.

Usually at ten on a Saturday night, senior staff gathered in one of the directors' cabins on Bathtub Row, martinis and cigarettes, a mélange of accents arguing or laughing. Yet here was the Detonation Division chief with a magnifying glass, hovering like a vulture over the assemblies that had not fired that afternoon. Or their remains, because he had already taken them apart, pieces and wires scattered across the table.

"Hello, sir," Charlie said.

"Fishk." Bronsky remained bent forward. "Perhaps I am not only one wondering about today's result."

"I thought you wanted this stuff in the trash."

He kept the magnifying glass to his face. "I am angry then. Not so much now. Do you know why they fail?"

"That's why I came. To find the error."

"I do this already and learn nothing. You have a theory?"

Charlie scanned the table. Three weeks of fastidious design and careful soldering lay there, dismantled recklessly. A ballpeen hammer would have done as good a job. Any diagnostics would be pointless now. The error was therefore likely to repeat, and he would be blamed. "Maybe it's because we used ten detonators, instead of twenty-four."

"Ah." Bronsky straightened on the stool. "Someone has been indiscreet."

"Or honest."

"Now I see it is your turn for anger."

"Four, twenty-four, one hundred and four, I'll do my best. But I thought we were on the same side. Is it wrong for me to know what you actually need? Are you concerned that I might try to talk you out of a method that invites malfunction?"

Bronsky set the magnifying glass on the table with care. "Fishk, how much you are knowing about arcs?"

"Thanks to Chicago," Charlie answered, "more than I ever cared to know."

"Good." He took a sheet of paper and drew a large circle. "Imagine in three dimensions though."

"A ball."

"Yes, a sphere, this large." Bronsky held his arms about four feet apart. Then he drew bumps at various places around the circle. "Detonators in arcs around ball, all identical distance from one another. Calculating this is hard arithmetic, many arcs. But to make ball implode, each detonator must burst uniformly, identical force."

"Implode. I don't know that term."

"Opposite of explode. Pushes everything inward." He put the pencil down. "Ball we are create here on Hill requires twenty-four detonators. All must fire simultaneously for Gadget to work."

Charlie pondered this information. "Two questions. First, do you understand that twenty-four things cannot happen at exactly the same time? It has never been done."

Bronsky shrugged. "Many things happen on Hill that are not done before. What is second question?"

"You know how long I've been working on this ten-piece design. Why build and perfect it when you actually need something that can detonate fourteen more?"

"Goal is not device. Goal is knowledge." He waved his hand over the parts strewn across the table. "This knowledge, we will use many, many of times."

Charlie scanned the table's debris. "We will?"

Bronsky's face went blank. "Or, perhaps, just once."

23.

BY GRETA'S MEASURE, I was back-dooring. That is, I was not tell-ing Charlie. In fact, I was not telling anyone. It was my own private glory. My own private torment.

Chris Beatty followed me home that night. It was my idea, the invitation an impulse I followed without pausing to consider the con-sequences. The ruse was simple too. I asked the gals if they would mind dropping me first, then waited outside till he came marching down the sidewalk. I felt like I'd pulled off a little coup.

Chris arrived quickly, almost at a trot despite his arm in a sling, which struck me as maybe how he did everything. But he pulled up short. "Is this all right?"

"Twice around the block," I said. "And I'll still be in before curfew."

"Fair enough," he answered, with a smile to melt a girl's heart. Or at least her resistance. I imagined you could fill a school bus with the ladies who had thrown themselves at this man. Yet here he was, with me. He chose me.

"Come on." Chris tilted his head up the street. "Princess."

The charmer. I stepped up on the side of his good arm, and we set off. But his pace was so jerky and quick, I had to grab his elbow to slow him down. Which is how we ended up strolling arm in arm.

He was taller than Charlie. He smelled terrific, which believe it or not was the first time I'd admired a fella's scent. And he jabbered a mile a minute.

". . . Then there was the day in high school when you won that basketball game with foul shots—"

"My mother hated me playing that sport. She was afraid I'd break a finger and wreck my organ career."

"I was home from college for the weekend," he continued, almost as if I hadn't spoken, "and wandered over to school just in case. I couldn't just knock on your parents' door, hi, I'm the total stranger who pined for your daughter—"

"You pined?"

"—and then that big girl fouled you, it was such a blatant shove, the poor sport, though I also understand how competition is useful, and pushes us to do our best, and maybe she got carried away, but anyway bloop bloop you dropped those two foul shots as easy as unwrapping a lollipop, and the timer rang game over and you'd won."

He bounced from topic to topic like skipping a stone on the lake: the foul, college, lollipops. Which should I respond to? "Would you believe I had never made two foul shots in a row before?"

"Nope." Chris shook his head as if I'd uttered blasphemy. "In my mind, Brenda, you always make both shots. Because every time I've seen you try, you've done it. That makes me want to show off for you sometime, too: land a plane under some difficulty, one engine out or something. To wow you like you wowed me that day."

I decided it was easiest not to answer. Let him put me on a pedestal. We'd already finished our first lap, and I felt like we could have marched thirty times around.

"But you," he said at last. "Tell me about yourself, your brother, your dad serving, too, from what I heard. How is it all going?"

"Oh, Chris. It has not been easy."

I started to explain, but it was a mess. I wanted his sympathy, I wanted to impress him, I wanted to sound humble, I wanted to be honest, I wanted to conceal the existence of Charlie Fish. Chris took it all in, nodding along. When I finished, he just stopped nodding. Not one word in reply. That's how badly I did.

Yet when we rounded the last corner, he surprised me. "One more lap? Please?"

I turned his wrist to see the time. Ten minutes till. "If we don't dawdle."

He picked up the pace. "Can I tell you about flight training? It's pretty amazing."

"Please," I said.

Chris began chattering again, top speed about entrance exams and exercise and finding out he had perfect vision. I started to tell about having perfect pitch, but he was explaining his first takeoff, listing the dangers with such enthusiasm, I let him carry on, and we strolled into the wild blue yonder.

Yes, I promised to see him the next night. I was able to get away with it because Greta was occupied with her guy. We had one phone call the morning after the dance. Turned out Brian was on leave before shipping out to San Francisco, and from there, west and west till he reached the little islands that never surrendered. Time was short, hearts were beating, and her thrill was strong enough that only at the end did she ask about Chris. "Did he stay that obnoxious, or did he calm down?"

"He was a perfect gentleman."

"I'm so glad. With ones that cute, you never know."

"Cute is right."

"Conceited too."

I hesitated. "Is it conceited if it's all true?"

"No," she laughed. "Then it's just bragging."

I was standing in the kitchen and my mother in the living room, but I could feel her listening. "Terrible dancer, anyhow."

"You're a pal for taking him away. That dance with Brian was something special."

We rang off, she had to get dressed for a dinner date with her new beau, and I was glad. Her heart could run wild and there would be no room to think about me. Which meant I didn't have to spill about what I was doing.

And what was I doing? I told my mother it was dinner with Greta. Then I pinned on my hat and met Chris four blocks away. He was pacing on the street corner, and I hung back a second to look at him. "Handsome" was the wrong word. "Pretty" was more accurate. Pretty like a busy baroque melody. Pretty like a young horse. When he saw me, he threw down his cigarette and opened his arms wide.

"There she is, my future wife."

I made a face. "How about we try a first date, and take it from there?"

Chris kissed my hand royalty-style. "Resistance is futile, princess."

It took all of my moxie to stay self-possessed. "Buy me a steak and we'll see."

The restaurant was around the corner from our house, yet I'd never been. Candlelight, small tables. As the maître d' led us, women followed Chris with their eyes.

When my steak came, he pulled the plate over on his side.

"What's the big idea?" I asked.

"Patience, princess." He cut a small piece, stabbed it with his fork and held it toward me.

"What?" I said.

"Please," he answered, all smiles. "Indulge me."

I took that bite off the fork. Quick as a pickpocket he cut another piece for me.

"Again?"

"Indulge me, princess."

So, while his plate of fish went cold, Chris fed me the entire steak. It was the ultimate pampering: slow, luxurious, and I must confess, it became sexual. I had never experienced a man's keen attention to my senses. Yet here was another bite, his eyes bright. I felt arousal down to my toes. To this day, I wonder what would have happened if he'd attempted a seduction.

After the last bite, he sat back, victorious. I needed to collect myself, wiping my lips with the napkin, the cloth strangely rough. "The most delicious thing I ever ate."

It sounded so pedestrian, for the magnitude of what he had awakened in me. Chris only called the waiter over, asked for the check, and went to work on his fish. In minutes we were outside, heading to the theater.

I held his good arm with both hands. "What are we seeing?"

"Whatever's showing."

By then we were standing beneath the marquee. I tore my gaze away from Chris's pretty face, craned to see the title—*The Mummy's Curse* starring Lon Chaney Jr.—and realized which theater he'd chosen: the same one I'd gone to with Charlie on our first date.

It was an understandable coincidence. There weren't that many movie houses in Hyde Park. But the bottom fell out of my stomach, and all the steak with it. Here I was with one guy, walking into a place already made special by another guy. I scanned the room and there was nobody that I knew, no one who could tell on me, or come up to say hi and ask how Charlie was doing. No one to call me a back-doorer.

Except myself. "Excuse me," I said to Chris, extracting my arm. "I need to use the ladies'."

"I'll get tickets."

I closed myself in a stall, trying to slow the thrumming of my heart. What kind of girl was I? Was there anyone I could talk to about this situation, now that I had lied to Greta and my mother? Should I ask him to take me home? Or was my devotion to Charlie a bad idea, and should I trust infatuation instead?

I was standing at the sinks, washing my hands thoroughly as a surgeon, when a tall girl came barging in. Wearing a perfume that smelled of citrus and musk, she went straight to the mirrors to freshen her makeup. While I dried my hands, she spoke to her reflection. "You're with that lover boy, ain't you?"

I glanced around, realizing she was speaking to me. "Not exactly."

"Well, is you or ain't you?"

"I'm his date tonight, if that's what you mean. He's very nice."

"I bet." She snapped her compact closed, gave me a quick up and down. "His kind don't come knocking every day."

I wanted to leave, but felt momentarily powerless. "We've only met recently."

The tall girl worked a fresh red gloss onto her lips, then tucked the lipstick away in her little bag. She puckered at her reflection.

"You want to keep him? Make him happy. If not, though? Give a sister a shot."

She breezed back into the foyer. I followed, as her route passed near Chris. She took a good long gander despite me standing there watching, then sashayed past. He stood facing a full-length mirror, smiling at himself.

"Hello, stranger," I said.

"My CO said going home would make me soft and fat." He slapped his trim stomach. "I can't wait to prove him wrong."

I felt rattled in nineteen ways. "Um, should we go in?"

He stepped aside with one arm forward. "Ladies first."

I felt like I was with a movie star, that's how many girls' heads turned. The attention was a little thrilling. Like tasting an exotic food you didn't know you'd always craved.

Now? Now I look back and feel mortified. This was the place Charlie and I had run up and down the aisles. And I was profaning that memory. I could have insisted that we see another movie, in another theater. Or suggested we go for a walk, to continue our conversation. Or asked for dessert somewhere. A hundred ways I might have shown a speck of decency. Instead I nestled into the seat beside Chris, one last turn of my head as if to toss my hair back, though in truth it was to count how many girls were still watching, and settled in for the show.

The newsreel gave me no mercy. Oh sure, at first it was the usual "United News" introduction, the drawing of an attacking eagle, then martial music. After that, though, came the headline: "Submarine Operations Revealed."

I felt like someone had punched me. Charlie's work, right on the screen. A long, narrow ship sliced through the water, then sank from view. Young men peered through periscopes. A Japanese merchant vessel floated on the horizon. A torpedo hit the ship in the exact middle, it tipped on its side, Japanese sailors plainly visible. Cut to another sub, shirtless men fired a torpedo. When this one hit, it made a geyser. The enemy ship was lost in spray and smoke.

Oh, it was terrifying and brilliant. The next sub entered the harbor of a place called Nagasaki, and two torpedoes dispatched a coal ship at anchor.

"Such courage," I whispered.

"I don't know," Chris replied, louder than necessary. "Doesn't seem fair."

"Whatever do you mean?"

"When I fly over a place, the enemy can hear me coming, and see me once I'm in range." Someone shushed him from behind, but Chris continued at the same volume. "He shoots flak at me, maybe scrambles a fighter to take me down. We battle each other." He waved his hand dismissively at the screen. "With those sneaky underwater things, there's no fight in it at all."

I felt my dander rising. "Well, what do you know about it?"

But Chris laughed, easy as loose shoes. "Not much. But I sure like seeing how it stokes your furnace, princess."

"What do you mean?"

"I've made you peeved, Brenda. Damn, it makes you handsome. I'd gladly tick you off twenty times, to see you look so good."

When it came to disarming me, the man was an expert. Besides, I didn't have to persuade him. I could hold my loyalty to Charlie, and to submarine warfare, close to my heart and Chris would have no idea. I hadn't done anything wrong.

The movie was terrible. Slow, predictable. After one scene that was supposed to startle us, but didn't, I leaned over. "I am so very frightened."

Chris turned in concern. "Is this too much for you?"

I shook my head. "Just kidding."

"Oh. Got it." He sat back, so did I, and the movie refused to end. He put an arm over my shoulder, which I pretended not to notice. When the lights came up, neither of us said word one. On our way out, he held the door for me. "How about this idea?" Chris said, "Once we're married, you can choose the movie, okay?"

How is a girl supposed to answer that? It made the movie seem like a cartoon. All I could muster up was bravado. "Don't say it if you don't mean it."

"Oh, I mean it. You'll see, princess."

We were two blocks from home when I gave him a hug good night. It was a decent squeeze, if awkward with the sling arm between us. He went for a kiss but I turned and all he got was cheek.

"What time tomorrow do you finish work?" he asked, without a beat of hesitation.

"Five sharp."

"I'll be waiting here at six. Would that be okay?"

"I need to check with my—"

"I don't mean to come on so strong," he said. "But I've waited a long time to be with you, years, Brenda, and I only have six more days home."

My stomach did another flip. "Six days?"

He grinned. "That'll be plenty—if we make the most of them."

Chris surprised me and went for another kiss, on the lips, done and gone before I could pull away. He backed off, almost skipping. "Good night, princess. Sweet dreams."

He turned and ran up the avenue, his shadow shrinking as he passed under a streetlight, then growing suddenly tall as it rushed out ahead of him.

I stood there, on the street corner of my childhood, and bobbed with the buoyancy of joy. Or was it the speed of time? With Charlie, we'd had centuries to flirt, eons to get acquainted. I'd enjoyed being coy, until that unforgettable Christmas kiss. After that I still felt no hurry, I had the leisure to notice how he made me feel, how he calmed me and made me stronger, how my repertoire grew as I learned songs to play for him. It felt natural, nothing pressured or rushed.

Chris was the opposite. Six days until good-bye. Six evenings to spend in his company, assuming my mother would let me go out every night, and not press for details when I came home. Which was as likely as her learning to stand on her head.

All these years later, I realize how ordinary my situation was. Thousands of couples faced the same dilemma. Some collapsed under the weights of distance and time. Some boys died on the battlefield. Some came home in no condition to be anyone's husband. Many returned to marry and have kids faster than ever before, creating the Baby Boom.

Chris and I were a part of this gathering tide. I felt its undertow, pulling at my legs. But I did not run back to dry land, no. I waded deeper in.

THAT SUNDAY AFTER LUNCH, Monroe emerged from the bushes laughing and shoving with a crew of teen boys. The instant he spied Charlie near the barracks, he sobered, shaking hands with the boys one by one, the oldest of whom looked about thirteen.

"You all are good fellas," he said. "And you won't grow roots waiting on me to keep my side of the bargain."

The boys ducked around behind the building, while Monroe slapped his belly and sauntered Charlie's way.

"What mischief are you up to now?" Charlie asked.

"Wait right there." He ducked into the barracks, returning with a folding chair and a twinkle in his eye. "Come along a minute, would you, Mister Charlie? Got some fine entertainment."

Charlie fell into step beside him, realizing soon enough that they were marching toward the guard house. "You do know these guys have no sense of humor, right?"

"You just set a minute." Monroe unfolded the chair under a spindly pine. "It's time them grouchy dogs learned a little respect."

"Is the punch line of this joke that I get arrested?"

Monroe laughed. "Better by a mile. Just you watch."

"All right." Charlie took a seat as Monroe swaggered in his sway-hipped way over to the gate.

The guards scowled as usual, Monroe showed his pass, and they let him through. "Thank you, fellas. All clears, and job well done. Have a beautiful afternoon, hear?"

With that, he moseyed away down the road.

"What the heck?" Charlie said. He knew there were no rides going out till hours later, no buses to Santa Fe. Was Monroe actually strolling twenty miles to the next human being, without so much as a water bottle?

The answer came not five minutes later, when he came sauntering from behind the barracks. Monroe put a finger to his lips, swaying up to the guard house again.

"Hey there," he called, slowing to an amble. "How you-all doing today?"

The first guard began to check Monroe's pass, then caught himself. He glanced over his shoulder, down the rutted road, then handed back the pass.

"Perfect day for a constitutional." Monroe sauntered through the gate, waving his fingertips. "Adios, compadres."

Charlie sat back to see what would happen next. Giles came strolling up from the mess tent, and Charlie waved him over. "This is rich," he said. "Stick around."

Giles settled himself beside the chair. "If Monroe embarrasses those jokers somehow, it will make my day."

"Still smarting from the night we arrived?"

"You remember the hangover I had. They questioned me for three solid hours. And it later turned out that my pass was on the bus, just fell behind my seat."

Charlie smiled. "I bet you've got it with you right now though."

Giles reached into his pocket and waved the card in the air.

Another minute or two and Monroe sauntered along, grinning like a crocodile. With a wink, he marched right up to the gate. "Gents, I do believe I'll go for a stroll."

Both guards were ready for him, and stood blocking the gate. "Back to your post, mister, wherever it is."

"You saying I can't go for a walk?"

The senior officer growled. "I'm saying I don't like civilians, and I don't like you."

Monroe opened his arms wide. "What harm have I ever did to you-all?"

"You civilians think this is all a damn joke. No discipline, no order. Wandering around at all hours doing who knows what. Our duty is to protect you, but that doesn't mean we have to respect you. Now move along, unless you'd rather be detained."

He chuckled. "Here I've been thinking your job was to keep outsiders out. Now you want to keep insiders in?"

The guards stood shoulder to shoulder, saying not a word.

Monroe slapped his thigh. "End of the war comes, fellas, this right here is what you're gonna have for memories." He strode back to Charlie and Giles with a bounce in his step. "Now ain't you tickled?"

Giles shook his head. "There's a hole in the fence?"

"Leave it to the teenagers to find a gap," Monroe answered. "Getting them to show me didn't cost but two beers."

"Worth every penny," Charlie said.

"Double," Monroe laughed.

"Can I drag you tricksters off to Sebring's lecture now?" Giles said. "We might find out what we're doing here."

Charlie rose from the chair. "Why not?"

Fuller Lodge had been transformed, now neither dance hall nor place of worship. Chairs stood in rows wall to wall, with a lectern at the front, behind which hung a large periodic table of the elements. An easel stood nearby, holding flip charts. Though the boys were fifteen minutes early, they found nearly all the chairs taken. They settled for a pair in the front row, with Monroe behind them.

Charlie leaned toward Giles. "I have never seen so many people in here before."

Giles pointed at the periodic table. "Do they bring that out for square dances?"

Monroe leaned forward. "Where's the dang popcorn?"

A side door opened and Robert Sebring entered, followed by Robert Oppenheimer.

"Hellfire," Monroe whispered. "It's the man."

Oppenheimer, director of the entire Project Y, had bright blue eyes, hair wild in the manner of Einstein though not as long, and a neck as thin as a bird's. A brown suit hung loosely on his bony frame, draping as he bent to say something in Sebring's ear.

"If I may call us to order." Sebring rapped his knuckles on the podium.

There was no microphone, so the room took a moment to go quiet. Sebring cleared his throat. "You've all been told to stick to your knitting," he said. "To learn things based only upon your need to know. You have worked in silos of understanding, unaware of what others are doing, though it might help your work, just as yours might assist them. This has been official government policy—compartmentalization—to prevent any potential spy from possessing sufficient information to be damaging. This afternoon, that policy comes to an end. Oppie?"

Sebring stepped aside, moving to a low table where he found a glass of water and drained it in one go. Oppenheimer stood at the podium, gripping each side with one hand. "Hello everyone."

The crowd murmured a greeting.

"It is not possible to be a scientist," he said, "unless you believe that the knowledge of the world, and the power which this gives, is a thing which is of intrinsic value to humanity."

Charlie noticed that the man, as he spoke, had risen on his tiptoes.

"And that you are using it to help in the spread of knowledge. And"—he gave all in the room a stern look—"are willing to take the consequences."

Then he winked at them, as if to say yes, we all secretly share that willingness. He relinquished the podium and Sebring resumed his speech. "First, theory. Second, practice. Between them, an intermission."

He smiled in feigned casualness, and continued without notes.

"If you place your hand in still water, it will look as though your wrist has broken. This is called refraction. If you play on a swing, at the peak of your height you experience weightlessness. You see, it is easy to find exceptions to what we consider natural laws. The only force that we currently know to be universal, from our labs to the theoretical reaches of outer space, is in the atom. Protons in acute vibration, electrons orbiting at the fastest speed that anything moves, and as scientists discovered not twelve years ago, neutral particles that give the atom mass and stability. Unlike light, which is easily bent, unlike gravity, which can be defied on a playground, the power that holds these tiny objects together has no exceptions, anywhere, from the alpha of the periodic table . . ." At this he touched a pointer to the top-left corner, occupied by hydrogen. ". . . to the omega." Sebring hovered the pointer over the lower right, the heavy metals.

"Imagine if you could harness the energy that animates these atoms, indeed that animates everything in the universe. Suppose you could somehow slice these particles apart, and as they sundered, they made a small, a very small, *pop*. Are you with me?"

No one spoke. No one moved.

"For most of this chart, it is not possible to perform such a slicing. But when we investigate the heavier atoms—uranium, plutonium—we find less stability. In fact, people in this very room have successfully divided them into parts, using for a knife a single neutron moving at high speed. One uranium atom, if cut correctly, will divide into barium or radium or other things, with a minuscule *pop*. This we call fission. The division also throws off additional neutrons, which might slice other nearby uranium atoms. This we call a chain reaction. *Pop pop pop*. Do you follow me?"

Monroe leaned forward again. "Is this supposed to be the gunfight scene?"

"Shh," Charlie said. "I'm trying to understand."

Sebring glanced at them. "Is there a question?"

"'Scuse me, sir," Monroe said. "Please go on."

"Here is the crux of part one." Sebring faced the full room again. "Food for thought during intermission: If you put enough of these heavy atoms close together, and trigger them with enough neutrons, the chain reaction *pop* will exceed in energy any other process known to mankind. For generating electricity, operating the heaviest machinery, or enabling weaponry whose force exceeds our imagination. Once again: exceeding in energy any other process known to mankind."

Sebring left the podium to fetch another glass of water. In light of the enormity of what he had to say, Charlie thought the man was rather small.

The crowd dispersed onto the patio, with none of the hearty conversation that typified intermissions at Fuller Lodge events. Charlie and his pals wandered farther, across the grass to an empty basketball court. Monroe picked up a basketball and took a shot. It hit the rim and ricocheted straight back to him. "What do you fellas think?"

"Nomenclature," Giles said.

"Sorry?" Monroe dribbled the ball once. Low on air, it barely bounced.

"Part one was about naming things. The frightening part is still ahead."

"Maybe," Monroe said. "Mister Charlie?"

"I'm digesting," he answered. "My thing is math. Not atoms."

"Yes," Giles said. "Occhiolism."

Monroe laughed. "How come you don't ever use human people words?"

"It means an awareness of the smallness of your perspective." Giles rapped his knuckles on the bark of a pine. "Tree, right?"

"Looks like one to me," Monroe said.

"Yes. Made of atoms, collected in nice sturdy molecules. But if those atoms can be split? To make an explosive? Then it's no longer only a tree. Everything contains the potential for violent transformation."

Charlie tapped the basketball in Monroe's hands. "What do you think?"

"Well," he drawled. "I don't rightly know."

Giles made a face like a gambler who suspects he's being bluffed. "Try."

"All right." He took another shot, but it went wide of the whole backboard, rolling away in the grass. "Always hated this dang game."

"The innate athleticism of a scientist," Giles said.

"Come on," Charlie urged. "Tell us."

"Fellas," Monroe shook his head, "I am twenty-six years old, and don't know a thing about any of this truck. But I do have a PhD in chemistry from the University of Kentucky, so fresh the ink ain't dried. I predict, soon as we're back in there, we're gonna be hearing about beryllium."

Charlie trotted off to fetch the ball. "Why is that?"

"Neutrons. That element's a regular neutron factory."

"Explicate," Giles said.

"You know the knife he was yapping about? Neutrons to cut atoms apart? Beryllium's a knife thrower. With nine arms."

"Hey, guys?" It was one of Giles's friends from Electronics, calling from the patio. "They're starting up again."

"Be right along," Monroe yelled back.

They fell into stride beside one another. Giles was frowning and Monroe noticed. "Something in your craw?"

Giles nodded. "Charlie, you may want to skip this part."

"And miss the application of the theory we just heard? Not a chance."

"You may not like what you hear."

Charlie slowed. "Do you know something I don't?"

"In fact, yes," Giles answered. "Everyone in Electronics does."

Charlie's face grew serious. "Do you think I'm not smart enough to understand?"

"Oh I wish."

Monroe snorted. "What in hell does that mean?"

"That Charlie will understand more of Sebring's talk than I wish he did."

"Hey, fellas?" the guy on the patio yelled. "He's starting."

Sebring had already begun, as the boys crept across the front to their seats.

"The idea," he was saying, standing beside a flip chart with a

drawing that resembled a cannon, "is that adding one mass of uranium to another mass causes a chain reaction of great volatility. We
call it 'going critical.' In a lab, we dipped a control rod into a pile, and
instantly the activity was greater than our Geiger counters could measure. When we withdrew the control rod, the reaction ceased. This
design," he tapped the drawing, "modeled after a gun, shoots a plug
of uranium into a mass that is just shy of critical. The result is explosive. Another secret lab, in Tennessee, is amassing uranium for such a
device. Our task here is more complicated. Let's peel it off in layers."

"Exactly what I said to a gal at the last dance," Monroe whispered.

Giles chuckled but Charlie shook his head. He turned to whisper. "Sometimes you act like a six-year-old."

"Proud of it," Monroe said.

"First," Sebring said, "we have what its inventors are calling 'the
nut.'"

He turned to a fresh page on the flip chart, which showed a
sphere with a barrier through the middle. "Slightly larger than a golf
ball, with a dividing membrane in the middle. In each half, we pack
elements that generate free neutrons—on one side, polonium, and on
the other, beryllium."

Charlie glanced back at Monroe, who winked.

Sebring flipped the page. Now a larger sphere surrounded the
nut. "This vessel contains plutonium, which is much harder to make
and handle, but is potentially far stronger than uranium. The sphere
is roughly the size of a beach ball, to keep the plutonium dispersed so
it won't spontaneously go critical. Therefore we need an implosion,
to compress the plutonium into great density, at the same time the
inward pressure will break the nut's membrane and release a barrage
of neutrons."

A man on the far side of the room raised his hand. "May I ask a
question?"

Sebring stepped away from the chart. "Of course."

"The plutonium in the beach ball. How much of a pop will it
make?"

Sebring raised his voice for the rest of the room. "The gentleman's question is about yield. We estimate that four ounces of plutonium, via implosion, might equal the yield of twenty thousand pounds of TNT."

A murmur passed through the crowd.

"Four ounces makes twenty thousand pounds?" Monroe whistled. "Woo-eee."

"Oh, excuse me." Sebring held up one finger. "I misspoke, pardon me. I meant twenty thousand tons of TNT. Not pounds, tons."

Now the murmur rose into a hundred conversations, in every corner of the room.

"Are you sure you don't want to leave?" Giles asked.

"Are you nuts?" Charlie replied. "This is fascinating."

"All right, then. Here we go." Giles raised his hand. "Professor Sebring?"

"Yes, another one." He pointed at Giles. "If we could have quiet please?"

It took half a minute for people to settle themselves.

"Yes?" Sebring nodded at Giles. "What is your question?"

He gave Charlie a pained look, then turned forward. "How do you plan to accomplish this implosion?"

"I prepared for that one." He marched back to his easel, flipping to a page with an even larger sphere, with dotted lines inside indicating the nut and beach ball, and with nodes sticking up here and there on its surface like prongs. "In our current design, implosion will occur when traditional explosives, in twenty-four detonators equidistant around the sphere, provide uniform contraction and pressurization."

For the first time, Sebring smiled. "It's rather elegant, really. Twenty-four conventional devices fire at precisely the same time, the plutonium compresses, the nut bursts . . . *pop*."

This time though, as Sebring said the word "pop," he made a sphere with his fingers, then slowly opened his arms as wide as they would go.

"Hey." Monroe tapped Charlie's shoulder. "Ain't that what you been working on?"

But he did not reply.

Giles leaned closer. "Are you all right?"

"Good God in heaven," Charlie said at last. "It starts with me."

THE FASTEST I EVER became an expert in anything was lying. It happened overnight. Unlike the organ, which even the basics of take years to learn, in the few hours between saying good night to Chris and waking the next morning, I acquired the skill of deceit.

In childhood, I might have tried the rare fib to avoid punishment, but it had never worked. In adolescence, I was capable of no worse than exaggerating a sore throat, to gain an extra day for writing my book report on *A Tale of Two Cities.*

Starting that night though, and for a time long enough that it pains me to admit, I became an artist of dishonesty. It worked two ways: deceiving my mother, who I kept in the dark about all things Chris, and lying to my friends, as I invented excuses for my sudden social unavailability.

My mother made it easy. She left for the armory before nine, and until then I hid in the newspaper. An attempt to assassinate Hitler failed. The US sank the *Yoshino Maru,* drowning 2,495. Oh, Charlie.

She wouldn't reach the store till one and I opened at noon, which left my mornings free. Once the front door closed behind her, I made myself count to two hundred before calling Chris. He always had some fun idea. The Lincoln Park Zoo, where we visited the monkey house, and Chris mimicked the lazy orangutan until the ape became angry. Wrigley Field, which was exciting even without a game under way. The only idea I rejected was the Great Hall of Union Station. Instead we went to Dearborn Station, where I made a big noise about the tall clock tower and Chris suspected nothing.

One telltale sign my mother might have noticed was my play-ing. The organ held no interest for me. Sure, I wanted to keep my chops sharp for conservatory after the war, and not lose the progress I'd made. But for months, every new piece I'd learned had been for Charlie. I dug out the old books of études, and during any lull in customers, I'd turn on the church model. But the exercises were dull as a sermon, and painfully repetitive. What was the point?

My mother poked her head out of the office. "What about that Bach toccata you were working on?"

"I don't know." I flipped through sheet music. "I guess I'm bored with it."

"You seemed pretty interested last week."

"Yawn yawn yawn," I said.

"You know what I say about boredom." And she went back to work.

What my mother said was that boredom is a self-inflicted wound. She was wrong this time, I thought. This time it was a Chris-inflicted wound.

Or maybe even Charlie inflicted, because any time I swapped the études for my newer repertoire, I couldn't complete two measures without seeing his sweet, unsuspecting face. One day I ran across the sheet music for Chopin's Nocturne no. 2, the first sonorous piece I'd played for him, and the notes read like an accusation.

But Chris had a magnetic pull on me. The next day we wandered through the main branch of the Chicago Public Library, holding hands in the grand building—though the high-domed skylight re-minded me of Union Station—and between chatting and smooching in the stacks, we lost track of time. When the clock in the stately reading room rang twelve times, I realized I was late. It was pour-ing rain, too, no cabs available. My mother might arrive at the store before I did, and how would I explain that?

Finally a nice older gentleman let me have his taxi, and I tumbled into the back without a good-bye for Chris. When I reached the store at twelve forty, Mr. Kulak from the high school was standing outside. He saw me climb out of the cab and held his umbrella over my head.

"I hope I haven't kept you long," I said, fumbling with the key chain.

"Fifteen minutes, I'd say."

"I'm terribly sorry," I said. "I dashed out for lunch and everything took longer than I'd expected."

"And took a cab back? Business must be booming."

I blanched. "Silly of me, right?"

Would he tell my mother? Would he take his business elsewhere? I spun the key, the door unlocked, and he stepped aside to let me out of the rain first. "Are you here to order choir packets?" I asked.

"New year, new packets." He took only a few steps inside the door, peering around the store as if examining it. "Next time you might put up a sign, 'back at one' perhaps. Because I would have preferred to return later, rather than stand in the wet."

"That is a great suggestion, sir," I tossed my coat on the office desk and hurried back with a notebook to take his order. "Really great."

He eyeballed me the same way he had just been scrutinizing the store.

Nights were harder, but Chris always had a plan. I'd say I was going to one friend or another's, my mother would remark about how very social I was being lately, and I'd say something snippy: I'm twenty years old and don't need to sit at Mommy's knee every night. She might roll her eyes, but that would end the inquisition and out I'd go.

On the afternoon two days before Chris was due to leave, Greta called.

"How is everything?" I asked her, feeling my mother's antenna switch on in the next room. "How's Brian?"

"The greatest, Brenda. The best." She sighed. "Today he said that he loves me."

"Yikes, Greta. He loves you?"

"I know. I know."

"How did that feel? What did you say?"

"I burst out crying." She laughed. "It made me feel so good, Brenda. He sees me, you know? He sees big-boned old me, and he loves me anyway."

I heard my mother rise from her chair and go upstairs. "Do you love him?"

"I think so. What do I know, right? But I think I really do." She huffed a couple of shallow breaths. "My mother said I need a night apart from him. For perspective. She says I need to pace myself."

"Agony. What does your father say?"

"He says a girl must guard her reputation." Greta giggled. "Right now I wouldn't mind getting a reputation at all, as long as Brian was involved."

We laughed together, easy as ever. I could have told her then. I could have been a true friend. Instead I checked the clock, counting the minutes till I would see Chris.

"So look, Brenda." Greta was done laughing. "What say we go out tonight, maybe see a movie, or get a late coffee somewhere?"

I clenched, knowing Chris would already have left his house. Two more nights.

"I need to spill my guts about Brian to someone," she continued. "We've been having a magical time. It is all so huge."

"Greta, I would love that." I twisted the phone cord around my finger. "Really I would." I lowered my voice. "The thing is, I've been laid up with a stomach bug. That's why I haven't been in touch."

"Aw, honey. I'm sure sorry to hear that."

"It's almost better," I said, half-convincing myself. "But you know my mother the dictator. No going out till I'm one hundred and ten percent."

"She and my parents ought to take a vacation together."

"To the North Pole."

Greta chuckled. "Bye-bye. Bon voyage. Don't forget to write." I pictured her waving at their imaginary departure.

"Maybe in a few days?"

"You bet, best pal. And if you need anything . . ."

"Thanks," I said. My mother sidled down the stairs and opened the fridge about two feet away from me. "Congratulations about Brian."

We hung up and my mother kept her head in the fridge. "Greta's engaged?"

"No, but a serious beau. Until he ships out in six days."

My mother straightened to look at me. "Lucky thing you have Charlie."

"You bet," I said. "Lucky."

Half an hour later, Greta's invitation was my excuse for meeting Chris. No chance my mother would object. He'd planned a picnic dinner at Rainbow Beach. I would have loved to bring the food, but that would have been too much to manage and conceal. Besides, our picnic basket was somewhere in New Mexico. Chris had his father's Oldsmobile, and we held hands while he drove. It felt grown up. Without his sling he moved more easily, athletically. At red lights he tried to kiss me but I dodged him.

After sunset we stood at the edge of the sand, the beach surprisingly uncrowded. I realized I had always taken Lake Michigan for granted. Now I saw how special it made the city, to sit beside a huge body of fresh water, the sun gone down with the thinnest grin of a moon close behind.

Chris carried grocery bags from the car, while I followed with a blanket from the trunk. After folding the blanket double on the ground, so we would not feel the little rocks too much, I sat with my knees to one side, demure as a saint. He unloaded a jar of pickles, a wedge of cheese, a long summer sausage.

"Do you have a cutting board?" I asked.

That took the wind out of his sails. "I am an idiot."

"That's all right," I replied. "I bet we can find a flat spot on the rocks. Did you bring a knife?"

He burst out laughing. "Brenda, I am the worst picnic planner in human history."

I smiled at him. "At least you brought this blanket."

He shook his head, still chuckling. "It's my father's. For some reason, he always keeps it in the trunk."

"Well, good thing I'm not hungry. Do you have anything to drink?"

"I sure do," he said, pulling out bottles of beer. "And car keys can pop the top off."

So that was our picnic: pickles and beer. We tried biting off pieces of cheese, but it felt more like gnawing and after a first try I declined his further offers.

Chris told me things every other soldier had insisted he was forbidden to reveal: where he was stationed (a Second Division airbase in Lowestoft, England), what kinds of missions he flew (at first mostly supply flights, but now bombing sorties at night). He told me his crash was due to equipment failure, a landing gear strut that buckled, and while he broke his arm in five places, two men were killed. As he spoke, I remembered girls in high school fawning over the quarterback, and wondered if I had become one of their kind. I considered myself awfully lucky to have the attention of a guy like Chris.

"You know," I interjected at last. "I've never dated a pilot before, so maybe it's different, but most boys keep mum about their military things."

He smiled. It wasn't just his teeth and lips. It was his eyes, his whole face. "See, I don't have to worry with you like with other girls, Brenda, because one day you'll be my wife and we'll share all of our secrets, so today is . . . I don't know, practice?"

I picked at the label of my beer. "How are you so sure?"

"Brenda." Chris put his things aside, not hurrying, calm as could be while my insides were fluttering, then inched forward. "I'm sure because I love you."

I didn't know what I was supposed to say. Greta had burst into tears. Why did I want to run away up the beach?

In the year I'd known him, Charlie had never said such a thing. Neither had my mother, though I knew she would walk through fire for me. My father had said it three times: the night I made those two foul shots, after an organ recital when I was fifteen, and the day I graduated from high school. I'd said "I love you too, Daddy" right back.

192 | *Stephen P. Kiernan*

Not that night. "You seem like a good guy, Chris. Maybe a great guy. But you barely know me."

"Well, you haven't exactly thrown the doors open. Introducing me to your mom, things like that."

"Well, I—" He was right. I'd kept him entirely separate. But the secrecy was all about Charlie, about protecting him. And maybe protecting myself, if people knew what I was doing. "I haven't met your family either," I said, going on offense.

"There hasn't been time," he said. "Besides, I feel like I've known you all my life."

"When's my birthday? Who's my best friend? How many kids do I want to have?"

"None of that matters," Chris said. "I mean, it's important, it's all important. But no answer you could give to those questions would change how I feel. Besides, I know your personality, I know your character. That's what I love."

He had doubled down. The guy was taking all of his chips, piling them in my lap.

"Brenda," he whispered, leaning closer. "Don't you love me a little bit too?"

"Maybe," I said, suddenly feeling like an honest human being again. I didn't have to make any declaration I did not feel. "I might."

Chris jumped to his feet. "Look at this place," he crowed, his arms wide. "Look at this beach, look at that moon. What is all this, if it's not love?"

I did not reply. And when he stormed away, I did not follow. I sat with my head down, picking at his father's blanket.

Today I try to remember what I was thinking about while Chris was gone. I search my memory. But it's a blank. Except for one little observation: his arm worked pretty well without that sling. And one little calculation: Rainbow Beach was not huge. It would take only a few minutes for him to reach the far end, and turn around.

I had never been with a boy so pretty. Nor one so accomplished. I might never have the opportunity again. Maybe there was something wrong with me.

Soon I saw the occasional glow of a cigarette, drawing nearer. Gradually it became Chris, moving at his usual brisk pace. I stood as he approached.

He was speaking before he reached me. "I get it now, Brenda. I understand." He flicked the butt away. "See, I feel the pressure because of shipping out in two days, but you have all the time in the world to choose a guy. What's the hurry, right?"

He arrived at the blanket. "I'm not afraid of the war, you know. But if I can't have you—"

I interrupted him by planting a kiss on his lips, full-on, and I could tell it took him by surprise because he nearly fell over. Which made us clutch each other more, as I became aware of the warmth of his body from the march up and down the beach, and the thrum of his heart in his chest.

But there was a surprise for me. This man who'd made me a puddle by feeding me steak? Turned out to be a lousy kisser. Stiff, wooden, he pressed his lips against mine with no passion. Again I couldn't help wondering: If Chris loved me, why didn't I feel it?

We parted, two steps backward, suddenly shy. "Let me take you home," he said.

"Please."

On the way to the car we held hands again. Also when he drove, and he stopped judiciously short of my house.

"Can we have dinner tomorrow, please?" Chris asked. "I have a million things to do, and my dad wants to spend the afternoon together. But the evening . . ."

"Of course," I said. "I didn't say I have no feelings for you, Chris. I'm not one hundred percent sure, that's all."

His hands wrung the steering wheel. "Maybe I can help. Maybe I can think of something perfect for tomorrow night."

"I'll look forward to it." And that was the truth. I kissed his cheek and hopped out, waiting till he drove off before I started down the sidewalk toward home.

* * *

My mother was up, reading in the living room. Her new favorite novel was about a girl growing up in Brooklyn, which I imagined made my mother think of her childhood in Chicago, though I hadn't read a word of it.

"Hi," I said. "How's the book?"

"Great," she answered. "How was dinner with Greta?"

"Pretty good," I lied, easy as slipping out of my shoes. "I heard a lot about Brian."

She nodded. "If you're still hungry, there's chicken soup on the stove."

"Actually, I am." I started for the kitchen, then paused in the doorway. "Why'd you make that? You hate chicken soup."

"I didn't make it," she said.

"Who did, then?"

Finally my mother lowered her book. "Greta. To help you recover from your stomach problems."

My mouth went dry. "I can explain."

"You'll need to, if you want to keep her as a friend. But I do hope you're feeling better." She lifted the book again; it was like a wall.

I came back to the living room. "Mother, you can't just—"

"Don't you say one word to me in your peevish voice," she said. "I don't have the patience for it."

"I said I can explain."

She closed the book on one finger. "And you'll expect me to believe you. May I tell you something, Brenda?"

I put my hands on my hips. "I have a feeling you will, whether I want you to or not."

Making no reply, she opened the book again.

"Well, I'm not going to beg you for a lecture," I said. "Say what's on your mind." I stepped closer. "Please."

She placed the book on a side table. "You are a grown-up now, Brenda. You do not answer to me. All you answer to is your own conscience. I don't need to know what you've been doing, and I don't want to know. Any time you have to sneak around, it's not right. Do whatever you have to do to live in the light of day, my girl."

I dropped my hands, bare as if I'd just stepped out of the shower. "I am trying," I said. "I am really trying."

"If it made you lie to Greta, try harder."

"I will," I said. And I believed it. One dinner to get through, and then I would. Chris deserved a good last night before returning to the war. But I would leave sorting out the rest till the battles were ended.

"Good night." My mother picked the book back up and put her nose in it. I admire her for that today, admire her restraint when she must have been livid, respect her discretion when she must have been burning with curiosity. "Oh, and there's a letter from Charlie. I put it on your bed."

I couldn't open it that night, any more than I could have eaten a bowl of Greta's soup. I did not deserve anything good. Chris loved me, I did not know what I felt, and I had lied to everyone.

In the long arc of my life, that night was the lowest. The time I'd shown the least regard for what really mattered. Everything about my predicament revealed how little I understood what was important.

But now, with the wisdom of retrospect, I sometimes feel more empathetic about that girl, and the pain she was feeling, all of her own making. Perhaps this moment was her beginning. Twenty years old, the summer of 1944 coming to an end, the blood of countless boys darkening the soil of two continents, perhaps she was starting to grow up. Each person does it at their own pace, and maybe her time had come.

Every other letter from Charlie, I'd torn open the same way I unwrapped Christmas presents—fast as I could, to see the treasure inside. But this one? I placed it on the dresser unopened, angled against a picture of my brother holding up a fish he'd caught. My name in Charlie's handwriting would be there to greet me in the morning.

But when I woke, all of my thoughts were on Chris. His fast talking, his quick stepping, his fearlessness. Stupid as it sounds, the authoritative way he threw his finished cigarettes down.

Though I disliked how bad he was at listening. Often when I told him something, his reaction was plain silence, no dialogue, then on we'd go to the next topic that interested him. And the boy was vain. I never knew the world had so many mirrors.

But the way girls reacted to him was amazing. How they ogled me, too, on his arm or sitting with him. I'd never felt prestige before, and I found myself standing taller.

I stayed in bed till my mother left for the armory, not dozing but avoiding. As soon as she closed the front door, I got up to open the letter. I expected innocence, humility, trustworthiness—traits I'd thought were vulnerabilities now revealed with all their power. For the first time since I'd met Charlie, I felt afraid of him.

Dear Brenda: Everything here has intensified. The hours, the difficulty of the work, the impatience of our directors, everything. July has been unspeakably hot, and possibly the thing that has intensified most is what everyone expects of me.

Although I am a tiny part of a large and complex organization, it turns out that my little contribution is an essential one. Imagine an automobile, and my job is to make the ignition key. I still do not understand what the entire vehicle will be, but I know that the leaders here are smart men, and they believe that if it works, it will prove decisive in ending the war.

How could anyone be opposed to that? How could anyone not work his hardest to help make it happen? Every day more boys die in France, in Poland, in Guam. Sometimes I feel like half the world is waiting for Charlie Fish to finish his work, so the planet can start spinning properly again.

I believe I could handle all the pressure, Brenda, if only you were beside me. I believe I could do a great job for this country, if only I could hear your voice. I could sleep at night, instead of worrying hour after dark hour, if I could see your face for a few minutes while you play something lovely on the organ. This place would seem beautiful to me, instead of barren, if you were here.

I'm writing you an awful corny letter today, I know, and maybe I should apologize for it. But I'm not sorry. I have finally admitted to myself how much being with you improves my life. I hope that hearing these things, in some small way, improves yours too.

And if it does not, would you please do me the favor of letting me know? I long for you so many times each day, if you do not feel the same way it would be better for me not to continue to pine. And I won't be bothering you.

But boy, if it turns out you feel the way I do. . . .

Charlie.

It was too large for me to absorb. Too honest for me to accept. Somehow the period after his name meant that he knew—not about Chris, but all of the other things. That I had written one letter to his two. That mine were short, and more like journals than heartfelt communication. Here he was, mister sincerity, calling what I had not realized was my barely masked bluff. I felt about half an inch tall.

Folding the letter back into its envelope, I put it in a drawer and went downstairs. I had things to do. A list in my head.

My mother had left coffee for me and when I opened the icebox for milk, I saw the soup. Lighting a burner, I put the pot on the stove and stood waiting till the edges began to bubble, then ladled myself a bowlful. I brought it to the table, pushing the papers aside because I could not bear any news that morning. Spoon by spoon, I ate that soup, and drank the last drops.

Then I phoned Greta's house. Her mother answered, and when she said hello it seemed to come from a great distance, as if I had actually been sick after all.

"Greta's not here," her mother told me. "Out with Brian, of course. The grand adventure. Four days left."

"Would you please tell her that she made the most delicious soup I have ever tasted in my life?"

"Why, Brenda, that is sweet of you," her mother replied, which told me that Greta had not revealed my lies to her mother. It deepened my guilt, that she'd remained loyal. "I know she'll be pleased. She worked a long time on that one."

"I could really tell. Please give her my thanks."

"You get well soon," her mother said.

I went to work though it was two hours till opening time, propped the store's door open as if to welcome people in, and sat at the spinet model. But I did not play. Why prepare for a future I might never have? People could talk all they liked—Chris, Charlie, Greta—but nobody really knew when the war would end, and what things would be like. It was all guesses and fancy words.

My mother arrived promptly at one, took a long squint at me while unpinning her hat and stowing that giant purse. "I have to reconcile month-end numbers today," she said. "You mind the floor, all right?"

"Of course," I replied, my tone flat as a sidewalk, though she had already bustled back into the office. Also there were no customers who needed minding. Soon I heard her punching keys and pulling the crank on the adding machine. I rose and went to the front window, where I stood for the rest of the afternoon, willing myself not to check the time, watching the world go by.

Sometime in midafternoon I heard a match struck behind me. I turned and my mother was lighting a cigarette. "How long have you been there?" I asked.

"Long enough," she said. "Are you all right?"

I faced forward again. "Not one person has come in today."

She exhaled loudly. "The war has caught up with us. July numbers are terrible."

"Are we going to have to close the store?"

She sidled up beside me. "Your father was smart, and bought the building outright years ago. So there's no rent, no expense besides the light and heat."

"We're not making any money though, are we?"

My mother stood smoking for a while. "I have an idea, but it requires homework. If you don't mind holding the fort, and locking up, I want to do some digging."

"Fine. I have plans for this evening."

She picked a bit of tobacco off the tip of her tongue. "I expected as much."

"One way or another, this will be the end of the secrecy."

"One way or another?" She blew smoke at the ceiling, then turned away to fetch her hat and purse. "Why does that description not give me a particularly good feeling?"

Perhaps it was some form of self-punishment: When Chris asked where I'd like to eat, I suggested the place Charlie and I had our first date. I knew what I wanted to do, I'd practiced the words I would say—we'll figure it all out when the war is over. He wore his dress uniform, looking sharp and fit, and I stood taller just to be walking with him. When we reached the diner though, he drew back a step.

"Really?" he said. "I was hoping to treat you to something fancy."

"This place has been good luck for me."

Chris laughed, easy as flying a kite. "When we're married you can pick the movies, but I'll choose the restaurants."

"When we're married, I'll change the diapers but you will wash them."

He laughed again, maybe one degree less, then held the door and in we went.

The diner was crowded, and smelled of eggs. We took the one open booth. The poor guy had jitters all over him. Sewing machine leg, reading the menu front and back, then front again. He lit a cigarette, put it in the ashtray, and half a minute later started to light another one.

"Easy, Chris." I put a hand on his arm. "It's just me."

"Well, that's the thing of it," he replied. "Because nothing about you, Brenda, is 'just you.' Everything is special."

I shook my head. "Half a minute at Dubie's Music would change your mind."

"I don't think so," he insisted. "This week with you has been the greatest of my life, everything upside down since I saw you at that dance." He paused for a deep breath.

"Chris," I said. "Why are you so nervous? Is it your arm? Your family? Going back tomorrow?"

He flared his eyebrows up and down. "Something bigger."

"Bigger than all that?" I took his hand. "Tell me."

"Can I talk it through for a second, and you won't chime in?"

I nodded. "No chiming." And when you are done, I thought, I will tell you to call me when the war is over and we will see how everything looks, but until then, stay safe and fight hard and come home in one piece.

"Like I was saying." He reached for his water glass, and I saw that it was empty.

There, right there, I reached the pinnacle terrible moment. Because, of course, I remembered the night at that diner with Charlie, my belly full of pistachios I'd eaten out of nervousness, and when I wanted water the waitress would not bring it. He'd asked nicely, twice, but it never came.

Now Chris held his glass out as a waitress hurried by. "Miss, could you please—"

But she kept her pace right on past. He licked his lips, and I could see his nerves had turned his mouth into a Sahara. Another waitress passed the other way, plates balanced on both arms, and Chris raised a finger. "Excuse me?"

She bustled on to deliver those plates. He winked at me, stretching his good arm out into the aisle beside our booth. There was no missing it. In a second the waitress was hustling back, walking right through his outstretched arm, not masking her annoyance.

Chris stood up, uniform and all. "Goddamnit," he said, way too loud. "What does a United States airman home on leave for one more day have to do to get a drink of water in this lousy place?"

The room went still, silent, not a fork hitting a plate. A big man with gray hair emerged from behind the counter with a pitcher. He filled Chris's glass in one motion.

"Asking nicely never hurts," the man said. He looked me over, which felt comfortable as a searchlight, then set the pitcher down. "How about I leave this here, soldier, and you don't bother my other customers anymore."

"That'd be perfect." Chris sat back down. "Just perfect."

I watched the man return to behind the counter, impressed by Chris's forcefulness, and also embarrassed by it. Certainly he'd had a better result than Charlie. To my relief, the conversations started up around us again, the clink of silverware.

Then I turned to see Chris drinking—and the truth is, he looked amazing: his strong jaw, his muscular throat, the poise of his hand holding the glass. I had never known a boy could be so handsome just drinking water.

"Ahhh." He gave himself a refill from the pitcher. "Hits the spot."

"You were saying, Chris?" I prompted. Calm as a pond, all I had to do was wait out whatever he wanted to say. Then I could deliver my little rehearsed speech, and everything would be fine. "About being upside down?"

"Right," he snapped his fingers. "Also what you said last night, about how I barely know you. I said I would find a perfect answer and today I did."

"Then your day was better than mine," I said. It broke his stride a little, and I could see him weighing whether to ask about my day. Instead he charged ahead.

"I need to be right side up, Brenda. Especially until the war ends, and we bury Hitler and his boys under good American bombs. I need to know you better, too, is my point, I need all the time it takes to know a person as well as you possibly can. There is one thing we can do that would take care of both necessities, both at the same time, which is why it is the perfect answer. If I ask the perfect question."

He dug in a pocket. "And then, princess, if you give me the perfect answer."

On the table in front of me, Chris placed a little box. It was velvet and blue.

"Wait." I held up both hands. Now I understood his nervousness. I should have seen this coming five blocks away. "This is not going to happen, mister."

He smiled, suddenly calm. "It is already happening."

"No it's not." I stood. "You are not asking me. You can't."

He came forward, as if onto one knee. "I am about to, if you'd—"

"I have to go," I said, grabbing my things. Maybe I was a fool, maybe this was the only time a guy would ever ask me, maybe the war would take Chris, would ruin Charlie, would crush my selfish little heart. But I could not stay in that place one second longer.

"Brenda, don't be silly. This is our moment."

I moved away from the table, backing toward the door. "I hope you are all right over there. Truly I do. And come home in one piece. I'm sorry, but I have to go."

I ran from that diner at top speed. As far as I know, he did not follow. If he had, I suspect the big man behind the counter would have tackled him.

The sidewalk felt like a running track, hard and straight. I heard only the slap of my shoes and the sound of my breathing. Before I knew it I was home, panting by the front steps. Gone half an hour, but everything had changed. The lights were on inside. My mother knew nothing about what I'd been through, what trouble I'd invited onto myself, what hurt I had probably done to a decent guy who wanted to go back to the war confident that a girl would be waiting for him—even if he didn't know her—to have another reason to stay alive.

Some part of me also feared that Chris would chase me, would try to talk me into it. Out of weakness I might say yes just to keep from breaking his heart twice in one hour. So I hurried up the steps and into the house and shut the door tight.

"In here," my mother called from the kitchen.

"Oh, Mama," I said, hurrying in to her.

"Mama?" She turned from the sink. "Since when do you call me that?"

"Since now." I rushed into her arms. And when she put them

around me, I thought I would burst into tears. But I didn't. Instead I felt the most immense liberation. Gigantic. What kind of a monster was I, to cut a suitor cold like that, and feel only relief?

My mother pulled away, scanning my face. "Let me look at you."

"I'm all right. I'm really all right."

"Was it a bad boy you were mixed up with?"

I shook my head. "Not bad. But he was no Charlie Fish."

She smiled. "There's only one of them."

"I need to go," I said, expecting her to argue, predicting her resistance. "I can't stay here. I need to leave Chicago."

"Probably you do, Brenda."

"Excuse me?"

"Before you pack your bags though, look at this." She drew me to the breakfast table, where a map of New Mexico was already spread flat.

"This is the homework I had to leave the store to do today. Did you know that libraries subscribe to newspapers from all over? They have a whole room of them." She handed me a list she'd made. "These are jobs in Santa Fe, from the want ads. A church is looking for an organist and choir director. Land that, and all we'd have to do is find you a place to live."

"This is possible?"

"This is necessary, my girl. For about twenty reasons."

"And I would go?" I asked. "And live there?"

"I'm betting there isn't an organist of your ability in two hundred miles of Santa Fe. And working as a professional will keep you skilled for the conservatory."

My hands dropped to my sides. "Mother."

"I know," she said. Our eyes met. What she was suggesting meant something huge. She would be the only one of us left in Chicago. And I would follow my heart to New Mexico. For the first time in my life, I thought my mother looked old.

She lit a cigarette, making a slow upward exhale. "I know, my girl. I know."

2 6 .

AS IT TURNED OUT, he had learned everything he needed to know from Beasley. A tortoise with a soldering iron, Charlie squatted on the wide fabrication table, half-trusting the sawhorses that held it up, and built his assembly step by torturous step. How odd it was, that the stork man in a Chicago basement had brought him to this point: fourteen devices in a single circuit, more than anyone had built before, designed to detonate simultaneously. Leaning over the triggering place, and reaching four devices down the line, he touched the tester's sensors to each end. The white light blinked on, the indicator needle jumped. Easing down as if from a rickety ladder, he allowed himself a second to admire his progress.

"Why are you climbing around like that?"

Charlie jerked upright, catching his breath, and saw Mather leaning in the doorway. He took out a toothpick and needled his front teeth. "You look like a monkey."

"The testing device is too small," Charlie answered. "Short wires. I have to test the assembly in parts."

Mather smirked. "It wouldn't occur to you to connect more wire, so you could check the whole thing? Start to finish?"

"I tried that for two weeks." Charlie circled the fabrication table. "But whenever something didn't work, I had to diagnose piece by piece anyway."

"I heard two of your last ones didn't go off as planned."

"True. But ten did, which was a new record."

"Sounds like failure to me." Tonguing the toothpick to one side of his mouth, Mather sauntered into the room. Wires splayed all over the table, threading among little mounds of electronic parts. "Reminds me of a toy train."

Charlie climbed gingerly on the near corner, hunching the tester over more nodes. "Maybe, but it's a powerful toy."

"Still," Mather said. "It appears you deserve your nickname."

The needle jumped again. "I have a nickname?"

"Come on," Mather scoffed. "You were probably the first to know."

Charlie crept off the table. "I don't know what day it is. I can't remember the last time I showered, or ate an actual meal." He straightened, the tester's wires dangling. "Nicknames have not been a priority."

Mather took out his toothpick and inspected the tip. "Bronsky must have a string tied directly to your balls."

Charlie circled his project, then paused. "Did you hear that the SS killed fifty thousand Poles last week, to retaliate for the Warsaw uprising? Bronsky is not the problem. I have fifty thousand strings tied to me."

"What a good soldier you are," Mather scoffed.

"I hope not." Charlie arrived at the last four points in his circuit. Mather stood in front of them. "Excuse me," Charlie said.

"I'm in your way." Mather stepped aside, then leaned on another corner of the table. It began to tip and Charlie rushed over.

"Please. This is weeks of work. No touching."

"You," Mather said, hands high like he was under arrest, "are a man incapable of irony. Using it, recognizing it."

Charlie narrowed his eyes. "Why do you insist on being such a difficult person?"

Mather sighed, giving him a bland regard. "I wonder if you would understand."

Charlie set down the tester. "Try me."

"All right." He pointed with the toothpick. "For all of your gee-whiz ways, Fish, there have been times in your life in which you were the smartest person in the room."

"Oh, I don't know about—"

"Spare me the oh-shucks. You were admitted to Harvard, so you were likely first in your class in high school. Probably the sharpest mind in some college classes too. Didn't you graduate at twenty?"

"This project grabbed me before graduation," Charlie said. "But I was eighteen."

"There." Mather leaned against an empty desk, crossing his arms. "Now imagine being the smartest person in the room, for every room you ever inhabit. Imagine how tedious humanity would seem. How shallow. 'Hello, how are you today?' God help me."

"Is that your affliction, Mather? Too smart to be nice?"

"You mock me, which I may deserve. But I tell you this, Fish: Over in Theoretical, I am no big deal. Fermi has intellectual thunderbolts that reimagine the world. Just crossing the street, he realized that atomic reactions could occur. And Bethe, calculation by calculation, has such colossal brain power, I feel like an ant."

Mather straightened. "It may well turn out that this strange, perverse, remote place is the happiest I will ever be."

Charlie had no idea how to answer. Was the man indulging in unbridled arrogance? Or was he committing brutal honesty? He decided to change the subject.

"Tell me," Charlie said. "What became of your beautiful sister?"

Mather shrugged. "She's a WAC. Some hospital in London. Rarely writes."

"Maybe she'll meet a prince, like you always thought she deserved."

Mather paused before a blueprint of the Gadget, the sphere with nodes poking out. This version was more detailed than the one at Sebring's lecture, with measurements, dimensions, details about how much explosive would be placed in each node. "Prince or not, he'd better have a decent backhand."

Meanwhile, Charlie had turned from him, leaning over the last set of nodes. He touched the tester's wires to either end, and the little white light came on. "There it is," he announced. "The whole thing works. Fourteen detonators on one command."

"Bravo." Mather made to clap his hands but they never touched. "A relief, actually. Time to tell the boss."

Mather continued to study the blueprint. "He's unavailable just now."

Charlie wandered over, running his eyes across the sphere's detailed sketch too. Something bothered him, now that the assembly was complete. What exactly, he could not say. "Why is he unavailable?"

"Because it is five fifteen on a Tuesday morning. I suspect the Detonation Division director is busy dreaming of icy Moscow winters or summer days at Lake Baikal."

"Five fifteen on Tuesday?" Charlie said, suddenly feeling fatigue in all his bones. "I've been here since Sunday afternoon. Forgive me, but I believe I'll go for a walk."

He threw a sheet over the fabricator table, then snatched his coat.

"Trigger," Mather said.

"Excuse me?"

"That's your nickname. Trigger."

Charlie stopped. "You must be joking."

"It's what everyone says. In Chemistry, Electronics. Even in Theoretical. I'd wager that Oppie, if he is aware of your existence, doesn't know your real name. Only Trigger."

Charlie stood near the doorway, fuming. "That is unfair. I am not responsible for how this technology is used. If anyone is the trigger, it's Oppenheimer. I'm just a math kid, doing what he's told."

Mather chuckled. "You keep telling yourself that, Fish. It may help you sleep tonight, not to mention forty years from now. But everyone on The Hill is complicit. We are all building the Gadget. And we will all be guilty of the crimes it commits."

"I am not making a Gadget," Charlie said. "I'm making a circuit of detonators. You could use them with dynamite to build a road. You could use them in mining."

"You could," Mather said. "Though I prefer Sebring's description." He tossed his toothpick in the trash. " 'Weaponry whose force exceeds our imagination.' "

Charlie jammed his arms in his coat sleeves. "I'm going for a walk."

He was halfway down the hall before Mather yelled after him: "Trigger."

The barracks had barely begun stirring for the day. A few technicians were lined up at the sinks. Others stood waiting for a shower. One boy put finishing touches on a letter. Another kneeled on the floor beside his bunk, with closed eyes and folded hands.

Charlie staggered past, leaning forward as if gravity were drawing him toward sleep. Instead of untying his shoes, he stepped on their heels and pulled. Unbuttoning his shirt, he saw that there was no envelope on his pillow. Twenty-five days.

He slid a box from under the bed, and opened it. There were her previous letters, arranged by date. He shouldn't write to her again. He'd put himself at Brenda's mercy, and her reply had been no reply, for almost a month. Only an idiot would fail to admit what that meant. Only a fool would keep hoping.

Charlie stretched out on the bunk, still dressed. Fifty things happened every day that he wanted to tell Brenda. And no answer was not a real answer. Maybe she was trying to decide. Maybe she needed a nudge. Maybe she wanted one.

"Why not?" He took out pen and paper. But where to start? Should he take back what he wrote in his last letter, and the offer to let him go? Should he tell her what those twenty-five days had been like, not hearing from her? Whichever, of course he should write. Silence never helped anyone.

"Dear Brenda," he wrote. "Dear, dear Brenda." Charlie lowered his head to the pillow to think. What should he tell her about first? Three breaths, and he was asleep.

In midafternoon, he had company. Midnight snuck aboard, snuggling against the bend in his knees. Charlie ruffled her head, and she climbed over for easier petting.

Only then did he fully awaken, and see that her normally black fur now had large spots of white—on her front legs and dotting her chest.

"Where have you been, little miss?" His forefinger circled her ear. "What place have you been going where you do not belong?"

By way of answer, Midnight stretched out a white-tipped paw and began to purr.

2 7.

THE TRAIN TO LAMY felt eternal, but I did not think I was going to die until I boarded the bus to Santa Fe. Despite impressive squealing, the brakes had so little grip, I doubted they could stop a mouse on roller skates. You asked for this, Brenda, I told myself, clutching the seat back ahead of me. You chose this.

When at last I stepped off the bus into a broad plaza, clean August sun poured down on us all. The buildings were small, none more than two stories, and spotless. The air smelled woody and sweet, and lacked the familiar hardness of Chicago. Almost immediately I felt myself warming and relaxing.

Before that trip, I had never been farther from Hyde Park than eastern Wisconsin, at my aunt Claire's place on Lake Michigan. Now I'd covered twelve hundred miles, to work for people I'd never met, in a place I'd never seen. Before my trip, I spent an afternoon in the library scouring picture books of New Mexico: landscapes, Indians, and the Spanish people. Not one photo of a church organ.

Travel had tested me: a wrenching good-bye from my mother that left us both weepy and weak, the melancholy of leaving a city by train, seeing its back-lot debris as if to say this place was never what you thought, never as pretty or kind. I was suspicious of strangers in nearby seats, anxious about my luggage in a separate car. Away from home, all my confidence turned out to be bravado.

"Here you are, miss."

I jumped, but the porter only smiled and gestured at my bags on the sidewalk.

"Thank you." I tipped him a dime, hoping that was right. "Will there be a taxi along any time soon?"

"Not many taxis in this town, miss. Where you heading?"

I told him the address and he nodded. "Five blocks off, up that street there."

I watched closely where he pointed, saying to myself five five five. Although I felt intrepid, I could not wait to finish the journey, so I could write to my mother and Greta, sweet forgiving Greta, and tell them every little thing.

The only question was my bags. I could manage each one on my own, but carrying two would be a backbreaker. Three was out of the question. I poked my head into a little rug and pottery shop, dim and cool, abandoned by the looks of it. "Hello?"

"*Buenos dias*," said a woman I had not noticed, perched on a stool to one side. She had dark skin and the blackest hair, while around her neck hung a pendant of silver and turquoise. It was stunning.

"Yes, hello." I cleared my throat, and pointed out at the sidewalk. "I need to leave my suitcases here for a few minutes. Would that be all right?"

She replied in a string of Spanish, and the only word I understood was senorita. But her smile I comprehended just fine. I tapped the face of my watch. "Quick as I can."

I set two suitcases beside her doorway, toting the heaviest one first. Five blocks, and I set off in the direction the man had pointed. After a hundred steps I began to understand what people had meant about the thin air. I flushed warm, felt my heart speeding up, while the suitcase seemed to gain weight with every block. The cross street came along in due time, and I forged on till I reached the right number. It was a wooden frame house, with open stairs hugging one side of the building. On the porch sat a woman in a sleeveless white shirt, drying her hair with a towel.

"Hello," I called from the sidewalk.

She paused her drying long enough to give me a thorough once-over. "Come out of the sun there, before you cook yourself."

"Thank you." I hoisted the suitcase along brightly, not wishing to give any appearance of fatigue, though I felt like I could have slept for two solid days.

"You're the new girl." She said it flatly, with no wrinkle of curiosity.

"Brenda Dubie, yes."

She nodded, but did not volunteer her name. Instead she slid an inch down the bench. "Have a seat."

"Thank you, but I still have two more bags to bring along. Would you mind guarding this one for me for a minute?"

"Guarding?" She tossed her hair back, and was she suppressing a smirk? "With my life, Brenda Dubie. Anyone tries to grab your gear, I'll shoot 'em dead in the street."

Now I saw that she was indeed smiling. "In that case," I replied, "do me a favor and drag the body away when you're done? Last place I moved, by the time I'd brought all my luggage there was a whole pile of corpses."

She gave the least little laugh, one "heh." And I set off on trip number two. I was already thinking about how good it would feel to shed my traveling dress, which I'd put on in my bedroom in Chicago two days before, and sink into a warm bath.

When I returned the third time, more than a little damp between my shoulder blades, the young woman was brushing her hair out in broad daylight for any and all to see. Apparently, New Mexico was considerably more informal than Illinois.

"How many more suitcases you got?" she said.

"This is the last."

"Sit down a second, then, before you keel over."

"I believe I will," I said, occupying the bench beside her. "Thank you."

"It's a free country." She studied her brush. "I've been thinking."

I took a deep breath. Soon I would go inside, find the matron of the boardinghouse, introduce myself, and beg on bended knee for a glass of water. "Have you?"

"I see you hauling your stuff here, three trips, without asking for help of any kind."

"I didn't feel that any was offered."

"Yes." She started brushing again. "You took care of it by yourself. That's what got me thinking. Strong-headed, straight-backed, doing all that when everybody knows I'm the tough girl around here, I'm the one who gets things done and doesn't wait for a man to save me from fainting."

I gave the young woman another look. Her short sleeves revealed strong arms.

"I figured one of two things could happen," she continued. "Either we'd wind up fighting like cats, or we'd end up friends. Seeing as how there's already warfare enough in this world, and the two of us as joined forces could pretty much own this town, I calculate that we should be friends. Put her there."

She offered her hand, and I shook it quickly. "I like your math. My name is—"

"Brenda, yes. I'm Lizzie Hinks." She returned to the brushing. "Whelped in Roanoke, but my husband, Timothy, hails from here, and when he was called to duty I came to live with his family. He's a medic in the South Pacific, tell you about that later. His mom is a first-class sourpuss. We collided half a dozen times a day, always over nothing. I didn't want to find out whose head was harder, or go to jail for murder, so I moved here. Not bad, though Mrs. Morris falls an inch or two on the strict side."

"I haven't met her," I explained. "We exchanged letters."

"If Mrs. Morris was to go best two rounds out of three with my mother-in-law, I might not bet on either one—but I'd sure buy a ticket for the bout."

Right then I knew that Lizzie Hinks would indeed be my friend.

"What's going on out here?" A large, brassy woman barged out onto the porch, chesty and aggressive. "Jabbering to yourself again?" Then she spotted me. Hands on hips, she bobbed her chin in my direction. "And you would be?"

"Brenda Dubie." I rushed to my feet.

"You don't have to stand for her," Lizzie said.

"Manners are wasted on girls like you," the woman sneered,

before turning back to me. "I'm Mrs. Morris. Would you like to see your room?"

"Please."

She spun and strode back into the house, lily of the valley perfume trailing in her wake; Lizzie waved fingers in my direction. "See ya."

"Glass of water?" Mrs. Morris called to me. I raced to catch up and say yes.

I was on the third floor, she said as she led me up the stairs, which meant the room would be hot. There was a fan, but I was not to leave it on all day. Nighttime only.

"Here we are," she said, stepping aside from a doorway.

I inched past her into the room. Whitewashed, small, with modest furniture. It was indeed warm in there. I leaned out the window. The view was the back lot of another boardinghouse, by the looks of it, laundry on the line, girls chatting and smoking on the back steps.

"The outside staircase is fire escape only," Mrs. Morris advised, filling the doorway. "It is more ladylike to use the stairs inside the house."

I took a good gulp from the glass she'd given me. "I should go down for my bags."

"No need," Mrs. Morris said. "I give that Hinks girl a break on rent in exchange for bellhop services."

"And she loves every minute of it." Lizzie dropped two of my suitcases at the doorstep. I was impressed.

"Thank you," I sang after her, but she had already started back down the stairs.

"The reverend and I live on the first floor, so we are privy to all comings and goings. There are no locks on the doors here, to prevent concealment." She glared at me meaningfully. "There will be no smoking. No alcohol. No male visitors at any time."

This last item she said with a sort of forward lean, as if I had already committed some infraction. "Don't worry about me, ma'am," I piped. "I'm here to play organ in your husband's church, and direct the choir. No time or interest in making trouble."

"I have no idea what constitutes trouble in a madhouse like Chicago," she said. "But in my experience, religious liberals think dogma is optional and rules are suggestions. The reverend sermonizes vigorously against such evils."

I worried that I might have landed in a predicament. But I gave her a smile. "I look forward to hearing him preach," I said, "and playing hymns that uplift our spirits."

Mrs. Morris relented with her scowl, a guard dog accepting a new bone. "Maybe you'll be one of the good ones."

"Not if I can help it," Lizzie huffed, returning with suitcase number three. "Starting with dinner tonight." She winked at me. "My treat."

"Which reminds me," Mrs. Morris said. "Curfew is nine, lights out at ten, one hour later on Saturdays."

"One thing?" I said. "Has any mail come for me?"

She shook her head. "Nary a postcard." And with a stiff bow, Mrs. Morris and her lily of the valley perfume were gone.

I sat on the bed, too tired to unpack, yet not so exhausted that I did not wonder where Charlie was, what he might be doing at that hour, when I might hear from him.

"Come on, new girl," Lizzie said, reappearing in my doorway. "Reverend Mother is gone, let's go get a hot dinner and a cold beer."

"I don't know," I said, standing. "She didn't seem so terrible."

Lizzie shook her head. "Kid, you have a lot to learn."

August morning in New Mexico is sweet as berries. Lizzie was a contrast, storming into the kitchen with a hunk of bread in her mouth, but putting on the brakes when she saw me deep in the news. "What in the world are you doing?"

"What does it look like?"

"What possible good can come of reading a newspaper?"

"Are you serious?" I spread the pages. "Your husband is a medic in the Pacific, right? With this, you can guess at what he's doing, or how the war is going in a place he might be sent. Today for example." I turned the front page toward her. "We sank the *Tamatsu Mara*, four thousand four hundred Japanese dead. I think Charlie is involved in submarine warfare."

"Sub work in the desert? You're loco, kid."

"What better way to conceal it?" I went back to my newspaper.

But Lizzie snatched it away, tossing her bread end on my plate. "Come with me."

I followed her out to the porch, where she hiked her skirt above her knees, and dropped to all fours. "We don't need to know what our men are doing," she said. "Our job is to be ready when they come home."

With that, Lizzie straightened her back like a plank and began doing push-ups. "One. Two. Three." So that was where the arm muscles came from. "A man needs a woman strong enough to hold him tight, and to bear his babies. Nine. Ten. Eleven."

Her back flexed with each push, her arms pumped like pistons. Every inch of her was firm, and I felt a flush of envy. "You want to land this Charlie guy, I suggest you get going. Thirteen. Fourteen. Fifteen."

"You are insane," I said, laughing.

She concentrated harder, face reddening but her breath steady as she lowered and rose. "Nineteen. Twenty." She popped up. "There. I do them twice a day. And when Timothy comes home, I am going to squeeze him till he feels every one."

"Instead of reading the newspaper, you want me to do push-ups?"

"It's a free country," Lizzie said. "But if you're serious about Charlie, take my advice." She tidied her dress. "I'm late for work. Stay cool."

After breakfast I put the paper back where the reverend had left it—he'd gone to visit parishioners in the hospital before I came down—then climbed the stairs to finish unpacking. Where was Charlie? Why hadn't he answered my letter?

When I was small, five or six, I loved to hide in doorways and startle Frank as he passed by. A little sister's way of being annoying, but I adored how he would jump and shout, and then clench me and say, "Got me again." That's how those questions about Charlie were: waiting patiently for me to pass, so they could ambush me. The worst one: what if I'd traveled all this way, and Charlie never wrote me back, never came to see me?

My room was cool in the morning, shaded at the back of the house. No one was around, but I closed the door anyway. In barely enough space, I stretched out with a straight back, legs stiff, hands under my shoulders, and lowered my chest to the floor.

When I pushed up, first I felt the burden of my own weight. Exhaling hard, I pressed down with my hands and watched my arms wobble as my body rose. I had to bow my head, grimacing and straining, to make it all the way up.

"One." I sat back on my haunches.

"Miss Dubie," I heard a call from below. "Ready to see our church?"

"Be right there, Mrs. Morris." I snatched up the wide straw hat Lizzie had loaned me, and trotted down the stairs. The second push-up would have to wait.

Outside, the church presented quite a contrast with the spired steeples of Hyde Park. This house of worship was smooth adobe. Inside its wide wooden doors the place was echoey and cool. Colored light spilled through stained glass onto the stone floor. Mrs. Morris charged up the center aisle trailing lily of the valley perfume, her heels banging the floor like a mallet. I heard people speaking in front, and a man and woman emerged from the office area.

"Thank you so much, Mrs. Sanchez," the man was saying, at high volume.

"We pray for your family, senor," the woman answered in a Spanish accent.

"I can rely on you to keep this matter private, I hope."

The woman did not answer, but bowed repeatedly as she backed away.

"Very kind of you to come see me," he said, again too loudly.

Mrs. Sanchez hurried past, eyes down. But then Reverend Morris was shaking my hand, welcoming me, pointing at this and that feature of the church.

"A revitalized music program will strengthen our worship," he boomed. The man was stiff-necked, and he had a nervous tic: angling his chin forward, as if to stretch the muscles in his throat. "Another form of devotion."

"I'm delighted to be here," I said. "What became of your last organist?"

I'd asked in an offhand way, making conversation. But it must have contained blasphemy of some kind, because the reverend and his wife both froze solid.

"I'm sorry," I backpedaled. "I can tell I've misspoken."

"It was me," Mrs. Morris said. "I've been the music director everywhere my husband has been a preacher. But here, some circumstances arose—"

"Outside circumstances," the minister interjected. "And we agreed that someone new, with musical skill and a prayerful spirit, would be good for our congregation."

"As I wrote to you," I said, beginning a speech I'd rehearsed on the train, "I am not a deeply churched person. But I can promise you a strong music program and dependable choir conducting."

"I'm sure it will be fine," Reverend Morris said, overloud again. After which we all had a nice long awkward moment in the nave of the church. I was already planning my interrogation of Lizzie Hinks. She would know what these "circumstances" were.

"May I see the organ?" I said at last, sighs of relief all around.

"Of course," Reverend Morris foghorned. "This way."

The organ bench and choir loft stood in front, to one side, instead of in the balcony over the entry. That was helpful, because I preferred to see what was going on directly, rather than reversed in a mirror as a balcony required. However, it meant I had a better view of the pulpit than of the choir, which would make conducting a challenge.

While the Morrises stood shoulder to shoulder, I slid onto the bench. It was a decent organ: three manuals of sixty-one keys, stops for flute, reed, trumpet—plus a swell division, which promised good volume. The console, though not ornate, was warm, reddish cherry. I slipped off my shoes and admired the two octaves of pedals.

"Pretty instrument." I switched the organ on. "With a nice array of stops."

They nodded enthusiastically, but oddly, without saying anything. I saw Mrs. Morris wringing her hands. And then a note began to play, ghostly, all on its own.

"It seems we have a volunteer," I said, cool as an ice cube. One by one I closed the stops, and when I removed the lower manual the note ceased.

"There is an occasional cipher on that keyboard," Mrs. Morris said. "Sometimes I've had to confine my playing to the upper manuals."

"Well," I replied, "don't we all have good days and bad days?"

"That's where the Lord comes in," the minister boomed. "Faith keeps us steady."

What song to play first, to establish my ability and set them at ease? My last audition had been for Oberlin, a run through the literature of French and German composers, mostly hoping to impress three conservatory professors with the range of my repertoire. They showed as much response as a trio of statues, then recommended me unanimously for admission. Now the pressure was different, because I was rusty. I'd practiced very little during my whirlwind with Chris. Also I'd been playing popular songs instead of classical. I smiled, imagining how they would panic if I played "Alley Cat." But in truth only one piece would do: that difficult Toccata in D Minor by Bach.

I would not have to perform the whole thing to put them on their heels. In fact, I was only a few measures along when Mrs. Morris flinched—her eyes flattening as if someone just behind them had closed the blinds. Thirty seconds more music, and she marched away up the aisle, her shoes hammering.

I paused, hands hovering over the keys. "Is everything all right?"

"Excellent," Reverend Morris declared at top volume. His chin did that tic, tensing the muscles in his neck. "Continue, please. It sounds heavenly."

ALL DAY THE CREW would gather at the concrete bowl and blow things up. Gunpowder, TNT, ammonia-based explosives. They tried devices that blew in one direction, then two, then four. They compared a medium bomb detonating in four directions with a small bomb exploding in six ways.

Over the course of a day, some boys went slightly deaf. By the next morning the ringing in their ears would have stopped, but then they'd ride in a truck bed back down for another day of detonating.

Others grew blasé, retreating from explosions only as far as the site boss insisted. He had stopped using the air horn, instead blowing a referee's whistle he'd found in a closet at Fuller Lodge. It lay atop a pile of athletic gear, from back when The Hill had been a boys' school. The whistle was a small prize compared with another find: a pump, complete with needle, to inflate basketballs. Now, most nights after dinner, there were pickup games in which the boys appeared casual while choosing teams, but turned fiercely competitive the moment play began.

It was not unusual to see a guy at breakfast with a shiner, inflicted by a stray elbow during a rebound tussle. One morning a boy showed up at the tech area with his arm in a sling. Someone bumped him, and he'd broken his wrist.

"I'm half-tempted to prohibit basketball," the site boss threatened.

"You do that, sir," Monroe advised. "The boys'll hate you till the rivers run dry."

So they concentrated on the next detonation, a hexagonal TNT. And when it had burst, the first person down to the concrete bowl was always the same: Charlie Fish.

He'd measure how far the wood or metal pieces had flown. He'd study the burn marks on the concrete. He'd kneel with a protractor, assessing the angles of force. Then he'd write notes furiously while the crew set up the next explosion. The number of devices grew by painful steps—sixteen, eighteen—always with one or two not detonating. Therefore, even though Charlie continued to set records for the number of simultaneous explosions, each test was also a failure.

Sometime midafternoon, Bronsky's truck would appear on the ridge. Everyone could see Charlie stiffen. Collecting his papers of test results, he'd nod at the site boss—"Thanks again, sir"—before trotting up the hill to the truck. He'd hand the pages in the passenger-side window, then tumble in back. The truck climbed the dirt hill, reached the gravel road, and roared away out of sight.

Each night he would work in the lab, soldering, testing, soldering, building detonators, soldering. Only when he had enough designs to occupy the testing crew the next day would he step out into the fall New Mexican night. Never had he seen so many stars. The air smelled sharply of pine. He could hear distant conversations, as if from across a body of water. Charlie would reach Ashley Pond, squatting at its edge, and in the soft dirt with his finger he would write one letter: *B*.

The Allies had reached Paris in August. Hitler ordered his troops to destroy the city on the way out, but they had not obeyed. Brussels came next, liberated in early September. Hitler survived an assassination attempt, and Rommel committed suicide rather than be executed for his role in it.

Meanwhile, Brenda was waking and sleeping, eating and working, and not answering his letters. He'd sent three, without a word in return. In a way, he had his answer. A woman not responding to letters was, in a fashion, being quite articulate.

Charlie straightened and left that *B* in the mud. After stretching his back and neck, he wandered off toward the barracks.

"There he is," Monroe hailed from across the yard, veering in Charlie's direction. "Rarest critter in these parts: Charlatius Fishius."

"An uncommon sighting indeed," called Giles, who wobbled a bit himself. "I thought they'd gone extinct."

"You're looking at the last of its kind, right here."

Charlie stood still as they approached, a tortoise out of steam.

"The species may be extinct after all." Giles lifted Charlie's arm and let it fall to his side. "This one appears to be dead."

"Pity," Monroe answered. "A loss to us all."

"Hello, guys," Charlie said. "What did I miss tonight?"

They glanced at each other and both burst out laughing.

"Really?" Charlie said. "That good?"

"No," Giles protested, though he continued laughing. "It was terrible."

"I can't wait to hear."

Monroe tried a serious face but could not maintain it. "The fella nearly died."

"Till they turned the lab into a vomitorium," Giles said, and that sent them on another spasm of laughter.

Charlie sighed. "It's been a long day, guys."

"Of course," Giles said, sobering. "But it exemplifies the absurdity of this place."

"It went like this." Monroe held his hands wide, like he was holding a picture frame. "Don Mastick, nice chemist fella, expert at scoping the smallest reactions. Oppie loves that stuff, so Mastick's holding a glass vial, tiny, maybe the size of a sewing needle."

"This afternoon," Giles added. "Six hours ago."

"Setting in that tube, though?" Monroe hastened to say, peeved at the interruption. "Near about half the world's plutonium supply."

"Now I'm interested," Charlie said.

"Well, during the afternoon some of the liquid done gassified in there. When he held the vial in his hand, the heat was too much."

"So it burst?" Charlie said.

Monroe nodded. "Popped. Onto the wall, mostly, but a bit went onto Mastick's lips." His eyes were bright with delight. "Some, right into the bastard's open mouth." And he was off laughing again.

"That's not funny," Charlie said. "Do you know how dangerous—"

"Rest assured," Giles patted his arm. "They contacted senior medical staff immediately. Hempelmann and the others. They concocted a nonreactive solution to rinse out his mouth. He swished it, then spat it, every fifteen minutes for three hours. They tested the spit and it was a good recovery."

"But then." Monroe wiped away a tear. "I don't know why this part kills me, but it does. They run a counter on his breath from six feet away. Mastick's still hot as a barbecue. So then . . ." He started chortling again.

"They pumped his stomach," Giles interrupted. "And collected the contents. That's a beaker I shudder to contemplate. And when it came time to salvage the plutonium from the organic material—"

"Who did they give the job to?" Monroe thumbed Charlie in the ribs. "Who?"

"I have no possible idea."

"*Mastick*," Monroe all but yelled. "They made the poor bastard titrate his own barf." And he was howling with laughter again.

Giles chuckled along, while Charlie stood shaking his head. "You guys are great. Honestly. But can I please go to bed now?"

Monroe kept grinning. "You know, Mister Charlie, a thing I admire about you?"

"What is that?"

"That you can work all day on detonators, and still sleep at night."

"Hey," Giles said. "Play nice."

"No offense," Monroe protested. "I can't get but about three winks, myself."

"Nor any taken," Charlie answered, patting Monroe's arm as he walked past, aiming for the barracks. "I'm too tired to take offense at anything."

* * *

He was soldering in his sleep. A giant in-box bent under the weight of designs he was to build. The instant he finished an assembly, some soldiers snatched it up. Brenda stood by, tapping her foot. In the logic of the dream, she could end his work with a word, but she kept silent. Charlie wanted to see where the finished detonators were going, but whenever he turned his head someone would press on his stomach to make him focus on the device before him. As he surfaced into wakefulness, it turned out that Midnight was kneading the blanket on his belly with alternating paws. He rubbed her ears back, which she tolerated for half a minute before hopping down to begin her day's expeditions.

The barracks were quiet, the others boys already at work. Charlie shuffled to the latrine, squinting at a pinup calendar to see that it was Saturday. Tonight, he might have some fun. If he was not too exhausted. Or too blue about Brenda. Or required to build something for Monday.

Probably he had slept through breakfast. But he scanned the row of empty sinks, and for the first time since arriving at The Hill, he had his choice.

Charlie was waiting by the mess hall for a ride to the concrete bowl when Monroe arrived with the power wagon. Stopping to let boys unload, he gave a sloppy salute.

"So I missed it?" Charlie asked.

"Yep, but you done good, Mister Charlie."

"I did?"

"Sixteen went bang without a hitch. New world record."

"Two of them misfired?"

Monroe shook his head. "Didn't fire at all."

Feeling like a rock had dropped in his belly, Charlie put a hand on the truck for balance. A moment later, Bronsky's yellow pickup came idling along. The driver slowed, and Charlie moved over to receive his lecture. But the department director only pointed over his shoulder. "We have leave assembly on big table. Perhaps please by tomorrow you are find what failed and why."

"Sure," Charlie said. "Yes, sir."

The truck pulled away, and wearily Charlie started toward the gate to the labs. At the same time the guards stepped forward, he reached for his pass.

"Hey, Mister Charlie," Monroe called. "See you at the dance tonight?"

"I wish," he mumbled. The guards inspected his pass and waved him forward.

When Charlie had presented his assembly for testing, it was laid out on a grid atop the fabrication table. Now a rough wooden crate sat in that place. He dragged it to the edge and peered in: wires, devices, cables, all in a mad knot. He turned the crate over and dumped the contents out.

It looked like a spiderweb that had trapped itself. Merely untangling the thing would take hours, and that was before a single diagnostic test. There was no one to help him, no one to share the work. And if he succeeded, what then? Was he a hero, or a monster? How would his invention be used?

Charlie fell back into his chair. Detonation wires dangled a few feet away. Without thinking, he took the positive one and clipped it to his left sleeve. Calmly, he attached the negative to his right. He completed the circuit. He was the Gadget.

The building's custodian passed in the hallway, a local man mopping the floor. He circled back though, and poked his head in the doorway. "Everything all right, senor?"

"Excellent, fantastic, splendid," Charlie told the man. He lifted the wires and let them fall on his chest. "All clears."

ALREADY I KNEW LIZZIE well enough to wait before asking. I gave it three whole days, though I was ravenous with curiosity. Meanwhile, Mrs. Morris was friendly to me as a scorpion. Each Sunday after I played, trying harder, aiming for perfection, her hostility was less hidden. And the reverend—between daily services, visiting the sick, and the funeral of a woman who'd lived her whole life in Santa Fe and therefore drew quite a crowd—was not around the house much. We all knew when he'd come home, though, because that voice boomed up the stairs like it was amplified.

"Thank God he's quiet during sex," Lizzie joked one day, though the very thought scandalized me.

It was after dinner, and I'd just come from the washroom. "You are so saucy" was the best reply I could muster.

"Probably he waits till we're both not here, so they can be as loud as they want."

"Probably you should spend less time imagining other people's private activities."

Lizzie laughed. "Believe me, kid. If my Timothy were here, I'd be thinking about his and mine and there'd be no room for anyone else's."

"Naughty." I whapped her with my washcloth. "Come drink with me at La Fonda."

"Your treat this time?"

"Why not?"

"Church collection money paying for booze." She slid into sandals. "I love it."

Off we went, into the warm evening. The moon hung high in the clear desert sky. Lizzie took my arm and we strolled like sisters.

The hotel bar was packed as a theater showing a new Bogart movie. Guys in their twenties, loud as a college party. Dozens of them, but no Charlie. One funny thing: None of them were dressed like ranchers or vacationers. No locals either. No girls. No one in uniform. Just a gang of pale guys with short hair, many wearing glasses.

We found a table outside, beneath a string of bare bulbs. I waited till the waitress brought our drinks, then dove right in. "Why is Mrs. Morris strange about me now?"

"What do you mean?"

"She was friendly till I played the organ. Now I'm the skunk at her garden party."

Lizzie shook her head. "It's your imagination."

"You'd think she'd have a sweeter personality, wearing such sweet perfume."

"That's just a cover-up. The woman's a genuine grouch."

"But not to me, at the beginning. Now she leaves the church anytime I play, almost at a run. And she's much less friendly around the house."

"Are you really good at the organ?"

"I'm not terrible."

"Maybe she was. Maybe it was a big problem with her husband, that she was a lousy organist and the choir hated her, and he had to hire you to keep his job. Your talent and youth stick a knife right in her pride."

I sipped rum and tonic like a mouthful of candy. It was wonderfully cold. "It feels bigger than that."

"Well, you've never had someone more talented than you rub it in your face."

"I don't know about that," I said.

"I bet there have not been too many situations that humbled Brenda Dubie. You seem plenty confident."

I squirmed. "I'll tell you one way I am definitely not confident: push-ups."

"Oh ho." Lizzie brightened. "Let's see what you've got."

"Here?"

She pointed. "Behind my chair. No one will see but me."

Clambering around, I tucked my dress between my knees and used my best form.

"Three?" Lizzie laughed. "That's all you've got?"

"I started out with less." I stood, a little wounded. "You don't have to be mean."

"I'm sorry," she said, "but three?"

I slumped into my chair. "I'm not sure why those stupid exercises are so three-alarm important, anyway."

"Because." Suddenly serious, Lizzie leaned toward me. "Is a woman who can do only three push-ups worth going to war for? A man needs something to desire, to keep him alive. Your guy is working day and night on some math thing that wipes his brain out. My guy is training for the Pacific invasion, preparing to see his buddies killed, maybe do some killing himself. You want a man to come home when this is all done, and think you are the only thing he has ever desired, and the only thing he will desire for the rest of his life. Then you go make babies like your life depended on it."

I couldn't argue. Someday the war would end. Only that morning I read that we'd torpedoed the *Junyo Maru*, 5,620 men. Hitler was in retreat too. Sooner or later, our soldiers would put their rifles down, and come home. And the mathematicians? What would happen to them?

"Do you think I am being punished?" I blurted it out without thinking.

"Whatever for?"

"Charlie never answered my letter saying I was moving here."

"Have you written him again?"

I shook my head. "I came all this way. He should write to me."

"You and your pride," Lizzie said. "Did you consider maybe your letter got lost?"

"None of the other ones did."

"You're disappointed in him, when actually he might not know you are here? And weeks are going by?"

"I don't know."

She gave me a long look, straight on, like I was a salesman feeding her a line.

"What?" I said. "What is it?"

"Maybe you want to be punished. It's odd to cross half the country for a guy, then not contact him. Maybe you did something wrong, so you're punishing yourself. Otherwise you would have written him twice, gone to the police, tracked him down somehow."

"You're out of your mind." My voice rose a little. "Presumptuous too. I want to be punished? What kind of crazy idea is that?"

Lizzie sat back with her drink, confident as a bird on her perch. "A correct one."

Normally when we returned from a night out, the boardinghouse's downstairs windows were dark. Only the stairway light would be on. But that night the whole place was lit up. Two drinks in my belly, I hadn't noticed. But Lizzie grabbed my arm and made us stop.

"Who's that for?" she whispered.

"What do you mean?"

"They're not up listening to the radio." She pointed at the lit windows. "So they have news. Is it for you, or me?"

"Lizzie, that is a terrible way to think."

But her fear was naked to me, just then, and contagious. "If it's me," I said, "I'll need your help. And if it's you, I promise to stand by you."

"Oh, Brenda." She gave me a quick hug. "I do love my fella."

"And he's not in combat yet."

"And your brother is in a motor pool, away from the fighting."

"They're going to be all right," I said. Which was pretending, because aside from submarine kills, I knew nothing about anything.

We were standing in the entryway off the living room, clutching each other's hands, when Reverend Morris cleared his throat. "Brenda?"

My mouth went dry. So it was me. Why did he have to be so damn loud?

"Hello," I said, chipper as a Monday morning. "How was your evening?"

"Your mother called," Mrs. Morris announced, icicles dripping from her words. What had I done to her, anyhow?

"Is everyone all right?" I asked, my voice cracking a little.

Mrs. Morris did not look up from her needlepoint. "We knew better than to pry."

"She would like you to phone her," the reverend boomed. "We discussed it, and we are willing to make a long distance call for you."

I glanced back and forth between them. "Is it too late to do it now? I mean, thank you. But could we?"

Mrs. Morris only pursed her lips, and pulled a needle through the canvas.

"Of course." Reverend Morris rose from his chair.

I followed him into the study, where he picked up the black phone and dialed the operator. He read her the number from a slip of paper. I tried to imagine my mother giving him our number, and what it might mean. Lizzie marched right across that living room to stand beside me. What a pal. I held her hand.

"It's going through now." He handed me the phone.

"Hello?" My mother sounded throaty.

"It's Brenda, Mother. Is everything all right?"

"Sweet girl. How nice it is to hear your voice."

"Who is hurt, Mother? What happened?"

"Why, no one is hurt, Brenda. Hold on." She coughed, I could hear her doing something, then she came back. "How are you, my girl?"

I felt confused. Her voice sounded fine. "Is there some kind of emergency?"

"Not at all. I'm just waking up. I told the Morrises there was nothing wrong."

Something inside me went cold. I turned and Mrs. Morris was concentrating on her needlepoint, calm as a sleeping cat. Why had she scared me like that? "Is that so?"

"After you left," my mother was saying, "the house was too empty to bear. I closed the store for a bit, and went to Aunt Claire's. You remember."

"On the lake in Wisconsin, I sure do."

"Well, I've been wanting to call anyway. But when I came home and saw the letters, it was the perfect excuse. But no one's hurt, honey. I've heard from your father and Frank and it's business as usual."

"What letters?"

"Why, from Charlie." She paused. I could picture her, probably lighting a cigarette. My father hated when she smoked in bed, but he wasn't around to object. "There were four here when I got home. One was addressed to me, asking if you were all right because he hadn't heard from you."

I didn't know what to say.

"I thought there must be some confusion. Is everything all right down there?"

"We crossed signals when I got here, that's all."

"But two of the letters were postmarked after you arrived."

"Um. He lost the address here and thought they'd be forwarded. It's all fine now."

Lizzie shook my hand off like it was dirty. Scowling, she crossed her arms.

"Oh good. I'll send them right away." In the pause that followed, I could picture my mother pinching a bit of tobacco from her tongue. "How is Charlie?"

I looked at Lizzie, who I could tell was hearing every word. "He never gets enough to eat. But, Mother, I can't stay on the line too long. The Morrises—"

"I understand."

"I'll get a pile of change together and call you from a booth soon, okay?"

"My big girl," she marveled. "I'm keeping the store closed for now. Call me soon?"

"I'll do it tomorrow."

And I placed the receiver back in its cradle.

"Everything okay?" Reverend Morris all but shouted.

"Fine, yes." I moved into the living room, Lizzie at my heels. I could feel her seething. "Thanks very much."

"We can't make a habit of this expense," Mrs. Morris told her needlework.

"Of course not," I answered, continuing to the stairway. "I'm grateful to you."

As I started up, I could hear Lizzie a few steps behind me, heat coming off her like a radiator. When I turned to say good night she had stopped at the top of the stairs.

"See what I mean about Mrs. Morris hating me?"

Lizzie opened her mouth, but hesitated. "We gave ourselves quite a scare over a couple of mismailed letters."

"Silly, isn't it?" I said.

"And you lied to your mother."

"It's too complicated to explain."

"Will you write to Charlie now? Since he obviously doesn't know you're here?"

"I'm going to wait till his letters arrive. So I know what he's thinking before I write back."

"He's thinking 'What the hell happened to Brenda?'"

"It'll all work out fine."

"Or is Charlie part of your 'too complicated to explain'?"

"No." Unable to look her in the eye, I fiddled with the doorknob. "It's all me."

She pursed her lips, then moved away to the head of the stairs. "I sure do wonder what you did."

Lizzie switched off the lights, and stood unmoving. After giving her eyes a few seconds to adjust, she made way to her room in the dark.

THE FUN WAS NEARLY over by the time Charlie arrived. He'd return to the lab later, but the band had been calling to him through the open window since sometime after eight. Now it was past eleven. He'd untangled the mess and found the misfiring culprits.

On the patio outside Fuller Lodge people stood in groups, chatting and smoking. A few couples had wandered toward Ashley Pond or Bathtub Row, smooching in the shadows. A song pulled him forward, though, into the music and the light.

People were matched in squares, and the first dance of the new grouping began. So Charlie had missed his chance. But he could still enjoy the atmosphere, and he slid along the side wall to be nearer the band. As always, the caller started with simple steps until the dancers were acquainted, gradually adding more complicated combinations. Maybe he'd been working too much, Charlie thought, because the people weaving in and out of their squares resembled the wiring he'd been grappling with all night. It reminded him, too, of the time he climbed behind the organ at Harvard, and saw all the tracking cables and controls. Was everything on earth a manifestation of a human desire to knot things in clever ways?

Monroe sidled up. "Keep dancing, kiddies. Keep having your parties. Don't you fret one second about the silly old war."

Charlie turned. "How much have you had tonight, Monroe?"

"Not a drop." He shook his head. "Stuff ain't working no more."

"Music does it for me."

Monroe scanned the crowded dance floor, couples close along the walls, men drinking steadily at the back. "I see all this"—he waved an arm at the room—"And I think here's a right nice summer camp, have another drink, everything's ducky, go make babies, you lovers, and what's to complain about excepting the milk being sour?"

Charlie gave him a long look. "You're sounding a little sour yourself."

"Lately I ain't feeling too chipper about what we're doing here."

Charlie nodded. "I hope we beat Hitler before this project reaches its goal."

"You think any of these guys will ease off if that happens? Cause I sure don't."

The caller interrupted to say it was quitting time. Some dancers protested, until he said the bass player had been nursing a sick stomach all night, and needed to quit. The crowd applauded the band, and only seconds later took up a chant: "Will-ly, Will-ly."

"Two minutes to midnight," Monroe marveled. "Can't miss a hundred and twenty seconds more fun."

The whole room joined in, clapping along, "Will-ly, Will-ly," until a bright-cheeked man emerged from a side room, holding his giant accordion by one strap.

"Hello there," Willy Meehan said into the microphone, and although everyone cheered, Charlie could hear the slurring of drink in his voice.

Sure enough, it took him two tries to swing the fabled Stomach Steinway into place, straps over his shoulders and the instrument wheezing into position. Then he cranked the mike down to point straight at the accordion.

Charlie inched closer. He loved that miniature organ, its hokey optimism. It reminded him of lunches with Brenda in Dubie's Music, about a hundred years ago.

Willy bent to the mike to speak. "Here's something different," he said, before straightening, and beginning a tune.

The melody was familiar, Charlie knew he would place it in half a minute, but the surprise was in the tempo. It was slow. A waltz, sweet and low and easy. Some of the couples took up proper position, and began to dance. Others stood awkwardly—they'd been content with the light contact of square dancing, but were unprepared for the intimacy of actual touch—no longer gliding past each other, but moving together, two by two.

"Do you know this song?" he asked Monroe.

"Course I do. 'Night and Day.' And this here is the first slow dance I've ever seen on The Hill."

A sweet sadness had filled the room, almost like nostalgia. Couples paused their canoodling to watch the dancers. The drinkers stopped talking. And the dancers held their partners close, swaying in time.

"Lord," Monroe said. "I about could bust out crying."

Charlie felt it, too, surprised by the tender melancholy that Willy brought to the song. He was playing it with his eyes closed.

It was over in minutes. The dancers parted slowly, everyone giving strong but sober applause. Someone came pushing through the crowd, Charlie could not see who.

"Is that Oppie?" Monroe asked. "Why's the boss here?"

They were the only ones close enough to see Oppenheimer grab the musician's arm and speak through clenched teeth. "What in hell are you doing?"

Willy blinked a moment. "A slow number, sir. No harm in it."

Oppenheimer shook his head hard, as if trying to fling water from his face. "Don't you ever, ever do that again."

Already people had gone for their hats, their jackets, the moonlit walk home. Oppenheimer spun on his heel and hurried off. Willy remained onstage with the accordion against his chest. "What did I do?" he asked, but everyone had turned away.

Monroe muttered to Charlie. "See what I'm talking about?"

They spoke little on the walk back. It was a quiet night, the air calm beneath a high fat moon. Charlie imagined Brenda in Chicago, under that same moon. Behind the barracks a bonfire burned low, coals glowing and a few boys gathered. They heard Giles's laugh like a siren call.

Monroe paused outside the barracks. "Mister Charlie, what if we make this thing, and it works, and it's like Sebring said in his lecture. The big pop."

Charlie held the door open. "Hitler has killed countless innocent people."

"But are you and me killers too?"

"Shut that damn door, will you?" someone yelled from inside. "Mosquitoes."

They hurried in, easing the door shut so it did not slam. Most of the barracks was dark, a few guys reading or chatting, writing letters. Not the rowdiest Saturday night.

"Have you been going to the debates?" Charlie said in a hush.

"All of 'em. You?"

"No." He rubbed his face. "It may seem hypocritical. But I feel like my job is to build one small part of this incredibly complicated Gadget, and hope the war ends before the rest is ready."

"But what if it don't end?" Monroe leaned closer, his voice urgent. "What if old Hitler keeps on fighting? And here we have this great big thing, and we up and use it—Munich, *bang*, Berlin, *bang*—and slaughter lord only knows how many souls. What are we then? Seems a hell of a lot worse than plain old soldiers, taking plain old orders."

Charlie brushed his hair back with both hands. "I don't have an answer."

"You and me both."

They ambled down the aisle between the beds, reaching Charlie's first. They both stopped when they saw the envelope on his cot.

"That from your girl?"

Charlie picked it up. His name in Brenda's handwriting. "It certainly is."

"Been a while."

Charlie nodded. He sat on the bunk and stared at the envelope.

"Ain't you gonna open it?"

"Not quite yet. Not tonight."

"You been pining on her for months now. Why in the world would you wait?"

"Because." He lay back, the envelope on his chest. "We don't know what it says."

"So?"

"So what's the harm in being hopeful for one more night?"

"No harm in hoping," Monroe answered. "G'nite, Mister Charlie."

He ambled down the row to his bunk, and sat on it, thinking for a while. He heard the *thunk* of Charlie's shoes hitting the floor, then the purr of the cat that had joined him on the cot. Boys drifted off all around, while Monroe lay there, open-eyed in the dark, until Charlie had fallen asleep.

31.

THE LAST TIME I felt that nervous, Charlie was late for our first date. This time I was awake before the sun. There was no point in dressing yet, or doing my hair. I lay in bed, listening to girls across the back lot getting ready for work. My stomach felt like a beehive, but the clock was in no hurry. At around seven, Lizzie poked her head in.

"Hey, kid. What time's his bus?"

"Ten. He wrote me ten."

"I'm fetching my paycheck at the hospital. Do you need anything?"

"For three hours to pass?"

"They will." Lizzie finished buttoning her shirt. By then I'd seen her undergarments many times, she was casual about skin and lace. For me, those things made me shy as a dormouse. "Do you think you'll tell the boy?"

"Tell him what?"

"Tell him what?" she chirped. "Whatever your secret is, kid."

My stomach tightened its knot. "I don't want to hurt him."

"Which hurts more? Being honest or deceiving?"

"He has to suspect anyhow," I said. "I've been here for months, and this is the first we're seeing each other. I am terrible."

"Everyone is terrible," Lizzie said. "Also, everyone is trying their best."

"Is there anything you'll need to tell your husband when he gets home?"

Lizzie checked her lowest button. "Only the naughty thoughts I have about him all the time."

I smiled. "You have a dirty mind."

She smoothed down her shirt front. "Every chance I get."

At breakfast I waited till Reverend Morris finished grace before drinking any coffee. Mrs. Morris marched in and out of the kitchen.

"Did you see the mail?" he asked her. "I'm amazed it keeps up after all these months." He was loud as a bullhorn, and his neck did that odd tic of stretching his chin. Though I had no idea what he was talking about, he shook a stack of envelopes at me. "Pleasantly amazed, of course."

Mrs. Morris returned with eggs and bread for me, and I thanked her profusely. Which made her pause by my chair. "You're welcome, Miss Dubie."

So, my new demotion: I was no longer Brenda. Any other day, I would have been offended. Or wondered what I did wrong. Not that day. I needed to clean up, choose the right dress, prepare myself for Charlie. Silly old wimpy Charlie Fish. I was terrified.

He'd sent me an address to meet on East Palace Avenue, between the plaza and the cathedral. Even with dawdling I arrived early, so I meandered over to the big, two-steepled church. I was thinking I might sneak in to see its organ, but a funeral was beginning. Mourners in black lined the walk. Pallbearers carried a wooden casket up the steps. Not an omen, I told myself, just coincidence. In Cathedral Park I sat on a bench, good posture and my ankles crossed, until ten o'clock rang in the steeple.

At East Palace, a drab green bus was belching black smoke as it pulled away. A crowd of local Latinos clustered by an iron gate, people in bright-colored ponchos murmuring adios before dispersing. They parted almost like a curtain, and there he stood, his back to me as his eyes searched the street.

Until they came to rest on me. It was sunlight. In that instant of recognition, his eyes brightening, I felt like a complete fool. How could I have made him wait? How had I allowed myself to wait? Rooted in place, I shook my head like I did not believe.

"Oh my goodness, Brenda." Charlie stopped an arm's length away. "Oh my."

For once I was the shy one, holding back because the pull of him was so strong.

"Let me look at you," I said, though I was already doing it. He had developed some, muscled out in his chest, his arms like ropes. Though his forehead was even more prominent with the buzzed haircut, and a healthy tan that had lightened the color of his hair. Charlie in all his goofy glory, and I felt a thrill flutter through me like wings.

He set something at my feet. My parents' picnic basket. I laughed. "I can't believe you brought that here today."

"I took good care of it," he said. And the fear came over me: Had he returned the basket because this was the only time we would see each other, and then he would be swallowed back into his secret war job in the hinterlands, and I would return to playing hymns and sleeping in a boardinghouse, and this morning might be all we would ever have?

"Of course you did." I moved forward, to hug him, and doing so made me step into a shadow. Was that Chris, like a devil on my shoulder? No, I looked up and the sidewalk there had a roof over it, like a porch, to shield pedestrians from the sun. But I felt the darkness of my transgression as though it was the dress I wore.

There was only one way forward. I put my arms around Charlie and pulled him close. His back felt stronger under my hands, firmer. At first he did not hold me back, but I stayed right there.

After a while, who knows how long when your desire is that keen, his hands rose to my waist, thumbs on my hip bones as though I were naked. I did not flinch or pull away. At last he succumbed, wrapping his arms around my waist and drawing me against him, pressed together the length of our bodies. I felt the world falling away, a rush of relief and a sharpness of want. What had I ever been thinking?

* * *

I remember that day with Charlie as clearly as the day we met. Our childhoods had ended, blunt as a cinder-block wall. We did not yet know each other as adults.

I was the one who released the hug first. I wish I could take it back. But guilt about Chris still shadowed me, and the secret of it came momentarily between us. "Come on for a walk," I said. "You don't know this town."

Why couldn't I have been kinder? How did I forget that life is short, and we ought to be our best in every moment? Charlie scooped up the picnic basket, offered his arm, and we promenaded. Or no: I led and he followed. Despite my conscience, in some deep, awful way, I still thought I was better than he was.

Lizzie was reading on the bench when we approached, feet tucked under her rump. "Hello, lovebirds," she called.

"This is Lizzie," I said to Charlie, as she stood and shook his hand, giving him a once-over and not hiding it.

"So Prince Charming is real after all? I was beginning to worry."

"I'm feeling pretty real today." Charlie gave his arm a pinch. "Great to meet you."

"What do you do for work, Charlie? Where do you live?"

He ducked his head, a gesture of shyness that had irritated me back in Chicago, but that now I saw differently. Modesty, maybe. The opposite of bragging.

"Oh, this and that," he said. "I live outside of town."

"Oh." She nodded. "You're one of those Los Alamos guys."

"I, um—"

"Don't worry," she laughed. "I'm not a spy."

"That makes three of us," I said. "We're only here to drop off a picnic basket."

"Sounds perfect," Lizzie said. "Just be sure to smooch each other all the time."

Charlie blushed, and I did too. "Are all married women this brazen?" I asked.

"I like to think I'm special," she answered. "Leave the basket. I'll take care of it."

"Thanks," I said. And I don't know why, but I gave her a hug, quick and fierce.

"Oh go on." She fanned the air before sitting again. "I'm trying to read."

We ambled away—no planned route, no destination—a companionable silence.

"Who was that?" Charlie asked after a while.

"Who, Lizzie?"

"The woman hanging laundry in back. She gave me a double-barreled frown."

"Oh, that's Mrs. Morris. She hates me but I don't know why."

"Because she doesn't know you," he said. "Otherwise she'd love you."

That reply made me think of my mother, and how deft Charlie always was at dealing with her prickliness. He'd done it again with Mrs. Morris. I pulled him closer. "Tell me about your work."

"I'm not allowed to say," he answered.

"But you can tell me, Charlie."

"Actually, no. It's against the law, and might be treason."

"Do you have to take everything so seriously?"

"Brenda." He hesitated, which at the time I thought was insecurity but now believe was him showing patience with me. "It is serious. There are women on The Hill who don't know what their husbands do all day."

"What could the army possibly be up to that would require couples to keep secrets from each other?"

After another minute of strolling, he replied. "I guess I can say that my job is something like what I did in your parents' basement, only a million times more complicated. I've never had to work so exactingly or concentrate so hard."

"Do you like it?"

He stopped. "Do I like it?"

"Sometimes when I'm learning a complicated new organ piece, the difficulty is part of the pleasure. I've been working for months on the Bach Toccata in D Minor, for example, and it is pummeling me, but in a way I really enjoy."

He smiled, and without thinking I reached over and touched his face. Right this minute, all these years later, I am so glad I did that, because his grin grew even wider. It's an image I'll always treasure. "Charlie Fish, I sure have missed your smile."

"Brenda, I have missed your everything."

We stood a minute, feeling it, pleasure and pain at the same time. I was twenty years old, thousands of miles from home, standing with the boy I'd come all that way to see. I wondered if we were about to kiss. Would it be like before? Or would Chris ruin it?

Instead Charlie chuckled. "You know, you look just like Brenda."

I pressed my forehead to his chest. "I'm her. I'm really her."

After a minute we started along again. "The fact is," he said, "I do like it. I use my whole brain, it's wonderfully rewarding."

"Lucky you."

He'd been about to speak, but caught himself. "Your job's no conservatory, is it?"

I shook my head. "At least one of us is doing work we like. That's not bad for wartime, right?"

"Perhaps. But I dislike the pressure of my work, and the haste, and especially how the things I make might be used."

"Which is how?"

He shook his head. "That's the treason part. Tell me about your job."

"Well, hang on tight, because it's a lot."

And I deluged him: The reverend asks me to play hymns so basic, I'm ecstatic if I get to use a minor third chord in the tonic-dominant pattern. He preaches at the top of his lungs, though his sermons are not especially powerful. Yet the congregation loves him, they answer his bombast with gentleness. On the way out of worship the white parishioners press his hands or shake them, while the local Spanish people hold back, waiting their turn, and instead of handshakes they give him hugs, people making the sign of the cross. Last in line, always, is Mrs. Sanchez—who cleans the church and who I met on my first day. She hugs the minister with both arms, and I find it reassuring. The organ has potential, I continued, but badly needs repair. Without knowing how, I manage to annoy the minister's wife several times a day. The best thing by far has been the choir, because it mixes all the different kinds of people who live in Santa Fe, young and old, white and brown, and for some reason the people's voices here are wonderfully clear, unmannered, and mercifully on pitch. A shortage of basses, with the war on, but most choir members attend every rehearsal, and come on Sunday ready to sing their hearts out.

Charlie nodded all the while. When I'd finished ranting, though, I remembered how quiet Chris could be after I'd spoken—until he started talking about himself again. "Am I a terrible complainer?" I asked.

"No," he said. "I was thinking, it's a long way from 'the Hammond spinet has ninety-two tone wheels.'"

"Hey, mister, I loved selling organs. And it's ninety-one."

"But you should hear yourself." Charlie continued walking, gazing at the ground. "Your life is full now."

"It has to be. I'm making my own way."

"But you're not doing it with the hard part of yourself, Brenda. You're doing it with the lovely person that music makes you become."

"Go on." I gave his arm a poke. "Buy me lunch?"

He smiled again, ducking his head toward me. "I happen to be starving."

I took him to La Fonda, figuring he'd been there before. But he followed me to the table wide-eyed. We ordered food, and in an awkward quiet we waited for it to arrive.

"So this is the place I've been hearing about," he said. "Some of my crew comes here every Saturday night. Here and the tattoo shop."

"You haven't gotten one, I hope?"

"Never." Charlie wrinkled his nose. "It's a stain you can't wash out."

"Why do so many boys do it, then?"

He shrugged. Then fiddled with his glass, leaning closer, and again I thought he might kiss me. Instead he started talking. "Imagine I'm making a manual for an organ, Brenda. But instead of sixty-one keys, I keep making fifty-eight, and then I can't finish."

"Sounds like a lousy instrument." I sipped my water. "You won't be able to play all kinds of songs on it."

"Exactly. Like those keys, my job is very small. But until I complete my part, the whole project is stalled."

"You can't stall things in a war, Charlie." I could feel my heat rising. "Time costs lives. There are millions of boys fighting in Europe, the Pacific. Lizzie's husband will be part of the invasion of Japan—they say it will involve five million American soldiers—"

"With casualties of up to one million, I know."

"If you're working on something to help them win, you have to finish. You need to make all sixty-one keys."

"That's the trouble," he said. "I can't."

He looked downtrodden as a hobo. The responsibility weighed him down, I could see that in his slumped shoulders. But I didn't know how to help. I summoned some gumption. "I know what you do," I declared.

"What do you mean?"

"I've been following your success, in the newspapers." I was all but preening.

"I don't think so."

"Oh yes. The *Nagara*." I nodded, full of myself. "*Shinyo, Tamatsu, Yoshino.*"

"I don't understand those words."

"The subs, Charlie." I grinned. "I've kept track. I'm an encyclopedia on the topic."

"Who told you I am working on submarines? It's ridiculous."

"I memorized it all for you," I said. "The *Taiyo*, an aircraft carrier."

He laughed a little. "Brenda, we are in the middle of a desert."

I could feel my dander rising. "Don't make fun of me."

"I'm not. But submarines?" He smiled, and it felt condescending. "Really?"

At that, I snapped back. "You know why you can't finish your little part?"

"You have a theory?"

"You make it look like good manners," I said. "And humility, but that's not it."

"What are you talking about?" His smile was gone now.

"You complained about the math, you whined about the soldering. Now it's about finishing whatever it is you have to finish. Why don't you have a spine for once?"

"If you had any idea—"

"But can you tell me? Oh no, that would be *treason*." My mother would have chastised me, but I found pleasure in using my brattiest voice.

"It's not as simple as—"

"Yes it is, Charlie. Whatever your little task is, I'm sure you can do it or they wouldn't have chosen you. You're afraid, that's all. Afraid and weak."

"Brenda." He looked crestfallen. "What's gotten into you?"

"I came all this way to be with you, Charlie. I upended my whole life to give us a chance. But honestly . . ."

"Yes?" He sat straight in his chair. "Please, be honest."

"All right." I pushed my utensils aside, it felt like rolling up my sleeves. "The real reason you can't build this mystery thing is that you don't know how to be courageous."

His mouth hung slightly open. I could have stopped then, but no.

"Be a man, Charlie Fish. Be a soldier. We're surrounded by them now, just pick one and imitate him. If you can help end the war and you hesitate? You're not a man."

Charlie looked at me head-on. His reply surprised me, because it showed how he maybe knew me better than I knew myself. "Seems like you have developed a lot of expertise on what a man is."

"Yes," I said, confident as ever, and unconcerned about what pain

I might inflict. I was an idiot with a machine gun. "That's because I met one."

Charlie fell back, curled over like I'd punched him in the gut. "You did?"

"Of course. I've been surrounded by men," I backpedaled. "Real men."

"One. You said you met one."

"Yes," I blurted. "A pilot. Home to recover after getting shot down."

"Where is he now?"

"Back in the war."

"Being a man again?"

If Charlie had yelled at me, if he had argued, I might have changed direction. But his woundedness brought out some horrible predator in me, a creature that found energy in his hurt. "There is nothing wrong with being strong, and direct, and heroic."

"You went on dates with him?"

The simplicity of the question marked the beginning of my disarming. I'd had months to absorb the reality of Chris, but to Charlie it was all new. The first inkling arose that I might be making a mistake. "I did. A movie, a couple of dinners."

"Did he meet your mother?"

It was a surprisingly intimate question. The wall of righteousness that stood between my guilt and Charlie started to crumble. I shook my head.

"Did you kiss him?"

Charlie and I had not yet kissed hello, even after all those months apart. We had not kissed at all that day. How could I tell him the truth? At what point did honesty become cruelty? The pain was written on his brow, which was creased like an old man's.

"No," I lied. "He tried but I wouldn't let him."

Charlie fiddled with his silverware, eventually arranging it in a straight line. "I don't know how the existence of a pilot you dated in Chicago erases the technical complexity of what I'm being asked to build."

"Because you say you can't make this thing, and I say you *won't*."

Charlie nodded, sliding his spoon up and back. "That might be true."

"Then be a man."

Charlie faced me then, and I saw that the rims of his eyes had gone red. Rubbing them with his wrist, he stood, dropped some bills on the table, and walked away.

"Charlie," I called, but he kept going, across the square and around the corner.

At that moment the waitress arrived, setting a plate before me and one at Charlie's place. "Do we need anything further here for now?"

"We're fine," I said, casual as a millionaire, *la-di-da*. But in truth, I felt nothing but cruel, a stranger who had just driven away the most decent man I knew. On that golden afternoon, I sat by myself and wondered what the price of my behavior would be.

"ALL I AM SUGGESTING," Giles said, using a tire iron to nudge a smoky log end into the coals, "is that the war may conclude before we achieve our goal."

"That would be fine with me." Charlie sipped his beer, then tossed a twig into the bonfire. "I'd prefer it if no one ever used the Gadget."

"You two," Monroe scoffed, staggering into the light, his arms piled with wood. "Dumb as a pair of fence posts."

"Pray tell how we are dumb," Giles said.

Monroe dumped his load on the ground. "My daddy," he said, adding logs to the fire. "Couldn't bear a whiskey bottle in the house. Said it was challenging him night and day to drink it. Oppie and them others? Same thing." He continued piling on the wood. "That Gadget is their whiskey. No rest till they blow up something big."

"What if there's peace first?" Charlie asked. "The Germans have been in retreat since the Battle of the Bulge ended in January. The Soviets freed the Lodz ghetto, and liberated those horrific camps. We are genuinely winning."

"Look at it the other way." Monroe circled the fire before the wind could blow smoke in his face. "Of one hundred and sixty something thousand Jews in that ghetto, near about a thousand were left, right?"

"So the newspapers say," Giles said. "All the rest were killed or forced to move."

"And them people in Auschwitz, you saw the pictures, right?"

"Living skeletons. It was terrible. What's your point?" Charlie said.

"Any of that making you fellas feel peaceful? Or less interested in cutting Hitler's fool head off? Cause the military guys, you know they all saw that truck, and got twice as happy to show the Third Reich what a good hard American boot in the ass feels like."

Charlie laughed.

"It's true and you damn well know it."

"What about Japan?" Charlie said. "Would they ever use the Gadget over there?"

"What in hell for?" Monroe set another log on the flames, jerking his hand back to avoid a burn. "We're already fire-bombing them into ashes. Ain't one of their fighters or flak guns can touch our big bombers, so we can drop as we please."

"Nevertheless, they're making us earn every inch," Giles said. "Iwo Jima was a slaughter." He took a long draw from a bottle of whiskey.

"Go easy there," Monroe said. "Save some for a thirsty brother."

"How about that photo of the marines raising the flag?" Giles marveled. "I'm astonished the emperor didn't surrender right then."

"That boy? We'd have to drop the Gadget right in his fool lap before he'd give up," Monroe said. He took the whiskey bottle and drank long. "Anyway." He shuddered. "Anyway it'd be mighty hard convincing the world we were justified in flattening Japan, when they can't barely shoot back."

"This is why I'm going to the debate tomorrow," Charlie said. He tilted his head back to gaze at the clear winter stars. "I want to hear the big guys hash it out."

Monroe studied him. "Again the crazy man believes the world makes sense."

"Or hopes it will someday."

Giles kicked a log with his heel. "I wish you were heading to Santa Fe instead."

"Change of subject," Charlie said, tilting the bottle to finish his beer.

"It's a long-distance version of opia, you know what I mean?"

"Afraid not," Charlie said.

"That's the ambiguous intensity of looking someone in the eye, which is both invasive and vulnerable."

"Change of subject," Charlie repeated, and they all fell silent. The new logs began to catch, and the three of them moved back from the growing heat.

"Hey, is Trigger in here?"

Lying on his bunk, Charlie winced and did not answer.

"Trigger?" the soldier called again. He was baby-faced, with little on his uniform to show rank or accomplishments. Soldiers rarely entered the barracks. He stutter-stepped forward. "Charlie Fish?"

"Right here," he said, sitting up. "What's the matter?"

"No matter, sir. But my superior officer, Captain Halsey, found something."

Charlie set Midnight aside, her belly now entirely white, and stood. "Yes?"

"Well," the soldier said, removing his hat. "The captain's wife had a baby last fall, and sent him a big envelope of pictures. He said it got wet on the way here, but all he was paying attention to was the photos. Today, when he was looking at them for the ninety-ninth time, he discovered something stuck to the back." The soldier held a regular envelope. "He ordered me to deliver it pronto, with his apologies."

Charlie recognized the handwriting immediately. He had gone three months without a letter from Brenda, an agonizing dry spell. But the postmark on this one said Chicago, September—more than two months ago. Perhaps everything was about to be explained.

Charlie raised his eyes. "Please tell the captain no apology is necessary, and I appreciate him sending this along."

"Will do, sir." The soldier put his hat on and hurried out.

"Poor fella seemed like he was scared of us civilian heathens," Monroe said, ambling over. "It might be catching."

"How does a newbie like that know my nickname?"

"Hill's a small place," Monroe said. "So what'd he bring?"

Charlie handed him the letter and sank down onto his bunk.

"Well dog my cats," Monroe said. "Probably all through this war, guys write letters home, then get killed. Right? So the letter comes a month behind the news that he's dead. This puts me in mind of that sort of thing."

"Brenda is not dead," Charlie said.

"Naw. Only you never talk about her or see her no more." He tapped the envelope against his leg. "Coals outside are still hot, you know, and paper burns quick. I could solve this problem for you in about ten seconds. All clears."

Charlie shook his head. "Thanks anyway."

"Suit yourself. But you ain't gonna read it now, are you?"

"I don't know."

"See, there's the difference between us, Mister Charlie. I'd rip this thing open right quick, and rid myself of the worry."

"What's inside that envelope won't change while I think about what it might say, and how that might affect me."

Monroe shook his head. "Pure craziness, but what the hell. Enjoy." He dropped the letter on the bed, and shuffled to his own bunk. Charlie gazed at the envelope, not touching it, till the barracks chief called lights out.

On the way into the debate, boys crowding in the Fuller Lodge doorway, a steady snow falling and no one taking much notice, Charlie felt a tug on his arm. Bronsky was there, as if he'd been lying in wait. He tilted his head to one side, then marched off in that direction. Charlie stepped out of the line to follow.

The detonation team leader strode through the hallway of offices and out the side door. He wore rubbers, Charlie noticed, so his shoes would remain unmarred by snow or mud. Charlie double-timed to catch up with him outside the building.

"Perhaps we take walk?" Bronsky said.

Charlie thought one was already under way. "Is there something you need, sir?"

"Place we can speak freely."

Charlie glanced suspiciously over his shoulder. "Is there a spy on The Hill?"

Bronsky rolled his eyes. "Fishk, don't be fool. There are twenty, if not more. I mean privacy from leadership, who is all attend debate."

By then they had reached Ashley Pond, skirting its eastern shore and following a walkway toward the tech area. Snow fell past the lights, spiraling in the wind. Along the row of buildings, steam rose from their heating vents.

Bronsky pulled up short by a bench. "Here." He indicated that Charlie should sit.

"I'll stand, thank you, sir. Is something the matter?"

Instead of answering, the man removed a glove and swept snow from the bench. He sat in the place he'd cleared, then brushed the other side free. Charlie considered, then took a seat beside him.

"Fishk, what you do know about me?"

"Not much, sir. That you are Russian. That you're in charge of the detonation team. That you picked me to build the Gadget's trigger."

"All Project Y information. Not Bronsky."

"In that case, I don't know anything, sir."

He cleared his throat. "I am born Kiev, November 1900. When I am young, my family is involve in Russian civil war. My father is intellectual full of ideas: rights of individual, limited power of state, independence of Ukraine. Others agree, so they create White Army, which Lenin's Red Army proceeds to slaughter. I am younger than you are when my family flees to Berlin. I am good student, attain PhD, become professor at excellent Harvard University."

"I didn't know that. I went to college there."

"You never take my chemistry class."

Charlie leaned forward and the man appeared to be smiling. But the shades closed quickly. "Lenin's army kills perhaps seven million people, perhaps ten million. Soviet is formed, which now fights Nazis on Eastern Front."

"That part I know about," Charlie said. "The bloodiest part of the entire war."

"Hitler retreats every day. But the land does not go to peace. It goes to Soviet."

"Well." Charlie peered back in the direction of Fuller Lodge, snow clouding the view, then ran his hands up and down his thighs to keep warm. "Not much we can do about that from The Hill, is there?"

"Exactly why I bring you here," Bronsky cried. He swatted Charlie's leg with his empty glove. "Exactly. What we can do."

As usual when he did not understand, Charlie's strategy was to say nothing.

"Outside observer would say: Fishk is smart boy, work hard, likes challenge."

"Thank you, sir, I—"

"Inside observer? Fishk cannot finish job, is not spy or bad guy, but is not in hurry to see Gadget used."

Charlie stared at his shoes. The toes were darkened from melting snow.

"You stick at eighteen detonators for months, until I say you need help. Then twenty-one, again for months, until I add detonator team. Now is twenty-three, for so far five weeks."

"Are you implying that I am delaying the Gadget?"

"I am not imply. I am state as fact. So tomorrow, I add to detonator effort David Horn. He is my doctoral student at Harvard, very smart, I recruit him here."

"You don't trust me anymore."

"Trust is peacetime luxury, Fishk. I am worry about Soviet. Seven million, they have kill. If they defeat Nazi, will they be our new foe? Will war extend? Or, we use Gadget, only country with Gadget, Hitler is gone, and Soviet goes home."

"I'm incredibly close, sir."

Bronsky pulled his glove back on. "Help from Horn will make faster."

"Or get in my way."

He stood. "Debate is in Fuller Lodge. Here is no debate. Here is decision, and courtesy of telling you directly."

"Give me a bit more time," Charlie insisted. "I've earned that request. Please."

The team director paused, brushing snow from his coat. "Perhaps."

Then he marched off into the technical area, vanishing in a cloud of steam. Charlie sat back on the bench, snow falling like feathers from a burst pillowcase, as only then he became aware that the air all around him was cold.

He snuck in along the wall. For a debate, the room was oddly silent. Also dark, thanks to the snowstorm, with lights on only at the front. The chemist James Wilson, an expert on isolating explosive uranium, stood between two desks, at each of which two men sat. But no one was speaking. Charlie squatted beside Giles and Monroe.

"What have I missed?"

"Anecdoche," Giles said.

"Which means?"

"Everyone is talking and no one is listening."

"But hell," Monroe added, "you're right on time for the fireworks."

Charlie peered around, aware that the room was full of tension. The men at the desks stared toward the back. Wilson stood with crossed arms. "We deserve an answer."

Whoever he was addressing did not respond. Charlie saw dissatisfaction on every face. Why weren't they debating?

"The whole idea of this project," Wilson continued, "was civilian control of a potential military instrument, because that device could exceed the military's capacity for restraint. We have men here"—he gestured to the desk on the left—"who see the war as nearly over, our role ended before it began. Professor Joseph Rotblat, for example."

An affable-looking fellow nodded his head.

"While other men"—Wilson gestured to the right—"say that eventually some nation will obtain atomic knowledge, and the rightful possessor ought to be a democracy, so everyone participates in these decisions—namely the United States."

Wilson stepped forward. "But after three debates, we remain stalled by the moral implications. We already know the army's answer. We do not want President Roosevelt's answer. They are not men of science. We want *your* answer. If we have the courage to demand it, you must have the courage to say it."

Charlie wished he knew who Wilson was speaking to. He felt the silence's pressure. One of the men at the desks lit a cigarette. No one else moved.

Finally a chair slid on the floor in back, and a man came forward into the lights. It took a moment for Charlie to see who it was: Oppenheimer. Wilson immediately gave ground. The Los Alamos director was painfully thin, his head balanced on a neck too slender. He arrived at the front of the room, and stood rubbing his face with one hand.

"A demonstration," he said. But there was a catch in his throat. He coughed and began again.

"We must build the bomb, because someone will. I trust our government and people to manage that challenge better than any other nation. Also, we are so close. The uranium Gadget is theoretically sound, no test is needed, only a sufficient supply of materials. The plutonium Gadget has greater potential yield, but we need a test to know if that is attainable as a practical matter."

He crossed to the man who was smoking, and asked for a cigarette. As Oppenheimer lit it, and took a long draw, Monroe leaned toward Charlie. "The lives being saved or lost, while he up and has a smoke."

Oppenheimer returned to the front. "I will personally encourage General Groves and the oversight committee that the Gadget must not be used on human subjects. Its power is too great. Rather, to prove decisive American military superiority, and the futility of opposing our army and navy, we ought to conduct a public demonstration."

He took a long draw on the cigarette. "We will build a Gadget to prove that it can be done, and to show that our nation alone possesses the capability. Perhaps we will also fabricate the impression that we have dozens more, ready for use. Then we will demonstrate it, for all the world to see. Hitler will understand its significance. Nothing more will be necessary. Therefore, a demonstration."

Oppenheimer did not take questions, or remain to elaborate. Instead he strode up the aisle, grabbed his overcoat, and charged out into the swirling snow.

Returning to the barracks after the debate, Monroe and Charlie trudged through growing drifts. Giles had stayed to argue with boys from Theoretical. Not until they'd passed Ashley Pond and the tech areas did Monroe speak. "So, Mister Charlie. You think Oppie believes that horse manure?"

"He has no reason to lie to us," Charlie said.

"Sometimes you are as naive as a mouse. One nibble of cheese can win you over."

"He could have said, 'I want to drop this thing on Berlin and Munich, and you are all ordered to build it.' Telling the truth costs him nothing."

Monroe considered a moment. "Maybe it don't matter if Oppie believes that demonstration noise, long as the fellas do."

"What fellas?" Charlie asked.

"All of us, I reckon. Now we can keep right on going."

"I'm not following you."

"I mean," Monroe said, kicking a clod of snowy clay, "Oppie gave us cover, morals-wise. Building a Gadget for demonstration, everyone can work without having to answer the ethical questions. If someday the bomb gets used on humans after all, well, that was someone else's decision, and our consciences are clear."

"If I'm naive," Charlie said, "then you are cynical."

"Could be," Monroe said. "Or maybe he just gave them all an out." He realized they'd reached the barracks. "'Nother loop round the pond?"

"Thanks, but I've got a letter I've been saving." Charlie opened the door. "Glad to see the Southern boy enjoying the snow, though."

"Like ice in whiskey."

Charlie watched Monroe wander into the darkness, until someone inside the barracks yelled to close the door, he was letting the heat out.

Dear Charlie:

By the time you read this I will be ready to go. To New Mexico, I mean.

I have made this decision without asking you for two reasons. One, it could take weeks of letters back and forth for us to get comfortable, and arrange the details, and I cannot wait any longer. And two, life here is changing quickly enough that there is no point in staying in Chicago.

Last week all we sold was one accordion. No pianos, no organs, no sheet music or lessons. One blessed accordion, and it was a beginner's model.

Also I think the war is wearing on my mother. I test her patience, when she has almost run out. I hate to say this because I am going to miss her so much, but I think she might be happier if she does not have to take care of me. She is closing the store, so she won't have that responsibility either.

But the main reason I am coming is you. Your last letter told me I should say good-bye if I am done with you. Instead I am doing the opposite. You're a smart guy, you can figure out what that means.

I have landed a job, and a room in a boardinghouse. I am coming to Santa Fe.

I read the train schedule. Now I appreciate how difficult

the trip must have been for you. I have one reassurance to make it easier: you are waiting at the end of it.

I appreciate everything about you much more now. I am not afraid to say it. Or write it, anyhow. There is a kindness about you, and it brings out the kindness in me. Which is a thing I think everyone would say is good. Ha.

Charlie, I hope I won't be crowding you, or interfering with your work. I hope I don't get grouchy, like I can sometimes. Because this is all a leap of faith for me. The thing I imagine over and over is an evening, after you're done with work, and we go for a walk. It's slow, because there is no hurry, and no destination except returning to where we started. And we see so much of each other, we are talking about ordinary, everyday things. And when it's done, we have a good long kiss, because oh how I have missed your kisses, Charlie.

I put my new address down at the bottom, where I'll be in two weeks.

Your Brenda

FIRST THING THAT MORNING, I did my push-ups. Nine; I was getting up there.

By then I checked more than my makeup in the bathroom mirror. I raised my arms and marveled. They were leaner, they had a shape. I hoped Charlie would like it. I knew full well that I did not have many more chances with him. Maybe only that day, our first meeting since he'd received my lost letter.

Which didn't mean that he shouldn't be a man, but maybe I did not have to tell him so. Life as a young woman—admittedly a headstrong one—felt like threading an endless succession of hurdles. All I'd wanted was to study in a conservatory and find a solid guy. Was that too much to ask?

The night before I'd decided to stay in, rather than go barhopping with Lizzie and the girls from the boardinghouse behind ours. Charlie would not arrive till the afternoon, his letter had said, because of work. But I wanted all my wits.

No one was at the breakfast table, which was a relief because by then my presence caused Mrs. Morris no end of aggravation. If I tried being extra polite, she recoiled like a dog resists a leash. If I played some new hymn on Sunday, she would all but bare her teeth. That day there was bread, cheese, and dark coffee. I opened the paper and out of habit could not help looking for submarine exploits.

I had an extra reason, anyhow. Lizzie's husband was training for the invasion of Japan that fall. He wrote once a week: California was sunny, he was getting in excellent shape, and there was fresh fruit everywhere. But medics' orders are to run to a wounded soldier's side, even in the middle of battle. So Lizzie refused to read the paper. She said it scared her too much. I did the reading for her, and delivered good news whenever I could. The *Akitsu Mara*, 2,246 dead. The *Mayasan Maru*, 3,456 drowned.

Only years later did it occur to me how odd that was, that I considered thousands of deaths to be good news. I suppose that is one of the things war does, turns your ideas of right and wrong upside down. Death, for any reason, is no cause for celebration.

That April morning, the paper was mostly about Okinawa, where a battle had begun ten days before. It seemed as terrible as Iwo Jima—which lasted five weeks and cost 6,800 American boys. From Europe, though, the news was thrilling. Prisoners at the Buchenwald concentration camp had overpowered their remaining guards and killed them. Already the Soviets had liberated Auschwitz-Birkenau. Allied troops were within fifty miles of Berlin too. If the European war ended soon, maybe Lizzie's husband would not have to be in the invasion. I had no reason for this theory, only hope on my friend's behalf.

I left the table to go dress, and saw that the door from our stairs into the house had been left open, as had the back door. That allowed a cooling breeze to blow through, but when I passed the living room I saw that the wind had pulled a section of the newspaper apart, spilling pages all over the floor. I went in and began picking them up.

All at once there was a great row from outside, behind the house. I tucked the pages under a flower vase and went to the window. It was only open a few inches, but I could hear everything. Reverend Morris was shouting at the top of his lungs, while Mrs. Morris tried to hang laundry on the line.

"Damnation and hellfire, woman," he boomed, his big voice louder than ever. "How many times must I tell you?"

"I can't let these things stay dirty any longer," she said.

But the minister yanked a shirt from her hands and balled it against his chest. "I don't want to see it. Do you hear me? I won't see it."

Mrs. Morris turned away and began clothes-pinning a sheet to the line.

"Don't you ignore me," he bellowed. His neck did that tic to one side, chin tilted. "I am speaking."

"What do you want me to do?" She turned and I saw that her face was shining with tears. "Is it wrong to wash his clothes and put them away nicely?"

"Put them away?" he yelled. "I will never put any part of him away."

Reverend Morris looked around, taking in me at the window, the girls watching from across the back lot, his wife standing next to a laundry basket, looking like she'd just been slapped. With one last roar he grabbed the clothesline and yanked till it snapped. Sheets and shirts fell to the ground.

Then I heard the back door open; he was coming inside. I bolted up the stairs.

Lizzie was standing in the hall, facing out the window.

"You saw all that?" I asked.

"Everyone within half a mile heard it too."

"Do you know what's going on?"

"Oh, Brenda." Lizzie moved past me and sat on the bed. "I'm not allowed to tell."

"Is it really all that terrible?"

She nodded and said no more.

"You can tell me," I insisted.

But she shook her head. "Actually, I can't. It's not mine to tell."

"So frustrating." I went to the window and Mrs. Morris was below, reaching up, attempting to knot the broken clothesline. Did everyone have a secret that caused them pain? The thin rope fell, but she bent to grab it, stretched upward, and tried again.

All of this took place in my morning before Charlie. Sometimes life is a heart filled to the brim. So I went wandering, and of all places, I found my way to the church.

Reverend Morris had given me a key to the side door, to practice the organ or conduct choir rehearsal. That Saturday the door was already open. I hadn't been there since Wednesday, so I knew I was not to blame. But that was only part of my concern.

I peered around in the gloom, but no one was inside. In the nave, I called loud and plain: "Hello?" It reverberated in the stone chamber. "Anybody here?"

When there was no answer, I decided someone had simply forgotten to lock up. Perhaps the minister, perhaps Mrs. Sanchez—the lovely local woman who dusted the stone floors every Friday. Often I'd heard her singing to herself, a soprano high and light, but could not convince her to join the choir. Whenever I asked, she ducked her head shyly and redoubled her stroking of the floor with the silent dust mop.

I switched on the organ, pulling a few stops into action, and heard a new cipher. Already I'd had to forgo one manual, thanks to an A-flat key that would not stop playing, whether I touched it or not. Now there was one in the second manual, G above middle C. So not only were two keyboards broken, but the notes were dissonant with each other. If the ciphers started up in the middle of a song, together they would ruin it.

I changed stops to silence both manuals, and confined myself to the remaining one. Normally I like to make contrasts with the stops, for example giving a background chord in reeds, while the melody plays in a high, clear flute. With one manual, there could be only one sound. It would be like playing a violin with one string: You might get all the notes, but reaching them would have you running up and down the neck all day.

I felt at a particular disadvantage because I wanted to work on the Bach toccata. Someday I might apply to Oberlin again, and I ought to keep ready. I opened the sheet music, checked my posture, and began.

The opening was an announcement, a trumpet declaring the arrival of a king. Next, the melody was doubled with another octave. But in a few bars, the piece became complex, layered, and Bach's brilliance took over. Intervals I'd never encountered anywhere else not only happened often, but made sense and propelled the music in new directions. Too soon I reached the difficult fugue passage in the middle. The coda at the end was a madness of tempo changes, but the fugue was where I stalled. Nearly all of it was in sixteenth notes. I dropped to half tempo, I tried one hand at a time, I closed my eyes and envisioned the correct motions. No dice. I dropped to quarter tempo, as though the fugue were a dirge, a funeral march. Suddenly there emerged a song of sorrow, a mourning that Bach had hidden beneath the clip-right-along version. The more I played that passage at quarter speed, the more I imagined a man in 1700s Germany, hugely successful yes, but still someone who knew something about sadness.

Naturally I felt that same emotion welling in me. There was no hiding from it. My eyes teared up, and I lifted my hands from the keys.

"Thank God," I heard, and jumped in my seat.

"Hello?" I called out. "Who's here?"

"Reverend Morris." His voice boomed from the balcony. "No need to worry."

"I thought I was alone."

"That last passage was quite moving." Loud as ever, even in an empty church.

"Thank you. It's so difficult, I have to play it slowly."

At first he did not respond. I saw him moving from one side of the balcony to the other, before he came to the railing. "You witnessed my tantrum this morning."

"It wasn't my intention, sir."

"You could have held pillows over your ears and still heard it."

It felt strange to have so personal a conversation shouted back and forth between the ends of a church. "It's between you and Mrs. Morris and none of my business."

Again he did not answer right away.

"Whatever it is, I hope the pain lessens for you over time."

"No," he barked. "I do not hope that. It would mean that my love for my son had diminished. It would mean that his sacrifice had lost its power to scour the soul."

This time I was the one who didn't answer. His son? His sacrifice?

"I cannot promise that I will never lose my temper again," he continued, the volume a trifle lower. "But your presence here has given my wife a break and me a bit of solace. I do not want you to leave. So I can promise you that at least I will try."

"It had never occurred to me to leave."

Well. He let that one echo around for a bit. He sat down, in the last row of the balcony, and then he knelt.

I closed the sheet music and made my way back outside. That church was full to the brim of things I did not understand. Oh, Charlie, it was April, where were you? I found a bench, watching the pigeons strut and coo, and waited for my life to begin.

When Charlie stepped off I was standing there, in people's way I suppose, but I did not care. I did not want him to spend one second searching for me. Before he had come all the way down the steps, I was moving—arms around his neck, kisses on his face.

"Brenda," he chuckled. "I'm blocking everyone."

I pulled back, still holding one of his arms, drawing him away from the crowd and down the sidewalk. Then I kissed him on the mouth.

Now I had smooched my fair share over the years, I make no apology for it. The boys were heading to war, or home on leave, and desperate for a little female touch. Nor did I mind, thank you. I knew tall, short, fat, and thin, good kissers and bad. You never knew how it would be with someone, no predicting till you were actually lips to lips.

But kissing Charlie was of a different order. I knew it then, I marvel at it now. The chemistry, the way he defied my ideas of manliness right up to the second our lips touched. Then he was the full ticket, and a ride in a jalopy too. When Charlie kissed me, I felt like I was falling, and the only answer was to hold on tight and keep kissing.

My letter had melted Charlie, and now he was giving me another chance. There in his embrace I promised myself, the world, the sky: I will not hurt this man again. I will not hurt this man again.

Here is the thing you learn when you don't interrupt, when you're not perpetually barging in on someone's ideas and speech: they finish their sentences just fine, and their thoughts are not weaker for reaching completion. I spent those hours with Charlie genuinely listening for what felt like the first time in my life. When I answered him, I was as opinionated as ever, but not so brash, not quite so certain. He did not have to play defense. I think I could feel him begin to relax.

Also I could not take my hands off him. Touching was like being fed. We spoke in low voices, almost whispers, and we ambled for hours, keeping to the shady sides of the street. We saw marigolds, and paintbrushes, and a kind of daisy that grew in clumps low to the ground. Had the people of Santa Fe planted a path for us? It felt that way.

And as long as I kept my restraint, Charlie opened.

"It's a kind of weapon we're building," he confided. "A new kind."

"Why is it difficult for you to participate?"

"Imagine a gun that you can shoot, but not aim. Maybe its bullets knock out an entire foreign battalion. Or maybe it will kill all the babies in an orphanage."

"But you're not the one firing it, are you?"

He shook his head. "I make a minor component. Which is also a crucial one."

"Well." I stayed close with him, thinking about what I was going to say before I said it. "The people shooting it are on our side, right?"

He nodded. "Very much so."

"Then we have to trust them, Charlie. You can do your part, and know that you are helping the war effort in a way that you know best. Then you can be done with it, and let them do their part in a way that they know best."

"Quite a few people on The Hill feel as you do."

"But you don't."

We kept walking, in a city that seemed strangely deserted. Where was everyone? At one point we turned onto a lane bordered with forsythia, one whole flank of the road a riot of flowers. Charlie paused by one of the bushes, the yellow sprays dangling toward us as if wanting to be touched. He brushed his hand against a branch, making it swing. "That Bach piece you've been working on. Imagine if you had a chance to play it on the organ Bach himself used, the one he composed it on. You're outside the cathedral, and you can hear it playing. Not much would stop you from getting inside and having a try, right?"

"It would be the dream of a lifetime."

"That's where the fellows are with this weapon. They are dying to get inside the church. In fact, they want to be the first ones in."

"But not you."

He smiled. "But not me."

I reached into the bush and pulled at a stem of forsythia. It didn't give easily, but I worked it back and forth until it snapped free, and then I gave it to him.

"Brenda. We shouldn't take—"

"Don't worry," I reassured him. "I planted this whole street here, last fall, so that we could walk here today. No one will mind."

We had a late-afternoon meal, enchiladas sharp with spice. While I'd grown accustomed to the local food, it was obvious Charlie had not been eating it. After an especially hot bite, his face reddened and he glugged down water. Afterward we meandered, wasting minutes like a millionaire dropping pennies. We kept time by the church bells tolling the hour, no more exact than that. Still, I felt a knot in my belly when they rang seven, his bus leaving at quarter after. As we rounded a corner onto East Palace, it was already idling in place. Boys with suitcases climbed aboard.

"More arrivals for The Hill?" I asked.

"They never stop coming."

There was a calm between us, a mending of our affections. Until

I saw something out of place: Lizzie, her hair unkempt, running up the street. I grabbed Charlie's arm, as if to brace myself.

"There you are," Lizzie said. She was panting.

"What is it?" Charlie asked. "What's the matter?"

"Reverend Morris needs you right away. The memorial begins at seven thirty."

"Memorial? We don't have any funerals this week."

"You don't know?" Lizzie's eyes went wide. "It's been all over the radio."

"What happened?" Charlie said. His tone was dark, as if he already understood.

"The president's dead," Lizzie said.

"What?" I shook my head. "That's impossible."

"Roosevelt died of a stroke. Truman is president, and nobody knows who he is."

Charlie flopped his hands against his sides. "Now everything is up in the air."

"Come right away, will you, kid? The Morrises are on the warpath."

"Tell them I'll go straight to the church."

"Good to see you again, Charlie," Lizzie said, trotting off.

The last people were boarding the bus. Charlie glanced their way. "I should go."

"Me too." But I grabbed both of his arms at the elbow, holding on. "Do you still think I should be a man, Brenda?"

That again. I had to be honest. "More than ever."

Charlie handed me the forsythia bough. Then he turned and took his place in line. I stood waiting, ready to wave the flowers and blow him a kiss at the perfect moment. But it never came: when he climbed up into that bus, Charlie did not look back.

34.

THE BARRACKS WAS IN an uproar. Boys were yelling at one another, arguing, a few came to shoves.

"I am willing to bet you," an Electronics technician bellowed, "I will bet anyone here that Truman does not know we exist."

"Don't be stupid," a Chemistry guy snapped. "You have no way of knowing what he does and doesn't know."

"You wanna bet me?" The first boy charged up the aisle, hand out to shake on the wager. "You wanna bet?"

"We overlooked something massive," Giles said in normal tones, yet it silenced the whole room. "Of all the variables we've been considering—thousands of them—FDR dying was nowhere on the list. That's a fairly gigantic thing to miss."

"Well, the horse already run off," Monroe said from his bunk, where he lay with his hands behind his head. "What in hell do we do about it now?"

Giles stood, stretching as though his back hurt. "Some of us need to go somewhere, away from the Gadget mission, and see if we can think of anything else that goddamn important that we completely missed."

He marched out of the place, which remained silent for half a minute, before the technician from Chemistry said, "What if they shut us down?"

"What if they want to use the Gadget right away?" the Electronics guy yelled.

And the top-volume argument picked right back up again.

Charlie remained on his bunk, petting Midnight—who raised her head to make him scratch under her chin.

Business as usual, that was the order in the following morning's memo. "Our enemies may see this interval of political transition as a moment of weakness. But we know that the peaceful succession of leadership is a hallmark of American democracy. The military remains fully engaged, with a stable chain of command, which includes all work here on The Hill. Reckless rumors to the contrary, orders are to stick to your knitting, and continue with business as usual."

The memo would have carried greater weight, the boys agreed in the mess hall that morning, had it been signed.

"There's no names at the bottom," one fellow said.

"No authorizing office identified at the top either," another replied.

Charlie thought the memo created more suspicion than it allayed. Besides, the day was anything but business as usual when he arrived in his tech area, and found a man sitting in his chair. "Hello, Charlie."

It was his professor John Simmons, all the way from Chicago. He gave that same trademark smile that had won over so many young mathematicians eighteen months ago. But Charlie saw something different upon seeing it this time—not warmth and fellowship, but calculation and manipulation, and it stopped him halfway to his desk.

"Uncle John. What brings you to The Hill?"

"Well, I expected to hear a hello, first." He rose and held out his hand.

Charlie shook it, but warily. "Of course. Pardon me. Hello."

Uncle John released his grip and turned to the table where Charlie's latest assembly effort lay splayed on large sheets of plywood. "You've come a long way since the Dungeon, I see."

Charlie inched up to his side. "What is Beasley up to these days?"

The professor's face darkened. "It's none of your business." Then the smile returned, winsome and bright. "Nothing like this work here, I can tell you that."

Charlie found himself wondering: Had the man always been a phony, only now he was somehow able to see it? Or had his uncle's warmth been sincere, until the war had tainted it?

There was a long silence, and as always when he did not understand a situation, Charlie kept quiet. But Uncle John said nothing, surveying the wires and switches before him, while the moment stretched longer and grew more awkward.

"Back in Chicago," Charlie said at last, "I was hard pressed to build one device. Now I construct whole arrays. This circuit here, if you can believe it, controls—"

"Twenty-four detonators."

Charlie caught himself. "Twenty-four, yes, sir."

"You know, son." The professor crossed his arms, casual as could be. "You seem to have found yourself right in the bull's-eye of this project."

"I don't know about that, sir. I just—"

"No point being humble," he interrupted again. "I've been briefed."

"Yes, sir."

"Some very senior fellows asked me to fly down from Chicago just to see you. It's rare that a pawn determines the checkmate." He smiled. "I hear they call you 'Trigger.'"

"Not so much to my face."

"It fits, if you ask me. But only." The smile vanished again. The man turned his warmth on and off like a lamp. "Only if the things you build actually work."

Suddenly Charlie knew why his uncle was there, and what this conversation was intended to accomplish.

"Before me," Charlie said, "no one had ever built a switch with more than eight detonators. I have managed to set one new standard after another."

"All the way up to twenty-three."

"Do you know how difficult it is to make two things happen at exactly the same time? Much less twenty-four things?"

At that Simmons turned to face Charlie. He tilted his head to one side as if he was about to tell a story—maybe a nostalgic one from Thanksgiving years ago, or one about an old friend from school days. Yet Charlie set his stance as if to dodge a punch.

"I don't know about you, but in these last few months I have really come to hate war. I've known too many people who died, or had loved ones die. We've won great victories, but the enemy remains as dangerous and determined as ever. It's ugly. Very ugly. Nothing would make me happier than to see the world at peace."

"I agree completely, sir."

"Do you really? Because it seems like you are standing in the way. The pawn has become an obstacle. Not only to ending this war, but ending all war. *All* war, Charlie."

"I'm not sure I follow you, Uncle John."

The professor leaned over the table, opened an assembly, and began flipping its switch on and off. Charlie raised a hand toward him, but the switching continued.

"Excuse me, sir," he said at last, "but that piece took ten hours to build."

"What's that?"

Charlie pointed. "It has to be ready for testing in two days. The whole assembly."

Simmons closed the switch without apology, and began to pace at the end of the table. "What does it mean to be at war, Charlie?"

"A friend of mine here says war is when someone is shooting at you."

"By that measure, you are not at war, are you?"

Charlie shook his head. "No, sir."

"Well, I *am*." He was not smiling anymore. "My definition of war is when a government slaughters law-abiding citizens, when it invades peaceful neighboring nations." His voice rose, and he paced faster. "When it preaches a gospel of the state crushing individuals and their freedoms, when it attacks my country, when it kills our boys. Then, Charlie, then I am at war sure as hell. And I will be at war until that government and its leaders and its entire goddamn idea is wiped from the earth."

By the end, Simmons was shouting. Charlie stood perfectly still. His uncle was not trying to persuade him. This was something else, and Charlie waited to see what it would be.

Meanwhile, the professor had stopped pacing. "Look at what's happened to me. A mathematician, calling for blood." He shook his head. "I'm not ashamed though. That is how important this project has become."

Simmons arrived at a chair Charlie had stood on, the day before, to add a piece to the middle of the assembly. Simmons turned the chair around and straddled the seat, forearms resting on the chair back.

"Imagine a day that brings an end to armed conflict. No longer will madmen be tolerated when they choose to make war. Would the next Hitler dare smash the ghettos of Poland, murder those innocent people, start years of terror and waste, if he knew we possess a weapon to obliterate not only him, but his entire capital city?"

"I hadn't considered—"

"Would the emperor of Japan attack Pearl Harbor, if he knew the extinction of his family's bloodline, and those of a million other residents of Tokyo, is only a few hours of air travel away? No, those men would never attempt such terrible things again."

"Do you really think so, Uncle?"

"The Gadget will do much more than deliver victory today, Charlie. Our power to annihilate will bring an end to war."

Charlie wandered to his desk, the array of papers, calculations, and designs. He thumbed the bar of a slide rule out and back.

"Everyone here is depending on you," Simmons persisted. "But that's not the real story. The future of mankind is depending on you too."

"I am the wrong guy to wager the future of mankind on."

"Then look at it this way. You are in debt. You owe a working detonator to your nation, after all the opportunities it's given you. Hell, son. You owe me."

Charlie pushed a sheet of paper aside. "What if I told you that I have not been stuck at twenty-three detonators on purpose? What if it really is that difficult to build?"

"You forget, Charlie. We're family. The same blood in our veins." Simmons stood, turning the chair right side around. "If you say you can't build it, I don't believe you."

And with one last flash of a smile, he marched out of the room.

The test the next day did not show twenty-three detonators working. Instead it was twenty-two. Charlie suspected the component his uncle had touched was the one that misfired, but he had no proof. Bronsky came by his desk after the test to say that David Horn would begin work the following day, in his own lab.

"One way or other, Fishk," he seethed, "we are have twenty-four soon."

Charlie worked nearly every waking hour, leaving the lab only for meals, or refills of coffee till his stomach burned. He stopped going to the barracks, sleeping instead under his desk like the senior scientists.

The exception was Saturdays. Then he caught the early bus to Santa Fe. A sign outside the last gate read: "Are you continuing to protect information?" and Charlie tried to stay awake till the bus passed it. Usually he failed, and slept the whole way down. Those days with Brenda flew past, whether they had plans to visit an adobe village, or simply take a stroll. She was kinder then, softer. Once she took him to her church so he could hear the organ, which had fine tone but many mechanical problems.

Nonetheless Brenda played the Bach Toccata and Fugue in D Minor with high proficiency, though after the fugue part he lost his fight with exhaustion. At the end, instead of applause Brenda was surprised by silence. When she found Charlie stretched out on a pew, sound asleep, she did not snap at him, or say he had insulted her playing. Instead she lifted his head to rest it in her lap, and sat with him there till the bells tolled seven, which meant it was time to catch the bus up to The Hill.

Back inside the fence, he skipped dinner and went straight to his desk.

That month showed a world in convulsions. Each new development stirred Charlie's hopes—and fervent discussions in the barracks—over whether the Gadget would be needed. Not two weeks into Truman's presidency, Mussolini and his mistress were executed, their corpses hung upside down in public in Milan. The next day, American forces liberated the camp at Dachau. Everyone saw the photos of skeletal men, women, and children. Also that day, Hitler married Eva Braun—their love like a dark flower, blooming from all the spilled blood. What did it portend?

The answer came in the papers of May 1: Hitler and his bride had committed suicide. A day later, after murdering their six children, Chancellor Goebbels and his wife also killed themselves. Then a thousand Germans committed mass suicide in Demmin.

"By their own hands," Giles declared at the bonfire that night. "By their own hands they set us free. There's no need for the Gadget. Surrender is imminent."

"It don't say much good about my morals," Monroe said, pausing to swig from a bottle. "But damn those boys make me happy, doing our job for us."

Sparks rose in the spring twilight, climbing, lost in the stars overhead.

"I don't care if our work amounts to nothing," Charlie said. "If we don't have to finish, and all those innocent people—"

"Mister Charlie?" Monroe said. "You're half a mile ahead of yourself. Stop talking and start drinking."

Charlie shook the length of his body, like a dog fresh out of a pond. He reached for the bottle. "I believe I will."

3 5 .

FOR THE FIRST TIME, when Charlie stepped off the bus I was not there to greet him.

I can still imagine it: the other passengers filing off, a few heading into the government offices, others meandering one way or another. He'd be standing alone.

That image made me give up at last. The organ had too many problems. I switched it off and headed for East Palace Avenue. At some point I'd have to tell Reverend Morris, before the wedding at three o'clock: there would be no music that day.

Charlie looked hungry, exhausted—until he saw me. Then he rose from the bench and held his arms wide and I swear I felt warmth from him all the way across the street.

"What's the matter?" he said before I had reached him. "Something is wrong."

"Oh, Charlie." I ran into his arms. "I'm sorry I kept you waiting."

He pulled me close. "Brenda, that's the way of wartime. Like me making you wait for me all week. I live for the day we do not have to wait anymore."

"I'm afraid it won't be today."

"Tell me what's wrong."

"The organ," I said. "There's a cipher in every manual now. All three. If I can't have at least one working properly, I can't possibly play the wedding this afternoon."

"What can I do?"

"You fixed that one in my parents' basement."

"That was basic stuff, Brenda. Split pipes."

"Charlie, I have nowhere else to turn."

The silence that followed was unique. Somehow that single sentence changed him, altered Charlie's whole relationship to me. For the first time, I was asking him for help. Unguarded, unvarnished, I needed him, and he recognized it.

"Let's take a look," he said. "Maybe we can get one of those ciphers to quit."

An hour later, he had abandoned that idea. Whenever I opened a stop, on any of the three keyboards, a random note would begin playing on its own.

"It's a different note on each manual," Charlie called from beneath the console. His legs stuck out like a mechanic's under a car. "You have three separate problems."

"You're not making me feel much better."

"I don't know how you've been able to play this instrument." He slid out, his sleeves and back covered in dust. "Let me see the music for today."

"It's typical wedding stuff. This is not the time to get appreciative—"

"What keys are the songs in? Maybe we can try a different approach."

We spread the pages on the church floor: E major, A minor, and D major.

"Only one uses the A-flat note—that's the cipher on your first manual. So I will disconnect that key completely. It won't sound when you play it, but it only occurs"—he scanned the pages—"six times. So the gap won't be too noticeable or frequent. If you stay on that one manual, I bet you can get away with it."

"Charlie, you are a genius." I gave him a good smack on the lips.

"Now I have to figure out how to disconnect a key." He blushed a little, then slid back under the console.

* * *

Charlie sat in the balcony during the wedding. Although I made it a point not to look, I liked thinking about him up there, seeing everything, hearing my playing on the limited instrument. It was a Hispanic family, the men wore dark suits and ties, the women dressed in brights: green and yellow and red. They were a prayerful group, heads bowed often. One elderly woman wept audibly the whole service. I loved her.

The music was more than satisfactory. Granted, I could use only simple stops. But the hymns were celebratory, with a nice triumphant finale, and I bet Charlie himself could not tell where the absent A-flats belonged.

As the congregation filed out, a white-haired uncle came forward. "*Senorita*, that was wonderful," he said, bowing with great formality. "Beautiful, beautiful music."

By the time Charlie came down, I was organizing for Sunday's service.

"Your playing," he said, pausing by the front pew. "You've improved."

I put the papers aside, crossed the aisle, and planted another kiss on his lips. I am not ashamed to say it: I wanted more. I wanted him entirely. I was sick of missing him, tired of being patient, done with having our lives dictated by the war.

Meanwhile, Charlie wrapped his arms around me, and it felt like we became one person. Would another guy propose at a time like that? Right after a wedding? While kissing in a church? What would a girl say if he did?

The moment passed, we released each other. Not five seconds later, Reverend Morris came back down the aisle.

"Lovely families," he boomed. "Well done, Brenda."

"Reverend Morris, this is Charlie Fish. He's . . . an organ repairman."

"Is that right?"

"Yes, sir," Charlie said. "I managed to quiet one cipher for the service today. But this instrument needs considerable work."

"It certainly does." The minister nodded. "And, Brenda, I commend you for finding him on short notice. But you might have asked what our repair budget is."

"If I may, sir," Charlie interrupted. "I'm sure we can come to terms that please you. My primary interest is in seeing this organ perform as it is capable. Particularly in the hand of a musician as skilled as Brenda Dubie."

"Is that right?" Reverend Morris said. "Do we have an ace here?"

"The ace of hearts," Charlie said. "You need an instrument that befits her talent."

"I suppose we do." The minister nodded approvingly. "Carry on, please. And I'll hold you to your word about favorable terms."

"Depend on it, sir." Charlie and Brenda wore sober faces, avoiding looking at each other.

Reverend Morris went into the sacristy to hang up his formal vestments, then gave them both a wave as he headed home for dinner. The second the side door closed behind him, Brenda and Charlie burst out laughing.

"An organ repairman?"

"It's true. An experienced one."

"Because I've now done it twice?"

"Charlie you saved me. And the wedding. I don't think the reverend could handle much of an upset right now."

"Why don't I spend a few minutes seeing if I can make any other easy fixes, and we'll save the hard stuff for another day?"

"Every person who comes to services here tomorrow will thank you."

"As long as you do, I don't care about anyone else."

I kissed him again, and we ambled back to the console. Charlie lay on his back and slid out of sight.

We stayed for hours. While he was absorbed in the work, I went to the sacristy and did push-ups. By then I was up to eleven. When I returned I noticed that the front doors remained open from the wedding, and with the sun angled lower, the light had turned to gold. I fooled with light switches till Charlie could see beneath the console. Then I sat by his legs, having found a toolbox, handing him tools as he called for them.

I had never really considered Charlie's legs before. Like the rest of him, they were skinny. But they were oddly graceful, too, like a dancer's. Whenever he stretched to reach something underneath, he had this unconscious habit of pointing his toes. It was like he was jumping, how ballerinas point their toes when they're in the air.

Every half hour or so, he would come out for a breather. Each time he emerged dustier, and dirtier, and wearing a bigger smile. "This thing has gigantic bellows," he said one time. "They could pump enough air for two of these sets of pipes."

We talked a minute more, I brought him a glass of water. He grinned the whole time like he'd just won at bingo. Then he flopped on his back and slid under again.

After the third or fourth break I realized: He was happy. Charlie was doing something that delighted him. He was humming under there, and I hadn't heard him hum since Chicago. He didn't want to break for dinner, though I heard his stomach grumbling. It pleased me to see this anxious man at ease, working but content.

This was the guy I had run around the theater with. The fella who gave me lovely gloves. Here I was, in a New Mexican version of sitting on the cellar steps. Saturday night and there was no other place I would rather be.

Eventually Charlie slid out and sat upright. "All my life," he said, completing a thought that must have started under the console, "I've believed that authority meant wisdom. That's why I obeyed it. Knowledge and prudence, based on education and experience." He wiped his hands on his trousers. "I was wrong. The Hill has convinced me. All authority actually means is power."

I wanted to hear more, but something had occurred to me: it had been a long time since I heard any churches toll the hour. "Charlie," I said, "what time does the last bus leave for Los Alamos?"

"Eleven. We'd better get moving." As he stood, he glanced at his wristwatch. And deflated entirely. "Brenda."

"What time is it?"

"Twenty past the last bus."

In a way I was pleased. It was an echo of the night in my father's workshop. I considered the tools scattered around me. "My fault. I should have been keeping track."

"Forget who's to blame. What do we do?"

"A hotel?"

"I only brought enough money for dinner."

I had a wrench in one hand, needle-nose pliers in the other. I dropped them in the toolbox with a clatter. "I'm sorry, Charlie."

"Enough of that." He squatted to bring his face level with mine. "No one put anyone in charge of the clock. Besides, now you're in good shape for tomorrow."

Collecting the other tools, I put them one by one into the box. When I'd finished, I raised my eyes and he was still squatting there. "I don't know what to do," I said.

"Why don't we try the East Palace offices? It can't be the first time this ever happened."

So I locked up the church and we hurried across town. The whole way, I knew what the answer would be. The iron gate was closed, no lights on, no one home.

An idea fluttered inside me, disobedient and exciting. It had come to me on the way over, and there by the iron gate it had me by the leg.

"Well," Charlie said. "We are in a bit of a pickle. Or I am, anyway."

My idea was full of risk: my housing, my job, my reputation. But it did not feel like temptation, it felt like opportunity. I could not imagine going through with it, much less convincing Charlie.

I put both hands flat on his chest. He seemed so skinny. Sometimes I forgot.

Out of nowhere I remembered a time at my aunt's place in Wisconsin, the summer I was eleven or twelve, and we went to a beach house that had a high dive. All my cousins were scrambling up the ladder and throwing themselves off. But I hung back, scared of the height. Even Bonnie, the eight-year-old, inched her way out and jumped from the platform.

"Go on, Brenda," my mother said, behind a fog of cigarette smoke. "A little courage won't kill you."

Funny how one sentence can reverberate through the whole rest of your life.

"Why don't you walk me home," I said to Charlie, "and we'll see what comes up?"

Which was how we wound up outside the boardinghouse, a quarter moon overhead and heading west. I whispered to Charlie. "Take off your shoes."

"Excuse me?"

"Socks too. And do exactly as I say."

Charlie chuckled. "Haven't you trained me to do that already?"

I put a finger to my lips. As soon as he was barefoot, I eased the door open.

"Really?" he whispered.

"A little courage won't kill you."

Today I am proud of that girl, and her boldness. Life has many high-dive moments, and some turn out to be belly flops. But Charlie was not sleeping in some park or hideaway, not if I could help it. Lizzie had been smart enough—or coconspirator enough—to switch off the light at the top of the stairs. That meant we climbed slowly, in the dark, every creak amplified.

At the top, I took Charlie's hand and led him to my room. The worst of it was over, and we could see well enough by the light of the moon. Closing the door, I had him sit on the narrow bed. The mattress creaked under his weight.

"What are we doing?" he whispered.

I leaned close, my lips an inch from his ear. "You are sleeping here."

He shook his head no, but I nodded and whispered again, "You can stay till it's almost light. No hanky-panky."

He gave me a look I did not understand. Pained, almost.

"Not that I haven't thought about it a hundred times," I added, the boldest thing I had ever said to a guy.

Charlie smiled. "A thousand times," he whispered.

"But not tonight," I repeated. Then I kissed his forehead. "I'm going to brush my teeth. You get comfortable."

When I returned, Charlie had stretched himself out on top of the covers and snug to the wall, leaving two-thirds of the bed for me. I grabbed his toes with both hands. "Hello, Charlie's feet." Then I made a spiral with my finger, so he turned away as I slipped out of my clothes and into a nightgown.

I lay down as gently as if I were made of eggshells. He curled around me as softly as if he were made of glass. The mattress sagged. We had no choice but to touch.

"Sweet dreams," I said, kissing his knuckles.

"You too, Brenda," Charlie whispered, his lips against my shoulder.

Moonlight poured through the open window, onto the floor like a blue-white spill.

That night was an agony. I remember it all these years later, clear as if I'd cut my finger this morning. I had just turned twenty-one, for heaven's sake, and Charlie was even younger. We had no experience with the opposite sex beyond kisses and hugs. And here we were, touching the length of our lovely bodies. Charlie's feet tucked up beneath my feet, his knees nestled behind mine, his hips snug to my rump like I was sitting in his lap. Longing filled me, top to bottom and hot at the core. I pressed his wrist to the bone between my breasts, and we lay with eyes wide.

At first it was a bath of pleasure. Warmth, and comfort, and melting into each other. Charlie smelled like dust from the organ repairs, but also leather somehow. Of course I wondered how I smelled to him too. An hour passed, I heard the church bells, and I was no nearer to sleep than when we'd put the church's toolbox away. We snuggled closer, but it only made things worse. Another hour. Another.

I ached for him. There is no other way to put it. I craved Charlie Fish in every cell. I experienced the physical pull that in the moment seemed naughty and wrong, but that I now know to be natural and right. It was a delicious yearning, and I wondered if Charlie was feeling the same torment.

He let out a huge sigh. Not the sound of a sleeping man, not deep or easy, but wide awake. That sigh contained all the hunger I felt, perhaps more. With that, I gave up on trying to sleep, pressed myself back against him, and decided to let the night pass under that powerful, unfulfilled spell.

There comes a day in the life of many women when the man they love is gone for one reason or another, and she would trade her best days now for her worst days before. That's me. Take the next month of my life, and I would gladly exchange it for that moment, Charlie's healthy young man's sigh, and I the woman in his arms for as long as the night would last.

AT DAWN HE WOKE with a start. Brenda was sound asleep, her face relaxed, her breasts supple under the nightgown, her legs tangled in his. Charlie moved with great care, trying not to wake her. When he rose the mattress squeaked in relief, but Brenda only rolled onto her other side, and he stood studying the curve of her back.

Then he tucked his socks into his shoes and tiptoed out. At the landing, the stairs seemed long and exposed, with windows opening into the house proper. Spotting the fire escape stairs, he climbed out the open window. Pigeons startled away at his appearance, cooing, flying out over the street.

It was a clear morning, early May, pale light pearly in the east. Charlie kept to the edge of each step to prevent creaking, and made it down without undue noise.

He tiptoed out to the sidewalk, intending to sit on the step and put on his shoes. But there was a woman by the front door, a woman in a housecoat who came down the walk to pick up the newspaper. She snapped it open and scanned the front page. Whatever she saw froze her in place.

Charlie spun on his bare heel and charged in the other direction, though it meant heading away from the bus. Shoes still in hand when he reached the corner, he glanced back. The woman had not moved. She was not reading the news, though. She was staring at him. Her face was streaked with tears.

* * *

Soon enough Charlie reached East Palace Avenue. As always, a group was gathered by the bench, but the early passengers were different from his usual afternoon or evening trips. They were all Latino—the cleaning help, the kitchen staff. They smiled and moved their things to make room for him.

"*Gracias*," he said, but not with confidence.

The woman in the office who had greeted Charlie when he'd first arrived in Santa Fe was now unlocking the iron gates. As always, the elfin boy hovered nearby, holding her coffee, taking the keys when she'd finished. She spied Charlie and said something to the boy, who nodded emphatically and disappeared into the offices.

Charlie would gladly have sat with the locals. But he'd been working under that organ for hours, hadn't showered, and suspected he was more than a little ripe. He leaned against the building and closed his eyes.

Instantly he wished he was back in bed with Brenda. They had been so warm together, so easily affectionate with their pretzeled limbs. He'd been excited by her body nearly all night too. He wondered if she'd noticed. Should he be embarrassed or proud?

"My mother thought you'd want to see this," a voice said. Charlie opened his eyes and the boy was holding a newspaper toward him.

But Charlie had been enjoying his reverie. "Thank you, but I'm fine."

The boy seemed confused, and held the paper forward again.

"All right," Charlie said. "Thanks very much."

"Very good." The boy ran with swinging arms back into the office.

Charlie leaned against the building again, wishing he knew what time the first bus departed. With no special interest or attention, he unfolded the newspaper.

GERMANY SURRENDERS. WAR IN EUROPE OVER.

Charlie lifted his head. The workers murmured in conversation, or napped. No one was in the street, no one celebrating. Didn't anyone know?

General Alfred Jodl, representing the German High Command, signed an unconditional surrender in General Eisenhower's headquarters, a schoolhouse in Reims, France, to take effect today. The successor to Adolf Hitler, German Chancellor and President Karl Donitz, has ordered all troops to lay down their arms. President Truman will address the nation later today.

The implications were so many and so vast, Charlie nearly fell over. What would he do in peacetime? Where would he live, and doing what job? Would Brenda stay here or return to Chicago? Might he actually get to see his family in Massachusetts again?

Maybe this was why the woman in the housecoat had been crying. Maybe someone she loved would be coming home.

Then another possibility struck Charlie: He might not have to finish the detonators. America might not need to use the Gadget. With victory, thousands of innocent lives might be saved. He lifted the newspaper higher so that none of the friendly locals could see him weep.

On the ride to Los Alamos, he read every word in that paper. There were celebrations in all the major cities, where the news arrived first. Photos showed crowds thronging the streets in joy. Churches were filled too. He imagined Brenda would be playing in the next few hours, and he was glad he had left the organ at least minimally functioning. The Germans had stopped fighting on all fronts, from Prussia to Prague to their own cities. High-ranking officials from America, Russia, and France had accepted the surrender. It was real. All wonderfully real.

The interior pages had other news, however. Thirty-seven days into the battle of Okinawa, US troops were making progress—sinking seven ships and controlling more of the island. But the fight was brutal. The Japanese had resorted to using child soldiers. The hills of the island were honeycombed with tunnels.

He crumpled the paper in his lap. Peace was still far away. No denying it, the news from Europe was exhilarating. Normal life would be possible again someday. Accustomed by now to the curves and ruts of the bus ride to The Hill, Charlie stared out at the view and wondered what would become of him when the last battle had ended.

The guards at the gate behaved like any other day: as friendly as porcupines, growling to see everyone's passes, grunting as they handed them back. Choir members were arriving at Fuller Lodge as usual, to practice before Sunday services. In fact, nothing on The Hill seemed different. Did they not know?

Charlie decided it would be better to arrive late to rehearsal, but in fresh clothes and having brushed his teeth, so he jogged across campus to the barracks. Behind the building the previous night's bonfire still smoldered, smoke spiraling into clear blue sky. The scent drew Charlie, and he saw one person still tending the coals.

"Look what the dog drug up," Monroe said, wearing a big goofy smile. "Right on time for the celebration."

"Where is everyone?" Charlie asked. "Why aren't there trumpets playing and people raising the roof?"

"Business as usual, Mister Charlie. A memo's already done gone out."

"But the people we were preparing to bomb have surrendered."

"Don't I know it." Monroe poked at the coals with a charred stick. "Apparently they's another enemy though. Only a rumor at this point, but the signs are promising."

"We're already firebombing the Japanese into extinction. This was always about beating the Germans."

"Well." Monroe wiped his mouth on his sleeve. "You try telling that to Oppie."

Charlie paced beside the fire. "You mean to say we should keep on working?"

Monroe shrugged. "More people in labs right now than any Sunday I can recollect." He spat into the coals, which hissed in reply. "What a species we are, right? Walking puzzles with fancy clothes on."

Charlie turned away, but stopped. "Have you seen Midnight lately?"

"The hour? Thanks to insomnia, every dang day. The cat? Not in a while."

"Me either." When Charlie entered the barracks, instead of the usual Sunday quiet of guys sleeping in, writing letters, folding laundry, the place was empty. He paused at the door, taking it in. Then he remembered he had choir practice. Hurrying to his locker, he pulled out a change of clothes. Time to sing some hymns.

LIZZIE AND I DID not get drunk immediately after we heard about the German surrender. First there was worship.

It began at breakfast, when Reverend Morris led us in prayers of thanksgiving. His voice choked every so often, as if someone had a rope around his neck, and whenever he started to think about all the lives lost, that person would squeeze the rope tighter. Mrs. Morris kept her chin raised, like her head was a glass of water filled past the brim, and leaning in any direction would cause something precious to spill.

That didn't keep the woman from darting her eyes at me whenever a prayer finished. If Charlie got out without me knowing or Lizzie suspecting, he certainly didn't wake the Morrises up. Still, I felt like it was tattooed on my forehead: Slept beside a man last night. Wanted him ninety-nine ways. Still thinking about it. Amen.

The surrender news arrived too late for Reverend Morris to cancel regular services, so he abbreviated them both, calling everyone back for a victory worship in the afternoon. Lizzie went back to bed before I could spill anything to her, while I headed to the church for the day.

Oh but I was sinful. Anytime I wasn't playing the organ or conducting the choir, I was thinking about Charlie, and how it had felt to have him pressed against me all night, especially when we were half-asleep and I could feel his excited manhood against my thigh, my arousal so strong it made me ache. Who knew that humans contained electricity? It was like he'd found a switch inside me, and I hadn't even known it was there until he turned it on.

Nobody noticed, not even when I missed notes during the meditation piece. The church felt giddy, a congregation that wanted not to sit and pray, but to whoop and cheer and gulp some gin.

Between hymns, I thought about what the surrender might mean. My father, Frank, Lizzie's husband, Charlie—all those people might be done with war work. Even Chris, who by then only crossed my mind when my conscience was after me. I hoped he'd come through the war intact, and could start his life again without the likes of me in his way.

Beyond that, everything was guesswork. I knew as I sat there, I would not jump a train back to Chicago without a burning reason. I would not reapply to conservatories until my father came home. I would stay in New Mexico as long as Charlie did.

For the afternoon service, the church was packed to the rafters. I was playing on a single manual, with no piano for backup if that A-flat cipher started up again. Walking a musical tightrope. I decided to warn the choir, so if the instrument failed I would give them a note from my tuning mouth harp, and they would finish a capella.

But Charlie's repairs held, and the music went as smoothly as it could. There was one odd thing: The organ notes did not sound at the same volume anymore. Certain notes boomed and others barely chirped. Fortunately, no one else noticed.

Reverend Morris was louder than ever that day. After inviting community leaders from the congregation to read scripture—Psalms about the Lord's victories, the Old Testament about the warlike power of His wrath—the minister came to the pulpit. Unfolding his notes, he delivered the sermon in a sustained shout.

"Mighty," he cried. "Mighty is the power of righteousness. Awesome is the hammer of justice. Tireless is the sword of vengeance."

The man carried on like I'd never heard him before, full bore and top volume. It did not feel that we were celebrating peace. More like we should stomp on our enemies and tear down their cities. Which I guessed we had pretty much done already.

As he gathered steam, Reverend Morris's face turned red, he pounded the lectern with his fist, he broke into a sweat. I was closest to him, of course, sitting below the pulpit. So maybe I was the only one to know that he was also weeping. It stopped my naughty daydreams, all right. His voice never wavered, though, not the least tremble.

"Damnation," he shouted. "Let heaven rain damnation on those who instigate war and slaughter the innocent. Let judgment deliver them to the eternal fires of hell."

But his eyes gave him away.

Only at the end did the minister diminish. His voice made him do it. He croaked, and coughed, and eventually paused. He did that tic with his neck.

"People in this community have lost loved ones in the conflict," he said in a hoarse hush. "People in this church right now. Some we know about, others keep their sorrow private. There is nothing wrong with keeping sorrow private."

Reverend Morris scanned up and down the pews, and then he gripped the lectern with both hands. "It is possible that . . . for some of these people . . . the enormity of their loss may have caused them to question their faith."

The place was quiet as if it had been empty. I wanted to sit back, to prevent my hands from accidentally hitting a note in all that silence, but I was afraid to move.

"Now we know," he continued. "Now we know that doing God's will, which is to bring peace to the world, requires sacrifice. My prayer for this congregation today, and for every person whose loved one made that sacrifice, is that victory renews your faith. May peace—"

He choked up again, and had to stop. I waited, everyone waited, while Reverend Morris took as long as he needed. I felt the pressure on him, what a time like this demanded of a preacher. If he had given me the least look, one eye blinked in my direction, I would immediately have begun playing a hymn.

But he never so much as glanced. Instead he took a deep breath, and let it go. I could feel half the room exhale with him. "May peace make it possible for you to believe in God again."

Then the minister nodded to me, like always after a sermon, and I played a two-minute meditation piece. He asked us to stand, and the congregation joined the choir in singing "A Mighty Fortress Is Our God."

Instead of the usual procession up the aisle, so he could shake people's hands on their way out, or receive their hugs, when the song ended Reverend Morris rushed away to the sacristy where—from my bench I was the only person who could see this—he ran straight into the arms of his waiting wife. She held him with her eyes tightly closed. Her hands were balled into fists.

I made some mistakes playing that last hymn. And after that day, Reverend Morris never raised his voice again.

Later that afternoon Lizzie arrived in the doorway of my room and shook a brown paper bag at me. "We have celebrating to do. Do you have any limes?"

I'd never tasted tequila. Her bottle was straight from Mexico, a gift from one of the domestics who'd come into her clinic with an infection and no money. But that did not improve the flavor. We drank it in shots, biting on a slice of lime after each big gulp. I kept thinking the next one would go down easier, but it didn't work.

"My husband?" Lizzie said, delaying her next shot by braiding her hair. "He has a big nose."

I laughed. "What in the world are you talking about?"

"Tim." She triangled a hand over her face. "It's practically this big. I have to lean my head to the side when we kiss."

"You are hilarious," I said.

"But you know what?" She leaned forward and whispered, "It's sexy."

"Do you never quit with the sex stuff?" I said, swatting the air.

"Wait till you're twenty-seven and married, kid."

I was about to protest as usual. But thoughts entered my head from the night before, and I kept quiet.

"He loves the smell of my hair," Lizzie continued. "When we

hug, he always burrows that big old schnozz in my noggin, and I can hear him sniffing. Taking it all in."

"Oh, sweetie."

She undid the braid and shook her hair down. Raising the glass, she threw back the shot in one gulp, chomped on the lime with her eyes squinted shut, and shuddered the length of her body. After a second, she opened her eyes again. "This war is not over till that man is home, and his face is buried in my hair, and I can hear him breathing through that fabulous big nose of his."

Lizzie held up the glass, and I knocked my knuckles against it. "Here's to big noses," I said. "And big love."

Lizzie poured me another shot, and sliced another wedge of lime.

Eventually I needed to use the john. When I stood, the tequila pounced on me, bending the walls, tilting the floor, interrupting my line of thought so much I stopped, and sat back down on the bed.

Lizzie laughed uproariously, and after a second I did too. Though if Mrs. Morris had come in right then and asked what was so funny, I doubt either of us could have begun to explain. After that, it was only a matter of time before Lizzie challenged me to a push-up contest.

"Now that the damn war is almost done, you need to be ready."

"I have things to tell you though," I said. "Big things."

"The end of the war is a big thing, kid."

"About Charlie, though."

Bottle in hand, she pointed at the floor. "No stalling."

Well, Lizzie didn't know it, but I'd been diligent. Push-ups every morning before I dressed, at the church during the day, and before bedtime. I'd made progress in secret. Also the tequila gave me confidence. I knelt, planked forward, and set out to tie my record: sixteen. But I hadn't slept much the night before, thanks to Charlie, nor eaten much breakfast, thanks to the Morrises. I began to slow at eleven.

"Not good enough," Lizzie said, squatting by my face. "Push it. Push it."

Twelve, thirteen. My arms burned. Fourteen.

"Don't you want your man to want you?" Her face was nearly as red as mine.

Fifteen. Sixteen. Slower than ice melting.

"Do it," Lizzie yelled. "Push it, Brenda."

Seventeen. I collapsed onto the floor, panting and spent. But Lizzie's face remained stern as ever.

"What?" I said. "What's wrong?"

"Nothing. It's stupid."

"It's not, I can tell." Dizzily, I sat up. "What is it, Lizzie?"

"A superstition I've had." She sucked on a used lime wedge, then winced. "Long as I did push-ups, Tim would stay alive. No matter what happened, if I kept at it, he would keep breathing. Now Germany is finished with. Maybe—" Her face softened, one pearly drop raced down her cheek. "Maybe he'll actually come home."

"No time for tears," Mrs. Morris said. Startled, we both whirled. She'd come up the stairs without our noticing. "Lizzie, your husband is on the phone."

"Timmy." She jumped up, grabbing the bedpost for balance, then hustled down the stairs. As Mrs. Morris looked after her, I tucked the tequila bottle out of sight.

"And you." She scowled from the doorway.

Did she know about Charlie? Was I about to get evicted? "Ma'am?"

Instead she nodded once, sharply, like her chin was cutting something in the air. "Good work today. The choir was on pitch." She hesitated. "Your playing also was fine."

A compliment? I was too surprised to reply. She turned and trundled down the stairs as well. I worked myself upright and staggered to the landing. "Thank you, ma'am," I called down, but she had already closed the door below.

With that, I was alone. Before the war, that was almost never so—home crowded with family, classes at school, fun with girlfriends, dates with boys. Since then I'd grown accustomed to solitude. I was changing. Even drunk in the middle of the day, I knew it. The European battles were over. I had slept all night beside Charlie. I was twenty-one, and so far from home it might as well be another planet.

The giddiness drained out of me as if I'd exhaled it. I collected the limes, washed the glass, put the bottle in Lizzie's room. Then I went back into my little monkish cell, and sat on the bed, and wondered what immense thing was going to happen next.

Charlie stepped off the bus the following Saturday into my open arms. I hadn't planned it, but I didn't care who saw. I suppose we'd both been expecting our usual awkward hello and gradual reacquaintance. Not this time. When the olive drab bus pulled into view, instead of my weekly butterflies, I felt lust. As he hugged me I planted a kiss right on his lips. And felt my hips tilt in a way they never had before, involuntarily toward him. Some boys stepping off the bus gave a cheer.

"Nice work, Trigger," one of them called.

I felt Charlie flinch, and I stepped back. "I'm sorry. Was that too much?"

He shook his head. "It was the name he called me. I hate it."

"What? Trigger?"

He seized both of my hands. "Do me a favor, Brenda? Never call me that. Not when you're angry, not as a joke, never."

"I promise, Charlie Fish." I kissed his neck. "I like your real name, anyway. It's like a big nose."

"What do you mean?"

"One of the things Lizzie likes most about her husband is his nose."

"Oh." He scanned the courtyard, people heading here and there from the bus, new arrivals climbing aboard with suitcases and travel papers. Then he put the world aside and looked at my face. "Hi."

"Hello." I snuggled against him.

"How are our organ repairs holding up?"

"Well, it's the strangest thing." I led him away from the name callers. "Not all the pipes sound the same volume anymore. Some are much louder."

Charlie nodded. "We need to do a voicing. Do you mind if I take a look at it?"

"I was hoping you would."

So, instead of the lunch I'd expected, or the smooching and caressing I'd dreamed of, we went to the church. Charlie tossed his coat over the back of a pew. Rolling up his sleeves, he came and kissed me long on the mouth. One second more and I would have glommed onto him for the rest of the day. But he turned his attention to the organ.

"What is a voicing?" I asked.

Climbing onto the wood molding behind the pulpit, Charlie peered into the pipes. "I don't know nearly enough to perform a full one. But it's a process of making the instrument fit the room, and making its parts work with one another. Giving the pipes the same volume is a basic start."

"But how do you do it? I only know Hammond organs, and they don't have pipes."

"Each one has an adjustable collar or a movable opening. But there are no half jobs. You have to do all the pipes."

I slid my dress sleeves up like he'd done with his shirt. "Ready when you are."

He smiled, and I realized how rarely Charlie smiled in those days, and how wonderful it was when a moment of lightness stole over him. We went to work.

Hours passed. The light through the church's big front windows crept across the floor as the afternoon passed. Mostly my job was to sit at the organ and play a note over and over, while Charlie did his business inside the nest of pipes—I'd peered in and it was a dusty, cobwebbed place. Little space to move, and no room for two.

I could have said the process was stultifying, a waste of my organ talents, a waste of his time. But I did not feel subservient at all. Charlie could not do the voicing without me. Likewise I needed him to make the instrument my livelihood depended on sound right.

At noon I went for sandwiches. When he came out to eat, Charlie had a dark smudge on his cheek. My impulse was to wipe it away. But I restrained myself. Too cute.

"I hope this isn't unbearably boring," he said, biting into his sandwich.

"Actually, I like it," I said. "I mean sure, it can be tedious to play a note again and again. But we're in a church, right? This feels a bit . . . well . . . sacred."

Charlie's old surprised face appeared. Like a long-lost friend. "Is that what's going on? I've been trying to figure out why this work is making me so darn happy."

"It doesn't hurt to do it together."

"Organ voicing can't be done by one person, Brenda. It takes two: one to play the note, the other to adjust it. That's the only way."

We gazed at each other. I know it was young love, and predictable. But take it from an old woman now: We had spent so many hours together being cagey, hiding our feelings, trying not to be at risk. All of that caution was finally falling away. I was happy to see Charlie happy. Today in my little apartment, I have a photo taken a few weeks later. He's standing in front of a clunky old Hudson, his face open as a book, and the grinning girl beside him is both me and not me. Brenda is the gal he's holding, yes, but so much life has happened since then, time has changed her in countless ways.

We do not get to keep anything. Best moments, worst moments, they rush by and away. So it may be corny that we stared at each other there in that church eating lunch on the floor, but we would never be those young people again, carefree despite the darkness that lay ahead. If I could freeze that instant somehow, or preserve it in amber, I would look at it a hundred times a day.

"Okay," Charlie said at last, crumpling up the waxed paper that had held his sandwich. "Better get back to work."

When he finished, I did wipe the dirt from his cheek. He watched me intently as I did it. Then he put his arm around me and we nuzzled to the front of the church.

"Brenda," he said, "I need to talk about what happened last time I was here."

"If you say anything other than that you loved sleeping with me, I will slap you."

He burst out laughing. "Pretty much the opposite. But thanks for letting me know where I stand."

"I can't stop thinking about it. The feelings are so powerful."

"Me too." He nodded. "That's why I'm sorriest about what I have to say next."

It was like he'd dropped a two-ton weight on my heart. I glanced around the churchyard, a few thirsty trees, a passing car. "What's that?"

"I'm going to do what you told me. I'm going to be a man. But it means I may not be able to see you for a while."

"Oh."

"Everyone is counting on me now."

I took a deep breath. "I can wait, Charlie. We've needed a ton of patience all through this war, both of us. I just hope it doesn't drag on."

"That's how lots of people feel," he said. "I think I'm allowed to say that they want our job done before the Pacific invasion happens."

"Lizzie's husband called last week. Victory in Germany didn't change anything. His unit is still preparing to go. If you can prevent that . . ."

"I'm so small in this, Brenda." Charlie rolled his sleeves back down. "A tiny part of a huge thing. But it turns out to be a very necessary part."

"Like one wheel on a bus?"

"One headlight. But it is very dark out." He heaved an enormous sigh. "Speaking of a bus, I need to be on the five o'clock run."

"You can't stay longer?"

"Afraid not."

"Then kiss me while you can."

And he did, as I pressed myself to him without shame or reserve, and he responded in kind. Our bodies clung like moths to the screen of a light-filled room.

I walked him to the bus, not talking much till we turned onto East Palace Avenue. "Do you know that I hate this street?"

"I do. My feelings about it depend on whether I am arriving or departing."

The old green bus was there, idling, all the other passengers already aboard. A church bell rang five times.

"How long do you think it will be?" I asked.

"Too long," Charlie said, kissing me once more, then trotting up the steps.

The engine belched black smoke, and there, on a window halfway back, he spread his palm out on the glass, an open hand till the bus turned the corner and I was standing on the sidewalk alone again.

IN THE END, CHARLIE used a car battery. Also two dozen flashlight bulbs. But simple components sometimes gave the clearest results.

How long had passed since he decided to finish? When you only sleep in naps between bouts of work, brief surrenders to the body's demands before returning to the calculating desk or the soldering iron—days were the wrong unit of measure.

Now Charlie stood at the head of the worktable. An assembly lay before him, spread out on two sheets of plywood. Turning that flat result into something that operated on the Gadget's spherical shape, that was a problem for someone else to solve.

It was odd, but for some components he felt a form of affection: They had always fired, always worked, while others misfired or proved to be duds. But now there were twenty-four of them, each with a lightbulb the size of a fingertip where the Gadget's explosives would be. If the lights went on all at once, those small bursts would crush the plutonium, pop the nut of beryllium and polonium, spray the atoms with neutrons, and produce a fission that would go critical in a few ten-millionths of a second.

As Sebring said in his lecture: pop.

How a car battery—purloined from a broken-down jeep at the vehicle depot—would fit inside the Gadget was not his problem. In fact, he had an intuition that something was not exactly right with the sphere's design. But after being told dozens of times, Charlie was sticking to his knitting.

He attached wires to the positive and negative terminals on the car battery. Lifting the initiator switch, Charlie examined the table again. Twenty-four devices, a maze of wires, a maze of questions for his conscience. He held the switch in his hand.

If only they had not called him Trigger. It was insulting. It diminished the complexity of his work. It implicated him in the Gadget's purpose. Charlie told himself for the hundredth time that he was neither building a bomb, nor slaughtering innocent civilians. He was a pawn, whose job was math involving arcs, and soldering. How the nation used those skills was not his affair. He was being a soldier. He was being a man.

Charlie glanced out the window. Dawn hinted vaguely in the eastern sky. Another full night in the lab. Maybe Uncle John and Oppie were right. Maybe demonstrating the Gadget would bring the Pacific war to a speedy end. Maybe it would prevent future wars.

"Right," he told the empty room. "And maybe tomorrow's Christmas."

With that, he closed the initiator switch, the contacts touched, and twenty-four flashlight bulbs switched on.

He counted twice to be sure. Yes, every single one of them. Finally he'd done it.

Charlie flipped the switch back, the bulbs instantly extinguished. On another day, he might have felt proud. Relieved. Triumphant. Instead he felt exhausted.

Also there was the nagging feeling that the design was not right. He'd done his part. Still, there was something wrong.

Charlie threw a sheet over the assembly, to shield it from dust and discourage prying eyes. He turned off the light at his desk— one that illuminated his soldering, as Brenda had taught him. At the door, he switched off the room light as well, then navigated the hallway by feel and the stairs by their creaking under his weight. Fatigue followed Charlie all the way, through the access door and out into the high-altitude predawn morning—where the light on the hills behind Los Alamos stopped him cold.

All this time he had seen the landscape of New Mexico as uniform, one muddy red with lighter or darker hues, but lacking entirely the variety of well-treed New England, and its million shades of green. People carried on about southwestern beauty, and he nodded along out of manners, with no idea what they were talking about.

Now the highlands were a daybreak rainbow: blues and purples at the base of the hills to vibrant yellow at the peaks. Above that, a sky whose blue was so pale it seemed white. A giant bird, he did not know what kind, sailed over without a single flick of his wings. Although the atmosphere lacked the dewy morning scent of lawns and fields back home, there was a freshness to the air, a cleanness. The scent of ponderosa was wonderfully sharp. He found that his shoulders were dropping from their clench up beside his ears. He took a deeper breath.

Two soldiers patrolled the tech area perimeter, rifles down, chatting in low voices. A dog trotted along inside the fence, heading in the other direction. Charlie had been planning to go to the barracks, but something about that dog made him change his mind. Instead he turned toward Fuller Lodge.

The front door was unlocked, the offices corridor dark. He ambled into the main hall, where there was neither dance nor lecture nor church nor party. Simply a large open room with a high ceiling, pine beams, serapes hung on the walls. Along one side stood glass cabinets, holding striking black pottery made by local Indians.

Charlie strode past all of that, to the far end, to the piano. The usual padlock hung on the keyboard cover, but whoever played last had left it looped through the metal bracket, unlocked. He sat, pulling the bench under him with a scraping noise that seemed to offend the empty space. He opened the top, and there were all the keys. He wished like anything that he knew how to play.

"Brenda," he whispered. She would know the perfect song for that moment too. And if it was a quiet one, he would get to see her face become sweet, unguarded.

Charlie placed his hands on the keys in the only way he knew how, the only shape, while pressing the pedal with his foot so the instrument would sound as loud and long as it could. Then with all of his strength: the G-major chord. He'd done it on a hundred organs, a thousand pianos, he'd played it one second before meeting Brenda.

And now, though the chord sounded powerfully—he felt it in his belly and heard it echo in the rafters—still it was no organ, the lodge no cathedral, those keys having no mighty pipes as loud as an entire orchestra. He played the chord again but arpeggiated, one note at a time from bottom to top.

And that was all. All he had, all he could offer to the woman in Santa Fe who held his heart. Given the speed of sound, how long would it take that G chord to reach her? Thirty-five miles, at give or take five seconds a mile, and the answer was a bit under three minutes, with Brenda's head on a pillow of the bed where he had slept with her, in the boardinghouse he had snuck in and out of—those notes arriving like the faintest shadows, helping her the littlest bit to awaken.

What a pleasant thought for Charlie, to imagine those sound waves, descending the mountains and crossing the desert to her ears. They rang in every other direction, too, circular ripples dispersing around the world, the gentlest whispers for anyone who needed them. And all at once he realized exactly what was wrong with the Gadget.

The usual tech crew began filing in at about eight, turning on lights and heating up soldering guns, making conversation as they eased into the day. By then Charlie was already surrounded by papers that bore a pigpen of calculations. Those who said hello to him received a bland "good morning," but he did not lift his head. He'd moved the large drawing of the Gadget's sphere beside his desk, along with the specification sheets. The pages he was writing on were crowded with arcs.

"Hey there, Mister Charlie." It was Monroe. "Word's out you don't sleep no more. Is it true?"

"As true as the rumor that you are never sober anymore."

Monroe grinned. "I'm sober right now. Course, it is early yet." He held a steaming cup of coffee out to Charlie.

"You're a savior," Charlie said, accepting the cup and taking a sip. "A saint among mortals. You wouldn't happen to have a couple of gallons of this, by any chance?"

"Well dang." Monroe patted his pockets. "Must be I left 'em in my other pants."

Charlie gulped down more. "What are you fellows up to this week?"

Monroe rubbed the bald top of his head. "I figured you'd know better than me. On account of we're dying to test your newest thing. All the talk at breakfast is you're about ready."

"It ran clean last night." Charlie waved at the table, where a sheet still covered the assembly. "There's still something not quite right though."

"Say, Charlie." Monroe sidled closer. "You getting enough to eat over here? Hungry horse can't pull much plow."

Charlie studied the Gadget design. "Do you know where I could find some sheets of metal? Maybe two or three feet on a side?"

"What kind? Steel and aluminum ain't the same thing."

"Well." He considered. "All kinds, I suppose. Yes, I'd need a sheet of each kind of metal we have around here."

Monroe scratched his chin. "Not to slow your thinking, Charlie, but I was asking about you getting enough to eat, which most times involves food. Not metal."

"Oh, I'm fine, thanks." Charlie waved it away. "I should wrap this little question up by noon or so anyway. I'll have a big lunch then."

"What little question is that?"

"Diffusion. If you have a pulse of energy in one place, how far does its force reach, and in what shape does it manifest?"

"I'm a chemist. You may as well be talking Chinese. But why don't I get my young boys to dig around in the toss-away pit? They's all kinds of materials in there."

"Perfect. Also I need a hammer, and large nails."

Monroe smiled. "If that's breakfast, I can't wait to see what you eat for lunch. Back in a jiffy."

He paused, expecting Charlie's usual effusive thanks whenever someone did him a favor. Instead Charlie fixed him with a piercing stare. "Are we doing the right thing?"

"Course not." Monroe laughed. "Didn't you hear Joseph Rotblat resigned?"

"What? Really?"

"World's highest expert on neutrons, and he's vamoosed. Said we were brought here to beat Hitler, which the regular army had already done. And Japan's got no bomb program. Time to shut The Hill down."

Charlie stared at his papers. "Is he right?"

"I've been arguing with Giles about that something fierce. He says everything's allowed in wartime."

"I think we're making a new definition of everything."

Monroe shrugged. "Then maybe Rotblat's right. Anyways, I'll be back with your metals in two shakes."

Charlie turned back to the pages covered with arcs, problem after problem.

Probably there was some equation, he thought, some calculus that would produce an answer in minutes. Lacking that knowledge, and unwilling to share the problem until he had solved it, all Charlie could do was try one set of numbers after another. When they did not work, he would change a single variable and see if that one succeeded. It was like throwing darts blindfolded, and hoping for a bull's-eye.

Midmorning, Monroe returned with the metal: eight square remnants from other tasks on The Hill. "Here you go, Mister Charlie," he said, dropping them on a desk with a clang. "Steel, tin, aluminum, a couple more. Hammer and nails, too, and I gotta admit, a boatload of curiosity about what you're up to."

"Just a theory," Charlie said. "Only a theory."

Monroe laughed. "Same thing Newton said, before that apple fell on his head."

"Can you skip the crew today, and help me out?"

"I don't much expect as they'll fire me."

Charlie led him to another desk, where he'd set up two wooden posts. "What we need is to bend the metal in a uniform curve, so that the two places that touch these posts are exactly nineteen inches apart."

"Why's that important?"

"Because that is the curve of the Gadget. We're copying its exterior."

"All right then." While Monroe measured nineteen inches on the first sheet, making notches to keep it exact, Charlie placed the hammer on a small scale, adding pieces of wood to its head until it reached the weight he wanted.

"I've calculated the force we'll need," he said, taking the tape measure, raising the hammer till it hung poised, six inches above the nail. "Ready?"

"This ain't gonna explode, right?"

"That's exactly my theory. Watch."

Charlie let the hammer fall, the nail drove through the sheet, and the metal dented for several inches in all directions.

"I knew it," he said, shaking the sheet in Monroe's face. "See what I mean?"

Monroe eyed him sideways. "You're looking a bit crazy right about now, you know."

Charlie laughed. "I'm sorry. I should explain." He held the sheet of metal out, a round dent in its middle. "The effect of the hammer is all near the impact. If you get as little as three inches away, there is no sign that I drove a nail through."

"Okay. Now what all does that mean?"

"It means"—Charlie seemed giddy—"the ignition won't work. The Gadget won't implode everything into a small, dense space. It will only crowd the plutonium a little, and make it slide up to places that weren't bent."

Monroe straightened. "You mean to say we're screwed?"

"For this metal at least, yes. We need to try the others."

"Why does this make you happy?"

"Because I figured it out now, instead of a month from now. When we would have wasted half a billion dollars of plutonium, and lost who knows how many soldiers."

Monroe stood, hands on hips, looking at Charlie.

"What is it?" He picked up another nail. "We need to test these other metals."

"Just thinking," Monroe said. "Some brain you've got on you, Mister Charlie."

"Get out of here," Charlie said.

Saying nothing more, Monroe reached for the next sheet of metal, and measured out nineteen inches.

By lunch it was clear that the detonator would not work. All the sheets had dented similarly. Charlie could not stop there, though, and he returned to his pages of arcs. At noon, Monroe brought him a sandwich. Charlie took a huge bite, then set it aside. Eventually Monroe rejoined his work crew, and later the other tech workers left for the evening. Charlie took no notice.

He needed a metallurgist. If only he could call his uncle John. But no, he was all pro-bomb now. He'd gone over to the other side. Funny, that was how Charlie used to think of the enemy.

The math told him there were two ways to make the plutonium work. The first was to use more explosives. That might rupture the exterior, though, flinging the plutonium unexploded into the open air. In other words, the opposite of crushing it down on that volatile nut. The second was to increase the number of detonators, though it had taken months to make twenty-four of them work together. That would create smaller explosions, keep the skin intact, and cause an effective implosion. Perhaps.

Now he dug through stacks of papers, reviewing his calculations. If you put the first detonator on the sphere's north pole, where should the others be located? How far should they be from one another? How many did you need?

Through the open windows Charlie heard a microphone from

Fuller Lodge, someone was repeating a code. It was a distraction, this strange, slow sequence of numbers, going on for what seemed like hours—until finally the noise distracted him enough to listen closely, and he realized that people were playing bingo.

He took a second bite of his sandwich and discovered that the bread had gone stale. He reached to put it back on the plate, but was already working his numbers again, and wound up placing the sandwich on the desktop. Bending over the papers, he dove into a universe of arcs.

When he finally arrived at the right answer, Charlie did not celebrate. He was too tired. Was it still Tuesday? Still the same day Monroe had helped him? Charlie had been awake since Sunday morning, so this was a new record.

After arranging the pages that proved his solution, tucking them into a manila folder, he brought all of the other papers to a metal bin in the corner. A sign above it read, Waste Documents.

"Isn't that the truth?" Charlie said, slapping his armload on top.

He arched his back, stretched his head from side to side, rubbed his face to wake himself up. Then he took the folder and headed down the hall.

Bronsky was arguing with someone, Charlie heard it from outside. He knocked anyway. At first the voices continued, but when he knocked a second time the debate ceased. Still no one invited him in. He worked up his nerve, and opened the door.

The Detonation Division chief was on his feet, face red as a beet, while Mather sat in a chair, feet on the man's desk, hands folded on his belly. The informality of it, their familiarity, halted him in the doorway.

"Fish," Mather said. "Like I always say, as stubborn as a salmon."

"Gentlemen."

"Fishk," the chief said. "I hear you have positive test on twenty-four nodes. Good news. We are schedule to test tomorrow at nine in concrete bowl. I hope it works."

"It works," Charlie said. "But it won't work."

Bronsky made a face. "Please to explain."

"You'll be able to blow up twenty-four little bombs tomorrow. And they're as close to simultaneous as humanly possible. But it doesn't matter. The Gadget won't work."

Mather scoffed. "And why not?"

"Diffusion." Charlie took a few steps into the office, placed the folder on the desk, then retreated to the doorway. "The metal will absorb too much of the burst. As the Gadget is currently designed, you will waste your plutonium and not get a reaction."

"Nonsense." Bronsky scowled. "Good men, smart men, have make calculate. In whole department, no dissent."

"It's right there for you to read," Charlie said, pointing at the folder. "All you'll get is an expensive metal ball with twenty-four dents in its shell."

Mather opened the folder, but only glanced at the top page before flipping it closed again. "Fish, you didn't just make an announcement. You brought us something to read, which means you've thought further. Did you solve the problem you found?"

He sighed. "I'm so tired, the numbers may be wrong."

"Whole concept is wrong," Bronsky said.

"What did you find?" Mather persisted.

Fiddling with the doorknob, Charlie spoke at the floor. "Thirty-two. It will take thirty-two detonators."

"And"—Mather held up a hand to silence Bronsky—"how do we build such a thing? When everyone agrees that twenty-four is the physical limit?"

"It's not possible."

Bronsky relaxed his frown. He faced Mather and nodded. "Where you would start, Fishk? What is step one?"

Charlie rubbed his face. "Step one is sleep."

"All right. We are seeing you at test tomorrow morning?"

Charlie nodded. "Yes, sir."

He had left the room and made it halfway down the hall before Mather yelled after him, "Nice work, Trigger."

Charlie was too tired to protest.

He had almost reached the stairway when the lights went out, yet another power failure. But by then, he was an expert at them. Charlie trailed his fingers along the wall, holding the railing as he went down the steps. Once he was outside, he found his way to the barracks by the light of innumerable stars.

39

THE SOLDIER HAD DIED nine minutes after the war ended. That was the first sentence of the first newspaper story I saw that morning. A tank detachment in Czechoslovakia had come under attack from a German unit that was unaware of the May 7 cease-fire. I read that the radio operator received a transmission that the fighting was over at the very moment his buddies were shooting at the Americans. When he told them to stop, they immediately did, and his captain raised a white flag in order to come forward and apologize. At first it appeared no one was harmed, but then they found the body of an unarmed mechanic's mate, a nineteen-year-old from Santa Fe.

Reverend Morris was already in action. Passing the table where I sat reading, he barely paused. "The service is today at three. Would you play that Bach piece you've been working on? The one I overheard the other day?"

"The Bach Toccata in D Minor?"

"Yes, at the end of the service. It's martial enough."

"I don't know that piece securely, sir."

He waved my objection away. "Play the portions you know. That opening passage will be perfect for this poor grieving family."

Poor grieving family? What could I say?

The turnout was huge, pews and balcony filled to capacity, people standing along the walls. Apparently the boy was from a prominent local family, and he'd been the high school's star athlete only eight months ago. Instead of delivering a sermon, Reverend Morris allowed the soldier's father to say a eulogy. All the stories he told were about when the boy was six. It slaughtered us.

Then it was time for the toccata. I reminded myself that the music was not about me, it was background—and the entire foreground was grief. That perspective gave me permission to skip the difficult sections and concentrate on the parts worth performing.

Sure enough, as the people filed out no one noticed I existed, much less that I was playing a complicated piece. Relieved at the end and not in the least insulted, I switched the organ off and organized the sheet music. As I finished, Reverend Morris was marching back, I presumed for the sacristy to get out of his vestments. I was out of sight behind the console, so I almost did not notice the woman who emerged from a side alcove, until she hurried across a pew and intercepted him halfway down the aisle.

He pulled up short on seeing her. His neck did that odd stretching tic. But when she opened her arms, he fell into them and they had a long, long hug. When they parted, she continued to hold his elbows. They spoke to each other too quietly for me to hear—not that I wanted to. I was mortified by the whole situation. I would have snuck away if I'd thought it would go unnoticed.

The woman was Mrs. Sanchez, who cleaned the church. Who always went last on the way out of Sunday services. Who had been meeting with Reverend Morris the first time I entered that church. Their conversation continued in murmurs. Whatever passed between them was not my business. I kept still, eyes down, resisting every urge to spy.

Finally they parted, Mrs. Sanchez bustling out the open front door. The reverend passed near enough to notice me. "See, Brenda? You played that piece wonderfully."

"Thank you," I said, in a tone as normal as his had been. But as soon as he entered the sacristy, I ran up the aisle and out of the church.

Lizzie was standing at her dresser, putting away laundry. The sight of her made me weak with relief. She took one look and stopped what she was doing. "What is it?"

"I'm not sure." I was breathless from running up the stairs. "I could be wrong."

"Out with it, kid. You look like you stepped on a scorpion."

"I think Reverend Morris is having an affair."

"What?" Lizzie frowned. "You're dreaming."

"With Mrs. Sanchez. I saw them together today, when neither of them knew I was there. It explains why Mrs. Morris is so angry."

Lizzie made a face I did not understand. She closed the dresser drawer and heaved a huge sigh.

"I'm right, aren't I?"

"You are wrong, Brenda." Lizzie said it in a low voice, the tone she used when she talked about missing her husband. "Very."

"All right, then. Spill."

She sat on the edge of the bed. "I'm not supposed to tell."

"My job, my housing, and my future depend on these people, and they have a huge secret. And supposedly you are my friend."

Lizzie was wearing an old shirt of her husband's, a long flannel one, and she wrapped it tighter before answering. "Promise you won't discuss this with anyone?"

I gave her a look that said whole paragraphs.

She shrugged. "They had a son. Dean. We never met, but word is that he was quite the looker. Anyway." She sighed again. I wanted to urge her to hurry, but I bit my tongue. "Anyway, he died on D-Day. Third wave on Omaha Beach. Reverend Morris took it very hard—they both have, but him especially. And because it has made him question his faith, he's tried to keep it a secret from his congregation. From everyone, actually."

"Then how do you know about it?"

"I was at the breakfast table when the telegram came. Mrs. Sanchez was there, too, to pick up her paycheck. They swore me to secrecy."

I went to the window and Mrs. Morris was hanging laundry again. She worked with an intensity, a tension, that now made sense. "I guess that explains all the hugs at the end of worship each week."

"This is a small town," Lizzie said, rising to stand beside me. "Everyone knows."

"Except me."

"After Dean died, Mrs. Morris started crying whenever she played the organ. The congregation could hear. Also she kept playing tons of wrong notes. The reverend told her to give it time, but she resigned."

"And they hired Brenda from Chicago."

"You were the first person to answer the ad."

I watched Mrs. Morris clothespin one of her husband's shirts to the line. What an agony she must have been carrying. "Why haven't I seen any photos of Dean in the house?"

"The reverend took them all down," Lizzie explained. "They're in a tug of war. She wants to build a shrine to their son. He wants to pretend the whole thing didn't happen. Once last fall, maybe six months after D-Day, I overheard him telling a visitor that Dean was off fighting in France."

"Why did they argue over her washing his clothes?"

"I don't know." Lizzie gnawed on a thumbnail. "Maybe if you put his things away all cleaned and folded, it means he's really gone."

"No wonder she resents me. I'm a constant reminder of her sadness."

"Maybe. But also she's a musician too. Imagine how you would feel if you weren't allowed to play anymore."

I leaned my head on the window frame, studying the woman below. "Maybe the purpose of war is not to kill soldiers on the battlefield, but to break hearts at home. Breaker of the most hearts wins."

Lizzie went back to the dresser, opening the top drawer, her fingers moving through the socks like she was looking for something. "All I know is I want my husband home, and a chance to have a future with him. That's my definition of victory."

"I need to be nicer to her."

"No harm in it, kid. But it won't make much difference."

"Why not?"

She closed the drawer without taking anything out. "Cause it won't bring Dean back."

40.

MONROE SETTLED HIMSELF BETWEEN Charlie and Giles at the crowded breakfast table. "I got it, fellas. The thing to do." He raised one finger. "We should all resign."

Charlie lowered his coffee cup. "What are you talking about?"

Monroe leaned closer, his bald pate shining from the overhead lights. "Pull a Rotblat, and quit this place. No us? No Project Y. No flattening of Japan."

Charlie shrugged. "I think the milk would still be sour."

"I'm dead serious," Monroe insisted. "Simple as opening a can of beans."

Giles shook his head. "Not simple, my friend. I wish it were."

"Name me one reason it wouldn't work."

Giles raised his head, scanning the crowded mess tent, soldiers at the entry while technicians and scientists poured in and out, or threaded through the lines looking for an open seat. "Brilliance adores momentum," he replied. "Do you see anyone here on the verge of quitting?"

Monroe panned the throng. "Not a dang one."

"Well," Charlie said. "I'd love to not have to build my part of the Gadget."

"But you will," Giles answered. "Won't you?"

Charlie stared at his plate. "Don't depress me."

"It's all right." Giles gave a wan smile. "'Conscience makes cowards of us all.'"

"Lemme guess," Monroe said. "Shakespeare."

"Well, look at you," Giles marveled. "*Macbeth.*"

"Red alert." Monroe pointed with his fork. "Competition's here."

Charlie glanced over his shoulder, spotting two men at the mess hall entrance: Bronsky and his star pupil, David Horn—brought to build the detonator assembly that the one person working on the task seemingly could not complete.

"Ain't got one-tenth your smarts, Mister Charlie," Monroe said, before shoveling a heap of scrambled eggs into his mouth, some of which spilled back on the plate.

"Must you always be such a perfidious mess?" Giles complained.

"Do you always got to talk like some kind of snob?" Monroe snorted. "Where I come from, a person says, 'You dang fool slob.'"

"Well then, you dang fool slob," Giles said. "Whatever makes you stop talking with your mouth full. Charlie, I think they're looking for you."

Charlie snuck a look, and both men were indeed scanning the crowded hall. Their stillness stood out amid the bustle. Horn was short, with thinning hair though he wasn't yet twenty-five, a crease between his eyes like you'd see on an old man, probably from thinking hard all the time. Charlie ducked low. "Do you think he solved it?"

"Doubtful," Monroe said. "But if he did, you're off the hook. Won't be Charlie Fish blowing the world to kingdom come."

Giles shook his head. "We haven't even built a Gadget yet, yet you keep saying it's murdering half the planet."

"You tell me, now that them Nazis are done for, one decent reason this project keeps going."

"Because the Soviets are probably racing to build a bomb too."

"For a war that's ended? To kill guys what are already dead?"

"For the world that will exist when this war is over. And they've spotted you." Giles gestured with his chin.

Charlie peeked, and both men were working their way through the maze of chairs. He stood. "Would you guys please take care of my tray?"

"All clears, Mister Charlie," Monroe said. "This goes right, you're gonna lose ten thousand pounds."

As soon as Bronsky saw Charlie stand, he changed direction, back toward the entry, with Horn in tow. Charlie understood: this was not a conversation to be had in public. As he followed them outside, a bead of sweat ran down his ribs.

Bronsky chose a bench uphill of the entrance, sitting comfortably. Everyone who passed would see them, sending as strong a message as if they'd met on the stage of Fuller Lodge. Horn stood a few paces off, unwrapping a stick of gum.

"Gentlemen," Charlie greeted them. "How's your day today?"

"Good news, Fishk," Bronsky said. "Very excellent news."

"Japan surrendered?"

Bronsky chuckled. "No, but we have cross a line today, from which is no retreat."

"What line was that?"

"Horn here." He waved a few fingers. "Have make an invention."

Bronsky, to Charlie, seemed as casual as a man on vacation—which made his stomach flutter. "Oh?"

"Doubler." Bronsky smiled, the first time Charlie had seen him do it. The man's teeth were crooked and gray, vestiges of a Russian childhood early in the century. "He invents device to split charge with precisely same delay in both signals. So: thirty-two detonators is work with two sixteen-part devices made attach to doubler."

"The same delay? How did he manage that?"

Bronsky shrugged. "Hard work. Now you build sixteens and problem is solve."

Charlie looked around slowly. Giles and Monroe were well down the lane to the barracks, arguing and laughing in a way that filled him with affection. A few feet away, Horn stood chewing his gum, eyes fixed on something in the distance.

"You are upset about wasted effort to reach twenty-four?" Bronsky asked.

Charlie shook his head. "We're going to be able to detonate it now, aren't we?"

Bronsky nodded, Horn hovering without bothering to conceal his eavesdropping.

Charlie ran his tongue over his lips, discovering that they were dry. Here it was. The Gadget would happen. The war with Japan was not over, the detonation problem was solved. He would build the arrays. This is what was going to happen with his life.

"In a way, it's a relief," he said eventually. "Now I know my part."

"Relief? It is excellent. We are need ten assemblies of sixteen, please."

"Ten? What for?"

Bronsky made a face, as if the question was insultingly stupid. "Five Gadgets."

Charlie stood stupefied. He had never imagined there would be more than one.

"You will please to inform Dr. Horn when you have finish? Perhaps five days?"

"That's possible."

"Good." Bronsky stood, brushing his pants legs as though he had spilled crumbs in his lap. "Then we are schedule assembly and test."

Charlie held as still as a pillar until they were a few steps away. "Hey, Horn, don't you have anything to say?"

The young man smiled, a bright and optimistic grin. "Nice to meet you, Trigger."

The Battle of Okinawa ended on June 22, 1945, after eighty-two days, a decisive Allied victory. Charlie read the papers closely. There were no signs of Japanese surrender—despite more than one hundred thousand casualties. Nor did the seventy-five thousand American casualties deter any plans for the invasion.

Then there was Ralph Bard's widely leaked appeal opposing any use of the Gadget. Charlie felt giddy at what the undersecretary of the navy had written to the secretary of war: "The position of the United States as a great humanitarian nation, and the fair play attitude of our people generally, is responsible in the main for this feeling."

This plea fell on deaf ears. There was no way out. One by one

Charlie constructed the assemblies, built with care and arrayed on his lab's long table. By then his soldering was as skilled as Beasley at his best. The devices were seamless and snug. Tested ten times, they worked infallibly.

Finally the night arrived when he finished the tenth one. Charlie put it through final testing, and it worked six times in a row. At that he switched off his iron, covering the hot tip with a welding mask as ever, and dropped into the wooden chair at his desk.

There was no one around, no one else working at that hour. There was no Brenda, no family back home in Boston. His work finished, Charlie was utterly alone.

Switching off the light to his work area, he navigated outside, through the tech area security fence, around Ashley Pond and away from all the buildings. He wandered past the junkyard, strange shapes of metal and wood in the dim light of a moon nearly set, until he reached the place where the outer fence passed closest to the cliffs.

And there he heard singing. Something classical, he recognized the melody from college choir, which felt like ages ago, and the person had a decent voice. Stepping with care over the rough rocks, he ventured toward the singer.

When he stumbled on a stone, the melody stopped. "Hello? Is someone there?"

He recognized the voice. "It's me, Charlie."

"My fine sir," Giles hailed him. "Don't jump."

"I wasn't planning on it."

"Excellent. Climb up this gully and join me."

Charlie scrambled on all fours to the knob, which overlooked the fence into a deep canyon. Warm air rose up the cliff face, smelling of desert honeysuckle. Giles sat on a flat rock, clutching a large brown bottle.

"Are you all right?"

"A relative question," Giles answered. "I'm doing fine, for one of the damned."

Charlie had no answer for that one.

"Remember when I used to talk about alchemy?" Giles continued. "The old lunatics trying to turn lead into gold?"

"Of course I do."

Giles raised the bottle to his mouth and took a long draw. When he'd finished, he ducked his chin back as if a boxer had jabbed his jaw, but his posture quickly recovered. "What a paradox, to discover that it was not mere analogy. We seek to divide uranium and plutonium, to make not gold but even rarer metals, plus the not-so-little pop that division makes. And just as in the days of alchemists, this is an upsetting of the natural order. Anyone who declares he can predict how much force our toying with nature will generate, well, he is lying to you. It's like a Zen koan: He who says he knows . . . does not know."

"Can I have a sip?"

"Of this rot?" Giles laughed. "You'll regret it."

"I finished the last detonator assembly."

"No wonder you're out walking where you shouldn't." He handed the bottle over. "For how many Gadgets?"

Charlie tipped the bottle and took a good slug. "God almighty," he sputtered. "This stuff is awful."

Giles nodded. "Agreed."

"Ugh." Charlie shook his head. "Anyway, five."

"Five?" He rubbed a hand over his chin. "We'd better drink more."

Charlie winced and tried again, afterward lowering the bottle with a shudder.

"Does that help?"

Charlie chuckled. "Not a bit. Where on earth did you get this nastiness?"

"Whiskey was Monroe's parting gift."

"Parting?"

Giles nodded. "Resigned at dinner. Waltzed up to a table of senior guys, and told them off in colorful terms. They had his gear and his carcass on a bus in under an hour."

"Monroe is gone."

"He said we would be murderers merely to satisfy our curiosity. He told two division directors their morals were 'lower than pig shit.'" Giles reached for the bottle, raising it in salutation. "Tonight's drunk is in his honor."

"Someone will make one of these weapons first. Our success might scare the others off."

"That justification and ten more are rattling around in my head. But we're probably wrong."

"Should we join Monroe, then? Next bus to Santa Fe?"

"Not all of us have Brenda waiting at the bus stop," Giles teased. "But no, Charlie. We're destined to complete this job. We'll end the war, and perhaps all wars. Or we'll bring on the ruin of humanity. There is only one way to find out."

"What about Oppie's idea of a demonstration?"

"I pray for that every day, and I am not a religious man. Ultimately, if your part of the business is finished, there's no turning back."

"None?"

"I have a suspicion that the exact point at which a scientist is satisfied is the exact same point at which a general becomes acutely interested."

"You think the army will take the Gadget and run."

"Five Gadgets," Giles corrected. He tossed a stone into the darkness. "Five."

After a long pause they heard the rock strike down below, one place and another, or perhaps the echo. Charlie imagined all the critters that would scatter at the sound. "Hey, what do you think became of Midnight? I haven't seen her in weeks."

"The same thing that will become of all of us," Giles replied with a bitter laugh.

"You are in a dark place, aren't you?"

"All clears," Giles said, as he tipped the whiskey over his head, pouring it into his open mouth and all across his face.

"Come on." Charlie yanked the bottle down. "That's enough."

They sat in a long silence. Eventually Giles pointed out at the landscape. "Do you know why I came here tonight?"

"No idea."

"You can only tell where the canyon is by what's not there. Where you see darkness, that's the end of The Hill. The roads have stopped, fences and guards and lights. You know what is left, out there? Do you?"

"Giles, maybe we should head back to the barracks now."

"An abyss, Charlie." He held his arms wide. "Everything past here is an abyss."

When Horn came for Charlie's detonators, he brought four men. They carried steamer trunks, into which they packed the assemblies like crown jewels. One of them did nothing but crumple papers to cushion the devices. Charlie sat at his desk, pretending to calculate arcs, unable to look away.

Horn stood by the door, observing. At one point he interrupted the packers. He reached into the trunk and rearranged one piece.

"Show more care," he said. When they had loaded everything, he nodded to Charlie and followed the others down the hall.

Charlie exhaled. He had not known he was holding his breath.

The next resistance came in the form of an official dissent. The Franck Report—written by senior scientists, Nobel Prize winners in chemistry and physics who had held secret meetings—issued a letter to President Truman opposing a bombing of Japan. The outcome, this document predicted, would be widespread international destabilization. Other nations would eventually develop their own atomic weapons, spawning a global arms race. The committee urged Truman to approve no more than a demonstration, on a deserted island and with the whole world witnessing, after which regulation of atomic weapons would be given to the brand-new United Nations, with a worldwide prohibition on the use of these bombs.

Charlie had great hopes. Franck was actually his uncle's boss.

He watched in frustration, however, as the report had no impact. Preparations continued. Starting July Fourth, he began making trips to Alamogordo—a giant plain beside the mountains that the original inhabitants had called Jornado del Muerto, the Trail of Death. It was a six-hour drive, down The Hill through flatlands, then out into open desert.

Hundreds of workers had preceded him. Project Y had purchased the land from a cattle rancher, and they turned the house into a command post, erected a tent city for scientists and technicians, and dispatched guards over the surrounding country. The original plan had been to patrol on horseback, but the land was too vast and water too scarce, so soldiers did the job in jeeps.

As far as Charlie could tell, his role was to observe, and try not to get too severe a sunburn. Each day at dusk he had a headache, from squinting in the desert sun all day. Metalworkers erected a steel tower one hundred feet tall, carpenters built observation shelters nine thousand yards from the tower. Long spools of wire tendrilled across the sand, linking the various facilities, and a construction crew bulldozed dirt over the wires. Charlie paced and watched and twiddled his thumbs.

He could not send letters to Brenda. That far into the desert, postal service was not among the amenities. Occasionally he would join other boys in the back of a power wagon and ride all those hours back to The Hill. But the trip left him dulled and he did not write then either. Giles worked nearly around the clock now, and with Monroe gone Charlie realized how few other friends he'd made. Although the work environment had always been intense, in the desert it ratcheted several notches higher.

There was a day when the atmosphere changed in Alamogordo too. It began one morning when a trailer-truck rolled out of the desert, a giant shape under tarps on its platform. With armed jeeps ahead and behind, it came to a stop near the operations center. A crane rumbled over, while men wrapped the covered object in chains. Lowering a hook, the crane hoisted the object and set it on the ground. Immediately a crew built a tent, shading the object from the sun.

Soon after, a car arrived with its own military escort, and a man stepped out with a suitcase handcuffed to his wrist. Armed guards stood by, as he ducked into the ranch house and shut the door behind him.

"Half of world's plutonium," Bronsky remarked. Charlie was startled. He had not known his boss was there.

"Is that right?" Charlie said.

The division director nodded. "Cost half billion of dollars to make. Imagine if we have try twenty-four detonators, and fail, and all this money is waste. Good work, you." He patted Charlie's shoulder and ambled away.

That night in a nearby tent, Charlie slept among strangers. In the morning, Bronsky pulled him aside. "You must see." Passing between guards, they ducked into the hidden object's chilly tent.

There it was: the Gadget, revealed. A dull metal orb, eight feet around, its casing secured by thick steel bolts, with holes all around for wires. The external detonators looked like cloves on a Christmas orange. Charlie marveled to see the actual thing, this device to which he had given so much thought, but always in the abstract. Now it was as real as the ground underfoot.

A team of scientists entered, chatting amiably. Bronsky leaned over to murmur, "They are arm Gadget now. Plutonium plug are slide direct into position, very snug."

Sure enough, two men removed the Gadget's cap. Two more carried a wooden box up a ladder. One opened the box while the other removed the plug, held it up for all to see, like a magician preparing his trick, then slid it down the opening.

Immediately Charlie could tell something was wrong. The man pulled the plug back, and slid it down again. Again it jammed. When he tried to remove it, the plug resisted. It was stuck.

"What in world?" Bronsky asked. "They have measure this twenty times."

The men on the ladder and the others all wore puzzled expressions. Finally one of them spoke. "Let's go wrap our heads around this. There must be some explanation."

"What in hell?" another man barked. "It's a little late to say we mismeasured."

"Please," the first man said, gesturing toward the ranch house. "In private."

The men filed out, Bronsky speaking to Charlie on the way. "Please to stay here."

Charlie waited hours. Every so often a scientist would come out to climb the ladder, peer inside the Gadget, and return to the house. When the door was open Charlie could hear men arguing. Meanwhile the sun rose, and the air in the tent grew warm. It was July, and soon the heat would be unbearable.

Then the Gadget clanked. Charlie jumped. The guards made eye contact to confirm they had all heard it. A soldier trotted over to the house and knocked.

A red-faced scientist opened the door. "We're trying to solve something here."

The soldier hooked a thumb over his shoulder. "It thunked."

"It thunked? What the hell?" The man jogged over, hurried up the ladder, and peered in the opening. "I'll be damned."

The other scientists came to see for themselves. By the time they'd each had a turn on the ladder, Bronsky had solved it. "Gadget was out in cold night, in cold tent. Passageway shrinks. Plug is in warm house, it expands. Leave them together, cold shrinks plug, down it goes. *Thunk.*"

The men laughed, scientists sealed the Gadget with more steel bolts, and the crane returned to carry it the nine thousand yards to the tower. Bronsky beamed as the crane inched away across the sand, the studded Gadget dangling.

"Looks like one of those medieval weapons, you know?" one soldier said. "The spiked ball at the end of a chain?"

"Or an egg," Charlie replied. A giant egg, the most dangerous egg of all time.

"First atomic bomb, Fishk." Marveling, Bronsky shook his head. "Is now arm."

* * *

Ordered to keep an eye on the Gadget, Charlie followed the crane toward the tower. It was nearly five miles away, but he had walked only a mile or so when a jeep picked him up. By the time he reached the tower, the crane had deposited its load and started back. Soldiers attached another hook, this one connected to a cable dangling down the center of the tower. None of the boys were scientists—Charlie knew because of the uniforms—it was all military, with one man very much in charge. Charlie considered it a failing that he could not tell the man's rank by the stripes on his sleeves. The motor on the tower lift was loud, so the boys' voices sounded like dogs barking.

The officer in charge yapped an order, the engine roared, and the winch overhead began to lift the Gadget. But it stopped after a few seconds. Even over the motor, Charlie and the others had heard the groan of bending metal. He backed away, craning his neck to examine the tower, and cupped his hands to yell to the officer.

"What did you say?" he shouted.

"The top girders are bent." Charlie pointed up. "The Gadget is too heavy."

The officer glared. "How about you keep your nose out of army business?"

Charlie stood there, flummoxed. He could see the iron pillars with his own eyes. They curved inward, toward the center of the tower. Meanwhile, the Gadget dangled fifteen feet off the ground. He inched closer again, debating whether to insist.

"Hey, Murphy," the officer yelled upward. "What did you build this thing to hold?"

"As ordered, sir. Four tons."

He turned to Charlie. "Hey, smart-ass, what's this thing weigh?"

"Ten thousand, eight hundred pounds, sir."

"If it falls, will it go off?"

"I wouldn't want to find out, sir."

"God *damn* it." The officer stomped away. In a matter of seconds, though, he had whirled on his heel to stride back. "Mattresses. You, you, and you." He jabbed his finger in the direction of various soldiers. "Requisition all the mattresses from the tents."

One soldier squared his shoulders. "Sir, regular army only has cots."

"So what?"

"Mattresses are for officers only, sir."

"I don't give a good goddamn," he said. "I want them piled here pronto."

"Yes, sir." The soldiers ran off toward a line of parked trucks.

"Hey, smart-ass," he said to Charlie, "I can't spare the hands here. You go too."

Fortunately it was midmorning by then, the officers attending to their duties. No one was around to object as the soldiers bundled sheets, pillows, and blankets, and left them on bare bed frames. The mattresses were thin, government issue, and dusty. One baby-faced soldier could not stop sneezing.

But they loaded the mattresses into the trucks. It was hot work, no wind and the sun beating down, their shirts dark with sweat. They climbed into the truck's cab, but the sergeant—Charlie knew his rank because the others called him that—announced that there would be a detour on the way back.

"Seaver can hold his damn horses, if you ask me," he said, driving over to the mess tent and sending them in to drink all the water they could hold. Charlie put his face under a spigot and gulped greedily. It didn't matter that the water was warm. He let it spill on his face, then wiped it around his sweaty neck and up into his hair.

Air pouring in the truck window dried and cooled them on the drive back out to the tower, and Charlie wondered if being in the military would have been so terrible after all.

The sergeant drove faster for the last mile. "Now let's double-time the unloading, guys, so we look extra sharp."

Seaver stood with his feet wide, frowning as they piled mattresses under the Gadget. The baby-faced soldier nudged Charlie. "Think this will help if it falls?"

He shook his head. "Not a bit."

But they unloaded all of the mattresses, making a stack almost ten feet high.

"Now we'll see what's what," Seaver said.

He ordered Murphy to restart the motor, and it bellowed and roared. Then inch by inch it hoisted the Gadget up into the center of the tower. Drawn back thirty yards or so, Charlie kept an eye on the upper girders. They did not seem to bend any farther. When the Gadget reached the platform, soldiers swung it away from the opening, the motor set it down, and Seaver turned back to his boys.

"Now. Let's get those mattresses back where they belong."

As Charlie helped again, a group of men on the detonator team came forward. They moved like links on a chain, each one's right hand holding the strap of a steamer trunk ahead, and left hand holding the strap of a steamer trunk behind. The last man was carrying a toolbox, which he swung up on his shoulder before starting up the tower steps. Charlie saw that it was David Horn, who marched past without noticing him.

For three days they wired the Gadget, inside an army tent atop the tower. Charlie wondered if the tent was intended to keep them cool, or to conceal their work. Meanwhile he waited outside the ranch's house with the growing crowd of technicians. Periodically the old windmill made half a turn in the breeze. But it was rusted, and moaned loudly enough that Giles covered his ears. "Sounds like a lovesick cow."

On July 13, Berthe came forward with calculations from Theoretical Division, and a prophecy. The chain reaction would not be limited to the bomb's materials. It would set the entire atmosphere on fire, annihilating the planet. Bronsky insisted that Horn's wiring team continue working, while senior physicists from other divisions met for a debate that kept lights on in the ranch house long after all the tents had gone dark.

On July 14, Berthe retracted his prediction. There had been a mathematical error.

Meanwhile a bulldozer inadvertently drove over the control wires, severing the connections between facilities. Glad to have something to do, Charlie took shovels and two soldiers and they unearthed the broken links. Under a scorching sun, he spliced and secured the wires, then helped the soldiers bury everything again.

"See there?" Bronsky crowed to the other division heads. "Science and army are cooperate."

On July 15, word came down: The test code-named Trinity would occur that night, at midnight. No one was permitted to leave or arrive. Charlie returned to his bunk and started a letter.

Dear Brenda,

I do not know what it means to be a man in wartime. No one is shooting at me. But hundreds of thousands of people are shooting at one another. What is my job? Am I simply a soldier, following orders? What has become of my conscience?

He put the paper facedown, as he had with his calculations back in Chicago, and went back outside to wait with the others. The humidity thickened all afternoon. At dusk, the wind picked up. Heat lightning glimmered behind the mountain range. Charlie stood outside the mess tent and Giles joined him. "Did you eat anything?"

Charlie shook his head.

"Me either," Giles said. "What if we actually have a storm?"

"It's July in New Mexico," Charlie answered. "Nobody imagined it could happen."

A long convoy of army trucks drove past, noisy behemoths trailing plumes of gritty dust. They were headed back to The Hill.

"Only three hundred are staying," Giles explained. "The official reason is to protect us, but I suspect it's actually to prevent sabotage." He scratched his arm. "Did you hear about the press releases?"

Charlie glanced at him sideways. "Do I want to hear?"

"There are three, already time-stamped for tomorrow. The communications chief showed me this afternoon. One, assuming the test makes a large noise and bright light, says an ammunition dump exploded, the fire is under control. The second one adds that gas canisters blew as well, so nearby communities had to be evacuated. The last one says there has been loss of life. I asked the officer what the blank space at the bottom was for, and he said that's where they'll put the names of the dead."

Charlie held his stomach and said nothing.

"He also told me they've informed the governor of New Mexico about the test. In case things go extremely wrong, and the army needs to declare martial law."

Charlie nodded. "You are my friend, Giles, and a good, smart guy. But you need to shut up now." He staggered away across the sand.

"If I don't tell you, Charlie," Giles called after him, "who can I tell?"

Charlie remembered with affection the thunderstorms of his New England childhood. Whether over the Fourth of July weekend up at Lake Winnipesaukee, or in late August back in Boston, the humidity would gather for days, building, until the scale tipped and the skies opened. If it happened during the day, the winds would strengthen, the leaves show their undersides, and the rain would deliver a deluge for half an hour or so, after which steam rose from the roads. At night, he'd wake to thunder rumbling in the dark and listen as the storm approached. Then the downpour unleashed, with lightning every few seconds until one bolt flashed simultaneously with the thunder, a great crash overhead, right above the house, and then the storm passed on, the flashes winked out, the rumbling faded, leaving the air washed and cool.

That night in New Mexico, the storm flickered with menace on the horizon, but drew no nearer. Rumbles came like muted drums, and the wind arrived in bursts of stinging sand, followed by ominous calm. Charlie sat at the tent opening, watching in perfect stillness.

Passing by, Giles pointed at the paper in his lap. "Another epistle to your girl?"

"I write to Brenda the way some people go to church."

"I'd like to meet her someday."

"I would not be here." Charlie waved one hand in a circle, as if to take in the tent, the desert, everything. "Hell, our nation would not be here, if not for Brenda."

A flash of lightning illuminated their faces, unmasked them to each other. Giles scuffed his shoe in the dirt. "You will tell me, won't you, when I need to be terrified?"

Charlie scratched his forehead with the pen. "You should have started being terrified two years ago."

By nine o'clock, Project Y leaders sent a message that countdown would be delayed till two A.M. By ten the wind had steadied out of the west, a light rain teemed across the desert, and the detonation was put on indefinite hold. By midnight the storm had intensified, sheets of rain slashing across the rows of tents.

Out of the darkness came Bronsky, holding an umbrella over his head though it had been inverted by the wind. Charlie observed the urgency in his stride, like a man on his way to a fistfight. He moved aside so his boss could enter the tent.

Bronsky held up a hand while catching his breath. Water dripped from his earlobes. "We are not find Horn anywhere."

"I haven't seen him," Charlie said. "I don't even know which tent he's in."

"Not important now." He wiped his eyes with fingers that Charlie noticed, for the first time, were long and graceful. The man would have made a good violinist. "We need to know danger level. If we have lightning strike, device will detonate, yes or no?"

"Hard to say, sir."

A flash lit the ground around the tent opening, puddles in the dirt.

"Do you see this?"

"I did, sir. Of course."

"What in hell? Are we safe?"

Charlie stood shoulder to shoulder with Bronsky, observing the rain. "How do you define 'safe,' sir?"

"Fishk, you have build detonators. Can lightning start them?"

"We never tested for external electricity, sir. We assumed the juice would be coming from us."

"*Chert voz'mi.*" Bronsky rubbed his eyes again, and Charlie noticed there were sores on the man's brow—made, perhaps, by anxious rubbing. Could the unflappable Detonation Division director be afraid? "So many geniuses," his boss said, "and here is thing we do not anticipate. What else are we forget to plan for? And what are we do now?"

"There are hundreds of yards of wire on the Gadget, and that platform is the tallest thing for twenty miles." Charlie squared his stance. "My advice would be to treat it like a lightning rod."

Bronsky hesitated, trying to tell if Charlie was joking. He opened and closed his broken umbrella. "Do you know they are have betting pool, up at command?"

Charlie raised his eyebrows in surprise. "They do not."

"One dollar each. Oppenheimer have bet on output of three hundred tons of TNT. Teller bet forty-five thousand tons. Ramsey says zero, total dud."

"Ramsey. Hasn't he always been a doubter?"

The sky flashed, the accompanying thunder coming five or six seconds later. Perhaps the rain had let up slightly, but Charlie was not sure. "What did you bet, sir?"

"I do not have dollar with me."

Somehow knowing his boss was worried gave Charlie a measure of calm. It meant that his emotions were reasonable. He put his hands in his pockets. "I'd imagine an enterprise as exacting as this one would have considered a variable like weather."

Bronsky gave him a hard look. Perhaps it was anger, but the man was often inscrutable. "Come, Fishk. Trinity test has job for you."

At once he set out in the storm, holding up the absurd umbrella though it spared him from not one drop. Charlie tossed the unfinished letter on his cot, flipped up his collar, and followed.

They skirted the command center, every light on inside, a man on the back stoop smoking. They came to a mud puddle that writhed and croaked, and only after they had passed did Charlie realize it was full of copulating frogs. Striking out across the open, they bent lower under the rainfall. When lightning flashed Charlie could not help wincing. But soon they arrived at the main barn, where they ducked out of the wet.

The lights were on in there too. Rain drummed on the sheet metal roof. Charlie saw two giant tanks wearing lead plating, knights in heavy armor. "What are those for?"

"Things various," Bronsky said, not elaborating. "Wait here." He went and spoke to one soldier, who directed him to another, who nodded at whatever Bronsky said, then both men returned to Charlie.

"Here," the officer said, handing him a rain slicker. "Won't help much, but won't hurt either."

"I don't understand."

Bronsky led him to a jeep, where another soldier sat behind the wheel. He wore a slicker too. "Driver is take you to tower. You relieve guard there, keep Gadget company."

"In the middle of an electrical storm?"

Bronsky nodded. "Is prevent sabotage." And he hurried away before Charlie could object. Thunder rolled across the sky. He stood, hands hanging at his sides. "All clears," he muttered.

"Ready when you are, sir," the soldier prompted.

"Right." Charlie navigated to the other side of the jeep. "I'm going to sit with the Gadget in a lightning storm?"

"Pardon me, sir," the driver said. "You'll want to have that slicker on before we set out."

Charlie, speechless, pulled it on halfheartedly, leaving one side exposed, as the jeep lurched out into the storm.

There were lights on at the tower, and when they pulled up, a pair of guards stood beside the metal steps. "Here you go, sir."

Charlie's side was drenched. He had tried to fix the slicker on the way out, but the ride was too rough. "The lightning has not let up one iota."

"Yes, sir." The soldier revved the engine. "I'll give the man you're relieving a ride back, but he'd better get down here double-time."

Charlie studied the boy at the wheel, who kept his gaze straight ahead. "Right."

The guards did not move as Charlie passed, nor register his existence as he began climbing the wet steps. He held the railings on either side, but they felt flimsy, little help if he should slip. A hundred-foot tower meant two hundred steps, and he put caution ahead of haste. One glance down showed him the lights of the jeep below, rain crossing its beams, and he continued the ascent. Charlie remembered climbing a fire tower on Mount Hope in Maine, back in his summer camp days. But that one was only sixty feet tall, other boys had already made it up safely, and it had been a bluebird sunny day.

On the platform, the wind was stronger and rain fell at a sharper angle. Charlie pulled back the tent flap to enter, and found a soldier asleep with his back against the Gadget. At once he flew into a rage.

"What the hell is the matter with you?"

The soldier blinked open his eyes. "Sir?"

"Don't touch this thing. Get off of it."

The soldier rose to his feet. "I didn't hurt anything, sir."

"You don't know that. How can you sleep at a time like this?"

"Three straight nights of guard duty, sir. Without so much as a break to pee."

That stopped Charlie for a moment. He went to the Gadget, which looked transformed from when he'd seen it hoisted. The exterior was webbed with wires of many colors, connecting his detonators. For the first time he saw the doubler—a giant steel case where sixteen wires converged. "This device is big," he explained, "but it's still fragile. Disconnect one wire and you've ruined everything."

"I don't even know what it does," the soldier said. "No one told me anything."

Charlie took a long look at him. Parched lips, no facial hair, an expression of fear. Thunder rumbled overhead. "This is not a safe place. You should go."

In seconds, Charlie heard boots scrambling down the metal steps. He ran his hands over the Gadget, checking connections one by one. They all remained sound. By then his temper had cooled, and Charlie knew he had overreacted. He drew back the tent flap. The lights of the jeep were long gone, a wet wind sweeping the sands.

"I have become Beasley," he told the storm, which replied with a gust in his face.

Then lightning flashed and thunder cracked simultaneously, and he knew that the worst of it was directly overhead. Charlie ducked back inside and eyed the metal floor. Perfect, he thought: everything was an electrical conductor. Who knew how long he would be up there? A tent flap in the corner snapped back and forth as though someone were shaking it. There was no question about whether the detonators would spark. One direct strike and he would be obliterated. Would he even feel it? It would happen in millionths of a second, his body blasted into its tiniest particles.

What was the name of that book he'd read as a child? The one in which a sailor boy is forced to stay high in the crow's nest, leagues and leagues from land, swaying and clinging while a hurricane smites his little ship and boils the surrounding sea. Charlie recalled that the boy survived the storm, but he did not remember how. He placed his palm on an open spot in the Gadget's shell, and waited for the world to end.

Eventually Charlie began to hum. Then sing. Then try to remember his part in every chorus piece he had ever learned. It was not pleasant, but unless a bolt of thunder was especially loud, he found himself half-forgetting his circumstances.

Hours passed, the rain a white noise punctuated by startling claps of thunder. He couldn't help wincing every time. Eventually Charlie heard something like a small hammer, tapping on the sides of the tower. Someone was climbing the steps.

Then the flap drew back, and Horn stepped inside the tent. "Hello, Fish."

"David." Charlie gulped with relief. "What a surprise."

"Two miserable hours in the latrine, or I would have been here sooner." He scanned the little enclosure, noticed the flapping bit of tent, and set a toolbox on its corner to stop the noise. "Nerves, I guess. Anyway, Bronsky found me a few minutes ago."

Horn continued inspecting the platform, saving the Gadget for last.

"An earlier guard fell asleep on it," Charlie said, "but I checked the connections."

"Thanks." Horn peered around the orb. "Looks intact."

"Are you my relief?"

"Yes. Though in my opinion, you shouldn't have been here at all."

"Oh, I don't know—"

"We can't delay the test, what with Truman meeting Churchill and Stalin tomorrow. The president needs to know if the Gadget will work." He placed both hands on the doubler, as if he were preparing it for some ceremony. "But it's my screwup, no question. I never thought to test for a storm."

At that instant, Charlie realized that he was not going to die that day. His shoulders lowered, his breathing eased.

"Anyway, your ride's waiting." Horn sat, pulling a paperback from his back pocket. "Humor essays, to pass the time. Wish me luck."

"Good luck, David," he said, then threw back the tent opening, and as quickly as he could, Charlie raced down the steps. As the other side of his shirt became drenched, he realized he'd left his slicker up on the platform. He did not care enough to go back.

The same soldier sat at the wheel of the jeep, but there was a passenger in back.

"There he is," Giles called out. "The babysitter's shift is over."

"Boy, am I glad to see you."

"Feeling's mutual," he replied. "You okay?"

"Better every minute."

Giles tapped the driver's shoulder. "Please get us the hell out of here."

At 2:00 A.M. Giles stood at the tent opening, watching the rain fall, and declared, "Chrysalism." He turned to Charlie, who was stretched out on his cot but wide awake. "Know what I mean?"

"Not in the least. What does today's ten-cent word mean?"

"Chrysalism. The womblike comfort of being sheltered during a storm."

Charlie rolled onto his side to face away. "There is no comfort tonight."

At 3:30 Giles roused in his folding chair. The storm had passed. "How about petrichor?" he asked Charlie. "Do you know that one?"

Charlie barely shook his head. He lay on his back, staring at the roof of the tent.

"The scent of the ground after a rain." Giles widened the tent opening with one finger. "I love it."

At 4:00 A.M., the countdown recommenced, with a detonation target of five thirty. Half an hour later, Horn returned to the command center. Charlie saw him climbing out of a jeep, and hurried over. "Thanks for relieving me out there."

Horn smiled. "We both feel relief at this point, right?" He bobbed from side to side. "Now I have to play goalie."

He climbed into another jeep, which took him to the relay tent. Charlie knew from the planning that this was where Horn would sit during the test, manning the only switch that, once the final orders came, could stop a detonation if something went awry.

The remaining boys also went to their assigned observation stations. For Charlie and Giles, that meant the southern end of the firing area, where a concrete bunker sat half buried in the sand, a row of windows facing north to the tower. The ease Charlie had felt after leaving the platform had evaporated. Now he held his stomach as though it pained him.

At 5:09, the twenty-minute countdown began. The announcement came booming over loudspeakers mounted outside the ranch's house, and radios at the observation bunkers. Charlie recognized the voice: Sam Allison, an affable physicist who sang to himself while walking the project's hallways. Charlie knew him from the choir, too: a clear, steady tenor. Around the Gadget, meanwhile, Charlie imagined there was an eerie silence.

The top command men occupied a separate shelter. It had a cluster of measuring equipment screwed and bolted onto the roof. One physicist handed out suntan oil, to protect the observers from ultraviolet light.

Outside the southern shelter, Charlie watched Giles poke twigs of different sizes into the sand. "I'm stealing Monroe's idea," he explained. "To measure how high the explosion cloud goes."

Charlie nodded wordlessly, then went off to relieve himself.

An MP at the bunker entry called the boys to find secure places. Charlie was surprised to see Mather there, calmly smoking against the wall. When he waved, Mather responded with a cool, slow nod. More boys sardined into the narrow space, clustering by the windows. A few remained outside. They'd been instructed to lie on their bellies with their feet to the tower, but none of them did it.

"Come all this way, and not see?" one said, chuckling. "Not a chance."

The MP stood near them. "You're civilian, so you don't have to obey orders. But it's my job to encourage you to comply."

"Thanks," the technician said, not moving. "Job well done."

Soon they were all hushed, smoking or talking quietly. They fidgeted. They ignored one another's odors. At the ten-minute mark—the milestone when, aside from Horn at his switch, human control ceased and the automated process began—Charlie rose to relieve himself again.

"Fish," Mather called. "You're as nervous as a cat."

"I'm fine," he insisted. "Too much coffee." And he headed outside.

"You'd be agitated, too," Giles told the boys, "if those were your triggers all needing to fire at the same instant."

"Never been done, can't be done," Mather said. "Even with Horn's help, Fish isn't smart enough. I've argued that for weeks."

Giles bristled. "We'll see."

Observation planes had flown south from Holloman Air Force Base, to monitor from the sky, their noise preventing conversation for a full minute. When Charlie returned from his moment outside the bunker, he stepped carefully over the other boys' legs to reclaim his place near one of the windows.

"Hey, friend." Giles shifted to make space. "You afraid that it won't go off?"

Charlie shook his head. "I'm afraid that it will."

A flare rose into the night sky: two minutes till detonation.

Mather let out a sigh. "I would not want to be Horn right now."

No one answered. They knew that even in silence, they had one another, while Horn at the switch was entirely alone. He would need to decide whether or not to proceed, based on an array of indicator dials, before the countdown reached six. After that the process was irrevocable. The observation planes arced up and away, out of range. A lovely shape, Charlie thought, the arc.

The one-minute flare rose, bright red in the black sky. As advised, everyone in the vicinity—inside and out, the MP included—lowered welding goggles into place. Silence draped on the bunker like a fog.

"Hey," Giles said. "Who wants to head out for a nice cold beer?"

No one laughed. Time had momentum, a weight they all felt. Ten, nine, eight. The signal surged down the wire. Seven, six, five. By then they knew Horn had not stopped it. Four, three, two. The greatest fuse in human history was lit. One.

The first instant was darkness, the whole sky black for the merest fraction of a second, followed by a light later calculated to equal the brightness of one hundred suns. It illuminated everything—stones, men's faces, the distant mountains—with a cruel and brilliant clarity. A blast of heat came next, as if someone had opened an oven door.

Even at that distance the temperature was hard to withstand, but the heat passed as it rose, a fireball billowing into the air, raging on itself. It ran through the colors of the rainbow, deep purples closer to the earth, bright oranges and yellows at the height of the climbing cloud. The pillar of power rose almost sexually before widening in every direction, a boiling head with broadening shoulders, and was that a flash of lightning inside the explosive cloud?

The scene took place entirely in silence, as if projected on a screen. Fully half a minute passed before the sound reached the bunker, a blast, then a roar that shook the earth. It growled, and endured, and carried so much dust and stones and sand that it scoured the observation windows. Instantly they became as opaque as sea glass.

The MP bent his head against the force of it. "Holy fuck."

Then the air rushed back toward the test site, pulling like an ocean's undertow, as an inferno ravenous for oxygen sucked everything toward itself. It surprised the men, some of whom glanced backward, perplexed, as if expecting to see another explosion in that direction. Meanwhile the burning shaft flowered upward into a toadstool shape, roiling orange like lava, climbing miles into the sky.

"We did it," Giles cried, shaking Charlie by both arms. "It worked."

Shouting huzzahs, the technicians threw down their goggles and rushed outside, watching as the furious cloud rose and spread. The men hooted and danced as though they were drunk, patting one another on the back, shaking hands. One raised his fist and shouted, "Take that, Mr. Emperor."

The MP's face was ashen. "Holy holy fuck."

"Cheer up, chum," Mather answered, skipping past. "The war will soon be over."

"*This* is what you people have been building all this time?"

Giles was squatting by his measuring sticks, and he called out. "Seven. The dust cloud rose seven miles."

But the others ignored him, their revelry careening outward, while pink in the east hinted at a day soon to begin. The plume reached its peak, then opened across the sky. Gradually the men calmed enough to clamber into trucks and jeeps, caravanning back to the command center, swerving and honking all the way.

They forgot one of their kind. In time he would have to march the whole five miles. When he arrived midmorning, sunburned and parched, the guards would speculate that he must have been caught in some unprotected place at the time of the blast. But that was hours later. Until well past dawn, he remained forgotten, squatting in a corner of the observation bunker, whispering one thing over and over: "Brenda. Brenda."

Charlie huddled in the dirt, his clothes soaked with sweat, his goggles still in place. Try as he might, he could not make his hands stop shaking.

41

Dear Brenda:

I have written and thrown away eighty pages to you. The world is immense and terrifying. I cannot come on Saturday this week, because The Hill has been closed for security and celebration purposes. I am not celebrating. I am not secure. I will take the Sunday bus, arriving at 10 A.M.

I need you.

Charlie

THAT WAS HIS LETTER, the entirety of it, which arrived on Friday afternoon. Seven sentences, and it changed everything for me. I had always known that Charlie was sensitive, and that the world might take advantage of him. But that letter revealed the depth of his vulnerability, in a way I had not admitted to myself before.

All I wanted was to hold him close, listen to whatever was causing him pain, and provide what comfort I could. All the times I'd counted days or hours till I would see him suddenly felt trivial. He'd said *"I need you."*

But 10:00 A.M. on a Sunday? That was the worst possible time. I played the 8:30 worship, then hurried over to East Palace Avenue, knowing I would have to hustle straight back for the service at eleven. The bus must have arrived early, too, because it was long gone and there was Charlie, standing alone on the sidewalk, peering from side to side, his hands moving like he was strumming an imaginary guitar.

"Brenda," he cried out. "Oh, Brenda."

We threw our arms around each other, and I felt him go still. "Let me look at you," I said, pulling back. "Are you all right?"

But as soon as we parted, I saw the tremor return to his hands. I drew him close again, and the calm returned to his body.

One November when I was a girl, as my mother opened the fireplace flue, a small brown bird flew into the house. She screamed, chasing it around, while the bird zoomed in and out of the living room, and around the overhead light in the kitchen. Somehow I knew to wait. Soon enough, the bird landed on the curtains. It stayed there long enough for me to cover it with a wastebasket, and then I reached inside. At first it fluttered and flailed against my hand, but then it calmed, and I held it gently, and removed the basket. The bird turned its head from side to side, not struggling, not fighting, while I carried it to the front door, and set it on the stoop. When I let go, it did not move for a few seconds. Then it rose, zipping away into the trees.

Now it was Charlie, settling in the same way, calm as long as I held on. "What happened to you?" I asked.

He shook his head. "I'm not allowed to tell."

"All right," I said. "All right." I squeezed him close, arms around his back so I could feel the rise and fall of his lungs. "You don't have to. I can see for myself anyhow."

Charlie nodded. "The future will be even worse."

"We are going to talk about it later," I said, "as much as you can. But first I have to work. I don't want you waiting somewhere, or wandering around. You stay with me."

"Please," he said.

"We need to go." I took his hand and led him across town to the church. We went straight to the side door, where Mrs. Morris was waiting, making sure I saw her check her watch.

"I was wondering where you'd run off to," she said. "You should be playing now."

"Mrs. Morris, this is my sweetheart, Charlie Fish. He's had an upsetting incident, and he'll be joining us at worship today."

"Your sweetheart?" My landlady gave Charlie the once-over like an interrogator shining a spotlight on a spy, but he only ducked his head to one side. "How do you do?" She held out a hand. "Welcome."

"Thank you, ma'am." His voice was quiet, as if he had no spare breath. He let go of my hand only long enough to shake with her.

"Charlie, you come right with me." I breezed past Mrs. Morris, leading him to the front pew. "I will sit with you when I can. Otherwise I'll be right there." I pointed at the organ console, which somehow felt about half a mile away.

Charlie sat, but when I let go of his hand he seized me for a moment more. I peeled him off and went to my place. It did not feel like he was clinging. More like what his letter said. Needing me.

The service passed in a blur, though it was a pleasant relief to have the reverend speak at a normal volume. I played the hymns, I conducted the choir. Every time I glanced Charlie's way, his hands shook like he was in an earthquake. When I was able to sit beside him, he relaxed the moment we touched. What was I being asked to do?

After church we took a stroll, because that is how we started every visit, getting reacquainted. Usually we chatted, but that day we were quiet.

The thing I noticed most though? The thing about which, of all the unusual aspects of that day, I am proudest? I had strength. It was different from the uppity tricks of my girlhood, and from the interior drive that had helped me cross the country. This was strength of a giving kind: Charlie needed me, and I was solid as a tree.

We turned onto the block near the boardinghouse. I had not planned it, but there we were. "I'm certain this isn't something you did," I began. "I know your conscience, Charlie. I know you would refuse to do anything that went against it."

"But I did," he said. "I did go against it."

"I don't believe it. It must have been something you saw."

He answered with a nod.

"Something truly horrible," I continued. "But you can't tell me about it."

"If I did, it would be treason. They would have grounds to shoot me."

"So you have a terrible secret?"

Charlie swallowed hard. "The worst. And it is not over yet."

We had reached the front walk of the boardinghouse. "Fine," I said. "I don't need to know what it was. You don't have to tell me. Just pretend you have. Because I believe you. I agree that it is horrible, and I sympathize completely."

I reached for the door, letting go of him for a second, and his hands fluttered immediately. "Oh, Charlie." I reached back and he clung to me again. Like I was a lifeguard and he did not know how to swim.

I felt such a strange mix of emotions: worrying about what he had seen, discovering how much I cared about him, wanting his well-being, and hoping I possessed the strength for both of us. That was when the idea came to me. The impulse of a lifetime.

"Charlie," I said, "kneel down."

He searched my face. "What?"

"Trust me on this. Kneel down."

"All right." Charlie put one knee down and I stopped him.

"That'll be enough. Now, repeat after me."

"What are you doing?"

"You'll see. Brenda . . ."

"Brenda," he replied.

"Will you marry me?"

Of all the times I have seen Charlie's surprised expression, that is the one I will cherish all of my life. His face went as open as a newborn babe's. I heard a door slam somewhere but I ignored it.

"Say it," I insisted.

"I haven't even met your father, much less asked his permission."

"We'll ask him after the war." I put one hand on my hip. "Now are you going to do what I say or not? Repeat after me."

Charlie's face. Charlie's frightened, wounded, excited, beautiful face.

"Brenda." He pressed his eyes closed for a second, then opened them wide. "Will you please marry me?"

"Oh heck, Charlie. I sure will."

He stood and we hugged and laughed and kissed, and laughed again. How would I have known, or even thought to suspect, that we'd had an audience?

"What's all this?" Mrs. Morris was striding off the stoop. "What's going on here?"

"Mrs. Morris." Charlie practically leapt to his feet. "Do you think your husband could perform a wedding today?"

"Today?" I said.

"I don't want to wait another minute," he answered.

Mrs. Morris scrunched her face up, as if she thought we were playing a practical joke. "I don't know his schedule for this afternoon. But I suppose we can ask."

"Wonderful," Charlie said. He ushered her forward, then took my hand as we followed. "Brenda this is your best idea ever."

In fifteen minutes, the arrangements were set. Reverend Morris brought Charlie to the phone to request a few days' leave. He sat me at the dining table with a blank marriage license.

"Yes, you are both present," he said, checking a box. "Lucky thing New Mexico isn't a waiting-period state. And you are both eighteen or older, yes?"

"I'm twenty-one," I said. "Charlie is twenty."

He turned the paper around, pointing. "Sign here."

I wrote my full name, and felt like I was becoming weightless.

"I'll have Charlie sign when he's off the phone," he said. "You should get ready."

I ran upstairs, effortless as if I'd grown wings.

Lizzie was about to work a Sunday shift. "Hey, kid," she called from the hallway. "What's the ruckus downstairs?"

"Charlie and I are getting married."

"No kidding?" She poked her head into my room. "That's great news."

I bit my lip a little. "Right now."

"Yahooooo." Lizzie rushed in and bear-hugged me, leaning me from side to side. "Fantastic. But wait. What are you going to wear?"

I stirred the dresses on the curtain rod that passed for my closet. "One of these?"

"Hang on."

She hurried away, and while she was gone I ached for my mother. This would have been our moment, our sweetest shared experience. But for Charlie's sake, I could not delay. Too many decisions depended on waiting till the war was over. It might break my mother's heart, but Charlie could not wait, and neither could I.

Lizzie returned with a sweet white outfit, trimmed in blue. "This was going to be my welcome home dress for Tim, if I lost enough weight to fit in it. But I never will." She held the dress up against me. "What do you think?"

"Honestly, Lizzie? It's perfect."

"Try it on. I have to get ready or I'll be late, so come show me."

The dress had thirty cloth-covered buttons running up the front, starting below the navel and finishing at the throat. The buttons were small, so it took some time to fasten them all. Makeup was next, then my hair. Finally I went to Lizzie's door.

"Va-va-voom," she said, laughing. "Prim and proper, Brenda, but *muy caliente*."

"Whatever that means," I said, laughing with her.

"It means this dress fits you perfectly. Approximately. Anyway, it's my wedding present."

I gave her a hug, unable to prevent a few tears of delight.

"Cut it out," Lizzie said, thumbing my makeup smooth. "You'll wreck your face."

"I need to get going."

She gave me a long look, wistful and sweet. "I guess those push-ups paid off. Go have a great life, kid."

Mrs. Morris sat on the organ bench, shaking her head at the droning notes. "All these ciphers. How have you managed to play this thing?"

"The first manual is clean," I called from the aisle. "But there's no A-flat below middle C."

"We need to make some repairs around here."

"I know just the guy," I answered.

Charlie stood at the altar, beside Reverend Morris. He had his hands in his pockets, in an attempt, I knew, to keep them from shaking.

Mrs. Morris closed all the stops to the lower manuals, and used the top one to play "Here Comes the Bride." But what made Wagner's old chestnut work was that Reverend Morris knew the words. I'd played at a dozen weddings, but I'd never heard the verses.

Here comes the bride, all dressed in white,
Radiant and lovely she shines in his sight
Gently she glides, graceful as a dove
Meeting her bridegroom, eyes full of love.
Long have they waited, long have they planned
Life goes before them, opening its hand.

I could only smile. Long have we planned? Try forty-five minutes.

I would have loved my family to be there, to be holding Daddy's arm, to see Frank maybe at the altar as best man. But I had been on my own long enough that walking alone seemed as right as Charlie being my destination. I held a few posies Mrs. Morris had snipped from her garden, and the simplicity of it all felt beautiful.

Her playing was not bad either. I couldn't help noticing—heavy-handed, but accurate. But what struck me was that she was smiling as she played. It was the first time I'd seen her happy.

By the second verse her hands were confident. She and the reverend made eye contact, and the look between them was as poignant as anything I'd seen before. He stood tall and calm, no sign of his tic.

Asking God's blessing as they begin
Life with new meaning, life shared as one.

Entering God's union, bowed before his throne
Promise each other to have and to hold.

Charlie gave me that hundred-watt smile, which calmed every butterfly in my belly. He took his hands out of his pockets and from halfway up the aisle I could see their tremor. But I was not afraid. I remembered the things my mother had said about men damaged by war, and I believed in Charlie, I believed in his ability to overcome whatever had horrified him.

In a few more steps it did not matter anymore, because I reached him. I have never stood taller.

Mrs. Morris hurried over to serve as witness, right at my elbow. The reverend smiled at me, at Charlie, and then took a long fond gaze at his wife.

At last he cleared his throat. "Given that one of you has already attended worship once today, and the rest of us twice, I'll get right to business." He took my flowers, handing them to Mrs. Morris, then instructed Charlie and me to join hands. We did, and I felt full to the brim. This was the boy whose strong fingers had opened the box of sheet music, back in Chicago a lifetime ago. This was the man who had slept beside me, against me, and for whom I had felt desire in every cell.

Reverend Morris recited the vows, and Charlie repeated them first. Then it was my turn. I barely remember. But I do recall feeling my feet on the floor, my shoes on the hard stone of the church, and everything about the moment was solid and real.

I don't know at what point Mrs. Morris started holding her husband's hand. But I noticed when we reached the part with the ring, and it turned out she had loaned Charlie one for the day, a gold band, simple as can be. He slid it onto my finger to tell the whole world that I was his now, and he was mine. Somehow the preacher and his wife holding hands made the moment even sweeter.

He told us to kiss, and as we did, in my heart I made a long speech about my commitment, while I received from Charlie the promise of lasting pleasure. Then it was all done but the blessing. Reverend Morris raised both arms over us. "Let us pray."

We bowed our heads.

"To the mystery of the universe that brought us and all creation into being," he said, "we dare to beseech the heavens and the Almighty. The world has been a dark and violent place for too much of the lives of these beautiful people. May the war end before their youth does, while their love is green and young. May their efforts and energies turn away from rations, coping, and loss, and instead create a generous future of family, community, and abundance. May they keep music at the center of their happiness, too, whether they are fixing instruments or playing them. Wherever they may journey in the years ahead, may they make a joyful noise."

Amen. Then Mrs. Morris scurried back to the organ and struck up Mendelssohn's "Wedding March," while Charlie and I kissed again, and started up the aisle. Reverend Morris, robes trailing, ran down the side so that he would be waiting for us at the church doorway. Once Mrs. Morris finished the song, she dashed out the side door. He shook Charlie's hand, and gave me a warm embrace. We stepped out into a sunny New Mexico afternoon in July, and were greeted by a cascade of rice.

"What in the world?" Charlie said.

There was Mrs. Morris, by herself, holding a burlap bag of rice, digging into it, and throwing a heaping handful into the air.

As a wedding gift, Reverend and Mrs. Morris let us use their car, an ancient black Hudson with a full tank of gas. They'd also called a member of the congregation who owned a small adobe in Taos, who said yes, we could stay there for a honeymoon. Mrs. Morris produced a camera, and ordered Charlie and me to pose in front of the Hudson. I have that photo on my dresser to this day. Me and my husband of five minutes.

Then hugs all around, everything smelling of Mrs. Morris's lily of the valley perfume, and we climbed into the Hudson. Sunshine had made the seats scalding. The car started right up, and with me at the wheel because Charlie preferred it, I eased away from the curb. A glance in the rearview mirror lifted my heart even higher: Reverend Morris with his arm over Mrs. Morris's shoulders, and her arm around his waist, and both of them waving with their free hands. Taking a deep breath, I pulled away as Charlie reached over and took my hand, and off we drove into the rest of our lives.

The adobe was small, two rooms with a kiva fireplace and a stack of split wood. The place smelled of ashes. When I slipped off my shoes, the red-tile floor was cold.

"No lights please," I said, and dug in the drawers till I found matches for the candle in the center of the breakfast table. I was surprised by how much light it gave.

I had never said I loved him. Maybe it was because of how rarely those words were spoken in my family. Maybe it was the way Chris had declared his love as a way of possessing me. Maybe I was plain scared. But Charlie had never said it to me either. I thought this was the time, we smiled at each other, I breathed in.

Charlie kissed my cheek and turned and got busy building a fire, and the moment was gone. In no time the kiva crackled and snapped as the wood caught. It took him one trip to bring my small bag of things, and he had nothing to carry for himself.

He tossed the bag on the bed, then returned to me in the kitchen. We spent a minute admiring the fire, enjoying it, before we turned to look at each other, perfectly aware of what came next, modest, shy, but utterly ready. Charlie started to undo the buttons of my dress—there were so many, so small, and his fingers slipped. I could feel his impatience, and it thrilled me.

He'd managed to undo five buttons, perhaps six, when he drew back and examined the dress more closely.

"Buttons, buttons," he said, laughing, grabbing my hips. "Too many buttons."

It was a rough kind of contact. But his urgency pleased me, showed me the depth of his desire. Though I was nervous, I found myself relaxing. As if a knot within me chose that moment to untie. I brought his hands up below my collarbone. "Rip it."

"What?" he said. "I don't want to ruin your dress."

I shook my head. "Just rip it off."

He put his mouth on mine and I arched up to meet him, as he gave a strong pull and the fabric gave way, and I heard the most wonderful sound—better, more glorious than any organ or choir: dozens of buttons skittering away on a red-tile floor.

"I FOUND SOMETHING INCANDESCENT for you," Giles said, ambling into Charlie's lab. He arranged some pages, placing them on the desk with a flourish. "Take a gander."

"You've never come in here before."

Giles shrugged. "Any department other than Electronics is intellectually unclean. I thought you knew."

Charlie laughed. "Somehow it slipped my mind." He began to read. "Wait," he said, and started over. The front sheet was mostly text, with a few signatures at the bottom. The other pages were all signatures. "Holy cow, Giles. Where'd you get this?"

"From the place where we don't say how we obtained something. But it's real. Leo Szilard delivered it to James Byrnes, our soon-to-be secretary of state, personally."

"It's dated the day after the Trinity test."

"Yes." Giles sat beside Charlie. "Szilard found seventy compatriots, from Oak Ridge, Berkeley, and Chicago."

Charlie scanned the list. "I know one of these guys. We called him Steel Wool."

"It's measured, and wise, and addressed to the president."

"Listen to this," Charlie said, reading from the first page. "'The development of atomic power will provide nations with new means of destruction. The atomic bombs at our disposal represent only the first step in this direction, and there is almost no limit to the destructive power which will become available in the course of their future development. Thus a nation which sets the precedent of using these newly liberated forces of nature for purposes of destruction may have to bear the responsibility of opening the door to an era of devastation on an unimaginable scale.'"

"Rather articulate, don't you think?" Giles said, deftly collecting the papers. "Like Oppie, they say the president should conduct a demonstration—"

"This dissent is important. It shows we're not the only ones with doubts."

"Yes, but I'm afraid the outcome is not entirely unexpected. All seventy signatories have been removed from weapons development."

"What?" Charlie shook his head, as if to clear it. "Szilard is an American citizen."

"What can I tell you? The man who discovered atomic chain reactions is no longer permitted to work on atomic research."

Charlie began to pace behind his large assembly table—which had been bare for nine days. "What do you predict Truman will do about this?"

"I predict that Truman will never know," Mather announced from the doorway.

"Hello, Mather," Giles said, not turning much in his seat.

"Hello, gents." He sidled into the room. "Fish, I wanted to know if you know what your uncle John's plans are. I'm weighing what I might do next, since this war is about to wrap up. If he had the clout to land you here, imagine what he might do for me."

Giles rolled his eyes. "You are as sour as the milk here, you know that?"

"And yet in days to come, my conscience will be clear. Can either of you make that claim?"

"What do you mean?" Charlie asked.

"Silly Fish." Mather shook his head in mock disappointment. "Let me ask you first. Has anyone briefed you on the success of our test last week?"

"I saw it with my own eyes."

"Yes." Mather idled down one side of the assembly table. "But the details?"

"What details?"

"Oh, for example, who won the pool on how big the explosion would be. Anderson drove one of the lead-shielded tanks out to ground zero, and his samples confirmed a yield of eighteen point six kilotons of TNT. So Rabi took the pot."

"Who cares?" Giles said, conspicuously studying his fingernails.

"Such as the tower was vaporized at detonation," Mather persisted. "The winch, the platform. Nothing left but a crater. Solid steel turned into air."

Charlie turned to Giles. "Is that true?"

Mather smiled like a poker player proud of his hand. "Did anyone tell you about the glass?"

"What glass?"

"The detonation heat was so intense, it melted the surface for hundreds of yards in every direction. It turned the sand into green glass. They're calling it Trinitite, after the Trinity test. Isn't that deliciously banal?"

"You are poison," Giles said. "You know that?"

"That's not nearly the best part," Mather continued. "You'll recall that the test took place at five thirty A.M.—"

"Five twenty-nine and twenty-one seconds," Giles snapped.

Mather frowned. "By eight thirty, the other detonators you built, for four more Gadgets, were loaded aboard the USS *Indianapolis* in San Francisco." He reached a corner of the assembly table and continued idling along. "With four sets of Horn's doublers, all destined for Tinian."

"For where?" Charlie asked.

"Tinian. It's one of the Mariana Islands, the size of five Manhattans, ten days' sail from San Francisco. Bristling with bombers. Also, a special hangar that holds a special bomber for a special crew. People on Tinian know all about the Gadget. For instance, a bomber can't load it in the hold like any ordinary bomb. It's taller than the clearance under the aircraft. The clever people of Tinian dug a trench with a ramp. They'll roll the Gadget to below ground level, drive the bomber over, then hoist it in. The aircraft will groan, I've been told. Five tons in one pull will strain any bomber's frame—"

"What is your point?" Giles interrupted.

"My point?" Mather came to a stop. "There will be no more tests. No flowers in the desert sky. From here on, it is all real. All war. And the destructor? All yours."

Charlie fell back against the table, a hand over his mouth.

"I do wonder, though. Do you think the Japanese people will like green glass?"

"Get out of here." Giles jumped from his chair. "You disgust me."

Mather was already at the door. "Over in Theoretical, I've had nothing to do with any of this. My hands are clean. Yours might have been, too, if you were smarter."

Giles threw a wastebasket, but Mather was gone before it struck the wall.

In the quiet afterward, Charlie went over and picked up the trash can, one by one putting the spilled papers back into it. After a moment he stopped, and sat on the floor.

"What is it?" Giles asked.

Charlie rested a forearm on the trash can's rim. "What have I done?"

"Your job," Giles said. "Like any other soldier."

Charlie stared down into the wastebasket. "So we pulled the trigger. Now we wait for the bullet to hit."

43.

I COULD NOT PREDICT what condition he might arrive in, in those first weeks, but I knew what my mood would be: always ready.

Charlie's workload had fallen so sharply, he could jump last minute on the bus, sometimes three times a week. He might arrive tired, or hungry, or more often distracted by worries about his work. It was a weight on him, never completely absent.

But my point of view? The last thing I'd expected: a dormant part of myself that Charlie had awakened, a secret he had called forth.

I was wanton. The great discovery of that time was how ferociously I desired. Charlie's quiet gave me confidence. I could trust him, and entrust myself to him. He fed my imagination, he enabled my abandon. I became reckless and obsessed. I would picture being with him in all sorts of forbidden ways. The best ones I would keep in mind for the next visit. No matter what I asked, he said yes.

"I had no idea about you," he murmured in my ear one afternoon.

"I didn't know either," I answered, and it was true.

Oh we were babies, and virgins, and I'd had no idea of my body's capacity for joy.

On Monday my mother would send some money. "Buy yourself a dress." On Tuesday I would shop instead for underthings—the more scandalous, the better. On Wednesday I would display them on the bed for Lizzie, who clapped her hands and laughed, or called me naughty, or grumbled that she could not wait for her husband to come home. My excitement was so great, I had no sense that I might be torturing her.

On Saturday morning I would dawdle as I dressed, assessing myself in the mirror, my breasts lifted by a new brassiere, my backside complimented by stockings that stopped at the top of my thighs, secured by garters of lurid red, and then one thin layer of respectability draped over the whole outfit, some demure sky-blue dress, innocent as a robin's egg, while I sashayed to East Palace Avenue to wait for him, my heart full of filthy secrets, an animal in heat.

Of course I was not entirely an innocent. I'd danced with quarterbacks and necked with captains, and there was the whole misguided dalliance with Chris. But Charlie was the first man I genuinely desired. And with incredible specificity. I thought about his strong hands, his hips surprisingly powerful and steady as an oil derrick, the high arches of his feet and what I might do to curl his toes. I lingered on memories of his kisses, and how they made me bold. I imagined pulling him to me as my lover, his face in my breasts, both of us thrilled by lust.

Sometimes I'd say no to myself, and push those thoughts away, they were occupying too much room in my mind. I'd jump out of bed to start the day, or go dust the organ keys in the church, or switch the shower to cold and then towel myself roughly to smooth the goose bumps away. Yet bit by bit the love notions would return, like a spell, a reverie all my own. Damn that wonderful Charlie Fish.

There were two problems. First, we still had not declared our love. I discounted that, though, because our bodies were saying it so zealously. But it nagged at me.

The second one was harder: We had nowhere to go. He'd applied for family housing on The Hill, but the waiting list was six months long. We could not live at the boardinghouse. Mrs. Morris reminded me with a wagging finger that men were still not allowed inside. I might be wed, but the virtue of the other girls must be protected.

The result was a perverse kind of sightseeing. Charlie and I would stroll the streets of Santa Fe, respectable as old folks on a constitutional, while both of our heads periscoped right and left in the hunt for a place to mate.

An empty house. The deep doorway of an out-of-business restaurant. On the seat of an abandoned truck. Once, against the retaining wall of a religious high school, after class hours but with me biting my lip to keep quiet just in case. The search made our hunger keen, hours spent seeking a safe spot made things urgent, and the chance of being caught made us aggressive. We had to move quickly, we had to finish fast.

That meant no time for coyness, no luxury of negotiation. It was right here, right now. We caressed each other's every inch with our fingers. We lavished the sensitive places with our tongues. We tried positions, ideas, attitudes. He stood before me proud, in broad daylight. I presented myself to him naked, inviting complete examination. I held his manhood and studied it like a marvel. He weighed my breasts in his palms.

"All I have been doing," I confessed one day, "is remembering when I pulled you into me harder, and how perfectly your cheek fit my hand."

Charlie nodded. "I can still feel it."

"And what have you been doing?" I asked him, a creature at play.

"Giving thanks for how you distract me from dread."

"Dread?" I said, grabbing him roughly to me. "None of that now."

And on we went. We were kneeling, straddling a chair, gripping a tree. We were lavish and base. For all my bossy ways, Charlie dominated me, and I was pleased to be his mistress, his release. Where did this surrender come from? How could I make it never go away? And then the next time again there was no place, every time we had to find a place. What a way to intensify desire. What a way to become expert in each other.

On those rare times when the hideaway we'd found allowed it, we would stay, holding each other in sweet silence.

I knew what pleasure I gave Charlie, and how already I was developing a mastery of certain deeds that he craved. He learned my wants as well, generously. He clung to me, he kissed my throat, and I thought: yes, I will give you anything.

Now, with the perspective of time, I know that this happy interval marked the end of a phase of young Brenda's life. In my secret heart, I continued to believe in my sophistication, my intelligence, my allure. Even as I indulged Charlie's least whim, I continued to hold myself in lofty regard. I had not yet told my mother that we were married, which I believe was a last vestige of that girl who considered herself superior. Some part of me—despite all the intimate connection with Charlie, despite the wild ecstasy he provoked in me—still believed that I was rescuing him. In a very few weeks, I would learn that it was entirely the other way around.

If I could reach back through time, from now to then, old woman to new wife, I would admire that girl, the sheen on her skin from the love she has just finished making in some basement or grove or parking lot. As she collects her garments one by one, I would tell her, enjoy it, savor it, because your days of self-lauding are almost at an end.

I've gone back and checked the records, and I remember correctly: the summer of 1945 was extremely hot in the Southwest. I disliked it for walking, for making the organ go out of tune, but especially for lovemaking. We dripped on each other. We grew sticky and fragrant. Sometimes I delivered Charlie to the bus, confident that our afternoon athletics would help him sleep for most of the ride, and in the heat I ambled back to the boardinghouse, also knowing that my clothes were disarrayed and I smelled of dried sweat and sour skin. But I was married, so no apologies were necessary. For all I cared, the world could take two steps backward off a cliff.

Besides, as I navigated a town stunned by summer, I was already on patrol, searching for the next place we could tryst, hoping it was in the shade. After one of those walks, as I lazily reached my room, Lizzie was about to leave for work.

Assessing me in her savvy way, taking it all in, she hesitated at the top of the stairs. "Tell me, kid. What are you doing to prevent a baby?"

I shrugged. "Not a thing."

"Want some help with that? Anything you'd like me to pick up at the hospital?"

"I'm fine," I said, not entirely understanding. "We'll be fine."

"Really?" Lizzie made a surprised face, tried to hide it by looking down the stairs, then spoke in that direction too. "Okay then. Off to the races with you."

She trotted down without another word. I turned and did a series of push-ups.

The next day Charlie visited, the air was humid and still. I wore a white cotton top, a lace bra beneath to present me to best advantage. Our search for a secluded spot was unsuccessful. By coincidence, we were only blocks from the church—where I had already declared we would never go to make love—when the skies opened. By the time we ducked under the church's stone archway, I was drenched.

"Oh my," Charlie said, a devilish grin on his face.

"What is it?"

"You." He pointed at my chest.

The wet shirt had become see-through. It clung to my body, left nothing to the imagination. Remembering my fantasy, I pulled his face between my breasts. My lover.

Two seconds after I released him, the church door opened, and there was Mrs. Morris. She seemed every bit as surprised as we were. Before I could speak, Charlie whipped his wet jacket off to drape it over me.

"Hello, Mrs. Morris," he said. "Didn't we get caught by the weather?"

"Come in," she said, shaking her head, not scolding but instead somewhat amused. "I'm sure we have some towels in here."

While we wiped ourselves off in the nave, she hurried up to the organ and switched it off. So she'd been playing again. Which maybe explained her good mood.

By the time we dried out, Mrs. Morris had taken her umbrella, wished us a good evening, and set out for home. Charlie stood up from the pew we'd been sharing, and crossed to the organ. Turning it on, he also switched on the lamp over the music stand. When he saw what piece I'd played most recently, his face lit up too.

"The toccata? I love it. Brenda, would you please?"

I ambled over. "Only the opening, Charlie. I don't have the fugue part in hand."

"Anything. Aside from hymns, I haven't heard you play in centuries."

I sat on the bench, my husband standing beside me, towels draped over our shoulders, and despite the limited stops and two broken manuals, I began.

Yes, the opening was powerful. Yes, the world fell away. When it came time to turn the page, I did not have to do the usual hasty grab. Instead Charlie reached forward to do it, which meant that the former choir boy was reading the music along with me.

As the fugue approached, I felt confidence from how well the first passage had gone. Which was dumb, because it made me barrel right over the waterfall. Only a few measures into the fugue and my right hand stumbled on the melody, my left entered late, and it all became a ball of knotted yarn.

"Damn," I said. "It was going so well."

"Brilliant," Charlie said, touching the score. "This is the measure that stops you?"

I nodded. "Just about every time."

"Here." He pulled me around to face him. "Can you sing it to me?"

"What do you mean?"

"Just sing the melody of that measure, and the part after, if you remember it."

"Well, I can't. I don't know it. That's the whole problem."

Charlie leaned forward, reading the notes, then he squatted so his face was level with mine. And he sang. *"Ba ba-bum ba-bum bum-ba."*

"This is silly."

But he sang the measure again. *"Ba ba-bum ba-bum bum-ba."* Perfectly on pitch. When he did it a third time, I sang along.

"There, you see?" He smiled as if he'd been repairing organs all day. Scanning the page, he squatted again. "Now the next measure. *Ba-bum-bum, ba-bum-bum, ba-ba."*

And I sang with him. Two minutes later I could sing the whole right hand of that passage. We did it together.

"Now comes the fun part," Charlie said, touching the key to make sure we would still be on pitch. It reminded me of when he'd done that same thing, on the piano in our living room, before singing on Christmas Eve. So much had happened, so much changed, yet he was still Charlie, not wanting to be sharp or flat.

"Ready? And—"

I started again, this time without him. When I reached the third measure, though, he came in singing the part of the left hand. My voice in the upper register, his in the lower, we played that fugue with our voices. We'd made an organ of ourselves.

We sang about ten measures before I couldn't help it and burst out laughing. Charlie laughed with me. "We'll teach that toccata who's boss. Try once more?"

Oh, Charlie. What was this euphoria? This high delight? "Yes please," I said. "From the top."

The next day at breakfast, Reverend Morris announced that Charlie and I were welcome to use the Hudson again, from time to time.

"Provided you leave at least a quarter tank of gas," he said, "in case I need to visit a member of the congregation unexpectedly."

"Excuse me," Mrs. Morris said, "but just who is going to pay for the gasoline?"

"You could take it from my salary," I volunteered.

"Well." She rose to head for the kitchen. "As long as you return it in impeccable condition." Which I translated to mean we should not have sex in the car.

"That is incredibly generous of you," I said, as sincere as any newly married girl would be, when her means of deliverance has arrived.

"No reason you two should be cooped up around here," the reverend said. "New Mexico is a beautiful place."

Charlie and I began to learn that very thing, every chance we got. We were sightseers with a mission. He would find a potential spot, and pull over. Or I would spy something promising, ask him to stop, and say, "I want you to come with me."

He always did. East of Taos, among the sweet-smelling ponderosa. Beside the Cimarron River, in the whispering grass. Standing up, in a cleft of boulders near Albuquerque, not fifty feet from a busy road. In a vast empty expanse somewhere to the south, writhing in the dirt under a roasting sun till we sweated like thoroughbreds. Oh, that one is with me still. We yowled like cats, and finished with skin painted red by the clay. We tried to wipe it off each other, which only made the mess worse. So we stood naked, laughing, so revealed and intimate. I adored it.

I figured something else out too. Remembering when Lizzie asked how I would feel if someone took my music away, one Sunday I invited Mrs. Morris to play the closing hymn. Reverend Morris would be in the middle of worship and unable to object.

"Really?" she said, her face lighting up. "Honestly?"

Which was how I helped her more than I'd realized. She remained stern as ever, but it became not her only mood. One night climbing the stairs I heard something from the main house, and stopped to listen. Yes, she was laughing. The next Sunday I asked Mrs. Morris to play two pieces.

Meanwhile Charlie and I explored as much of New Mexico as that gas tank allowed: pueblos and Indian dwellings, cliff towns from centuries ago, deep dry gulches—where if it rained for as little as five minutes, they could flash-fill and flood and sweep us away. Always I asked the same way: "I want you to come with me." And he would.

Then we found the falls of Nambe. Way up in the hills, far from prying eyes, where the water was cool and tumbling, and the sand as soft as cotton sheets. We were gentle that day, my body unusually welcoming, and Charlie moved with a kind of certainty I hadn't felt before. Afterward we swam, in no hurry to dress, Adam and Eve in a season of war, trying to make our own Eden.

I'd brought a blanket and we cuddled on the riverbank.

"What are you thinking about?" I asked him.

After a pause, he answered: "Japanese children."

"I'm sorry, what?"

"Tell me this," Charlie said, shifting his hips, changing the subject to my favorite topic. "From our lovemaking so far, what do you like best?"

My first impulse was to describe a particular position, or maybe a place and moment that had brought special release. But I thought before answering.

"I like trust best," I said eventually. "How safe I feel with you, how I can count on you to be a good guy, and how that allows me to let myself go. I enjoy not being afraid."

Charlie was smiling. "Great answer."

"What about you? What do you like best?"

His smile faded. Charlie stared into the distance. He kissed my forehead absently.

"What?" I said.

"Well, the thing I like best with you is how the world goes away. My work, the war, everything becomes small and distant. All I can think about is you, and what we are doing, and how fantastic it feels. It's like we're on an island."

"Yes," I said. "A universe of two."

But then. As I snuggled closer against him, and the river gossiped at our feet, I had the smallest, most subtle and secret feeling that there might be something else in that universe. Who can say where the idea came from? Of course it was impossible, we'd only just finished making love. There was no way my body could be aware of anything that quickly. Yet I genuinely had a sense of being changed. Something inside me had begun. Without understanding how, I felt myself enter an entirely new kind of knowing. We had become more.

44.

GILES SPOTTED CHARLIE ON the bench outside the mess tent, and tottered over with a grin. "I have something unexpected to show you."

"This is the place where I was introduced to David Horn," Charlie replied. "Back when we didn't know how to detonate."

"I submit that you two solved that problem rather well," Giles said.

"Does that make Horn a hero, therefore? Or a villain?"

"Both, of course." Giles held his arms wide, as if to indicate the mess tent, the technicians passing by, the truck traffic below. "Like all of us."

Charlie mused a moment. "What do you know about the guillotine?"

"They used it in the French Revolution to decapitate aristocrats. Why do you ask?"

"I read up on it in the Santa Fe library."

Giles sat beside him, a palm on each knee. "Educate me."

"France had many forms of execution—hanging, burning at the stake. Punishment was based not on the crime but on the condemned person's economic status. In the 1700s, the government decided capital punishment should be egalitarian, regardless of the criminal's class."

"A rather brutal form of equality, by the sound of it."

"They also decided to separate torture from execution. Killing by the state might be just, but should not be inhumane. The courts hired Tobias Schmidt, a German whose trade was building harpsichords, to make a machine that killed people without pain."

"Fascinating. And this has been an item of interest for you why?"

"Because Schmidt failed. The execution itself probably didn't hurt, but there was plenty of suffering." Charlie counted down on his fingers. "In knowing that certain death was coming. In walking out to the scaffold." His voice accelerated. "In placing your head in the groove. Perhaps you smell the blood of those beheaded before you. Perhaps the crowd jeers, mocking your terror. Perhaps it's raining. Perhaps you shit yourself."

Giles turned in his seat. "Charlie, are you all right?"

"But the agony, you see," and he formed a circle with his thumb and forefinger, as if holding a paintbrush to make a fine point. "The pain is all in the anticipation."

"Ah." Giles sat back. "Now I understand you."

"I have been nervous countless times in my life. I'm afraid twenty times a day. But never before have I lived in such a complete state of dread."

Giles put an arm over Charlie's shoulder. "You are speaking for all of us here."

"Whatever happened to Oppie's idea of a demonstration?"

"He was speaking as a scientist," Giles replied. "But the actual masters of this project are military, and the only language they speak is victory."

"Victory without annihilation might be possible."

"Perhaps. But we will never know."

Charlie rubbed his neck. "So we place our heads in the groove, waiting for the blade to fall."

"My friend, that is a dark thought. But look." Giles pointed. "An amusement."

Down the slope, Mather had ducked his head out of the tent. He spied them and strode in their direction, a bounce in his step.

"Gentlemen," Mather hailed them. "And I use the term loosely."

"Hello, Mather," Giles said. "What brings you over from Theoretical? Desire to rub elbows with the rabble?"

"An appetite for intellectual consensus. The elusive idea that by now, all of us might find agreement about where we are and what presumably will happen next."

Instead of answering, Charlie began to pick at the paint on the bench. Giles scratched himself under the arm. "Elusive would be an understatement."

"What dissent can there be? We've seen the power of our creation. Are we now to toss it on the junk heap? A footnote in the physics textbooks of tomorrow? 'Oh yes, there was this minor invention in '45, but we moved past that.' And so on."

"Perhaps we don't merit mention at all," Giles said.

"Less than two and a half years from the birth of this project to the test three weeks ago?" Mather chuckled. "I believe future generations will judge our achievement to be the fastest transformation of human power in history."

"Then why am I filled with dread?" Charlie asked, continuing to pick at the paint.

"Because you are not a warrior," Mather said. "The rest of us, in a moment of doubt, would march to the library and read old newspapers. In two minutes, you can find editions from the second week of December, three years ago. The photos alone will persuade you: burning ships, sinking in the harbor, hundreds of men trapped inside. A more intelligent person might find an inner resolve."

"Like Szilard?" Charlie said. "And the seventy others who signed his letter?"

Mather made a sour frown. "The test frightened them, that's all. Had they waited ten days before all of this clucking and squawking, they'd have returned to reason."

"What about the Franck Report, then? Other men who lack resolve?"

"Exceptions to the rule, Fish. One hundred thousand people across the country work on the Manhattan Project. Any group that large will have dissenters. Among any random hundred thousand Americans, five hundred will refuse to say the sky is blue."

"Ha," Giles said, though it was not at all a laugh. He peered up, a perfect noontime in early August. "The sky is not blue."

Mather pulled his chin back at the affront. "Fine. Plead ignorance if you like. But you are as culpable as all the rest of us."

"I know," Giles said. "I feel it."

"You're even more responsible, Fish." Mather nodded in Charlie's direction. "If Giles here accomplished nothing in Electronics, dozens of others could do the job. If I made no progress in Theoretical, it would not matter." He turned, idling away down the hill. "Only one of us is Trigger."

Charlie jumped to his feet, but Giles grabbed his arm.

"I should have decked him back in Chicago," Charlie fumed.

"It would only give him pleasure. That's how confused that boy is."

"Damn it, though." Charlie sat back down.

Giles waited half a minute, letting the situation cool, before he spoke. "Now may I show you the thing I mentioned?"

Charlie smiled at his friend. "Anything to change the subject."

Giles unbuttoned his cuff, rolling up the sleeve. "Drumroll, please."

He paused as a young soldier jogged past them, into the mess tent. Aside from seeing that his shirt was dark with sweat, they took little notice. Then Giles raised the sleeve, to reveal a blue tattoo on the inside: a hardy stem, with thick flowerets at the top.

"Broccoli?" Charlie asked.

Giles laughed. "Cauliflower, actually."

"I don't understand."

He turned his wrist so the inking was right side up. "Remind you of anything?"

Charlie squinted, then made his surprised expression. "The Gadget?"

Giles laughed. "It was the only design close to what we saw. The detonation."

"I thought you hated tattoos. You told Monroe it was graffiti on the body."

"I do. And the banality of this vegetable makes it all the more hideous. But now that I know what we've accomplished, I *want* to be marred. We should all be marred."

The soldier came running out of the mess tent, spotted them, and dashed up to the bench. "Is one of you Charles Fish, detonator division?"

"That's me," Charlie said.

The soldier bent at the waist, panting. "I've been all over, sir, looking for you. The tech area, the barracks."

"Now you've found me." He sat up. "What can I do for you?"

"You're wanted in the division director's office, sir. It's an emergency."

"No satisfying that man," Charlie said to Giles as he stood. "What does Bronsky want now?"

"It's about your wife, sir."

"Your wife?" Giles interjected. "Since when do you have a wife?"

"What about her?" Charlie asked.

"Well, sir." The soldier gulped. "Apparently she's dying."

45.

AT FIRST I THOUGHT it was a heavy period. Some months are like that, who knows why. Then it persisted, grew heavier—what my mother called "the curse" was making me light-headed. One night at bedtime I mentioned it to Lizzie.

"Sorry, kid." She gave my arm a bump. "I've had one myself. You'll bounce back."

"What are you talking about?" I asked. We were standing in the hallway, she in one of her husband's long shirts and me in a light summer nightgown.

"Miscarriages. They can make a gal awful blue, too, so keep an eye out. But you two shouldn't worry." She laughed. "You'll probably make sixteen babies before you're done."

"Yeah." I chuckled feebly. "We'll have to keep trying."

Lizzie winked. "Practice makes perfect."

I wandered back into my room. So we did conceive that day at Nambe Falls. Only the baby didn't survive. It would feel so different to realize these things, I thought, if my husband were there to share them. I lay on the bed and hugged my stomach.

But the bleeding kept up, day after day. Sometimes I felt a sharp pain too. Once I was better, I would send Charlie a note letting him know what had happened.

Wednesday during choir practice, we had finished warm-ups when I raised both my arms to signal the call to attention—the moment everyone breathes in for the first note. I felt stabbing pain in my shoulder. My knees buckled, the room went dim.

Next thing I knew I was in an unfamiliar bed, sore like someone had run a sword into my belly. A hospital, I knew by the bleachy smell. Bandages ran across my abdomen. I wanted water but there was no one to ask. And it was too much work to raise my voice.

I dipped in and out of consciousness with no sense of time. I remember Lizzie coming to see me, straight from her shift and still in her nursing uniform, trying to look tough. But she held a wad of tissues and I watched her twist them into a knot. The Morrises came, too, several times. I stirred to half-awake one night and they were both at the bedside. They were kneeling, heads bent, and I wondered: What did I ever do to deserve being prayed for? Then I was out again.

Eventually I could speak, but only in a whisper because more than that hurt too much. Another time when I woke it was Reverend Morris by himself, standing at the bedside and sobbing, tears pouring down his face.

I blinked, he was gone, and I wondered whether it had actually happened.

One afternoon I opened my eyes and who should be standing there but Charlie Fish. His face was creased with worry. It made him look so adorable. I raised one hand, which I admit took some effort. He took it and kissed my knuckles. That was when I felt like I really began to sleep.

Every time after that, Charlie was there. If he left my bedside, it was only when I was way down deep. Because anytime my eyes opened, day or night, they saw him.

Once it was early morning, not light yet, and Charlie was asleep in the hard hospital chair, looking about ten years old. I was so glad to see him, I cried a little. A nurse came in, all bustle and business, checking my pulse and temperature, while Charlie woke and peered around with a confused expression.

The next time I woke, Charlie stood on one side, caressing my hand, and when I turned to see who was holding my other, well. My mother. All the way from Chicago.

She leaned down to kiss my jaw, under the ear, and she whispered. "Baby girl, you are going to be all right. You rest now."

As if I had any choice. And yet, each day I did grow stronger. I ate a few bites of bread. I sipped water through a straw. A doctor came in, a handsome man with gray in his sideburns, but he had a terrible limp. That was the war for you, I thought: Two good legs and he'd be preparing for the invasion of Japan like Lizzie's Tim. Maybe that bum leg had saved his life. Or maybe he'd hurt it in the war already. He stood at the foot of the bed, clipboard in hand, and spoke to it rather than to us.

"Ectopic pregnancy. The embryo did not attach to the uterus as it should. Instead it attached to the right fallopian tube. Why these things occur is a mystery. This failure caused a rupture, leading to internal bleeding that persisted until the patient collapsed."

"Failure?" I said. I had failed in some way?

"In emergency surgery," he was reading from the clipboard now, "we sectioned the damaged area to prevent further bleeding, and removed compromised tissue." He lowered the clipboard to his hip. "The patient has lost one side of her reproductive system. Obviously the fetus did not survive. Internal bleeding was advanced, requiring six units of transfusion. The left side reproductive tissue remains intact, so the patient remains able to conceive. Questions?"

If there were any, I was too fuzzy to participate. "Failure." That was the word that accompanied me back to sleep.

But I had done one thing right: I had married Charlie Fish. Lizzie, the Morrises, they stopped in each day. They chatted with my mother, which felt odd, two different parts of my life connecting, my elbow meeting my knee. She was there most of the time. But Charlie? Always. I measured my healing progress by the expression on his face. The less worry he showed, the less worry I felt.

One morning they made me stand. The pain made me think of magicians, and their trick of sawing a woman in half. They made me prove I could get on and off the john. That afternoon, I walked all the way to the nurses' station, gripping my mother's arm for balance.

"You're doing great," she encouraged me. "I know how you feel, too, because the incision is like a C-section. Which I had when I was delivering you."

I stopped in the hallway. "I never knew that."

She shrugged. "It never merited discussion before."

"I suppose not."

"Every time I look down, in the shower or changing clothes or whatever, I see a reminder of the birth of my baby girl."

We started shuffling along again. "Mother, are you going sweet in your old age?"

"You had me worried, kiddo. And with all of you gone, Chicago has been quiet."

"Are you all right?"

She swatted at the air. "Let's just say your mother appreciates her family."

"You *are* going sweet—"

"For the love of Pete." She stepped sideways. "Charlie, you guide her for a while."

He'd been right behind us all along.

"I'm going to the waiting room for a smoke," my mother said, leaving the two of us alone in the corridor.

"Shall we turn back now?" Charlie asked.

It was like someone uncorked a bathtub, my energy drained so fast. "Good idea. What have you told her, anyhow?"

"She knows we're married, if that's what you mean. And since you got pregnant, I imagine she knows that we—"

"Enough," I said, but the exertion of saying it made me pause for breath. "How come you don't have to get back to The Hill?"

"I'll need to, soon. Though I'd sure rather stay here."

We passed rooms with the doors half-closed. Inside one, someone was coughing hard. Then I shuffled on, with pathetic, tiny steps. "He said we might still have kids."

"I had no idea we were so close."

"Neither did I."

We smiled at each other in that hallway, a sad smile, but underneath it was something new between us. Like we were growing roots. I felt happy and sad and deepened all at the same time.

We'd reached my room and Charlie helped me back into bed.

I held on to him a second more, which made him lean down, so he bent all the way and kissed me.

"Don't," I said. "I haven't washed or brushed my teeth or anything."

"But you're alive," he said, and kissed me again. Like he meant it.

Which of course was the moment my mother barged back into the room. Seeing her daughter on a bed, holding a man who is kissing her, I imagine required some mental adjustment. It did for me.

"Excuse me," she said, backpedaling. "I should have knocked."

"Not at all," Charlie said, strangely at ease in that awkward moment. "I needed to check on the patient's condition, that's all."

She laughed. "What's your diagnosis?"

"As sassy as ever."

"Some conditions just can't be cured, kiddo."

"You two," I said. "Don't you go ganging up on me."

Finally the nurses told me I'd be going home the next day. Well, back to the boardinghouse anyhow. My mother went to make sure my room was ready.

"I need to go back tomorrow too," Charlie said. "But your mom's going to stay another few days, and I'll be down on Saturday like usual."

I patted the bed, and he sat on the edge of the mattress. "You know what I want?"

"To be fully recovered?"

I rested the side of my fist on his thigh. "For this war to be over, so we can start our lives together right."

Charlie's face went blank. He didn't answer me.

"Hello?" I said. "You don't agree?"

He sat there, staring off, and only gradually returned to me. "Sure. Of course, yes. But ending the war . . . that's more complicated."

"The hell it is. We pound them until they surrender. Then everyone—Lizzie, my mother, my brother, my dad, you and me—we can bring things back to normal again."

"Okay," he said. "Then let me say that ending it is more complicated *for me*."

"What in the world does that mean?"

"I don't even know." He stood, backing away from the bed. "I'm going to get a little air, okay? Be right back."

He rushed out of the room, the first time he'd left my side in nine days. What had I said?

That night the ward was strangely quiet. No nurses disturbed my sleep with a thermometer or stethoscope or blood pressure sleeve. Usually in the small hours I could hear the radio down at the nurses' station, big band jazz turned down low, but not that night. I didn't hear the ping of call buttons, either, which was unusual. Even in bed, I could tell something was going on, something was different.

Then I slept, and by morning I'd forgotten about it, and was busy getting ready to go home. After breakfast they brought a wheelchair for me. Which Charlie pushed so slowly I wanted to smack him. Once again the Morrises lent us the old Hudson. I told everyone not to make a fuss, but to be honest it took some doing to land me in the big backseat. Charlie drove, slow as a snail while my mother had a cigarette, blowing her smoke out the open window.

Lizzie was at work, but the Morrises were home—and behaved odd as a pair of harlequin ducks. They hovered and fluttered, and created a traffic jam at the door. I didn't understand why till I reached the foot of the stairs and glanced to the left. Their living room was packed. Funeral, wedding, nothing had brought that big a crowd to the house before. My first thought was that I would have to play for a service of some kind.

"What's going on?" I asked. "Somebody die?"

"Don't you worry about any of that," Mrs. Morris said. "Not your business."

"They're all basses, wanting to audition for the choir," Reverend Morris joked.

"Yes, and today is Christmas Day," I said. But then I was concentrating on climbing the stairs, and lifting a leg that high required more stomach muscles than I realized, which meant a serious flare of pain with each step, and the exertion of two flights required all of my attention.

Soon they had me situated in bed, with extra pillows, a jug of water, and a little metal commode to spare me trips to the john. Charlie was going to be late for his bus. My mother tried to shoo him along, saying I'd be fine, but he stuck around till I was set and secure. I admit it, I was exhausted.

"I hate to go," he said. "But I think you'll be okay."

"Course she will," my mother said. "I'll be here three more days, and then you'll be back. Once this war is done, we'll all be together in Chicago, happily arguing with one another."

Charlie winced at that. Why would he not want the war to be over?

He gave my mother a long hug. "You're family now, Charlie," she said, patting him on the back.

"I like it," he answered, grinning. "I'm a Dubie and she's a Fish."

She ducked back into the hallway while he came and leaned over me. "Your job is to get well, Brenda. We'll both do our jobs, and everything will turn out all right."

I caressed the side of his face. "Come back soon."

He kissed me once more, and paused in the doorway, one hand holding the frame. "Now I know I am definitely a man in wartime."

"Why is that?" I called weakly from the bed.

"Because I am leaving the woman I love."

It was the first time he'd said it. He'd done it perfectly too. I saw his words register on my mother's face in the hall. Charlie hesitated for half a breath, poised there, waiting. Then he knocked twice on the door frame and I heard him running down the stairs. By the time the outer door slammed I knew what his hesitation had been—a moment for me to announce something similar, to express my thanks for all his tender care, to say, "Charlie, I love you too."

But my mother had been there, and I'd felt self-conscious. So even after all the devoted hours he'd spent by my side, long days and nights of steadfastness, Charlie went back to The Hill without a declaration of love from his wife. What kind of monster was I? What childish, selfish person?

My mother came in, tucking sheets and fluffing pillows, matter-of-fact. Which told me that she had noticed my failure to respond too.

"There," she said when everything was snug. "I'm going downstairs for a smoke, then I'll be back."

Oh, Charlie. That moment, when my heart hurt more than any other part of my body? That was the first time this girl knew what it is like to lie in a bed of remorse.

46.

ON THE EIGHTH OF August, the bus to Los Alamos was nearly empty. Two local men sat in the rearmost seats, a canvas duffel of plumbing tools on the floor between them. The driver ground through the gears, swearing mildly at a reluctant clutch. Otherwise Charlie was alone. The route out of Santa Fe narrowed, the roadside homes and shops dwindling, and then none. The bus turned west across the Rio Grande, laboring as it climbed the winding road to The Hill.

Charlie showed his pass at the front gate, found himself waved summarily through, and thought the soldiers seemed less hostile. Maybe the Trinity test impressed them enough that they realized the scientists were not a complete waste of food.

The bus stuttered to a stop outside the mess hall, and Charlie descended into a strange quiet. Normally in midafternoon on a Wednesday, the place would be bustling. He heard two cooks arguing, but none of the other normal hubbub. No one was walking around. He'd been away nine days, an eternity in the tight timetable of The Hill. Now it seemed the world had ended while he was gone.

Hitching up his pants, he set out for the barracks. They were nearly empty, two men on cots at the far end, both snoring loudly enough that Charlie thought each should have wakened the other. On his tightly made bed, the blanket was unmarked by visits from Midnight. Changing his shirt, he headed for the lab. What assignment would Bronsky have for him, now that the detonators were finished?

As he passed Ashley Pond, he noticed a gathering in Fuller

Lodge. Chairs stood in rows, many of them filled, while someone's lecture droned at the front of the room. On a Wednesday. Normally he would have swept by to eavesdrop. Instead he picked up his pace till he reached the tech area gate. The guard barely glanced at Charlie's pass before waving him in. Something was definitely going on.

When he reached his desk, the only orders on it were the usual weekly directions for dealing with documents—which to preserve, which to destroy. No checklist of tasks, no criticisms of recent work. Under that sheet, the mess of calculations and designs he'd left incomplete when he'd heard about Brenda. He fell into his chair, flummoxed.

"Hard to get comfy now, isn't it?"

He turned and Mather sauntered in. The man was like a rash that would not quit. But Charlie knew he would explain things. "Where is everyone?"

Mather shrugged. "On a hike? Taking a nap? Drinking themselves blind?"

"On a Wednesday?"

"You poor boy," Mather said, his grin revealing an evil delight. "You don't know."

"Know what? I've been at the hospital with Brenda."

"I heard. Everything peachy now?"

"Not quite peachy," Charlie said. "Please don't be coy. What is going on?"

Mather held up one finger. "Wait right here." And he scuttled away down the hall.

Had The Hill's work been shut down? Had Truman done something? He went to fill his cup at the lab sink, but when he turned the knob nothing came out.

"The water shortage is worse," Mather said, returning with his arms full of newspapers. "Apparently a tanker truck is on its way. But no more showers this week."

He reached the assembly table, and dropped the papers so that they landed with a slap. "Feast your eyes, Fish. Come learn what Trigger has done."

His heart fluttering, Charlie saw himself as if from outside his body, crossing the room and bending over the newspapers. On top, the *New York Times*. Its headline was in capital letters, stacked in three lines across the top of the page:

FIRST ATOMIC BOMB DROPPED ON JAPAN;

MISSILE IS EQUAL TO 20,000 TONS OF TNT;

TRUMAN WARNS FOE OF A "RAIN OF RUIN"

"It happened," Charlie said, rubbing his neck. "The blade came down."

"What are you talking about?" Mather asked.

Charlie read on. On August 6, 1945, at 8:15 A.M., Japan time, the *Enola Gay* released an atomic bomb over Hiroshima. It detonated while six hundred yards in the air. The fireball reached three hundred thousand degrees, making a ground temperature of five thousand four hundred. It demolished every building for two miles.

He opened to the inside pages. There were many stories, including one explicitly stating that the bomb had been developed in Los Alamos. "I need to warn Brenda."

Mather chuckled. "She knows, I'm sure. Unless she's been under a rock."

"In fact, she has."

There was no immediate estimate of the number of people killed, but the articles quoted President Truman at length. "We are now prepared to obliterate more rapidly and completely every productive enterprise the Japanese have aboveground in any city. We shall destroy Japan's power to make war."

Charlie sat back. "I can't continue."

"But we're only getting started." Mather flipped the *Times* aside, and there lay the *Albuquerque Journal*: "U.S. Announces Atom Bomb; Hope for Earlier End to War."

Charlie pushed it away, only to see the *Pittsburgh Post-Gazette*, which also used capital letters. "DEADLY NEW ATOMIC BOMBS BEGIN DEVASTATION OF JAPAN."

Charlie straightened. "I don't need a newspaper to tell me what the Gadget does."

"Then try these. A day later."

The first thing Charlie saw was a death toll estimate of one hundred thousand people. One hundred thousand. One blurry photo showed a city leveled, every structure gone but one or two chimneys standing bent and alone. Complete destruction.

"Dear God," he said. "Have the Japs surrendered?"

Mather snorted. "Incredibly, no. Call it an indication of how persuasive a demonstration would have been."

Charlie scanned the various front pages, fanned on the table like a hand of playing cards. "We don't know that."

"The emperor saw an entire city destroyed, and still did not quit. So actually, Fish, we do know."

"We will never know for certain."

Mather shook his head. "You sound like the editorials. All bleeding hearts."

Charlie shuffled through the pages. "Where are they?"

"Move over." Mather flipped to the bottom of the stack. "Here are a few. All half-informed, and too late to matter."

Charlie closed his eyes. If Giles had delivered this news, he might have cried. If it were Monroe, they would have wept together. Why did it have to be Mather?

"Let me see." Blinking, he leaned over the opinion page of the *St. Louis Post-Dispatch*. But he had begun to tear up, and could read only fragments. The editorial asked the reader to imagine Denver obliterated in an instant. Science had "signed the mammalian world's death certificate, and deeded an earth in ruins to the ants."

He opened the *Milwaukee Journal*. There was a map of Milwaukee, with circles to show which parts of the city would be obliterated, which ones ruined, which ones burned. The editorial predicted "a self-perpetuating chain of atomic destruction" that could destroy the planet like "a forest fire sweeping before high winds."

Last came the *United States News*. "We cannot be proud of what we have done. If we state our inner thoughts honestly, we are ashamed of it. . . . Since we lately had been warning the people of Japan against air attacks on certain cities, we might have warned them against staying in the specific area where we first wished to demonstrate the destruction that could ensue from the continued use of the atomic bomb."

Charlie wiped his face on his sleeve. "Wow."

"Yes." Mather nodded. "Apparently everyone has forgotten that our firebombing was every bit as catastrophic. Use a new tool, and your critics suddenly have amnesia."

"That wasn't what I meant," Charlie said.

Mather sniffed. "One struggles to comprehend precisely what you do in fact mean by the great philosophical treatise known as 'wow.'"

"How did you manage to come by all of these papers?"

"Bronsky trusts me." He shrugged. "The army sent someone to Albuquerque to bring him the latest news."

Charlie found himself tidying the papers, folding them closed again.

"It's all right," Mather said. "He was finished with them anyway."

Charlie kept folding. "I want to put it all away."

"There's more, you know. Not news, but evidence of your role."

Don't answer, Charlie said to himself. Don't take the bait. He went to his desk and, as ordered, began sorting papers into two piles: keep, destroy, keep, destroy.

"Your math, you see," Mather continued. "It was instrumental."

"I don't want to know."

"Of course you do," Mather scoffed. "It's history now anyway. Remember that day, long ago in Chicago, when you had to calculate the timing of an object falling from thirty-five thousand feet to other various heights?"

"Of course," Charlie said. "With no idea why. It was absurd."

"We weren't permitted to tell you," Mather replied. "That wasn't absurdity. It was caution."

"Caution? With me? I've been loyal, and kept all my secrets."

"But you're weak," Mather said. "Who could predict what you might do?"

Charlie took a stack of papers to the bin labeled Documents to Destroy and dropped them in. "I am finished with this conversation."

"Now I've hurt your feelings," Mather said, "when I meant to pay you a compliment. Because of course what you were calculating, in all your wrestling with *pi*, was the fall time of the bomb. All of your hypotheticals proved conclusive."

Charlie returned to his desk without answering.

Mather went to the window, hands on his hips like a landowner surveying his fields. "You are the one who calculated the forty-three-second fall."

"So?" Keep, destroy, keep.

Mather glanced out the window. There was no activity, no one hustling across the tech area. The place was deserted. "So after forty-three seconds, a B-29 going three hundred and fifty miles an hour would be six miles away."

"Mather, you are tiresome. What's your point?"

He turned from the window. "You proved that they would survive, Fish. The B-29 crew, I mean. Your math demonstrated that they could drop this gigantic bomb, and be far enough away when it blew, and the detonation would not obliterate them. See?"

Charlie shook his head. "Not really."

"The military didn't have to recruit men for a suicide mission. Your math made the whole thing possible."

Charlie rubbed his face with both hands. "I feel like I've been used."

"On the contrary." Mather shook his head. "You have received advancements, based on legitimate accomplishments. I would not have predicted it, Fish, but you have come a long way since Chicago."

Charlie took a sheet from the destroy pile and turned it over. He poked around and found a pencil. "How many men do you estimate worked in that math room?"

"I don't estimate. The exact number was thirty, plus our manager Cohen, that worthless windbag."

"All right." Charlie did quick division on the paper. "That's three thousand, two hundred and twenty-six each."

"Meaning what?"

"Meaning the number of Japanese people killed in Hiroshima per math person."

"Don't be infantile." Mather began pacing. "Their nation started this. The imbeciles are *still* fighting us too." As if insulting someone was balm, he calmed, half-sitting on a desk. "Those bastards invited this destruction on themselves."

At that, Charlie realized what the conversation was actually about. Giles would have spotted it sooner, but it was apparent to him now: Mather was filled with guilt. He had come here not to deliver news, but to shed culpability. Whether by exaggerating Charlie's role or by blaming the Japanese, the man was seeking exoneration.

Charlie knew with every cell in his body that this was not something he could give. Especially given the culpability he felt himself.

"Tell me, Mather," he said. "Whatever became of your sister? The pretty tennis player you said none of us would ever touch. Did she make it through the war all right?"

"My sister." Mather laughed to himself. "My untouchable sister."

"Last I heard she was in England."

"Nursing assistant at a war hospital, that plucky gal." Mather picked a sheet of paper up from the desk. "One anecdote from her last letter should suffice."

As he spoke, he folded the paper this way and that. "One day she was delivering some documents, an innocent messenger for some VIP, scurrying through the ward, when a surgeon shouted at her to assist him. It was an emergency. Well, she has the heart of an authentic do-gooder, but no medical training whatsoever. He said it didn't matter, this boy would die of infection if he did not amputate immediately, and there were no nurses available. He pointed to where she was to secure the delirious fellow's leg." Mather put the paper down to hang his hands out in the air, holding an imaginary thigh. "She put her hands on his swollen skin, and it was hot to the touch. The surgeon placed a blade against the skin, and the moment he applied pressure, the wound burst. My sister was not wearing a mask, of course, and it sprayed into her face."

"That is a horror," Charlie said.

"Blood, pus, who knows what hideousness." Mather dropped his hands. "Poor boy probably died within the hour anyway. But my sweet, dutiful sister remained at the bedside, as ordered, until she found herself holding an amputated leg. Then that lovely girl asked the surgeon, 'Where do I put this?'"

He picked up the paper again, crushed it into a ball, and tossed it toward a wastebasket. It missed and bounced away on the floor. "You don't need a battle to destroy you. That nice tennis girl? That beautiful tomboy? Wrecked. Utterly wrecked."

"Is anyone going to get out of this war intact?" Charlie asked. "Anyone?"

"Did you know," Mather said, rousing himself, sitting up straight, "Fish, did you know that our armed forces set aside certain cities as ineligible for fire bombings? Apparently we wanted them kept pristine for the Gadget."

"What do you mean?"

"If your atomic bomb blows down charred timbers, where's the glory? They set a few places aside, intact. A better canvas on which to display the art of annihilation."

Charlie sat with his head down for a full minute, struggling not to vomit. When he looked up, Mather was staring at him. "I'm having a difficult time with all of this."

"Consider mankind as a species," Mather replied. "Is it a collection of angels, who make music and art and automobiles? Or is it a mob of monsters? These are the questions I ask."

"And what do you think, now that we know how to split an atom?"

"What I have long suspected," Mather said, a smile coming to his face. "Our species is capable of anything."

47

MY MOTHER STAYED TILL the stitches came out, then caught a train back to Chicago. Lizzie waited two solid days before coming to the doorway of my room, a look on her face that made me think she was going to say she was seriously ill.

"Here's what you need to know first," she said instead.

"About what?" I was flat on my back. I'd managed to make it downstairs twice each day, even shuffling half a block from the house the second time, though the climb back up the stairs was still daunting. I had dressed for the day's first salvo, but paused before starting the struggle to get my shoes on.

"First you need to know that my husband, my powerful lover Tim, was scheduled to ship out from San Diego in three weeks."

"For the invasion, yes. You told me."

"He's a medic," she added. "So he'd be running right into the gunfire."

"Let's sincerely hope that doesn't happen."

"You believe that, don't you? And we should take any steps we can to prevent it?"

"Lizzie," I sat up, no easy task. "Of course. What's this all about?"

She rubbed a finger under her nose. "Our country took steps."

"Good. Did it work?"

"Not yet. But I need you to be thinking that way."

"You're scaring me a little," I said.

"We've been keeping something from you. Mrs. Morris wanted to wait longer, but the hell with her."

"Is it about Charlie? Is he all right?"

Lizzie hesitated. "He's fine. Though he's also probably not entirely okay."

"Tell me," I said. "Say it plain."

Lizzie took a deep breath. Her fingers were in a knot. She shook them loose and sat on the bed. "There is a bomb. Well, two. Bigger than any bomb ever."

"Does our side have them?"

She nodded. "We dropped the first one on a city called Hiroshima. It killed a hundred thousand people."

"What?"

"The second hit the city of Nagasaki. They say that one killed seventy thousand."

"Why kill the whole city? Were they some kind of military fortresses?"

"No. Just regular cities. But we killed everyone."

"That's not right," I said, standing up. I had to hold the wall a second, while my blood caught up with my body. "Unless . . . has Japan surrendered?"

Lizzie shook her head. "I can't imagine why not. The photographs in the papers are horrifying. The cities look flattened. Nothing left."

"That sounds savage."

"I'm not heartless, Brenda." She unclipped her hair so that it fell around her face. "I feel bad for the women and children and old folks who got cooked by that bomb."

"Naturally."

"But their country started it," she continued, reaching back to braid her hair. "They are the ones who refuse to surrender. The hell with them. Now they know we will make them fry." She quit braiding and pushed her hair to one side. "They'll quit soon. And my husband will come home in one piece."

I considered that for a moment. "What does all this have to do with Charlie?"

Lizzie sighed. "The bomb was made here, kid."

"What do you mean, 'here'?"

"Los Alamos. In a giant secret lab. Other labs helped, but this was the main one. Charlie works at the place that made this bomb, that killed all those people."

Oh, an old conversation came back to me: Charlie talking about building a giant gun, with a bullet so huge it could not be aimed.

"How great are we, right?" She was smiling. "Now Tim won't die on some island ten thousand miles from here, and we are the greatest warrior nation ever. Also cold-blooded murderers, but who cares, if it means your man is coming home."

"I thought Charlie was doing math."

She laughed. "He was. Math on how to flatten an entire city with one punch."

I sat down on the bed. Had I underestimated Charlie all this time? No. I knew him. I knew that his work had been tearing him up. I remembered the day he could not stop shaking. That man would not contribute to a weapon so destructive. "I'm telling you, Lizzie. Charlie doesn't know anything about bombs. He's a mathematician." I set my jaw. "I don't believe you."

"I thought that might happen," Lizzie answered evenly. "So I brought this."

Reaching behind her back, she pulled a rolled-up newspaper from her belt and tossed it on my lap. "This is from five days ago. See for yourself, kid."

The *Santa Fe New Mexican*, August 7, 1945. One glance told me everything, the headlines in a cascade down the page: "ATOMIC BOMBS DROP ON JAPAN." Above it, in smaller letters, "LOS ALAMOS SECRET DISCLOSED BY TRUMAN." Below, "Deadliest Weapons in World's History Made in Santa Fe Vicinity." At the bottom of the page, "Now They Can Be Told Aloud, Those Stories of The Hill."

I scanned the page, not knowing where to begin. "I don't understand."

Lizzie stood and went to the door. "I've been your friend for a while now, Brenda Dubie. I've bucked you up and bailed you out, and listened for a thousand hours. I just spent nine days at your bedside, without so much as a thank you. And when I tell you the news that is going to bring my husband home, there's no congratulations. No 'I'm happy for you.' No 'Now you can have those babies you've been wanting, instead of being a widow at twenty-seven.' Just 'Oh, my innocent Charlie would never do such a thing.'"

She jabbed her finger at the newspaper. "He did it, little miss. He helped in the slaughter. And I'm glad. He could have killed twice as many people and I'd still be glad. Chew on that one for a while."

Lizzie spun on her heel and vanished down the hall. I heard her door slam.

I was alone with the newspaper. From top to bottom, I began to read.

It was all there: the bomb, the ruined city, the death toll. Suddenly all kinds of odd things made sense: the quiet night at the hospital, the crowd in the Morrises' living room, Mrs. Morris's hushed manner when she checked on me. And the credit was going to the people at Los Alamos. "Charlie," I said to my empty room. "What did you do?"

The answer, as I continued reading, was surprisingly plain: the gang on The Hill did this, they invented this thing, and the president was proud of them.

This was what Charlie had hesitated about. This was what had terrified him. And this was the thing I had pushed and urged him to do, with no idea what I was saying. What a reckless, arrogant beast I was. And he listened to me, he allowed me to compromise his conscience.

This was the most wrong I had ever been. All those times I thought of myself as superior? Now I knew better. Maybe the strongest thing a person can do is follow his conscience. Maybe this is the only kind of strength that matters. Now? One hundred thousand killed, and I hadn't said I loved him? Seventy thousand killed, and I'd told him to be a man?

I hoisted myself off the bed and struggled down the stairs. Flinging the door open, I staggered into the street. There were stitches across my middle and I was barefoot.

Should I head to the church, to seek spiritual comfort? Or go to East Palace Avenue, and take the next bus to The Hill? Or hike back up the boardinghouse stairs first, and apologize to my friend? Where could I shed the weight of my guilt?

I found myself immobile, standing in the middle of the boulevard. Even if my heart had known which way to go, my body hurt too much to take me there.

A car approached, long and black, swerving around me with a blare of its horn. The man behind the wheel gave me a long, angry stare as he roared away, and I had no argument to make in my defense. The damage my vanity had done.

Another car came along, but slower. The woman driving wore an expression of deep concern. All I wanted to say to her was no, I am unworthy. No, I have ruined him.

THE MORNING AFTER JAPAN'S surrender, Charlie's assignment was to police the detonation area. No celebrations, business as usual.

"Absurd," Giles said, climbing into the truck bed beside him. "The testing terrain alone covers fifteen acres."

"I don't mind," Charlie said, sliding over to make room, as half a dozen other technicians joined them. "Anything to keep me from thinking about this hangover."

Giles looked upward. "At least it's not sunny. We would roast."

The skies were gunmetal gray, horizon to horizon. The day promised steady rain, though none had fallen yet.

"And Nagasaki." Charlie tried to swallow but his mouth felt like sawdust. "Another two thousand two hundred and fifty-eight each. But who's counting?"

Giles gave Charlie a quizzical look, until the truck jerked forward, then chugged away from the mess tent.

"Moving at a civilized speed makes me miss Monroe," Charlie said.

"By now I imagine he has a terrible case of ellipsism."

"Which means?"

"The sadness that you'll never know how things turn out." Giles sighed. "I liked everything about Monroe but his driving."

On the ride to the detonation area, the other technicians chatted or dozed, but Charlie remained upright, scanning the hillsides on both sides of the road.

"What are you looking for?" Giles asked.

"Nothing," Charlie answered. "My cat."

Giles closed his eyes, trying to get comfortable. "If Midnight has any survival instinct at all, she is long gone from this place."

Soon enough the truck reached the clearing. Giles watched Charlie climb down, wincing with the effort. "I've never seen you put it away like that before."

"Your fault," Charlie muttered. "Before I met you, I'd never even tasted whiskey."

"Yet another reason that today is a proud day for our nation."

The team fanned out, Charlie and Giles lingering near the concrete bowl. They'd fill a wheelbarrow with debris—splintered wood and twisted metal—and haul it up to the road. Later a sanitation crew would come and cart it all away. After dumping the wheelbarrow, Giles pretended to climb in for a ride.

"Any other day, I would oblige you," Charlie said. "Today I would shatter."

"You know," Giles observed, as they rambled down the hill, "you've been hitting the bottle every night since you returned from Santa Fe."

"So have you," Charlie replied.

"But I'm an old hand. You're setting new records each night."

Charlie stopped, and Giles pulled up too. Beyond the scrub and ponderosa, the land fell away into a canyon. To the right, the road continued to Bandelier and the ancient cliff dwellings. The overcast skies made everything look vast and bland.

"Which would you rather have?" he asked. "Pain or numbness?"

"Pain is instructive," Giles said. "If your ankle aches, perhaps you sprained it. If your head hurts, possibly you need to drink less."

"What if the pain isn't something you can bear?"

Giles wiped sweat from his face. "Brenda did not die. Your grief about other things may not last forever."

"You know what we did. You know how vast the damage is."

"The planet does not contain enough whiskey to kill that pain. Only to dull it, and only temporarily. You need to find some other way to manage."

"I have no idea what that could be," Charlie said, lifting the wheelbarrow again.

A banging sound came from above, and they both turned. A pickup similar to Bronsky's came careening down the incline. The tailgate had fallen open, and with each bounce of the truck, it rose and slammed down.

"Here comes the rodeo," Giles said.

The truck rattled to a halt, its passenger climbing out: John Simmons, wearing a wide-brimmed cowboy hat. He glared in at the driver. "Nearly killed me, you idiot." But then he saw Charlie, and broke out his trademark smile. "Ah, there's my fine nephew."

Charlie muttered to Giles, "No rodeo, just a politician." But he came forward and introduced his friend.

Simmons took in the test area, the trees and detonation craters. "Gorgeous spot you've been working in."

Charlie made no reply, so Giles filled the pause. "What brings you to The Hill?"

"This guy right here," he said, clapping a hand on Charlie's shoulder. "Victory is only one day old, but some people already have big plans for Trigger."

"Please don't call me that," Charlie said.

"Sorry." He held up both of his hands. "Sorry. But look." He tipped his hat backward, as if he'd just unsaddled a mare. "We need to talk, son."

"I have to finish here," Charlie said. "In time for the afternoon bus to Santa Fe."

"Hell with that." Simmons made a dismissive wave. "I'll give you a lift."

"Um." Charlie stared down at the canyon. "A lift."

"Sure. Meet you at the mess hall at four. That way we can chat at our leisure."

The professor strode back to the truck, and they heard him speaking as he climbed in. "Now, are you going to drive me back like a sane person?"

They watched as the truck turned around and eased uphill.

"Phoniest man who ever lived," Charlie said.

"Isn't he your uncle?"

"That makes it harder. No one likes to realize their relative is a fake."

"Maybe," Giles replied. "But you told him you have to finish here, when you know that will take months."

"Guilty, Your Honor."

"What opportunity could he possibly have for you at this point? They haven't even signed the surrender documents."

"I have no idea or interest," Charlie said, as he started the wheelbarrow toward the concrete bowl. "Unless it involves whiskey."

Simmons did not have a truck for the ride to Santa Fe. He had a blue Ford sedan, which he parked directly in front of the mess entry, forcing hundreds of people to squeeze around him. Charlie came along with his face washed, wearing a fresh shirt.

"Now you're looking sharp," the professor said, opening the passenger door. "But, Charlie, did you hurt your leg?"

"No, why?"

"I thought you might be limping."

Charlie shook his head and sat in the car. "My legs are fine."

The road from The Hill, he noticed, was an entirely different experience if you weren't in a bus. Simmons drove slowly, and Charlie's stomach stayed in one place.

"You know, son, you've made us very proud with the work you've done here."

Charlie pursed his lips and said nothing.

"You're a hero to us all," Simmons continued.

"I am not a hero," Charlie said. "I was barely in the war."

"Nonsense," he said, chuckling. "I mean, sure, people died because of our bombs. But think of the countless people who did not die because of them. Japanese men and women. American soldiers. You saved hundreds of thousands of lives."

"Why am I suddenly reminded of my mother coming home from

a dress sale with a stack of boxes, telling my father how much money she had saved?"

The professor took a long look at Charlie before bringing his eyes back to the road. "Sometimes I forget how young you are."

Charlie ran his thumb along the door handle. "Uncle John, I feel very, very old."

They rode in silence for a while. Simmons cleared his throat and tried again. "What about all the wars you have prevented? The Hitlers that will never rise, because mankind fears this new weapon so much?"

"Only until other nations learn how to make atomic bombs. We did it, from zero to Hiroshima, in twenty-nine months. How long do you think it will take the Soviets?"

The professor chewed on his lower lip and did not speak. As the road turned toward Santa Fe, they caught up with the bus from The Hill. "Tell me this doesn't feel good," Simmons said. He accelerated and passed the bus, air roaring in the car's open windows. Slowing again, he patted Charlie's leg. "You know, this conversation hasn't been going at all as I'd expected. But I want to tell you about some options you have."

"Options for what?"

"Next steps, son. The future."

"There is a future?"

"There are several futures. And your uncle is in a position to help, as of about forty-eight hours ago. First option is that you stay on The Hill. It will remain a national research laboratory. I can offer you a post under Hans Bethe, who will be writing a history of the bomb project. An incredible honor to work with him, of course. Where you climb from there depends on how well you do. I'll be on the scene in a related role, to make sure your path is a smooth one."

"There's another option?"

"I am approved to offer you a spot in the PhD program in physics at Stanford University. You will work with Nobel Prize winners, in the best labs, with a brilliant research career before you."

Charlie shook his head. "I can't afford anything like that. I have a wife now."

"So I heard, and congratulations," Simmons said, flashing his toothy smile. "But you misunderstand. This offer would be a full ride: tuition, books, a housing stipend."

"How is that possible?"

"Let's just say that you live in a grateful nation."

Charlie had no reply for that. They had reached the outskirts of Santa Fe.

"You'll need to direct me," the professor said. "I don't know this town."

Charlie checked his watch. "I'm glad we're early. I have something I need to do."

"Happy to help." The rest of the ride they were silent, Charlie saying left and right as needed, till they arrived at East Palace Avenue. Charlie had opened his door when Simmons reached out to grasp his forearm. "You can study all kinds of physics there, you know. It doesn't have to be military."

"That's what I thought about math."

"This offer won't wait, son." He let go. "Promise me you'll think about it."

"Maybe." Charlie headed across the square. Outside a boot store, a man perched on a stool had an elaborate mermaid inked onto his arm. Charlie, having noticed him before, approached the man and they had a brief conversation. The man pointed up the street, angled his hand to the right. Charlie set off in that direction. Only then did Simmons drive away.

Five minutes later Charlie rapped on the glass of a tattoo parlor. A man so sunburned his skin looked like leather came to the door and mouthed no.

"It'll be quick," Charlie called through the glass. "Only a few numbers."

The man shook his head again. Charlie could see an eagle on his neck, stretching as the man moved. He waved a wad of bills back and forth.

The man threw back the latch. "*Entra entonces*," he said, shuffling to the back.

Charlie followed, saw the man sit on a metal stool, and took a seat on the wide chair beside it. "Numbers," he said, unbuttoning his shirt. He tapped his right shoulder. "On this side, a three, a two, a two, and a six. Black ink, half an inch tall." Then he tapped on the left. "Over here, I want a two, another two, a five, and an eight."

The man nodded. "With comma? Like two thousan'?"

"Exactly," Charlie said. "Two thousand, two hundred and fifty-eight."

The man nodded. "What is this numbers for, *senor*?"

"One hundred thousand and seventy thousand, each divided by thirty-one."

The man's expression did not change. "Five dollar, each side."

He pushed Charlie back in the seat, lit a cigarette, then left it to smolder in an ashtray. As he wiped the skin with alcohol, Charlie felt the cool of it evaporating. Then the man leaned over with his needle and ink.

"Is going to sting some, *tu entiendes*?"

"It's all right," Charlie said, closing his eyes. "Hurt me."

49.

HE LOOKED LIKE HELL, to tell the truth. Worst I'd ever seen him. Hunched over like someone had hit his sternum so hard it knocked the wind out of him, and he hadn't gotten his breath back yet. I'd planned to greet him with a declaration of love, to relieve my conscience and confirm it for him without a doubt. But his appearance sent that plan soaring away over the rooftops. He looked like a shell of himself, hollowed out and still. "Oh, Charlie," I said, pulling him into a bear hug.

"Ow, ow," he said, wincing. "Easy."

Only as I drew back did I notice the bleeding on his shoulders. "What on earth?"

"Nothing," he mumbled. "Not important."

Opening his shirt, I saw numbers on either side. "What are these about?"

"Reminders," Charlie muttered. "Souvenirs."

"Here, come out of the sun," I said, leading him to a bench away from the bus crowd. The emptiness felt worse to me than his shaking weeks before. At least that had an energy to it. This was scary. As we sat, too, I noticed that he smelled sour. "We need to take care of you, Charlie."

"There is," he held up one finger, as if he were interrupting me, "an order to the universe. A way things work, at the smallest level, and a force that keeps them intact. Now imagine the universe's sharpest knife." He leveled that finger, making a jabbing motion. "So sharp, it can slice the order of things in half. When that happens, even to a few small ounces out of all the matter that exists, the universe complains. And when something that powerful complains, it blows down everything for miles."

"You're talking about the bomb now."

"I did not discover any of it, Brenda. I did not even invent the knife. I only developed a way to get the knife out of its sheath. Now look at what's happened."

He was damaged. And it was my fault. "It was war, Charlie. Every man had to do his part. My brother, my father, my friends. This was your part."

"Sure." He nodded, but with his face scrunched up like smoke was getting in his eyes. "If you take the best warriors on our side— best tank commander, best fighter pilot, best machine gunner—how many do you think they killed? One hundred? Two hundred?" Charlie rubbed his face with both hands. "This is hundreds of thousands, Brenda. Not counting however many more who die from the radiation sickness we did not even know existed."

"Charlie, you said yourself it was a giant gun, and someone else was responsible for aiming it and pulling the trigger. You didn't make those decisions."

"I am talking about the universe, Brenda. We made it complain. And I am not certain that it is finished complaining."

"What does that mean?"

"If you dare to brush up against God, He is likely to notice."

By then I had reached my limit of crazy talk. This was my husband, after all. The guy my mother had said was likeliest to come out of the war intact. "Look, Charlie. We can chew this into little pieces over the months ahead. In the meantime, there is peace. The fighting is done. Our men will be coming home."

"It's true," Charlie conceded. "Things are already different on The Hill too."

"In a while we'll need to figure out where we go next."

Charlie turned to me then, and his expression softened. "Hi, Brenda," he said, touching his fingertips to my cheek. "Hello, my wife."

"Hi there," I said, taking his hand, kissing his palm. Here was my moment, to make the declaration I'd withheld. "Charlie, one thing I need to say—"

"You'd like to return to Chicago. I know. And I'm inclined toward Boston, for the same reasons. But you should know they've made me some offers."

He deserved to say his piece first. My words of love could wait. "Really?"

"A grateful nation moves quickly, I guess. Anyway I could stay in Los Alamos—"

"No." I waved the idea away. "New Mexico has been good for me, but not for you. The next thing Charlie Fish needs is to be in a good place."

"Thank you," he said. "I could go get a doctorate in physics at Stanford."

"Stanford University? In California?"

"For free. I'd work with the best people imaginable."

"Would you have to build more bombs?"

"Exactly the right question," he said. "I don't think so. There's acoustics. Optics. Radar, which is still in its infancy."

I could see how the discussion was bringing him back to earth, how his forehead relaxed. "Acoustics would be great, Charlie. After all your organ listening."

"Do you think so?"

As he spoke, I became aware of a little flame, burning in my heart. A silent candle I had sheltered from all the winds of the past two years, and all at once it seemed to have renewed heat and light.

"I do," I said. "But there is one thing."

He turned to me, the face of innocence. "Yes?"

"Do you think they have a music department at Stanford?"

"A university that renowned? They must."

It was all I could do to keep from jumping in the air and shouting. "Do you think it would be possible for me to study there, and maybe take courses in the organ?"

"What a terrific idea," he said, brightening. "I could see if my uncle can add it to the deal." Charlie banged his thigh with his fist. "I'll insist on it."

After all that, he still cared for me. I took both of his hands. "Charlie Fish, I don't care if it's California or Kalamazoo, I'll be right there with you."

I was ready to say more, to say everything, but he did not respond with the delight I'd expected. Instead his face folded into itself, and he started to weep. After a few seconds Charlie lowered his head, crying harder, then collapsed into me completely, a sobbing mess. His tears darkened the yellow shirt I'd put on specially for him.

I wrapped my arms around Charlie, careful not to touch his sore places, and rocked him back and forth. The feeling of newness, of giving comfort, was as strong as the weeks we'd spent learning the pleasures of sex. I had not yet declared it, but I was not done falling in love with Charlie Fish.

"I've always been interested in acoustics," he blurted out into my belly, before burying his face there again.

I nearly laughed. Instead I said, "Then it's settled."

The superior girl still had not learned. I thought I was saving him. I was wrong.

5 0 .

THE LECTURE HALL WAS only half-filled, as the semester began with many men still on active duty. Not everyone was eager to return to a classroom.

"In the course catalog you will see curriculum modifications," said Richard Zeno, world-class particle physicist and physics department chairman. He had bushy eyebrows, hair in his ears, hair in his nose. Behind him sat other professors, plus postdoc fellows, observing with undisguised boredom.

"I can't believe it," a boy to the left whispered. "The same room as Richard Zeno."

Charlie nodded, but he was paying attention to the speech. The demands for some faculty members to aid in the war effort, low enrollment, availability of research funding—all of these forces "may require an adjustment of expectations," Zeno said. "It could be some time before we are at full throttle. But I assure you, we will have no deficit of excellent instruction, no shortage of work."

Charlie's curiosity overcame his desire to make a good impression by listening closely. He pulled out the course listings. There were three optics courses on the list, but in reading the descriptions he realized they were about focusing techniques for aircraft bombing runs. He searched further, finding one course in his area of interest— "Foundational Principles of Acoustics"—and it was not offered until spring semester.

Zeno invited the new students to ask questions. A student to

Charlie's right raised his hand. "Will Stanford be helping to develop the hydrogen bomb?"

Several of the professors in back roused themselves at that question. Zeno pointed to a long-bearded fellow who, as he spoke, held his jacket by the lapels. "We intend to play a leadership role," the professor said. "There will be course offerings, lab work, postdoc and field opportunities, and presumably, jobs for those who excel."

Charlie saw heads nodding all around the lecture hall.

Another hand rose. "Will we be working on atomic electricity? Or just weapons?"

Zeno answered that one himself. "Funding at present is weapon-centric. But I fully expect that other applications of fission and fusion will gradually come to the fore."

He scanned the room. "One more?"

Charlie found his hand in the air. "What about acoustics?"

Zeno chuckled. "What about acoustics?"

"I'm only seeing one course in the catalog."

"Professor Fusco, yes. We expect him to return from Oak Ridge this fall."

"But that's the only offering in that discipline?"

Zeno turned to the professors, none of whom seemed interested. He smirked at Charlie. "That field will return to prominence the moment we find a way to win a war through the application of acoustics."

People laughed here and there in the audience, after which a department administrator came forward and described the registration process. After him, lunch.

Charlie took his tray across the cafeteria to a crowded table, an empty seat at the far end. The fellows nodded hello, while one at the head of the table was saying something. "I didn't hear one concrete example of how we'll work on the H-bomb. And who was that guy asking about acoustics? I mean, let's be deliberately irrelevant."

Charlie waved his fork in the air. "That was me."

"Well, then." The boy seemed not at all abashed. "How does that contribute to the betterment of America?"

Charlie scooped mashed potatoes with his fork. "Personally, I feel like I've done quite enough national betterment lately. Now I want to enlarge my mind." And he shoveled the food into his mouth.

"I knew it," a boy across the table said. "You're him, aren't you?"

"Him who?" said the loudmouth at the head of the table.

"Trigger. I heard he was in our program. You're him."

Charlie spoke with his mouth full. "I don't like that nickname."

"But you're a hero," the boy said. "You made thirty-two things happen at once."

"Actually it was sixteen. Two arrays and a doubler." He scooped more potatoes.

"I thought you'd be taller."

Charlie held his hands wide. "Sorry to disappoint you."

"Still," the boy said. "This is the detonator genius of Los Alamos, guys. Trigger."

Charlie stood, picking up his tray. "I don't like that name."

That night Brenda had dinner waiting, and she was wearing a snug red dress. They had rented a three-room bungalow with a tiny front porch a dozen blocks from campus. By then they had woken in the same bed for eight consecutive mornings, and the pleasure of it was so acute, Charlie lingered. Each day he'd had to run to campus to meet his first commitments.

"How's it going so far?" she asked, while they sipped iced tea on the porch.

"Not what I expected."

"In a good way?"

"Someone called me Trigger."

"Oh, Charlie."

"No acoustics till spring. But there's an electronics course that might be fun. A little soldering, perhaps."

She laughed. "I pity anyone who tries to compete with you."

Charlie put his glass down on the table. "I think I'm going to bed."

"Are you all right?"

He paused at the door. "I am the tiredest man on earth."

And he left his wife on the porch alone, dusk coming on like a premonition.

The next morning he was at the kitchen table, writing, when she came in. "Sorry I overslept." Brenda bent and kissed the side of his neck. "How did you sleep?"

"Next to you," he said, flipping the papers over into a folder, then hugging her waist. Brenda stood as still as a tree, not moving until he let go. He pressed his head against her belly, and she had to shift her hips—still tender. She grabbed a fistful of his hair, then released it and went to pour herself a mug of coffee. "Still healing, I guess."

"I know how you feel."

"Oh, but look at the time," she added, and when Charlie glanced at the stove clock, he jumped up and ran for the door.

By lunchtime that day, nearly all the students were calling him Trigger. Charlie went to electronics early, set himself up with a soldering bench, and amused himself with components until the room was full and the professor arrived. Papers and books tucked under one arm, he glanced at Charlie's work area and stopped cold.

"Gentlemen, there will be no use of the irons except under my supervision." He said it loudly, for the whole room to hear. "Is that understood?"

Charlie turned off his iron, removed his mask, and placed it over the hot tip.

The professor put down his papers and sidled over, arms crossed like a disappointed parent. "This is dangerous equipment, young man. Reckless of you to—"

Charlie moved aside, revealing the assembly he'd made. The professor tilted the device on one side. "Wicking, sweating, smooth wires. Where'd you learn all this?"

An undergraduate in the back row called out, "Los Alamos."

"Well, thank you for a job well done." The professor ambled to the head of the room. "You may know enough to teach this course. Others here may feel the same. But I'm the one with the PhD, so you'll not be touching equipment except as I direct." He faced the class. "Do we understand one another?"

Charlie went and found his seat, settling in at the small desk. "Yes."

"Sir," the boy in back said. "This man is a hero."

"He may well have been, and bravo, but he's a student now."

The next morning Brenda came into the kitchen and Charlie was writing again.

"The great American novel?" she asked.

"A letter to Giles." He turned the page over, tucking it into a manila folder.

"How is he doing?"

"I'm writing to him, as you see. He hasn't received this yet, much less replied."

Brenda had been on her way to the coffee, but instead she pulled back a chair to sit beside him. "I am not the enemy, Charlie."

He put down his pen. "Of course you aren't."

"What is upsetting you today?"

"You mean besides the Gibraltar of guilt I'm carrying around?"

"Plenty of people consider what you did heroic. That's why we're here."

"I was called a hero yesterday," Charlie said. "In front of a whole class."

"Well, isn't that sw—"

"I could have throttled him." Charlie shook his head. "What I did was maybe—possibly, theoretically—necessary. No more than that. Some people were excited by the difficulty of the task, but for most of us, we did our part only because it was needed."

"But, Charlie, you—"

"We faced no enemy. Nobody was shooting at us. I saw not one person die. Hardly heroic. In fact you could argue that making the bomb—my bomb, my damned bomb—was the consummate cowardice. I could not have been safer, sitting by your bed in the Santa Fe hospital, while the people of Hiroshima were getting ready for work or laboring in the fields or on their way to school."

"You just interrupted me twice."

"I—" Charlie caught himself. "So I did."

She took his hand. "You shush now. You had a small part in a giant victory, which is all any soldier does. You helped end the war, which is good for America and Japan."

"But the carnage."

"Do you wish we were still fighting today? That men your age were throwing themselves on some beach five thousand miles from here? Or that Japanese men were defending it to the death, however futile that was?"

"Of course not."

"Can you imagine the rage of every mother and father who lost a child in the invasion, if they found out later that we had the bomb and did not use it?"

"I hadn't thought of that."

"Enough of this guilt. Those parents love you. They don't even know your name, but they love you with their whole hearts. Now," she said, standing, "I am going to make us some breakfast, and you are going to eat it."

He bowed his head. "All right."

"And then," she said, "you are going to go talk to someone, some senior person, about how Stanford University can take better care of this excellent man and famous student."

Not two hours later, Charlie spotted Richard Zeno in the hall. "Pardon me, sir, could I speak with you for a minute?"

Zeno, his bushy eyebrows lowered, gave Charlie a long look. "Fish, isn't it?"

"Yes, sir."

"Come to my office in ten minutes."

Charlie went outside to march his nervousness around the building. It was a lovely fall day in Palo Alto, sun sparkling through the trees, the air sweetened with a scent another student had told him was eucalyptus. Gradually, his pace slowed. The campus was nearly empty, two students crossing the lawn from one building to another. On the far side of the physics building, a parking lot sprawled, most of its spaces empty.

Zeno's secretary was out, but the department chairman called from his desk. "Come in, come in." He waved Charlie to a seat. "Welcome to Stanford. How is it going?"

"Thank you, sir." Charlie placed his stack of books on the floor. "I'm glad to be here. But I have some concerns."

"Then I want to hear them. Be as frank as you like."

"Thank you." Charlie sat straight, hands on his knees. "My concern is that the work here, all of the priorities, are about atomic bombs."

"The study of physics has entered a vast new territory."

"Yes, sir. But I spent the past three years in that territory, and I came here hoping to gain knowledge in other areas."

Zeno scratched a sideburn. "Acoustics, wasn't it?"

"And optics, and radar."

"We'll likely have funding for radar soon. Peace won't stop that enterprise."

"But the work will be for military applications, I imagine."

"We live in an unstable world."

Charlie pulled back, taking a deep breath. "I've been contemplating withdrawing, sir. Not getting my PhD after all."

"Nonsense." Zeno stood. "No no. Fish, this is a preeminent graduate program. You'll find no better. What do you want? A teaching assistantship? A lab job?"

"I don't know, sir."

"That makes it hard for me to help."

"I don't want to learn how to become a better warrior."

Zeno ambled to his window. He gazed out on the quad, where

Charlie had just been walking. "I'd like you to think about it, Fish. What do you actually need from us, as opposed to what you need to reconcile within yourself?" With his thumb, he brushed his thick eyebrows back. "I want you to stay. I will make any reasonable accommodation."

"That is incredibly generous, sir."

"You do your thinking, and let me know."

"That's the best answer I could ask for, sir."

"Excellent." He came forward, hand outstretched. "Truth is, it raises our stock to have the likes of Charlie Fish in the program."

Charlie shook his hand. "I'm just a mathematician."

"Hardly."

Gathering his books, Charlie said nothing.

"In fact my colleagues will be green with envy," Zeno continued, sitting again at his desk.

"Why is that, sir?"

"Are you kidding? I got to have a private meeting with Trigger."

RIDING THE BUS WAS a sign that I was healing. The system was different from Chicago's straight lines, instead following a web of crossing routes. While Charlie was gone all day, though, I ventured out—each time a bit farther from our love cottage. Things had not been as passionate as in New Mexico. Which I blamed on Charlie's blues. Each day that passed without lovemaking, without even a casual caress, gave more mass to the weight between us. This was not about my lust, this was about finding our way back to each other.

One night in the shower, it became too much and I began to cry. I longed for his touch, his closeness, our bond. With me, though, sadness and anger are close as thumb and forefinger. Yanking back the curtain, I called out, "Hey, Charlie? Charlie Fish?"

After a moment, he poked his head in the doorway. "What is it?"

I gave him the same look as I had on the roads outside Santa Fe, and said what I always said. "I want you to come with me."

He undressed slowly, while I watched, and ducked in under the steamy stream. We touched tenderly, as if we might break. He knelt to press his face against the scar on my belly. I soaped the numbers tattooed by his shoulders. Then he straightened and kissed me on the mouth. Instantly the atmosphere changed. I handed Charlie the soap, and we were off and running. We stayed in that shower till the hot water ran out. Afterward I joked that I must have the cleanest breasts in all of California.

We were lovers again, yet still I had not told him that I loved him. There was an obstacle of some kind, an impediment—not to the feeling, but to the saying of it. I knew it was an unkindness, and I knew it was entirely my problem.

Each day after he'd dashed off to morning class, I did my push-ups. I'd lost strength in the hospital, and each push tugged at my scar, but I was back to nine already. As I dressed, I thought about how Charlie felt responsible for all those dead Japanese people. My belief that it had been necessary didn't change the fact that I had pushed him to do it, I had made him contradict his conscience. In a way, I was guiltier than he was. And the longer he took to recover, the more I regretted being mistaken.

Yes, the superior girl was realizing that maybe she did not have all the answers. If he'd refused to build the detonator, someone else might have. But the bomb would not be on his conscience.

I am still wrestling with this idea in my head, all these years later. There have been plenty of wars and battles since 1945, but I feel the restlessness of culpability. It pushes me out of my recliner, to the dresser, where I see that photo of us, standing in front of the Morrises' Hudson on our wedding day. It works every time. It reminds me that I did do one thing right. I did love him—even if I hadn't told him yet.

So, on those California mornings, it was out of the house for this girl. I'd hop on a bus, ride it a random number of stops, then climb down and investigate a new part of town. Streets were safe and people were friendly.

We'd had some hard good-byes in Santa Fe, of course. The Morrises offered us a ride to the depot in Lamy, and Charlie arrived late.

"Quite the valedictory from Giles," he said. "But I couldn't find the cat anywhere."

Mrs. Morris, with a hug that smelled of lily of the valley, thanked me for getting her playing music again. Reverend Morris said a blessing in a soft voice. As for Lizzie Hinks, we'd long made up by then, and after an awkward moment she tumbled tearfully into my arms.

"I hope Tim is home soon," I said, "and you make babies by the dozen."

"But first I have to ride back with Mrs. M," she whispered.

"She's not so bad," I said.

Lizzie grinned at me. "Yes she is."

The conductor called all aboard, Charlie hoisted our bags, I took the picnic basket, and we boarded the train to Denver—the first leg in our long journey west.

Charlie kept his promise, and persuaded Professor Simmons to find me a place in Stanford's freshman class—but the following fall, when the faculty would be back. My postsurgical energy sometimes flagged at odd times anyway, so waiting seemed wise.

I healed quickly, though, as young people do, and my mood lifted too. My father would be in Chicago by Halloween. Frank accepted a post in Nuremberg, maintaining prosecutors' cars until the trials were over, then he'd come home too. My mother's letters were giddy.

That was the tempo around us. Of course there was sorrow, deep as a canyon. One morning a woman on the bus wept from the time I got on till I stepped off in Redwood City. But the world allowed optimism now. The sun was coming out.

That day I saw the sign for Peale's Organs, a modest store, a few blocks from the water. Outside, three trucks bore the company name, beside the outline of a console with pipes. I hadn't touched an instrument since we boarded that train in Lamy. The idea of playing tugged on my heart like the moon pulls the sea. I marched right in.

A bearded man on the phone glanced at me and held up one finger. "Of course," he said. "We can fix that before Sunday."

I peered around, and there was no showroom. No display of Hammonds waiting for my fingers. The shop was a long narrow space with workbenches along both walls, a hammering noise coming from the back. I smelled sawdust. One man was carving a small block of reddish wood, while another was hand-buffing a pipe taller than he was.

"Can I help you?" The man on the phone had hung up. He held a pair of pliers. A square pencil was tucked behind his ear.

"I gather you do not sell organs here."

"No, ma'am. We repair them."

That idea held me in place for a moment. The two times that I'd seen Charlie working and happy, he was repairing the organ at Reverend Morris's church. Quieting the ciphers before that wedding, voicing the whole instrument a week later. I could picture him, crawling out from under the console, smiling and covered with dust. Not to mention the pipes he fixed with my father's basement soldering equipment. He was happy that morning too. "Do you have a lot of work these days?"

"Pretty much any church in the Bay Area has a problem, they call us. And with the war over, we've got a whale of a backlog." He used the pliers to scratch his beard. "For an organ store, ma'am, I'd guess the nearest one's in Palo Alto."

"Thank you," I said. "I'll give it a look."

But that was not what I had in mind. On the bus home I hoped that Charlie would be there already. I'd rush him right into bed, make him forget all about the bomb. Instead the house was quiet, as if waiting for me.

I went into the kitchen to see what I might make for dinner. There on the table was the manila folder, which held the letter Charlie had been writing.

"Brenda," I told myself, "don't you dare."

Then I sat right down and turned the pages over.

My brilliant Giles:

I am sitting in my kitchen, afflicted by rubatosis. I'm sure you already know that this is the unsettling awareness of your own heartbeat.

Where is your whiskey when I need it most? Where is your fine companionship?

I suspect that coming here was a grievous error. The war followed me. What we did followed me. It rubs salt in my wounds day and night. There is no peace.

Probably you have a million-dollar word to describe my emotions exactly. Do you also have a word for its cure?

I am a stew of uncertainty, a stone soup of doubts. I didn't need those tattoos after all. The numbers are with me forever.

I know how to be a good husband but

He'd stopped there when I came in. I wondered how he would have finished that sentence . . . but I can't because I am charred with guilt? . . . but my wife urged me to build something that killed hundreds of thousands of people?

Now that I had committed the crime of snooping, I went further—seeing what else was in the folder. Photos: Hiroshima after the bomb. A flattened Nagasaki. No buildings, no houses, no trees. Just rubble, a wheel but no wagon, the white spine of a horse. A picture captioned "Industrial Promotion Hall," the building still standing, but one whole side torn away, its tower looking like a hollow silo. The most striking picture was from high above, showing a rough circle of charred land, surrounded by ash-white fields. I studied that one, trying to imagine what Charlie felt when he saw it. And this was what I had driven him to do.

"Sweetheart?"

I jumped. He stood in the kitchen doorway. "Darling. You're home early."

I didn't bother to hide what he'd caught me doing. I just ran and threw myself against him. He held me, too, pressing us together till I felt his heart beating against mine. It was not sexual; it was like two people clinging to a lifeboat.

"Tell me," I said. "What do you most want me to know?"

"I want to quit," he whispered. "I can't bear being Trigger anymore. I want to be rid of the whole business."

I bent my neck so I could see the stove clock. I knew what to do, and if we hurried there was just enough time. "Then I want you to come with me."

"I'm not in the mood for that right now."

"I don't mean it that way," I said. "Let me get my purse and hat."

On the bus we were quiet. He was tired, but my leg jiggled nonstop.

"What are you up to?" he asked eventually.

"I was wrong to tell you to be a man," I said.

"That hardly matters now, Brenda."

"That's why I'm not going to push you today. You already

are a man. I'm only going to give you an idea. Then it's your own decision."

Charlie took my hand and kissed the knuckles. "Whatever you say."

I marched him from the bus stop to a place across the street from our destination. Then I turned Charlie so he could see for himself: the store sign, the trucks. "How about that?" I said. "Peale's Organs."

Charlie glared at me like I had three eyes. "I don't understand."

"Okay," I said, "I'll spell it out. Two things."

He turned his head. "Can we go home now?"

"Just two quick things," I said. "Bear with me, please."

In front of his face, he straightened two fingers.

"First thing." I tapped one of them. "I love you, Charlie Fish." The old surprised expression came back to his face, so familiar and kind, and I felt a flood of affection. "I admire you, I respect you, I love you."

"Why, Brenda," he said, "I just—"

"Second thing." I tapped his other finger. "I don't care what you do for a living, as long as you follow your conscience."

That seemed to take the wind out of him. "What if I don't know where to go?"

"I gave bad advice when I told you to be a man, then good advice when I made you propose to me, then bad advice when I said you should get a PhD. It's time for good advice again." I smiled. "Ready?"

"I don't know," he said. "I genuinely don't."

Oh my sweet, brilliant, humble husband. So much doubt on his face, such a mountain of uncertainty. I was unsure, too, but I could taste the potential. Besides, I knew that this time I was not motivated by self-regard. I was guided by my heart.

"It's time for you to leave Stanford," I said.

"Before you begin your organ studies? I can't do that."

"Any life that doesn't work for one of us isn't working for both of us."

He had no answer for that. I placed a hand on each of his shoulders, my palms probably right over his number tattoos. "Are you ready, my love?"

He looked up, eyes brimming. "All right, Brenda. What do I do now?"

I pointed. "Go on in there, right now. Walk into Peale's Organs, and ask for a job."

God bless that Charlie Fish: he did.

EPILOGUE

1986

DEEP FOG BLANKETED THE Bay Area, but my flight still landed on time. When we left San Francisco, Charlie and I had just celebrated our anniversary. Now, forty-one years later, I returned alone.

The university said they would send a driver, but I had not expected a young woman. She stood with a sign at the arrival area: *Mrs. Fish*. Before I'd said hello, her face brightened with recognition. "Hi," she piped. "I'm Gracie."

She wheeled my bag to the waiting town car, hoisted it into the trunk, then opened the rear door for me.

"I'd rather ride in front with you."

"We have another passenger back there."

I climbed in, slow on my pins, but after all those years what did I expect? The curly-haired girl in back was adorable as a poodle puppy.

"Anna Carson," she said, with a forthright handshake. "With the *Stanford Daily*."

"Student run since 1892," Gracie called from the front, starting the car.

Anna shook her head in apology, curls wiggling. "My publicist . . . and roommate. She's a music major, so she wanted to meet you."

"Well, I think you both are darling."

Anna frowned. "Darling," clearly, was not high on her list of desired compliments. "I was hoping to interview you."

I folded my hands in my lap. "That would be fine."

"Great." She flipped open her notebook. "So when were you last on campus?"

"Well, I was never actually on campus. Charlie was."

"Oh, right." She nibbled on her pen. "Now you live on the East Coast?"

"Beverly, Massachusetts. We were near Charlie's family, but the main reason is that he liked to hire boatbuilders, for their precision."

"How many organs has the Fish Company built so far?"

"Today's ceremony celebrates the debut of Opus 85."

"Do you have a favorite?"

That question made me pause. Out the window, everything we drove past seemed to have doubled: cars, buildings, houses. The quiet town of Millbrae was unrecognizable.

"I always used to say the next one. Now I'm not sure. The company will continue to make excellent instruments. I'm still adjusting to that happening without Charlie."

"I understand it will also be without you. Haven't you basically run the place?"

I smiled at her. Young women now were all about who's the boss. How could I explain the balance Charlie and I had found together? "Early on, I managed our travel. We were all over Europe, so he could study the great cathedral instruments, but we were also broke. It was a romantic education."

Anna scribbled away. Up front, Gracie craned her neck to hear me better.

"When Charlie launched his own business, I did everything I could to help him succeed—hiring workers, writing contracts, keeping the books. Everything."

"Is building organs difficult? Did you help with that part too?"

"Charlie could have built airplanes, printing presses, grandfather clocks. That's what it means to be a mechanical genius. But he chose organs. They require many crafts and skills, none of which I possess. My value was practical—billing, payroll, supplies. When those tasks were done, my job was to help with voicing."

"Voicing?" Anna asked. "What's that?"

"Making the instrument sympathize with itself, and with the room where it will live. My part was to sit at the console, playing a note over and over, while Charlie worked deep inside the pipes, making refinements."

"Can you explain that more?" Gracie asked.

Anna gave her a scowl, then tipped her pen at me. "Please."

"Voicing takes two people: one to play the organ, one to adjust it. No one wants to sit for two solid days playing a middle C with the coronet stop open, while someone else listens and tinkers. Other technicians said it was deadly tedious. But I didn't mind."

The car was quiet, except for the blinker as Gracie turned off 101 and headed toward the university.

I surrendered to an impulse. "Stop taking notes and I'll tell you the whole truth."

Anna considered my offer, then put her pen down.

"Charlie was making sacred instruments—for weddings, funerals, moments of the soul. The work was about saving his conscience. And because we were a team, about restoring mine too. So in a voicing? Every time I pressed a key, it was an act of love."

The girls were not so young, really. They looked to be about the age I was when I met Charlie. I hoped they would understand.

"How was all of this for you as a woman?" Anna asked. "Participating and contributing, but without undermining—and never pursuing your performing career."

"Please understand," I answered. "I did not abandon my aspirations for Charlie's. It was more like the time we sang the toccata together in the church: We merged our dreams. Each of us needed the other to make it happen. Each of us helped the other to find redemption."

She gave me a puzzled look. "You sang in a church together?"

"Never mind," I said. "Let me say it another way. Our lives together were like voicing an organ. Everything else goes away. There is no outside world. Only one person, playing a note over and over, and one person refining the sound. It's a universe of two."

In the silence that followed, I thought the interview was over.

But Anna picked up her pen again. "In all your travels, was there a favorite moment?"

"Oh, a thousand. But I'll share one. It concerns the Bach Toccata and Fugue in D Minor, a piece I've always struggled with. Charlie and I were touring German organs, and we stopped in Thuringia. The man who was supposed to meet us was late. To pass the time while Charlie investigated the pipes, I decided to play. Well, I was making a perfect mess of the toccata when he popped up like an imp beside the console. I snapped at him not to startle me, but he laughed. Then he told me this was probably the instrument Bach wrote the piece on, and definitely one he had played it on. Bach himself."

"Wow," Anna said. "Cool."

"We're here," Gracie called from the front.

Charlie was clever when it came to pleasing customers. He would complete an organ at his factory, for example, then invite whoever was paying for the instrument to come play it. They always did, even nonmusicians, pressing the keys with a mix of awe and delight at the giant sounds that resulted. Likewise, when he shipped an organ to the church or college or wherever it was going, he made a point of saying that his fee did not include unloading. The people receiving the instrument would have to remove it from the trucks themselves, and carry it inside. It belonged to them now. Sometimes the choir would perform outside during an unloading. Then Charlie's team would assemble the instrument, he would perfect the voicing, and there would be a debut.

Stanford was no different. The chapel entry was crowded with students, faculty, well-heeled folks who'd written checks for the organ. The building's exterior had a handsome mosaic, images of saints or apostles I suppose, but there was a hurry to introduce me around, and I didn't have time for a proper look. I smiled, shook hands, thanked people, and in general felt my husband's absence as though I'd come without my left arm.

Inside, the place was handsome: a floor of some unique wood, stained-glass windows, a lofty dome. Mosaics decorated the side walls, too, and I realized how accustomed I had become to the plain, forthright churches of New England.

The speeches were dull, until the university organist, a portly fellow with Ben Franklin glasses, took the podium. "This is the last instrument designed by Charles Fish," he said. "It is an exemplary piece of work—so responsive, so powerful, you feel a direct connection between your finger and the pipe."

He paused to adjust his glasses. "Please understand, I say this not to boast but to explain: We have here, in our chapel, an object as rare as an original of the Declaration of Independence. In the long arc of Fish's life, he managed to become one of the finest organ builders in human history. This university is immensely fortunate to share in the final act of his exemplary career."

The audience applauded. Career. I would have bet not two people in that place knew what Charlie did before he started making organs.

"We are grateful to Mrs. Fish for joining us today on his behalf," the man continued. I raised a hand and the clapping was polite. "Now, for the performance . . ."

He introduced the musician, whom I'd never heard of. To judge by the crowd's response, though, you would have thought he was the ghost of Harry Truman. Cheers, whistles, applause. I confess I felt a buzz of electricity.

My enthusiasm cooled, though, when the organist placed one hand on the console for balance, and bowed so low I wondered if he was joking. He straightened, making an odd flourish with one hand, and I thought, *What a dandy.* Then he slipped out of his shoes, showing everyone plainly that he was barefoot, a sign of respect for the pedals but so contrived I snorted behind my hand.

With a backward flip of his coattails, the man took his seat at the bench. It was all rather cloying, and I prayed he would not be playing Pachelbel's Canon. He opened stops, straightened his posture, cleared his throat.

Begin already, I thought.

And he did: It was the Widor. The Fifth Symphony by Charles-

Marie Widor, that is, a complete flambé of technique, and this musician was made for it. Minimum substance, maximum show. He had a way of swaying his head, of rising on his buttocks. If he had been my student in 1942, I would have smacked him with a ruler.

The man had chosen a piece to display himself, not the organ. He was impressive, yes, but mostly impressed with himself. When his right hand played primary melody, he would lay his left hand on the bench—calling attention to the music he made with only five fingers. I was annoyed, disappointed, then annoyed all over again.

But the piece is six minutes long. I used that time to examine the instrument. A lovely console, red poplar. Three manuals. Stops in four rows on either side of the keys. I couldn't see how many pedals there were, but I certainly heard them. Charlie would have been proud of his crew.

We traveled the world together. We built a business from nothing. We met great musicians, witnessed spectacular performances. Increasingly, and then for years, Charlie was happy—the kind of hardworking happy he had been in those Santa Fe days, all dusty under the church organ. We were partners the whole way.

My father did come home, and reopened the store. People had room for music in their lives again. Fifteen years later he became one of the first people in Chicago to sell the new electrified guitars from Leo Fender. Likewise with the B-3, an organ Hammond built for gospel music, which instead became popular for blues and soul. Soon he owned music shops all over town.

Frank came home, too, opened a three-bay garage in Wicker Park, married a great chesty tough girl named Marie, and they had a troop of boys. As gas stations became convenience stores, he went into that business with my dad as an investor, and made a comfortable life for his family. Maybe even rich. I'm not saying the war didn't touch Frank, sure it did. Years later, Marie had to put one of those accordion gates across the top of the stairs, because of his nightmare sleepwalking.

As for my mother, she was kinder to my father, as promised, and did one thing to spoil him every day. Coffee in bed, a love note hidden in the cash register. They added up. When I visited, I could see my parents were happier. She continued reading and doing crossword puzzles, but quit smoking. Too late, though. Lung cancer took her at age fifty-four. A decade later my father had a series of strokes, then died in his sleep.

At the reception after the funeral, a familiar-looking man came over to give his condolences. "Tom Beatty," he said, shaking my hand. "Sorry for your loss."

"Thanks for coming, Tom." I hesitated. "Do I know you?"

He shook his head. "You knew my brother Chris."

"Of course I did. Chris Beatty. How is he?"

Tom blinked at me. "Chris was shot down, in January of nineteen forty-five."

"I am so sorry," I said. "I didn't know."

"Turns out you were his only girl," Tom said. "I hope you were nice to him."

"Nice as I could be," I answered.

"He told me you broke his heart." The man had a set to his jaw. Was this some sort of reckoning? I was at my father's funeral, for Pete's sake.

"Not quite." I gave him a kinder face than I was feeling. "Anyway, I was a kid."

"Yeah." Tom nodded. "We were all kids." He bowed and moved away.

For a minute I was alone, and allowed myself to consider what aspects of Chris had stayed with me over the years. Not my brief infatuation with a guy who probably didn't really care about me, not my long guilt for emotional infidelity, but actually what he said in that first feverish burst of words at the dance: that life is short, we never know when our time will be up, so we can't waste a single opportunity.

"Here you go." My husband appeared with a glass of water. "Who was that?"

How had he known I was thirsty, when I myself hadn't noticed? I raised the glass to him. "Charlie, I love you."

He kissed my cheek. "You, too, sweetie."

After taking a big swallow, I answered: "Brother of a high school chum."

That was 1962, the last time I went to Chicago.

We never returned to New Mexico either. But I have seen pictures. They tore down most of the old buildings. Which were sick with radiation. Today Los Alamos is a prosperous little city. A bridge, with security gates like a highway tollbooth, spans a ravine to the national laboratory that still operates there. It looks like an office park, only without corporate logos on the buildings.

Most of what remains from that time is irony. Oppenheimer was investigated as a possible Communist, and lost his security clearance. In a farewell speech, he said, "The time will come when mankind will curse the names of Los Alamos and Hiroshima."

Meanwhile kids were taught, in case of a nuclear attack, to duck under their school desks, though half a mile from a detonation the temperature reaches nearly six thousand degrees. Desks wouldn't do much good. Not ironic enough? Holloman Air Force Base, where the Trinity test observation planes were based, has served repeatedly as a training ground for the Luftwaffe.

It's enough to make an old woman wonder: Who is an ally? Who is an enemy? Do we have to kill millions of people every few decades to figure that out?

Nambe, New Mexico, is now a park, with dams, waterfalls, and a reservoir. The place Charlie and I conceived our one and only time is now underwater. And Stanford, the school that cured Charlie of physics forever, is home to the last instrument he designed.

The ultimate irony, of course, is that the terror invoked by atomic weapons has actually, inexplicably, created a new form of peace. A tense one, yes. Dangerous, fragile, untrusting. Each new nation that obtains this immense power seems less likely to exercise restraint with it. Nevertheless, since Nagasaki in August 1945, the atomic bomb has been a threat only, a bluff never called. So may it forever remain.

* * *

The marionette on the bench who was torturing Charlie's legacy finally reached the end of the Widor. He extended the final C-major chord, holding it twice as long as the score required. I wanted to yell "Let it go," but at last he did, and while I sat back with relief, the place went mad with applause.

Oh, but he was changing music books already. Dear heaven, he was going to play another. I felt claustrophobic at the idea of it. Until I heard the first notes.

It was Buxtehude's Prelude in C Major, a true classic, composed by the man who taught the organ to Bach. An opening of melody played across several octaves, with rests that let the room ring, a sequence of chords to announce that everything so far had been mere introduction, a passage of light notes, as if to prove the composer was capable of being cheery, and then the full thrall of the instrument.

At once it became clear: This silly man at the console had been toying with us. He was excellent. His attacks were bright as trumpet blasts. His figures were robust and certain. His filigree was spotless.

And when the mighty passages came, the power and the glory, he knew exactly what kind of machine he was driving. All of us, every person in that room, had the bone-shaking, heart-quaking experience of a Charles Fish organ at the height of its might, 4,488 pipes in complete command.

I could feel Charlie, too, his integrity and patience, his humility and genius, as if he were sitting beside me. We had spent four decades together, I knew his steadfastness like no one else. I could hear it in that instrument.

When the piece ended I was the first on my feet. But in seconds everyone was giving the man a standing ovation. He took his annoyingly excessive bows, the university organist said something about a reception, and people began filing out. I sat to catch my breath, winded, as if I'd run a race. Which in some ways I suppose I had.

Anna reappeared, followed by a boy her age who had long black hair and the thinly grown beard exclusive to undergraduates. I was tempted to suggest he wait a decade and try again, but I noticed the camera on a strap around his neck.

"Would you mind terribly?" she said. "Maybe you could sit at the organ?"

"That I do not mind in the least."

Up close, the console was gorgeous. With care, it could still be so in three hundred years. Charlie had used his innovation of reversing the keyboard colors: instead of the natural keys being white and the accidentals black, as on pianos, this organ had dark keys for naturals and white for the accidentals. It looked opulent.

I slid onto the bench. A brass lamp illuminated the music stand. It matched the brass fish inlaid in the wood, Charlie's signature. Just behind stood the thirty-two-foot reed pipe, first of its kind, nearly touching the ceiling. This was one of the good ones.

"Turn this way," the photo boy said, and I obeyed. "Chin up," he commanded, and I did as I was told.

"Now let's get one of the performer . . . ," Anna said, leading him away. "Thank you," she called back with a wave. Then I slid around on the seat to face the instrument. The stops surrounded me, the pipes towered over me. My husband's final deed.

When Charlie was dying—his liver a mess of problems the doctors attributed to childhood diet, but we knew it was a result of radiation—one night he said, "Do you know what the smartest thing I ever did was?"

"Tell me, love."

He wrinkled his nose, which by then was as close as he could manage to a smile. "Married a girl way out of my league."

"No," I told him. "You married beneath you. She just rose to your level."

His tongue ran over dry lips. "You never got to attend the conservatory."

I held a cup with a straw for him, he took a good suck of water, then I set it aside. "You and me, Charlie. That was my greatest performance."

He relaxed then, surrendered to his deep fatigue, and I knew it would not be long.

Something about that memory made me shift on the bench, and

my elbow nudged a key. It sounded. Only a fraction of a second, but now I knew: Mr. Elaborate-Bow had neglected to turn the instrument off.

Oh, didn't I sit up straight? And open the trumpet stops? And put my worn hands to a shape so familiar, they might as well have been caressing Charlie's brow? In one gesture, both hands, both feet, I came down on a single unabashed chord. The one Charlie played in the Dubie's Music showroom in the fall of 1943: a great G major.

I let it sound, then released, then listened as it dwindled for the count of five. Such a room. Such expert voicing. The chord lived for five full seconds.

What came to mind then, of all things, was the charge Reverend Morris gave us at the end of our wedding blessing: make a joyful noise. Which is exactly what Charlie and I spent a lifetime doing, so why stop now? No question about what piece of music it should be either. My one and only performance of it. "Toccata" means touch.

Already I could hear men rushing down the aisle, to protect the instrument, I suppose. To stop me. But they were forty-one years too late. After checking my posture, I began, the opening notes like the peal of a trumpet. Which meant that no one dared interrupt—if not because I was the organ builder's wife, then because it was Bach, king of this instrument, calling on us all to pay attention.

I *have* paid attention, and learned one thing in this life: Whatever you love, no matter how fiercely, you will lose it one day. That is the only certainty. Therefore be as kind as you can. Don't fear your mistakes, as long as you learn humility from them. There is no such thing as perfect pitch.

As I continued playing, the organ came alive under my hands: pipes singing, bellows pumping to fill them. I could feel Charlie breathing through the instrument, so I did not fear the difficult passages ahead. I leaned into every note.

And that is how I was able to touch him one more time.

ACKNOWLEDGMENTS

"Seldom, if ever, has a war ended leaving the victors with such a sense of uncertainty and fear, with such a realization that the future is obscure and that survival is not assured."

—Edward R. Murrow, August 1945

I MUST IMMEDIATELY CONFESS two things.

The first is that this novel was inspired by an actual person. Charles Brenton Fisk, born in 1925, was a student at Harvard University who worked during World War II at the University of Chicago Metallurgy Department. Later, Charles served on the detonator team at the Manhattan Project laboratory in Los Alamos, New Mexico. After the war he attended Stanford University's graduate program in physics. He dropped out after less than a semester to work for a small organ company in Redwood City, California. Subsequently he educated himself in the organ, in classes at Stanford and by studying instruments across the United States and Europe. In 1972, he formed the C.B. Fisk Company in Gloucester, Massachusetts, which makes premium quality organs to this day.

I learned about this man from a brilliant essay in *The Georgia Review*, by Laura Sewell Matter of Albuquerque, New Mexico. But I need to be clear: The *real* Charles Fisk—who married twice and had two children—provided only the skeleton on which I sought to build a fully fleshed fiction. The Charlie Fish of this novel, therefore, is entirely imagined.

The second revelation is that this book, by engaging with the staggering complexity of atomic weapons and the byzantine intricacy of tracker-style pipe organs, commits many acts of egregious oversimplification. In many instances I blurred or minimized technical details. In reality, it was all far more complicated.

That is not to say that this novel disregards history. It follows the available record closely: holes in the Los Alamos security fence; a man ordered to guard the Trinity test bomb during the thunderstorm; accordion music during square dance breaks; and animals changing color due to radiation. The army really did pile mattresses under the Gadget as it was hoisted to the platform. The submarine strikes—including ship names and number killed—actually happened. All newspaper headlines and quotations came directly from those publications, verbatim.

Most crucially, dissent among people working on the Manhattan Project—the debates in Fuller Lodge, resignations after the fall of the Third Reich, the Bard letter, Szilard Petition, and Franck Report—was real. Quotations from those documents are also verbatim.

What liberties I took were few, and for specific narrative reasons: Charlie's train to New Mexico left from Union Station (though it actually embarked from Dearborn Station), because I wanted a departure setting that would make him think of organs. The physicist Robert Serber delivered his explanatory lectures in 1943, but Charlie had not arrived at the Hill yet, so I moved the lectures later and had them delivered by the fictional Robert Sebring. Newsreels about submarine warfare did not generally appear until early 1945, but I allowed Brenda to see one on her date with Chris in 1944. Monroe did a few things the physicist Richard Feynman actually had done, David Horn was modeled after Donald Hornig, and Igor Bronsky substituted for the Russian demolition team leader, George Kistiakowsky (who lacked a deep Russian accent and was a devoted poker player). John Simmons was a fictional stand-in for the actual director of Chicago's metallurgy project, Professor Joyce Stearns—who was the real Charles Fisk's uncle. According to several accounts, the milk at Los Alamos really was always sour.

This book draws on a wealth of literature; rather than being exhaustive, I'll mention highlights. Richard Rhodes wrote the definitive history, *The Making of the Atomic Bomb.* Life on the Hill became vivid through *Inside Box 1663* by Eleanor Jette, whose husband Bill worked on the Manhattan Project, and whose own science background enabled her to guess what was happening long before the facts became available. *Tales of Los Alamos: Life on the Mesa 1943–1945* by Bernice Brode revealed the daily challenges that families and spouses faced. *Los Alamos 1944–1947*, a photobook edited by Toni Michnovicz Gibson and Jon Michnovicz, provided a visual history. *The Manhattan Project*, edited by Cynthia C. Kelly of the Atomic Heritage Foundation, gathered an excellent oral history from 1938 to 2006. The incident of a man swallowing plutonium has been widely documented; I relied on the account by Eileen Welsome in her book *The Plutonium Files.* I learned that early atomic bombs were powered by a car battery in Eric Schlosser's terrifying masterpiece, *Command and Control.*

I also gained information from the Los Alamos Historical Society, the Bradbury Science Museum in Los Alamos, and the Atomic Heritage Foundation. An off-the-record scientist at the Los Alamos National Laboratory was generous with his time. His recovery research report taught me the geography of The Hill, indicating what happened where. John Canaday, in his book of poems *Critical Assembly*, offered a compass for navigating the personalities of The Hill. In an interview subsequent to her essay, Laura Sewall Matter expanded on Fisk's life in ways that were hugely helpful. Miranda Fisk, the real Charles's daughter, was kind enough to share stories of her childhood and memories of her father.

In September 2018, I had the honor of hearing in person the stories of two *Hibakusha* (survivors of the atomic bomb): Shigeko Sasamori, who was thirteen years old when she saw a bomber drop a large white object over Hiroshima, and Yasuaki Yamashita, who experienced the bombing of Nagasaki when he was six. The de-

finitive account in English, meanwhile, remains *Hiroshima* by John
Hersey.

Then there was the musical part. The novelist and screenwriter
John Fusco convinced me (partly in conversation and partly while
jamming) of the glory and delight of Hammond organs. Emory Fan-
ning, Middlebury College music professor emeritus, introduced me
to the pipe organ with patience and humor. There is nothing quite like
standing amid several thousand pipes when Emory opens the swell
division, and the volume rises tenfold. David Neiweem, music professor at the University of Vermont, was generous in explaining and
demonstrating the C.B. Fisk Company instrument in that school's
Redstone Recital Hall. Dr. Edward Elwyn Jones, University Organist and Choirmaster at Harvard University, introduced me to the Fisk
organ in Memorial Chapel—and treated me to a masterful performance in which I was the entire audience. I referred to essays by Jones
and others collected in *The Organ in the Academy*, edited by Thomas
Forrest Kelly & Lesley Bannatyne. I also benefited from *The Organ*
by William Leslie Sumner, *Making Music on the Organ* by Peter
Hurford, and especially the delightful history *All the Stops* by Craig
R. Whitney. Courtney Douglas, 2018 student editor of *The Stanford Daily*, was kind enough to send me articles from that newspaper
about the Fisk organ. Details about the instrument came courtesy
of Stanford University Organist Dr. Robert Huw Morgan, who also
made excellent suggestions for this book's repertoire of organ pieces.

Workers at C.B. Fisk Company—especially the patient and un-
derstated Dana Sigall—convinced me that tracker organ building
requires countless forms of craft and artistry. Although we never
met, I am indebted to the late Hannes Kastner for his recording of
Bach's Toccata and Fugue in D Minor, a performance I listened to
often while writing this book.

With so much for me to learn, this novel had a rocky start. But
the searing intelligence and endless generosity of my friend Chris
Bohjalian helped enormously. My trusted agent, Ellen Levine,
helped hone and focus the early going, especially when I delivered
an absurdly long first draft. My editor, Jennifer Brehl, who deserves

gold stars for patience and insight, also helped shave needless pages, and gave excellent suggestions literally from the first sentences forward. Paula McLain and Jana Seter Nuland offered generous prior help for which I remain grateful. Thanks to Hadley Bunting and Rev. Will Burhans for conversations about the nature of conscience. K.K. Roeder provided moral support, uplifting company during some creepy research, and a warm place to stay in New Mexico.

Early draft readers helped as dependably as ever: John Killacky (who wisely told me to turn down the violins), and Kate Seaver (who suggested that Brenda should not go upstairs to help her mother with the dishes, but instead should sit on the cellar steps and keep Charlie company). That idea opened a thousand narrative doors. Special thanks to my friend and go-to brainstormer, Dawn Tripp.

How many names is that? I've lost count, and probably have forgotten some deserving people, for which I apologize. This project depended on the help of multitudes. My gratitude to them is immense.

ABOUT THE AUTHOR

STEPHEN P. KIERNAN is a graduate of Middlebury College, Johns Hopkins University, and the University of Iowa Writers' Workshop. He spent more than twenty years as a journalist, winning numerous awards before turning to fiction writing. *Universe of Two* is his fourth novel. He lives in Vermont.